"*C*lever and charming."
Rachel Gibson

♥

"*H*ot and sassy!"
Susan Andersen

♥

"*C*hristie Ridgway's books are pure
romance, delightfully warm, and funny."
Jennifer Crusie

♥

"*R*idgway's smart, peppy style is reminiscent
of Jennifer Crusie, but her . . .
heroines stand on their own."
Publishers Weekly

♥

"*F*ast-paced, funny, poignant, and passionate,
Christie Ridgway captures
the very best of romance."
Christina Dodd

Avon Contemporary Romances by
Christie Ridgway

THE CARE AND FEEDING OF UNMARRIED MEN
AN OFFER HE CAN'T REFUSE
THE THRILL OF IT ALL
DO NOT DISTURB
THEN COMES MARRIAGE
FIRST COMES LOVE
THIS PERFECT KISS
WISH YOU WERE HERE

Christie RIDGWAY

THE
Care and Feeding
OF
UNMARRIED
MEN

AVON BOOKS

An Imprint of HarperCollinsPublishers

This is a work of fiction. Names, characters, places, and incidents are products of the author's imagination or are used fictitiously and are not to be construed as real. Any resemblance to actual events, locales, organizations, or persons, living or dead, is entirely coincidental.

AVON BOOKS
An Imprint of HarperCollins*Publishers*
10 East 53rd Street
New York, New York 10022-5299

Copyright © 2006 by Christie Ridgway
The Care and Feeding of Unmarried Men copyright © 2006 by Christie Ridgway; *Her Officer and Gentleman* copyright © 2006 by Karen Hawkins; *A Bite to Remember* copyright © 2006 by Lynsay Sands; *Never a Lady* copyright © 2006 by Jacquie D'Alessandro
ISBN-13: 978-0-06-076350-3
ISBN-10: 0-06-076350-7
www.avonromance.com

First Avon Books paperback printing: May 2006

Avon Trademark Reg. U.S. Pat. Off. and in Other Countries, Marca Registrada, Hecho en U.S.A.
HarperCollins® is a registered trademark of HarperCollins Publishers Inc.

Printed in the U.S.A.

10 9 8 7 6 5 4 3 2 1

For Jennifer Granholm.
You're right; you're the one who said,
"Why aren't you writing romances?"
Thanks for that and all the past, present,
and future (promise!) good times.
Love ya, Jen.

♥

Chapter One

"Leader of the Pack"
The Shangri-Las
"A" side, single (1964)

The rain was pouring down on the Palm Springs desert in biblical proportions the night he stalked into the spa's small bar. He was a big man, tall, brawny, the harsh planes of his face unsoftened by his wet, dark hair. Clint Eastwood minus forty years and plus forty pounds of pure muscle. Water dripped from the hem of his ankle-length black slicker to puddle on the polished marble floor beside his reptilian-skinned cowboy boots.

She flashed on one of the lessons her father had drilled into her. *A girl as beautiful as you and with a name like yours should always be on guard for the snake in Paradise.*

And as the stranger took another step forward, Eve Caruso heard a distinctive hiss.

The sound had come from her, though, the hiss of a

quick, indrawn breath, because the big man put every one of her instincts on alert. But she'd also been taught at the school of Never Showing Fear, so she pressed her damp palms against the thighs of her tight white jeans, then scooted around the bar.

"Can I help you?" she asked, positioning her body between him and the lone figure seated on the eighth and last stool.

The stranger's gaze flicked to Eve.

She'd attended a casual dinner party earlier that evening—escorted by her trusty tape recorder so she wouldn't forget a detail of the meal or the guest list, which would appear in her society column—and hadn't bothered to change before taking on the late shift in the Kona Kai's tiny lounge. Her jeans were topped with a honey-beige silk T-shirt she'd belted at her hips. Around her neck was a tangle of turquoise-and-silver necklaces, some of which she'd owned since junior high. Her cowboy boots were turquoise too, and hand-tooled. Due to pressing financial concerns, she'd recently considered selling them on eBay—and maybe she still would, she thought, as his gaze fell to the pointy tips and her toes flexed into involuntary fetal curls.

He took in her flashy boots, then moved on to her long legs, her demi-bra-ed breasts, her shoulder-blade-length blonde hair and blue eyes. She'd been assessed by a thousand men, assessed, admired, desired, and since she was twelve-and-a-half years old, she'd been unfazed by all of them. Her looks were her gift, her luck, her tool, and tonight, a useful distraction in keeping the dark man from noticing the less showy but more famous face of the younger woman sitting by herself at the bar.

Eve placed a hand on an empty stool and gestured

with the other behind her back. *Get out, get away*, she signaled, all the while keeping her gaze on the stranger and letting a slow smile break over her face. "What would you like?" she asked, softly releasing the words one by one into the silence, like lingerie dropping onto plush carpeting.

"Sorry, darlin', I'm not here for you," he said, then he and his Southern drawl brushed past her, leaving only the scent of rain and rejection in their wake.

Eve froze in—shock? dismay? fear? *"I'm not here for you."*

What the hell was up with that? Granted, life hadn't been going her way lately, but though she knew not to depend on men, surely she could depend upon their reactions! Blonde hair and blue eyes, long legs and big breasts . . . they'd never failed her before.

What did it mean? What was the world coming to? Rain in the desert. Men underwhelmed by her beauty. Next the dead would rise from their graves. A shiver rippled down her spine. Come to think of it, just a few weeks before that had actually happened.

"What the hell are you doin'?"

The sound of the man's next words released Eve from her paralysis. She spun around, but his wide shoulders blocked her view of the person he was speaking to. Eve could imagine her, though, huddling in her corner, big-eyed, her broken arm hugged tight against her thin body. She remembered the feeling herself, she remembered feeling lost and helpless as the darkness closed in, squeezing the air from her lungs, choking her throat. Her first experience with the claustrophobia that could still make her cower.

Then the light, the voice. *"What a pretty girl. I'd never hurt you."*

"Well?"

The man's impatient tone banished the memory, and Eve's pulse skittered. A second shiver bolted down her spine. *Move*, she ordered herself. Get between them again.

Or get out, her weaker self reasoned. *You're no Wonder Woman, we both know that. Do what you do best.*

Look out for #1.

Trapped by indecision, Eve heard the scrape of the barstool's legs and tensed. If Jemima Cargill decided to run for it, Eve would be right behind her. The Clint-clone looked that dangerous.

The younger woman's fingers gripped the man's slicker sleeve and yanked him forward. "Oh, sod off, Nash," she berated in a soft, pseudo-British voice, "and sit down and have a beer."

To Eve's surprise, he merely grumbled, then obeyed. Jemima Cargill, Hollywood's latest and greatest waif-actress, looked over her shoulder, all enormous dark eyes and sharp pointed chin. "Would you mind serving the dope a drink?"

Eve obeyed too, moving around to the other side of the bar, her wariness easing a little now that the big man was sitting down, even though he couldn't look less dopey as he narrowed his eyes at the young woman seated beside him. "Don't mess with me, Jem. I've been doing the whole trains, planes, and automobiles thing for the last"—he squinted down at the watch on his burly wrist—"thirty-eight hours."

"I didn't call for the cavalry," Jemima answered, her British accent evaporating into her usual California-speak. "As you can see, I'm just fine."

He relaxed against the back of his stool as Eve set the draft beer down in front of him. His voice changed too, still good ol' boy slow but now more frustrated. "Is that right? Then why is your arm in purple plaster and why is Allison sending faxes all across Europe insisting I play bodyguard?"

"Because she's an overprotective stage mother who's on her honeymoon and, shock of all shockers, she actually might love her new husband enough not to end it early."

Shaking his head, the man reached for his beer and then paused, staring at the wineglass in front of Jemima Cargill. "Tell me that's ginger ale."

The actress rolled her eyes.

"You're underage." The man swung his head toward Eve and pinned her with his gaze. His eyes were an eerie, almost-clear gray. "Ma'am, you're serving a minor."

"Ma'am"? First, "I'm not here for you" and now, "ma'am"?

"I'll be twenty-one in two weeks," Jemima put in. She glanced over at Eve. "In case you haven't figured it out, this is my big brother, Nash Cargill. On the monster-truck circuit, you won't be surprised to learn, his nickname is The Preacher. Nash, this is one of the spa owner's daughters, Eve Caruso, who—"

"Eve Caruso? Allison mentioned the name." Suddenly, he was really looking at her, and there was hellfire and brimstone in The Preacher's eyes, though his voice stayed as country boy laidback as before. "You're the one whose tell-all society column spilled my little sister's whereabouts."

Jemima rolled her eyes again, then offered up to Eve an apologetic smile followed by a little shrug. "Preacher, meet the Party Girl."

* * *

In the morning, juice and lattes were served at the Kona Kai's bar. Eve picked up her doubleshot and took it through the French doors into the small dining room where guests were served breakfast, lunch, and dinner at the appropriate hours. It was early, so the only two seated were her half sisters, ensconced at a glass-topped table in the corner. Téa, four months older than Eve, looked radiant but frazzled, the same way she'd been looking since her recent engagement. The three had been meeting two mornings a week, ostensibly to help Téa with the details of her upcoming wedding.

As if their older sister would let a single one of them go.

Téa's straightened hair was already starting to wave at the ends as she tucked the dark mass behind her ears and bent over a mile-long to-do list. Joey, two years younger, was tapping a white envelope against the glass tabletop in an annoying, impatient tattoo.

Eve stood where she was, waiting out the inevitable before joining them. It only took another ninety seconds.

Téa glanced over at Joey. "Would you *stop* that?"

Joey continued to tap. "Stop what?"

"That noise," Téa said. "Stop that noise."

Joey's eyebrows rose. "What—? Oh." She let the envelope drop to the table and started drumming on the glass with her fingertips instead. "Sorry."

Téa shifted her gaze from her younger sister's face to her ceaseless fingers. "You need to be still."

"Oh." Joey stared down at her hand and then flattened it, obviously forcing it to stop moving. "Sorry again."

Now with Joey more subdued, Eve moved forward with a smile, her mood lightening. Maybe her world wasn't so messed up after all, not when the Caruso sisters were as predictable as ever. Busy interior designer Téa, the responsible, good-girl oldest sister, who had only finally loosened up after falling in love and becoming engaged to Johnny Magee. Impulsive, always moving Joey, who threw her bottomless energy in a dozen directions, including a successful career in the family's one legitimate business, the gourmet food company La Vita Buona.

Eve supposed they saw the same girl they always had when they looked at her, too. The blonde in the middle of their tight brunette circle. The social sister—first to date, first to French kiss, first to discover the power of being female. She made a living by writing her "Party Girl" column, which ran in the Palm Springs daily, as well as articles for the Southern California luxury magazine *Wealth*. Starting next month she was going to be blogging on a new entertainment website, HipPop.com. Along with her investments, it should have been enough to keep her in classic clothes and trendy accessories, but then she'd taken a stupid, greedy risk.

Still, as Eve slipped into a seat at the table, she felt almost normal for the first time since October, when, in the same week that their missing father had been confirmed dead after sixteen years, she'd received an unexpected phone call from her stockbroker, followed by an even more unpleasant one from the Securities and Exchange Commission. "Good morning," she said to her sisters.

Still perusing her list, Téa *mmm*'ed and Joey continued frowning down at her hand, as if daring it to move. More of Eve's tension eased, including a nagging knot between her shoulders. Yes, she could believe her life was getting back on track. It really was. She glanced out the windows at the sheets of rain, refusing to see the strange climate change as a bad omen. "How about this weather?"

Joey looked up, then her gaze jumped over Eve's head, her eyes widening. "How about that man?"

The knot between Eve's shoulders jerked tight once more. She kept her gaze forward. "What man?"

Now Téa looked up too. "*Oh.* That big man."

Eve set her jaw. "What big man?"

"He's hot in one of those I-could-break-you-in-half-with-a-snap-of-my-fingers kind of ways. Check him out," Joey urged, "before he turns around and—uh-oh."

"Uh-oh, what?" The knot twisted tighter.

"Uh-oh you can't look now," her younger sister said. "He's coming in here."

"Tell me he's not coming to our table," Eve whispered, her fingers clutching her latte. Speaking of omens, she'd ended the night before with Mr. Break-You-in-Half-with-a-Snap-of-His-Fingers, and she didn't think it was a good one to begin the day with too. She didn't like big men, not that she'd ever let them know it.

"Nope, he's taking a seat in the far corner." Téa's brows drew together. "What's up?"

Eve tried shrugging off the new sense of disquiet he'd brought with him into the room. "That's Jemima Cargill's brother. He arrived last night and he happens to think I'm the devil incarnate."

Joey snorted. "Right. And you with all your angel looks."

"He does." Last night, Jemima had apologized for his behavior before towing him off to register for a room, but he hadn't looked the least bit apologetic to Eve. "It seems he blames me for her broken arm."

"I thought you actually moved her out of the way of that oncoming car," Joey said. "She tripped and fell all by her itty-bitty self."

"Shh," Eve said. At dusk a week before, she'd encountered the actress a block away from the spa. As they'd stood chatting, an oncoming car had swerved on the narrow, sidewalkless street, coming straight for them. Eve had pulled herself and the younger woman out of the way. "It was an accident. Jemima and I both believe it was nothing more than that."

Except the incident *had* left an odd aftertaste in Eve's mouth, which was why she'd been so apprehensive when Nash Cargill had walked into the bar the night before. She frowned down at the layer of froth on her latte. "Apparently Jemima's mother called on Big Bad Brother to look over the situation. To look over *me.*"

Her younger sister began to rise. "Well, I'll just straighten him—"

"No, Joe." Eve put her hand on her arm, though the unswerving loyalty would make a softer woman cry. "I can handle my own problems." Téa and Joey and their mother, Bianca, had done enough for her over the years. They'd been her family since she was three years old, when her father, Salvatore Caruso—Joey and Téa's father too—had brought home his daughter by his dead mistress to be raised by his wife. Eve owed them, not the other way around.

Téa was watching her closely. "Eve—"

"Forget it. Let's talk about something else."

Her older sister paused. "If you say so." Then she sipped from her own coffee. "How's the home-hunting going?"

Let's talk about anything but that. "Nothing's caught my fancy yet." She cleared the lying little frog in her throat. Without the cash to rent a new condo, let alone put out a down payment to replace the one she'd been forced to sell, she hadn't bothered looking. "Lucky me to have the rooms at the spa in the meantime."

Just something else she owed Bianca for, though she tried to pay her back by taking on odd shifts at the Kona Kai's bar. "What about you, Téa? In the last few days have you and Johnny found a place to start your lives of married bliss?"

Téa plucked the piece of paper in front of her and waved it in the air. "It's on the list. But it may have to wait until after the Superbowl."

"Why?"

Joey piped up again in that loud, youngest-sibling voice of hers. "Because our brother-in-law-to-be's gambling syndicate is really busy during football season."

"Shh!" Eve squeezed shut her eyes, keenly aware of Nash Cargill's looming—disapproving—presence in the back of the room. "Shh!"

"What?" Joey asked. "It's legal. Johnny pays taxes."

"Just keep it down, Joe," Eve said.

"Why?" their younger sister continued, without adjusting her volume. "You've never cared before that Johnny's a professional gambler."

Eve responded from between clenched teeth. "Just humor me, okay?"

Though it was true, she'd never been a stickler for rules or other people's notions of morality. But The Preacher on the other side of the room was making her uneasy. Sighing, she stared out the window again at the stormy, dark sky. The Preacher—and that nasty little lesson in legalities that had come down on her head a month ago. Besides, she'd started the morning feeling optimistic and didn't want the mood ruined by another episode of being looked upon as if she were a criminal. "Let's talk about what *you've* been up to, Joey."

"Are you sure?"

"Yes." Maybe the company had a new pasta sauce on the market. That would make a safe, banal topic.

"I've been visiting Uncle Benny in prison."

At Eve's startled look, her younger sister's face broke into a mischievous grin, and her voice rose again. "You walked right into that one. But it's true. Once a week, I've been going to prison."

"Shh!"

Téa was already shaking her head. "It's too late. We've really caught your big friend's attention this time."

For just a second, Eve wanted to slide down in her seat and under the table. But then she steeled her spine, forcing herself straighter in her chair. Never in her life had she been ashamed of her family. She wasn't going to start being ashamed of them now. "So what? Who cares what he thinks?"

No one, no man, nothing was going to make Eve Caruso hide again.

Joey idly picked up the envelope she'd been playing with before and glanced down at it. "Ooops," she said, sliding it across the table. "I found this on the front desk. It's addressed to you."

"Strange." Eve picked up the plain white envelope, her name handwritten on the front. Then she heard heavy bootsteps and felt a rustle of air that carried with it a fresh, masculine scent. Familiar, after last night. Her sisters' dark eyes widened, then flicked to her face.

"Mornin', ladies," a man said.

That man.

"Morning," Téa and Joey said together.

Eve said nothing as he walked behind her to position himself at the wall of windows to the left of their table. He stared through the glass as if fascinated by the overflowing pool and drenched patio furniture.

Her sisters stared at the man as if fascinated by him.

Eve took her own sidelong look. Dry, he wasn't any smaller than he'd been the night before. In faded jeans and a long-sleeved knit shirt, he appeared to be close to six-and-a-half-feet tall, with enough muscle for two men. Dark, shiny hair, with just a hint of a wave, needed to be cut. His profile was masculine. Arrogant. Annoying.

Her sisters were still staring.

Their reaction put Eve's nerves on edge. What was so very interesting about Nash Cargill? He'd obviously only repositioned himself nearby for improved eavesdropping.

Well, fine, she decided. If he wanted to eavesdrop, she'd give him a front row seat. She'd make it clear he couldn't ruin her mood, her day, her sense of who she was. Summoning up years of seduction experience, she shifted on her chair to high-beam a brilliant smile in Nash Cargill's direction. "Say, would you care to join us?"

The acting gene must run in the family, because he managed to look surprised instead of smug. A good ol' boy grin broke over his face. He'd be delighted.

Eve just bet. It took only moments for him to settle in the empty seat and for her to perform the introductions. She explained to Nash that Téa and Joey were her half sisters. She told her sisters that Nash drove monster trucks. Then she leaned toward him conspiratorially, letting him get a good look at the cleavage revealed by her V-necked top. *See 'em and weep, Cargill.* "We were just talking about our uncle Benny. He's suffering from a few . . . legal difficulties."

"Oh?"

"Oh, yes." She toyed with the envelope in her hands, sliding a fingernail under the flap to loosen the seal. There was a single business card inside. "It's really no secret," she said, leaning close to Nash to provide another eyeful. "Our family's mobbed up."

"Huh?"

It *was* no secret, so if he wanted to know more about her, she might as well be the one to tell him. "Our grandfather is *il capo di tutti cappi*—the boss of bosses on the West Coast."

His country boy grin faded by a tooth or two. "You're joking."

"Oh, you don't joke about the California Mafia."

"Eve . . ." Téa said, looking pained.

Eve ignored her. Her older sister held a lingering shame and anger about who the Carusos were and what they did, but not Eve. She'd come into the family by the back door, so to speak. Without them she'd be nothing, have no one. So she didn't cast stones.

But Nash Cargill now appeared to be made of them. Through narrowed eyes, he was just watching her, his face expressionless. After that first puzzled moment, he didn't seem any more affected by the information than he'd been by the glimpses of breast she'd been flashing him.

Arrogant, annoying man.

Didn't he realize she was warning him off? She was

telling him she didn't appreciate his suspicion. That she didn't care about his disapproval.

Under the cover of the table, she reached over with her fingertips to touch his hard thigh, right below the crease of his groin. Her nails scraped against the soft denim as she wet her lips with her tongue. "Be careful," she teased. "Now that you know we're a dangerous family, Nash."

Don't mess with me. I'm too much woman for you. Her nails scratched him a second time.

His heavy hand slapped down, covering hers. Holding it still against his solid muscle.

Eve jerked back to escape his touch, but he was larger, stronger than she was, and he kept her captive. Through her palm, she felt his thigh flex. Panic closed in like darkness.

"What a pretty girl. I'd never hurt you."

She tensed for that viselike pinch on her upper arm or that throbbing pain in her upper lip. Instead, a jolt of heat buzzed up her skin all the way to her breasts, tightening her nipples.

Startled by the sensation, she jerked her arm again. He let her go this time, and her elbow shot back toward the table, knocking the envelope and the business card inside it to the floor.

Nash Cargill bent to retrieve them and Eve let him, rubbing the top of her hand and avoiding her sisters' eyes, giving herself time to camouflage how much The Preacher's touch had rattled her.

She was breathing again when he straightened, the two pieces in his fingers. He handed them over separately. The envelope first. The business card second. She glanced down as she plucked it from his callused palm. White card. The official-looking bald eagle, the words SECURITIES AND EXCHANGE COMMISSION, and the other words, "Call me," scrawled beneath the investigator's embossed name. Her heart started thrumming again, as if Nash Cargill's flesh were still pressed to hers.

Calm down, calm down, Eve scolded herself. It wasn't so dire. After that single, terrifying meeting, she'd managed to avoid further contact with the SEC. This peremptory command could be avoided too. And it wasn't a bad omen, just like the unusual rain wasn't a bad omen, just like Nash himself wasn't a bad omen either.

But why then, she wondered, did all three together make her suddenly feel so certain her life was never, ever going to be the same?

Chapter Two

"Ramblin' Man"
The Allman Brothers Band
Brothers and Sisters (1973)

I thought you'd sworn off rescuing women?"

"This isn't 'women,' this is my sister," Nash said into his cell phone, stretching his feet in front of him as he stared out the third-floor window of his room at Palm Springs's Kona Kai spa. It was still raining like hell, but by midmorning other guests were wandering the grounds, past hedges and pots of flowers made only more green and colorful by the low-lying gray clouds. Some people headed for one of the several pools, and others took the path he knew led to the buildings where the actual spa services were offered. "Jemima told me she's having an all-over salt scrub and then a paraffin treatment on her hands and feet. You have any idea what she's talking about?"

"Not really," replied Bryan Matthews, Nash's VP of Finance. "But you could ask her—"

"This is my sister!"

"Okay, if you think that's too personal, then you could Google it, just like you could have Googled the Carusos, instead of asking me to do it."

Nash crossed one booted ankle over the other. "I keep forgetting how to spell that. G-e-w-g-u-l or g-o-o-g-u-l-l?"

Bryan sighed. "How many times do I have to tell you? Your big, dumb Bubba act won't work with me. I happen to know you have an MBA."

"Master's in Bad Ass, I keep telling *you*," Nash replied. "Which is why I need a pencil-necked, calculator-brained, business wonk like yourself to do all the detail work."

Not to mention the fact that he hadn't been sure he could see or think straight after a day and a half of transatlantic and transcontinental travel followed by too-few hours of jet-lagged sleep. But now that he'd seen for himself that Jemima was in good spirits despite the broken arm, Nash was inclined to believe that her stage-mother Allison *was* overreacting.

A little more assurance and he could report back to his former stepmother with good conscience that all was well in California. Then he would leave his baby sister in Palm Springs and get on with the rest of his life—which included returning to Europe, where he'd been traveling on a semi-vacation with the monster-truck exhibition circuit until the frantic faxes had caught up with him. "So, Bry, what'd you find out?"

"There really is a California Mafia."

"No shit!" Flabbergasted, Nash jerked back his feet and sat straight in his chair. "I thought she was pulling my leg." More like his chain. Party girl Eve Caruso was too damn beautiful for her own good and obviously accustomed to getting her own way. It had taken every ounce of willpower to keep his drool inside his mouth and his gaze off those spectacular breasts she'd served up to him at the breakfast table with such cool aplomb. "Tell me more."

"The Mafia moved out West during Prohibition days. In Palm Springs, it was a big operation that included gambling along with the hooch, but then games of chance were pushed out by the authorities and taken eastward to Vegas."

Which reminded him. Hadn't the little sister, Joey, spilled that big sister Téa's husband-to-be was a professional gambler? Jesus, just another unsavory point in this family's dis-favor. "The Carusos stuck around Palm Springs, though."

"Yep. And Cosimo Caruso, the grandfather of the Caruso girls, took over the local action in the 1950s, solidifying his power in all the years since."

Nash scowled and swore under his breath. "Jemima sure knows how to pick 'em, doesn't she? First time on her own and she takes up with these kind of people. She's supposed to be on a relaxation break before reporting to her next movie." He looked around the room, at the bed piled high with pillows and a thick white comforter, the tempting little minibar, the hedonistic whirlpool tub he could see through the bathroom doorway. "I suppose the spa is built with mob money then."

"That's where you're wrong. The Kona Kai was bought a few years back by Bianca Caruso—wife of Salvatore, who was Cosimo's only son. Salvatore took over briefly as mob boss before going missing sixteen years ago. Seems his wife turned her back on her husband's family after his disappearance and worked her way through the ranks to become the spa's owner."

Slumping in his chair, Nash ran a hand through his hair. "So Salvatore disappeared, you said?"

"And was resurrected last October, in a manner of speaking. His remains were found in the crumbling walls of a lagoon built on a local property. An accidental death, finally confessed to by an old friend, who'd kept silent out of fear of mob retaliation."

"So the daughters—"

"Just recently found out that dear old dad is definitely dead and gone."

Nash thought of Eve's angel eyes and plump, heart-shaped mouth. How had she handled the news? Did her heart ache with the loss? Did she need—damn it! There he went again, falling right back into the old rut. Being someone's shoulder to cry on was highly overrated, and, he figured, strictly unnecessary when it came to that delectable little mantrap.

The woman's eyes were ice-blue, and the only thing he should be thinking about her mouth was how it was perfectly shaped to be wrapped around his cock. But even that was trouble, because *trap* was the operative word. He wasn't interested in being caught—he was too smart to mess with a superbeauty like Eve Caruso—and she was the kind who wanted every dude in the vicinity to be at her feet. Most men would think her heavenly face and luscious body were worth the grovel or two.

But Nash wasn't one of them, so he was going to keep his distance from that hot little honey. "If the spa's Mafia connection is that remote, then I suppose

I'm not worried for Jemima." He was already thinking of how quickly he could get back to Germany. There were still some days left of the tour.

"You haven't asked me the other question," Bryan said.

Nash opened his mouth . . . and couldn't recall what he'd been about to say. Through the window, Eve Caruso, mantrap, superbeauty, hot little honey, came into view. She had her hair pulled back in a cheerleader ponytail, and she was wearing stretchy calf-length pants and a matching sleeveless sports-type top. There were running shoes on her feet, and she seemed oblivious to the rain that splattered darker drops on her already black clothes. Nash thought of her dead father again, then his gaze dropped to the twitch of her round ass and he remembered instead that provocative scrape of her fingernails against his thigh. His dick shifted in his pants.

"Nash?"

"Huh?" Thank God he was getting on a plane today, because she was like an arsonist when it came to his sexual fire. The woman was a walking crime.

"I said, Ricky Becker has disappeared."

"What? When? I thought that when they released him from the mental health place, his mother promised the judge she'd keep a close eye on him."

"He went out for a burger and never came back. Ten days ago."

Nash pushed to his feet and paced the floor, moving away from the window. Ten days ago. About the time the notice of Jemima's presence in Palm Springs had shown up as a Hollywood tidbit thanks to Eve Caruso's society column, "Party Girl." Ten days ago. Just shortly before a swerve-and-run driver had caused

Jemima to trip and break her arm. Ricky Becker or simple accident?

Turning back, Nash looked through the glass. There was the mob boss's daughter, taking a path that a sign proclaimed led the way to the fitness center. He spun again and headed for his duffel bag, hoping he'd find his running shoes and workout gear inside.

It might not be the wisest of personal moves, but now he had no choice but to confront the so-sexy wise-girl once again. He couldn't leave Palm Springs until he found out more from Eve Caruso.

The fitness center was expansive, with three mirrored walls and a fourth made of windows that looked out over more lush hedges and an Olympic-sized pool. A variety of exercise machines, free weights, and black padded benches were scattered about the room, as well as half a dozen people using them. None of the half dozen was Eve Caruso.

Frowning, Nash let his gaze roam the area until he caught a glimpse of some movement through a doorway at the back of the room. Had to be her. He strode forward.

It was a large supply closet, and she was standing inside, facing shelves filled with stacks of white towels. Nash gripped the sides of the doorjamb. "Do you have a minute?"

Her blonde ponytail bobbed as her head jerked up. Whirling, she pressed her back against the wooden shelving. A hand flew to her throat. "You." She swallowed. "It's you."

"Hey, sorry." Her looks struck him like a punch in the gut. He felt the blow to his bones. From California to the Carolinas and all the little towns and large cities in between, big trucks and the men who drove them were undeniable magnets to hot-blooded beauties. Some of the guys thought they liked the vibrations of the 575-cubic-inch engines under their sweet, perky butts. Nash figured they believed a man who crushed cars for a living could also crush whatever looming problems they had in their lives—overdue bills, annoying ex-boyfriends, delinquent kids, you name it.

Consequently, he'd had his share of pretty women in his passenger seat. But those big blue eyes and that valentine of a mouth put Eve Caruso in a class by herself. "I didn't mean to startle you," he said.

Her hand fell back to her side, taking only some of the defensiveness out of her pose. "I'm not afraid."

And speaking of a class by itself, then there was her body—no! *Don't think about her body.* He wasn't here to wallow in her attractiveness, remember? Nash willed his gaze to stay trained on her face. "We need to talk."

She gestured toward the room behind him. "Outside—"

"No. Here's good." He glanced over his shoulder. For all he knew, a tabloid reporter was lurking on the treadmill, just waiting to overhear some dirt. The idea made him step inside the closet and reach for the door to shut it behind him.

"Don't."

He looked back at Eve. Her hand was up by her throat again, and she was plastered once more to the shelving. "I *am* scaring you," he said.

"Of course not," she replied. That hand dropped again, and she cleared her throat. "I'm fine."

Yeah, right. Nash stepped back to give her more breathing room and wondered just exactly what he'd done to earn her distrust. He'd given her no real reason to be so wary. For years he'd managed to keep the Mr. Hyde inside of him well-hidden.

"I'm *fine*," Eve repeated and reached around him to grab the doorknob herself. She shut it with a decisive *thunk,* then went back to her position by the shelving. "So, what else is it you want to know about me and my family?"

In the enclosed space, he could smell her. It wasn't an expensive perfume, as he might have expected. Instead she smelled . . . soapy. Yeah. She smelled like suds in a bathtub, one naked leg gleaming wetly—

"Mr. Cargill?"

"Mr." Cargill. Why did that one little word suddenly change the scene in his head? Now he was the headmaster and she was the naughty student sent to his office for a well-deserved spanking.

A smile suddenly played around that sweetheart mouth of hers.

Damn it! Damn woman could probably read the fantasy growing in his mind. Damn woman had likely *planted* it there. Aware he'd lose power points by showing the least reaction to her, he wiped any expression off his face and crossed his arms over his chest. "I want to talk about my sister. About the day that car nearly ran her down."

"I thought Jemima told you already."

"She's pretty hazy on the details. Her memory mainly consists of you tugging her to the side of the road and then her falling on her arm. Was there really a car?"

"What do you mean?" She frowned at him, and even that looked more like a sexy pout than anything else. "Of course there was a car. Or do you think I make a practice of pushing down famous starlets just for the fun of it?"

Pissing her off wasn't what he wanted either. He needed her cooperation. He needed *information*. "That's not what I think. I said that wrong, okay? Look . . ."

There was a flush on her cheekbones. "Look, what?"

He still hesitated. But damn it, he had to go forward or else he wouldn't be able to leave Palm Springs and the proximity of this tempting, too-hot-for-his-own-good woman. She was the kind of female that could make a fool of a man. "Is there some sort of confidentiality agreement we could come to so this won't end up as part of your gossip column?"

Her dark blonde eyebrows slammed together. "I write society news. I don't gossip."

"There's a difference?" He couldn't help himself, and then instantly regretted it when he saw sparks flare in her eyes. There was no need to add extra heat to the air around them. "I'm sorry. But this is about Jemima, and I need to be careful."

Eve turned her back to fuss with the stacks of towels on the shelves. "Believe it or not, people, your sister included, are *pleased* to be mentioned in my column. If celebrities didn't want to be famous, they'd find different lines of work."

Hell, he knew that, not that he felt like admitting it at the moment. Monster trucks were an entertainment industry too, and he'd appeared in magazine articles and on sports pages and been delighted every damn time by the publicity. "Chalk it up to my overprotective instincts."

"Not every woman needs a protector." From the steely look of her spine, it was obvious Eve Caruso didn't. She was probably thinking she could make a phone call and get good ol' Nash wacked if she wanted to. Being a California Mafia Caruso no doubt gave a woman a certain brand of confidence.

"Well, I hope you're right about Jemima," he said. "Because here's the part I would like to keep between ourselves. There's a young man—a nineteen-year-old—who's been following her. He was living at home with his mother, but he disappeared right before Jem broke her arm."

Over her shoulder, he could see Eve's fingers white-knuckle the towel she'd been shifting. "She has a stalker?"

"I don't know if Ricky Becker is up to his old obsession or not. I only know he's not at home in the Valley sitting in front of his mother's boob tube like he's supposed to be. Did you get a glimpse of the driver of the car?"

Her ponytail waggled as she shook her head. "It was almost dark, and the headlights were on bright. I couldn't see anything but that the car was steering for us."

Nash sighed. "I was hoping you'd tell me it was some little old lady from Pasadena or an aging golf duffer who'd briefly mistaken the gas pedal for the brakes."

"Jemima's stalker has threatened her?" Eve's voice sounded more breathy than usual, and she was still clutching at that towel.

"The mental health people claim he isn't a danger to himself or others. But you never know, do you?"

"Yes." And now there was an odd catch in her voice. "You never do."

Nash, though sworn off his former role of white knight, still heard the husky sound as an unignorable note of female vulnerability. Taking a half step forward, he put his hand on her shoulder.

She flinched, then wrenched her body away from him.

"Hell," he muttered, yanking his hand back. It was A-OK for Eve Caruso to initiate a flirtatious touch—to his upper thigh, of all places—but devil forbid she let a man touch *her*. Just further evidence she was a siren he should steer his big, manly boat away from.

Frustrated with himself, with the situation regarding Jemima and Ricky Becker, with wondering whether he should apologize for merely trying to be goddamn kind, he swore again. "Hell," he said again, slamming his right fist into the palm of his left hand. The punch landed with a gratifying, fleshy *pop*.

That made Eve Caruso leap for the ceiling.

He reared back as she now whirled, and his shoulders hit the door an instant before she was grasping the knob with both hands. It turned, and he stumbled back as it swung open. She flew forward, leaping over his size 15s on her way to fresh air.

Her face was pale, her forehead glistened with sudden sweat.

Staring after her as she bolted from the fitness center, he felt a tingle of worry trickle down his spine. Damn.

Something was up.

And though he didn't want to know what had Eve Caruso's panties in a twist, it was obvious that he couldn't leave Jemima here with this volatile situation and with these volatile people anytime soon.

Chapter Three

"Walking in the Rain"
The Ronettes
"B" side, single (1965)

Outside the doors of the fitness center, Eve gulped in breaths of cool air. *Calm down. Slow down. You're safe now,* she thought, pulling every emotion back inside, like a turtle taking to the protective cover of its shell.

She'd almost lost it. Confined spaces, or pitch darkness, or, heaven forbid, both together could do that to her. But she'd escaped, so there was no sense in attracting undue attention with a mad dash.

Her pace slowed to a sedate stroll. She couldn't outrun certain of her demons, she knew that, but with her checking account, her savings account, her stock portfolio, and her IRA as dry as the desert should be, her pride was one of the few things she had left. She was going to hang onto it with both hands, both feet, and even her teeth, if necessary.

No one would ever know she was terrified of enclosed spaces, big men, and being flat-broke.

Not her family, and not the imposing, annoying Nash Cargill.

She supposed he thought she was nuts for rushing out of the closet like that, but what the hey? He disapproved of her already anyway. There'd been a little moment, just a flicker of an eyelash, during which she'd thought she'd had him where she wanted—wanting her. But then his jaw had hardened and he'd turned all handsome and domineering big brother again.

Jemima Cargill might have a stalker. God.

Eve pushed the thought out of her mind, rubbing her hands against her upper arms to smooth out the sudden case of goose bumps.

It was the dismal, intermittent rain that was spooking her, she told herself, not a sense of precognition. And it certainly was the dismal rain and the chilly temperatures that had driven most of the spa patrons away from the lush grounds and into the massage rooms, facial chairs, or the pricey, private bungalows.

The Kona Kai had been a Palm Springs landmark since the 1950s, a favorite haunt of the Hollywood set and other wealthy clientele because the residential area was separated from the public facilities by thick walls, guarded fences, and tight security. The guestbook was kept strictly confidential, and because of that, during the high season from October to May there was never a shortage of grateful residents recuperating from plastic surgery, a messy scandal, or simply a bad starring vehicle.

Eve waved at the young attendant who manned the wrought-iron gate leading to the spacious cottages and one-bedroom suites. Without a key card or an invitation, no one would make it past him, and she was pleased by the physical reminder that as long as she kept to the Kona Kai and kept her cell phone turned off, she could ignore the little two-word order on that morning's business card from the SEC investigator. *"Call me."*

She wouldn't.

Her bungalow wasn't far, along a cobbled path made almost mazelike by shoulder-high trimmed hedges of yellow hibiscus and glossy-leaved gardenias. Intersections were marked by huge clay tubs spilling over with multicolored flowering annuals. The flora looked somewhat wilted by all the rain, and you couldn't see the usually stunning, rocky ripples of the surrounding mountains through the heavy layer of clouds weighing down on the valley, but Eve clung to an Annie-like hope that the sun would come out tomorrow.

The creature on her front doorstep reinforced the feeling. At the sound of her footsteps, the dog-sized, ragged tomcat lifted his head from something he was investigating on the mat. As usual, his fierce expression seemed to soften.

"Hello, cat," Eve murmured as he trotted toward her. Her sisters called him Adam—hah hah—because of his odd affection for Eve. He'd shown up as a stray a few weeks ago and adopted her. "We orphans have to stick together," she said, bending to rub the crown of his orange head between one ear and the half of the other that still remained. He pushed against her ankle with his chin, almost knocking her over.

She staggered to keep her balance and found herself staring down at the—what was it?—thing the cat had been nosing by her front door.

Goose bumps prickled her arms again and then

tumbled down her spine. The stiff and still thing was the corpse of a yellow canary.

"He brought you a gift."

Eve swung around at the familiar voice. Bianca Sabatino Caruso, Téa and Joey's mother, and the person who had taken in her husband's offspring by another woman twenty-five years ago. Eve. When his mistress had died, Salvatore Caruso had brought home his three-year-old blonde daughter, just four months younger than his oldest, to be raised by his wife.

Now nearing fifty, Bianca was petite and slender, an elegant woman who looked more French than Italian. More Brie than Parmigiana Reggiano. Next to her dark beauty, at times growing up Eve had felt all arms, legs, and washed-out hair. Looking at Bianca and then at her dark-haired and dark-eyed half sisters, Eve had always wondered what had happened to the evidence of her own Italian descent, figuring it must have been buried beneath the genetic heft of stolid Swedish or Norwegian DNA.

She'd felt apart, even though Bianca had never, ever treated her that way.

"He brought you a gift," the older woman said again.

Eve blinked. "Who?"

Bianca gestured to the purr-er at Eve's feet. "Adam. Cats will do that."

"Oh." Eve glanced down at the tom winding around her ankles, making like a throaty motorboat. He'd never done such a thing before, and it seemed out of character. What she liked best about the cat was that he didn't try to curry her favor like most males who hovered in her vicinity. Gifts didn't seem his style. He appeared to believe his presence in her life was present enough. "I suppose the bird didn't just fly here and knock itself out on my front door."

Another nervous shiver rolled down Eve's back, and Bianca—though not maternal-*looking* she still possessed fully functioning maternal antennae—drew closer and put her hand over Eve's forehead. "Are you all right, *cara*?"

"Of course." That *"Call me"* threat from the SEC notwithstanding. Eve didn't know what more they could want from her. When the investigator had contacted her last month, she'd been forced to explain herself. One of her former gentlemen friends, Vince Standish, respected, upstanding CEO, had whispered a juicy little stock tip in her ear during a charity lunch. A hush-hush merger. A sure thing if she moved fast, because the news was being released the very next day. Only the very next day Vince Standish had turned out to be not a generous ex-lover with a surefire financial tip but a vindictive weasel who'd paid her back—for ending their relationship—in the lowest way possible.

By using her own greed to do it.

Bianca frowned. *"Cara?"*

So maybe Eve *was* sick, because it made her ill to think about how she'd run with the tip—liquidating what assets she could and taking out short-term, high-interest loans against what she couldn't—to risk every nickel she had and then some. When the real details of the hush-hush merger had been made public, she'd discovered that the company she'd invested in had been on the losing side of the deal. It was now worth nothing. After having sold her condo and her car and anything else she could think of to cover the loans, she was worth nothing as well.

But she couldn't let Bianca know that. The older

woman had done enough for her. "I'm fine. Good." Eve stepped back, in case the woman's palm was some sort of parental lie detector. "Do you need any help in the lounge tonight?"

Bianca shook her head. "Are you sure you're all right?"

Ignoring the question, Eve used the toe of her shoe to nudge the dead bird toward the nearby shrubbery. "Here, cat. You can have it back."

The big tom just looked at her. Like Bianca was still looking at her.

To escape their dual regard, Eve kept her gaze on the dead bird. Suddenly hating the idea of leaving it unprotected against the elements, she knelt. A sharp-edged rock was lying nearby on the damp earth. She picked it up and went to work digging a small grave.

Maybe it was the activity that prompted Bianca's next words. "Eve, we . . . we haven't talked much about finding your father's remains."

"What's there to say?" Eve kept her voice casual. "We'd already accepted his death years ago." Perhaps the others had. The truth was, however, that even though he'd been missing since she was twelve years old, she'd always held out hope that Salvatore had been somewhere in hiding and that someday he'd return. Was that so strange? It wasn't easy to accept being truly alone in the world.

Above her head, she heard Bianca sigh. "I never talked enough about the past with you girls."

Squelching her squeamishness, Eve used her rock to push the pretty yellow bird into the little hole she'd made. "It doesn't matter." And she certainly didn't want to talk about it *now*. Her current modus operandi was to ignore or avoid all unpleasant things.

With the exception of Nash Cargill, she'd been doing okay.

What would Bianca have to say about the past anyhow? That it had been a strain on the marriage to raise this other, extraneous daughter? That it hadn't been easy loving the living symbol of her husband's infidelity? Eve had drawn her own conclusions about that while looking at herself in the mirror every morning— deciding that the secret to an unbroken heart was controlling your feelings for a man and thus not letting him control you.

Rock still in hand, she swept the mound of dirt she'd made over the dead bird. Covering it up. "Let's talk about something more pleasant," she said, even managing to throw a sunny smile over her shoulder. "Do you have another hot date tonight?"

"*Eve.*" A flush tinged Bianca's European cheekbones.

It lightened Eve's heart. "Oh, you're as bad as Téa. Always so prickly and secretive when it comes to men. We know you've been seeing that guest who's been staying here for the last few months. What's his name?"

"Well . . . I . . ."

Eve took pity and grinned. "So are you seeing 'Well . . . I' again tonight, or what?"

Shaking her head in obvious exasperation, Bianca crossed her arms over her chest. "No, as a matter of fact, I'm not. But I did invite an old friend of you girls to have dinner with us, if you can make it."

With the corpse buried, Eve rose, rock still in her hand. "My calendar's free tonight. Who'd you invite?"

"Sandra Dailey."

The rock fell to the pavement from Eve's slack fingers. "Sandra."

"I remember her from your school days at Our Lady of Poverty. She stopped by the front office to say hello."

"To say hello to you?"

"I suppose she was hoping to run into one of you girls."

Me. She was hoping to run into me, because I keep ducking her calls.

"So I invited her to dinner tonight and told her I'd try to get you three together as well. Wasn't she a particular friend of yours?"

"Téa's. She has always been closer to Téa." When they were seventeen, Sandy Dailey had dropped Eve as a friend after some unpleasant accusations. Eve hadn't particularly missed the friendship, though, busy as she'd been with dating Sandy's former boyfriend.

That was the problem with living in Palm Springs, that was the problem with the whole Coachella Valley, for that matter. The surrounding mountains made it a very, very small world.

"Sandra works for the government," Bianca said. "One of the acronyms. I forget which now."

The SEC. Sandy Dailey was the investigator who had explained to Eve, at their meeting, about illegal insider trading and the punishments that could be handed out. Think Martha Stewart. Think Martha Stewart at Camp Cupcake. Behind bars. Incarcerated. Locked up.

Claustrophobia for days on end.

Though Eve had gained nothing—lost everything!— from her single foray into victimless crime, Sandy Dailey had told Eve to keep herself available for further questioning.

And Eve, sticking to her modus operandi, had avoided the woman's phone calls ever since.

But now, oh hell, unless she wanted to ignore Sandy's obvious emotional blackmail and take the chance the other woman wouldn't spill her secrets to Bianca, Téa, and Joey, Eve was now going to have to call *her*.

Chapter Four

"Flirtin' With Disaster"
Molly Hatchet
Flirtin' With Disaster (1979)

Nash felt like a stalker himself, lurking beside the driver's door of Jemima's toy SUV. By definition, a "utility vehicle" shouldn't come in colors like red or blue or—good God—pink, but here he was anyway, leaning against a Pepto bumper to make sure his little sister didn't skip out on their lunch date. At least the weather—clear skies and 80 degrees—was sunny, even if his outlook wasn't.

He'd put her manager and her agent in L.A. on the Ricky Becker–watch from their end, though the police had told them the same thing they'd told him. The crazy kid wasn't crazy enough to be locked up. He hadn't done anything scary enough . . . yet. It was that *yet* that was keeping Nash close to Jemima until someone got a bead on little Ricky's whereabouts.

Scowling, Nash checked his watch. She'd said five

minutes . . . fifteen minutes ago. Now, it could have been her usual lax notion of time, but she'd been squawking about his bodyguard stance since he'd told her about it yesterday—that is, when she hadn't been avoiding him altogether. Was she trying to ditch him again?

Five minutes later there was still no sign of her.

Damn it all, he thought, his fingers curling into fists. This situation was going to make him nuts. He was used to confronting obstacles head-on and then crushing them. Circling problems was for those pretty NASCAR boys, not for a monster-truck man like himself.

From a row away in the spa parking lot came the unmistakable metallic *click-click-click* of a solenoid trying to engage the starter. It labored again without catching. And then again.

Nash's clenched hands eased. Smiling, he straightened away from the SUV. Now here was trouble he could do something about immediately. He'd feel more relaxed after some hands-on problem solving.

The solenoid clicked a few more times as he made his way around a classic Caddie and an onyx Navigator. He reached the hapless motorist just as she exited the driver's side of a battered blue Hyundai. His stride hitched and he stared, not sure which startled him most—swank Eve Caruso in a beater of a car, or sexy Eve Caruso buttoned up in a black business suit, her glorious blonde hair confined in a tight roll behind her head.

Her gaze landed on him and he could read her first thought in the expression on her face. *Damn*, she was thinking. *Just my luck.*

For some reason, it made him grin. "Need any help?"

She slammed shut the door and stomped to the front of her car on businesslike black heels. "Believe it or not, I can change a tire and," she said, reaching for the hood latch, "even locate a car engine." She proved it by lifting the hood and propping it open.

He was quiet for a moment as she stared down at what was inside. Then he rubbed his chin with his hand. "Beyond that, uh, what can you do?"

He didn't need to see her eyes to feel the snap in them. "Nothing, double damn it."

Grinning again, he ventured closer until he was near enough to sniff her naked-flesh-and-bath-bubbles scent. "Are you on your way to a social engagement?"

"Something like that," she said, without looking at him.

"You're dressed like you're going to a funeral."

Her laugh was short and bitter. "Something like that, too."

Nash frowned. He'd been needling her some, sure, but he hadn't meant to hit a tender spot. "Are you all right?"

Her shoulders stiffened. Then she took a slow turn and leaned back against the car's grille in a pose that struck him as more practiced than provocative. Her voice purred. "Now what makes you think I'm not one-hundred percent peachy-keen?"

With his gaze on her plump mouth and her throaty words echoing in his ears, Nash's hormones jumped like Shaq on a thirty-point night. But he poured a metaphorical cooler of Gatorade over them and shoved his hands in his jean pockets. "Maybe because you're all dressed up with no way to get there. In case you don't know, that *eh-eh-eh* noise your engine is making can mean only one thing."

A frown developed between her perfect blonde brows. "What's that?"

"That you need me, darlin' "— he was back to needling her, for some unknown reason—"whether you like it or not."

"You mean, whether I like *you* or not."

Since he figured they both hoped she didn't, Nash let it go. "Now, move aside," he said and, without thinking, put his hands on her upper arms to shift her out of the way.

At the contact, they both froze. He remembered how she'd jumped when he'd touched her in the closet the morning before. Her gaze lifted to his, and he didn't know what the hell she was remembering.

He didn't care. At the feel of her beneath his hands, his hormones were hopping around like pro ballplayers again—or maybe more like junior high schoolers—and he couldn't look away from that perfect face. Eyes of the deepest blue, high cheekbones, small straight nose, and that mouth, oh God, that mouth. Somewhere, some man had written sonnets to that mouth.

Nash was more of a limerick man himself, but her lips could drive even him to loftier heights.

His fingers tightened in possession, just as she side-stepped away.

He was left staring down at the grimy Hyundai engine instead of Eve Caruso's over-the-top beautiful face. Good. Thank you. Perfect.

"I'm in kind of a hurry," she said.

He slid a glance at her. She arched an imperious eyebrow. No doubt men fell all over themselves to do her bidding. God knows he wanted to.

So he took his own sweet time reaching for his pocket tool.

"If you can't fix it, just say so, okay?" Her voice was twenty-four karat sweet. "It won't make you look any smaller in my eyes."

Pausing, he turned his head her way. "If you were looking at all, you'd know there's not one part of me that's small, darlin'."

She lifted that damn brow higher.

He bent over the dirty engine. To his surprise, she stepped close behind him to peer around his shoulder. The air should have only contained the familiar, heady smell of grease and gas and oil, but she messed it up by adding the distracting perfume of girl. Frowning, he glanced at her again.

"I want to know what's wrong," she said. "So I can take care of it myself next time."

Translation: I can take care of myself *all* the time.

"Your battery connections are corroded," he said, scraping the white gunk away with the screwdriver he'd pried from his Leatherman. "You have to keep these clean. I'll tighten them down, and then we should wash them with a baking soda solution."

"Do we have to? I really am pressed for time."

"What?" he scoffed. "You can't be late for some charity lunch?"

"That would be rude, wouldn't it?"

Her snippy tone irritated the hell out of him again. "Like me, you mean?"

He didn't have to see the eyebrow to know it was arching once more. "You're the one who called me a gossip."

"It's a silly job you have," he muttered, bending further down.

"Oh, that's right. It's not something *meaningful* like playing Tonkatrucks with the other big boys."

Oh, fine. He felt a smile tugging at his mouth. He might now own a multi-million-dollar business, but it *had* all started out with a passion for Tonka and Matchbox. "Why do you do what you do?" he asked.

She was quiet a moment. "Because it's fun." She was quiet again. "Why do you do what you do?"

He straightened to look down at her. "Because it's fun."

She smiled. So did he. No games, no pose, nothing but two people who at the moment had a meeting of the minds.

Maybe that thought occurred to her as well, and like him, made her uncomfortable, because then they both frowned. He wasn't supposed to be near her, let alone appreciate anything about her. Certainly she didn't appreciate *him*.

But his gaze wouldn't shift off her angel face. "Are you seeing someone?" he heard himself say, his voice abrupt.

He silently groaned as the question floated awkwardly in the air between them.

"Am I seeing someone?" she repeated slowly, giving him plenty more time to wish he could kick his own ass.

Why had he asked her that? Take-care-of-herself-or-not, this woman was trouble, she was trouble with a capital Too Effing Sexy. He didn't want a barracuda in his life any more than he wanted the babes with their bad credit and their bad exes.

"That's quite an interesting question." She seemed to mull it over, then her fingers found his skin. To be precise, her fingernails lightly scratched along the bulge of muscle on his forearm, ruffling the hair. His scalp prickled. His cock stirred.

His only defense was to lift an eyebrow as coolly as she. "It's a simple question."

"Well . . ." She drew out the word to the same length as her next stroke of nails, then gave a small shrug that could mean anything.

Frustration made him fist his fingers again. He'd walked over to find a relaxing "hands-on" experience, and instead he'd found Eve Caruso and all her grind-his-back-teeth beauty. His _"Are you seeing someone?"_ gave her the upper hand, but he knew better than to let it show. He stared her down, freezing his muscles even as his blood heated.

Perhaps she sensed his strong will, because her touch altered as she stroked down his flesh. Instead of her nails it was a soft fingertip, tracing a circle on the top of his hand.

Witch. Tracing a heart.

His teeth ground again. Didn't she have all the moves down pat?

Her tongue touched the bow of her upper lip, leaving a wet spot in the matte pink perfection. He still couldn't look away.

"Nash?" Her voice was soft. Faint.

He had to lean closer. To hear, he told himself. "What?"

Only a breath separated them. "What is it you want?"

"Bonjour!"

At the sound of Jemima's cheerful voice, Nash nearly choked. He jerked back from the superbeauty, pulling free from her touch and the hypnotic net of attraction she cast out without a qualm. His head whipped toward his sister. "You're late."

"Je suis désolée." Though she switched to English, her

French accent remained. "Ees so confusing, this passion for time you *Americains* feel."

Nash rolled his eyes. "Can it, kid."

Her grin was impish and unapologetic. "So sue me. I got held up on a call with my agent about the new script." Nash wondered about that. The last he'd seen her, she'd been chatting up some guy swathed in bandages.

Jemima's gaze darted between Nash and Eve. "What have you guys been doing?"

"Fixing her car," Nash said, turning away to return the hood to its closed position. "It should start fine now."

"Actually," Eve corrected, "we were sharing our romantic—"

"Mistakes," he said without looking at her. Indulging in that last piece of conversation had been a definite mistake.

"Oh, *mon frère* has made tons of those," Jem said blithely, waving her hand in a Gallic gesture. "He's the king of mistakes."

Nash swung around to glare at his sister, while speaking to the other woman. "Eve, didn't you say you had to be going?"

Though he refused to look at her face again, he could feel the smile playing at her mouth. Hell, her touch was still ghosting over his flesh.

"Not when this is getting so . . . intriguing."

"He's got a fat file folder of Farrahs," Jemima informed Eve. "Though he's claimed to have sworn off of them."

"Farrahs?"

Jemima looked so damn innocent. It was going to be a shame that he'd have to concoct some horrible payback for this little stunt. He pinned her with his gaze. "If you know what's good for you—"

"It happens to be a popular name amongst the women who follow the monster-truck circuit," Jemima said. "Nash has dated—what?—seven of them?"

"Two." So this was how his sister was going to punish him for his big-brother protectiveness. Frustration was rising again, but there was no point in letting either woman guess they'd gotten to him. He leaned against the front fender of the Hyundai and gave a go-ahead gesture to Jemima. "Do your worst, brat."

"It's a hobby. He's rescued a half dozen Farrahs from bad jobs, bad choices, or the bad boys they've hooked up with."

"I'm sure they're suitably grateful," Eve murmured.

"Not grateful enough, according to Nash. He claims he's climbed off his white steed for good, because he's tired of those women going off with his best CDs, his best T-shirts, and, ultimately, his best friends." Drawing in a breath, she darted him a look. "But what *I* think is—"

They were all spared the brat's psychoanalysis by the ring of a cell phone. After pats all around, it was found to be coming from the device in Eve's suit jacket pocket. One look at the screen and her face leached color.

He found himself stepping forward. "Eve—"

"I'm late. I have to go." She hurried to her car door.

Getting there first, he opened it for her. It wasn't that he was a gentleman, he was just damn glad that she was going on her way. Finally. Pale or not. Who cared?

She slid in. He slammed shut the door, his hand on the frame of the open window. "Have fun," he said.

Her gaze met his. She didn't look like fun was on her horizon, but her lips curved in a quick smile. "Thanks," she replied, her fingers brushing the top of his knuckles. Without his permission, his hand turned and captured hers.

Their palms met, and a hot spark jumped up his arm and sent a heated message to his groin. Oh, hell. That ol' black magic was damn sneaky, wasn't it? It didn't care if you wanted it or not. If the chemistry was there, then, *poof! sizzle! bang!* it had you under its spell. Her spell. Though the look in Eve's eyes told him it was a mutual misfortune.

However, she managed to pull away first. Shaking his head, Nash watched her back out and drive off. So much for his hands-on problem solving, he thought, letting out a sigh. It had only left him feeling more frustrated than before.

Chapter Five

"Stop, Look and Listen"
The Chiffons
"A" side, single (1966)

In a Denny's halfway between Palm Springs and Riverside, Eve sat on orange vinyl and stared out the dusty windows. The glass double-entry doors were just a dash away, but she pressed her knees together and curled her toes in her pumps to keep herself in her seat.

Sandy Dailey pushed the saucer piled with plastic thimbles of creamer across the fake-grained table. Eve already knew they were lukewarm and ten minutes from spoiling. She'd take her coffee as black as her mood had been since she'd been forced to phone the SEC investigator. Sandy had agreed to cancel her dinner at the spa the night before if Eve promised to meet with her this afternoon.

"So," Sandy started. "Why don't you tell us again how it happened."

"Us" being Sandy and her younger associate, a boy-accountant who looked more like Tobey Maguire than a government investigator. Still, since he was male, Eve should catch his eye and unbutton her jacket or lick her lips or find some excuse to touch him, but she couldn't muster the energy. "I explained the first time we talked, Sandy."

Under the SEC's questioning, Eve had sung like a canary, still reeling from the double whammy of the discovery of her father's remains and the betrayal of Vince Standish within days of each other.

"Tell us again." The ten years since high school graduation had honed the bones of Sandy's face to razor-sharp lines. Her gaze was sharp, too, and trained on Eve's.

"Eleven months ago Vince asked me to marry him. When I refused and broke off our relationship, I thought he took it well. I thought we remained friends."

"Apparently not." Sandy sounded unsympathetic.

Eve shrugged. "Apparently not. After the merger actually went through, my broker said it was as if I was a hundred and eighty degrees off. Now my new stock—the stock I'd been tipped to invest in—was worth only pennies on the dollar. That's when I figured out Vince had planned it that way."

"He's not a man who takes disappointment easily," Sandy replied. "And you still haven't confronted him?"

"Why give him the satisfaction?" Instead, she'd pretended to everyone that her decision to sell off her condo and her Mercedes had been due to her moving up—although she had yet to find the exact right replacements. She'd sold everything she could to pay off the loans, including eBaying a bunch of trinkets and taking a trunkload of clothes to a designer consignment boutique in a city seventy miles away, where no one would recognize her.

Sandy tapped her chin with a blood-red fingernail. Eve had worn a dress in that exact same shade when Sandy's ex had taken her to Sandy's prom. Eve wanted to ask the other woman if that was what had prompted this little shakedown, but not with accountant Tobey at the table.

"You remember I told you we can put you away for this."

Eve suddenly felt the walls closing in on her, just as she had the first time Sandy had brought it up. Jail. Prison. No way out.

Darting a quick look at those wide double doors, Eve gripped her fingers together in her lap. "It seems hard to believe," she managed to say, though she'd done enough Internet research to prove that Sandy's threats weren't empty. "You have all the records. You know I'm now broke."

"When it comes to insider trading, it's the intent that matters, not the result. The SEC prosecutes all kinds of people, from CEOs to custodians. From winners to losers. We don't want anyone to think they can fly beneath the radar."

Eve squeezed her fingers together again. *"Have fun,"* she suddenly remembered Nash Cargill saying as she'd prepared to drive away to the meeting, and she choked back a half-hysterical giggle. *Hey, Preacher, are we having fun yet?*

"You have nothing to say?" Sandy prodded.

Sadist. "Only that I think it's time I talked to a lawyer." Though she had no idea how she'd afford one, unless she went to Bianca or her grandfather. Unless she wanted all the Carusos to know how the inconvenient bastard daughter had screwed up. Screwed up at this time, when her grandfather was preparing to retire and the family was in flux. Wouldn't they be happy she'd brought the authorities one step closer into their lives?

"What made you do it, Eve? On some level, at least, you had to know it was wrong."

Like stealing boyfriends was wrong? But she hadn't made an extra effort to get Scott Chambers to call her when they were seventeen. She just hadn't hung up on him when he had. As for taking advantage of the insider stock tip . . . she was a Caruso, wasn't she? Didn't that give her a genetic excuse for her crime?

It had been less than a week after they'd uncovered her father's remains that Vince Standish had whispered that little financial secret in her ear. All sorts of bad memories had been surfacing during those days, and his tip had appeared so harmless. With less than twenty-four hours to act, she hadn't mulled it over long. Truth to tell, it had seemed a piece of very good luck at a very dark time.

But Sandy wasn't soliciting Eve's explanations, she suddenly realized. This was less about rubbing on old rival's nose in her mistakes and more about . . .

"What is it you want, Sandy?"

The other woman's expression didn't falter. She was quiet a moment, then she shrugged. "Standish has toyed with the SEC rules and regulations before. I want him, and with your help I think I can get him."

Not that Eve felt very charitable toward Vince at the moment, but *she* wanted something more than him getting his comeuppance. "What do you have in mind? And more importantly, what's in it for me?"

Chapter Six

"Trouble No More"
The Allman Brothers Band
Eat a Peach (1972)

Late that night, Nash pushed open one of the French doors leading to the Kona Kai's small lounge, a beer on his mind. His gaze honed in on the babe at the bar, and he slowed his stride. Her back to him, Eve Caruso sat perched on a stool, her blonde hair streaming in soft waves over her shoulders.

It was late, he was irritated after a day of shadowing his sister, and he definitely wasn't ready for another round with the superbeauty. After this morning he'd again promised himself to keep his distance from her.

But he still wanted that beer, so he decided to cross the bar area to reach the front desk through the second set of French doors on the other side of the room. He'd get the person manning the reception area to fetch a draft for him and then he'd escape back to his room via another route. It wasn't a cowardly move—just cautious.

And as her throaty chuckle wrapped itself around his dick and tugged, he congratulated himself on his quick Plan B.

If only he hadn't then slowed to see who'd made her laugh. If only she hadn't then seemed to sense a presence behind her and swung around.

If only she hadn't been apparently tipsy enough to lose her balance and nearly land at his feet.

Catching her around the waist, he re-righted her just as she let loose another husky chuckle. "Uh-oh. I almost fell for you." She beamed up a smile at him. "Would you like a drink? I'm buying." Her voice lowered to a stage whisper. "But only because I get a discount."

"I thought I was the one you were buying drinks for, Evie," the man on her other side complained. He appeared to be two times more hammered than "Evie" and four times her age.

She plucked a spear of olives from her martini glass and sucked on the third and last little greenie. The old dude watched her hollowing cheeks with a disgusting intent. Sighing, Nash pulled out the stool next to hers and took a seat. Old habits died hard, didn't they? But the good news was, though she might need a chaperone, she was too drunk to be dangerous to him.

He glanced at the young man who came to stand on the other side of the bar. "Beer," he ordered. "Whatever you have on draft."

"And another martooni," Eve put in. "My dad used to call them that. Martoonis."

The bartender grimaced. "Eve, are you sure—"

"Of course I'm sure! Vodka martooni, very, very, very dry. With one, two, three olives." As she held up three fingers, she glanced over at Nash's face, then stiffened. "Oh, no. Oh, no, no, no."

"What?"

Her valentine lips turned down in a stern frown. "No sermons tonight, Preacher. I've had a trying day, and tonight this party girl wants to party on without interference."

The bartender slid the beer and the martini in front of them. "She doesn't drink much," he told Nash. "I've been watering down the vodka and she's still sloppy."

"I am not sloppy." She straightened her spine and pushed her hair behind her ears. "You tell him, Nash. You tell him I'm not sloppy."

"You're not sloppy."

"And *you're* not sincere."

Now *that* sounded more like the superbeauty he knew and was suspicious of, so he grinned. "Car work for you okay?"

"Purrr-fectly." She scooted her stool closer, propped her elbow on the bar, and peered up at him through sooty lashes. "Maybe I should put you on retainer. What's a private mechanic go for these days? And what could I possibly provide as down payment?"

The drunk on the other side of her slung his arm around her shoulders. "I'll pay you, Evie, I'll pay you anything you want. Just come back to my room with me."

Nash didn't think twice. He gripped the geezer's wrist, removed the offending appendage, and let it drop. "You're done, dude."

"But—"

"Done." Putting on his I-crush-cars-for-a-living face, Nash rose and stepped closer to the older man. "The lady doesn't want you or your money."

Maybe he sounded menacing, too. His only intention had been to get the guy out of Eve's face, but he couldn't say he was sorry to see the man push away from the bar and stumble off. When Nash settled back onto his own stool, Eve slid him a sidelong look and pulled the olive spear she'd resumed sucking out of her mouth again.

"I could have taken care of that myself, Preacher. I'm not one of your Farrahs."

That reminded him. He had to ask the front desk to make a 3:00 a.m. wake-up call to his little sister, with Nash's compliments. "Can't we forget about that? The Preacher and the Farrahs?"

That sent her back to her martini glass for another gulp. "Absolut-ely! Get it? Absolut-ely. As in the vodka. Tonight we're here to forget."

"I'll bite."

Her blue eyes went innocent-wide and her voice breathy. "Promise?"

Shaking his head, he laughed. "You *are* sloppy."

"What's that supposed to mean?"

"A few martinis and you lose your subtlety, darlin'."

She stared at him, obviously indignant. "I do not."

"I'm afraid so. Too much vodka and the vamp is way overdone."

Her jaw dropped. It made him focus on her puffy bottom lip and the wet texture of her pink tongue. "I've never overdone anything in my life."

"Whatever you say."

"I say I'm right." She slapped the top of the bar. "I've been wrapping men around my little finger—with subtlety and without an ounce of 'vamp,' mind you—since I was a toddler in petticoats and a pinafore."

Oh, he could see it. Pink ribbons, too. "Maybe you're getting old, then. Stale."

She blinked. She blinked again. "Huh?"

"You know, used up. Your wiles, your charm. Maybe they wear out or something." A smile was struggling to break free. This was the most fun he'd had since he'd entered the record books five years ago with the longest monster-truck jump in history. He gestured toward her. "After a few years, your tits sag and trying too hard sets in."

She stared another second longer at his face. Then she glanced down at her spectacular chest, then up at him again. "Take that back. I'm only twenty-eight years old."

If she'd been sober, he wouldn't have had a prayer of survival. He knew that. But God, he felt as if he was taking a few points back for every male she'd slain from toddlerhood until today. "But going on twenty-nine, right?"

He braced—okay, barely—for the insulted super-beauty's next reaction. In her vodka-induced state, he figured she was virtually harmless.

So when she slid to her feet and stood between their seats, he only grinned, despite the fact there was nothing the least bit funny about her stiletto heels, denim worn as tight as a suntan, and T-shirt that was tickling the belly ring in her navel. When she gripped one of his knees to swivel his stool to face her, he didn't protest.

It was only when she stepped between his veed thighs that he felt his smile die. The inner leg seams of his jeans kissed the outer seams of hers as she moved closer. Her naked-except-soap scent filled his head. "That sounds like a dare to me."

Christ. Even martooni-d she was a force to be reckoned with. He breathed in another gulp of that wet-flesh perfume of hers and forced himself to hold still as she slid her arms around his neck. By pure instinct, his hands cupped her bottom, and now that they were there it would have been a waste not to appreciate the round, firm curves.

Wasn't there anything about this woman that wasn't all-out, over-the-top, more-than-her-fair-share spectacular?

His cock battled his zipper to answer that one.

And she glanced down as if she knew. Of course she knew, he thought, watching the satisfied smile that curved the corners of her mouth. "You are trouble," he murmured.

"But not too much for you to handle, right?"

This was a game to her. But hell, he'd started it, so he squeezed her butt. "I seem to be handling it just fine, don't you think?"

"Let's put that to a little test." She pulled his head closer.

He resisted. Frowning, she tugged harder, but he was as strong as a bull and didn't budge.

Her sky-blues met his eyes in surprise. "Don't you want to kiss me, Nash?"

"No." It was the honest truth.

"No?—" She broke off as her gaze jerked over his shoulder. "Oh, God."

In his arms, he felt her body tremble. "What?"

"Oh, God," she muttered. "Oh, God, can this day get any worse?"

He tried turning his head to see what she did, but she caught his jaw in one very cold hand. "Listen to me," she said, all signs of tipsiness gone. Her voice was clear and crisp, as if she'd been slapped to alertness.

"All right."

"In a minute, you're going to kiss me. Then you're going to pick me up and walk me out of here. Do not pass Go, do not collect two hundred dollars, do not pay any attention to the pair of men loitering in the doorway."

"Which one am I specifically not paying attention to?"

She didn't question how he knew. "The younger, dark-haired one who is channeling his inner Chili Palmer."

So it was a gangsterish, Travolta look-alike he was shielding her from. And *shielding* was the operative word, he knew, because another tremor shook her body.

"On the count of three," she whispered. "One . . . two . . ."

Hairs leaped high on the back of Nash's neck. He didn't wait for three.

Chapter Seven

"Don't Ask Me No Questions"
Lynyrd Skynyrd
Second Helping (1974)

Eve's mouth was softer and hotter than Nash had ever imagined. And despite himself, over the last forty-eight hours of their acquaintance he'd been imagining it a lot. "God," he murmured against her lips. With his hands on her ass, he pulled her closer, and his thighs clamped hard onto hers.

He swept his tongue along her lower lip. Through both their shirts he felt her nipples tighten and another tremor shake her body.

Because of his kiss . . . or because of Chili?

She was playing this for the man in the doorway, he reminded himself, or for some game of her own. With that in mind, he eased his hold on her. She didn't take him up on the hint, though. Instead, she speared her fingers in the back of his hair and pressed her sweet little tongue into his mouth.

A fire ignited in his belly and he yanked her to him again, her nipples now as hard as his cock. She slanted her head to change the fit of the kiss and then he took over, sliding into her mouth so that he filled her the way the rest of his body was aching to do.

She trembled again, and he didn't let it stop him from savoring her mouth, her wet heat, the almost-pornographic pleasure of those showstopping tits against his pecs and that perfect ass against his palms. But she wasn't protesting; instead, she was melting against him, like soft butter spread on hot toast.

He had to get her naked.

The imperative need of that thought shocked him free of the sexual haze. This kiss wasn't for real. Looping his thumbs in her back pockets, he jerked her away and lifted his head.

Her eyes were half-closed, her mouth was open and wet.

"Shit," he muttered. But instead of diving back in like he wanted to, he cast a swift glance over his shoulder. Just as she'd said, two men were standing in the doorway between the lounge and the spa grounds. One was gray-haired, short and wiry, while the other was younger, taller, dark-haired, wearing a khaki-colored designer suit and an expression so cold that Nash figured he must practice it in a mirror every morning.

If the man had been staring at him, he would have stood his ground, but it was Eve who had his focus, and Nash remembered he was supposed to get her out of here. He planted a quick kiss on her mouth, then curled his hands around her waist. "Let's go, Party Girl."

He boosted her up, and she slid her long, swimsuit-model legs around his waist, leaving his erection nestled two layers of denim away from heaven. *Jesus*, he thought, stifling a groan. She was going to kill him with lust alone.

Her eyes opened all the way, and her gaze met his. Despite the startling kiss, their provocative pose, and the man in the doorway she wanted to avoid, she was still cool as a cucumber. She could even arch that damn brow. "Apparently you need monster equipment to drive those monster machines."

"Take it as a compliment," he said, striding toward the door and the two men he intended to push through without hesitation. "Because what I have to tell you, isn't."

"What's that?"

He shifted her a little higher and kept his eye on the two men eyeing them. "Darlin', not only are your tits starting to sag," he murmured in her ear, "but you're getting a bit bottom-heavy, too."

And whether it was due to her surprised laughter or his brisk pace, the duo at the door parted and let them through without incident.

His stride ate up the path that led from the public areas of the Kona Kai to the gate separating them from the private suites and bungalows. The guard held the wrought-iron open for them, and Nash walked through. He kept going until he heard the clang that signaled it was shut. Then, without warning or ceremony, he dropped the party girl to her pretty feet.

She stumbled a little on landing, but he resisted the urge to hold her up. Hold her again. Kiss her, long, and hot and wet. He couldn't let one fake smooch lead him away from good sense or the questions he wanted answered.

He got right to it. "So what just happened?"

"You hustled me out of there. Thanks." She tried to put her hands in her front pockets, but those X-rated jeans were so damn tight they only fit her index fingers. "Good night."

In disbelief, he watched her turn on one pointy toe of those bad-girl pumps. "Where the hell do you think you're going?"

She glanced at him over her shoulder. "For two aspirin and a big glass of water, unless you know better hangover prevention."

There was no need for aspirin or anything else. Something had driven the drunkenness right out of her. That's what he wanted to understand. "Hold it right there."

Her feet stopped moving, but she did the whole eyebrow arch again, from over her shoulder. "What?"

"I just sucked face with you and you think you can walk away without an explanation?"

She winced. " 'Suck face'? I haven't heard that since seventh grade."

The superbeauty made Nash feel like seventh grade. Flooded with hormones, fascinated by the female half of the world, more than ready to flex brand-new muscles. In seventh grade, Nash's height had jumped from five-and-a-half feet to six, and his father had halted his Monday through Friday threats to beat the crap out of him. He'd waited until the booze-binge weekends instead.

Nash put his mind back to the matter at hand. "I want to know what was going on back there. Who's this Chili, Eve?"

Still keeping her distance, she turned. Shrugged. "Nino Farelle. He's an . . . associate, I guess we'll say, of my grandfather."

"Cosimo Caruso. Don of the California Mafia."

Her mouth curved. "You've been doing your homework. I wasn't sure you believed me."

Nash strode closer to confront her toe-to-toe. "Are you seeing this Nino? Is that it?" He'd asked her earlier that day if there was a man in her life, and now he realized she'd never answered. "Christ, Eve, did you use me to make him jealous?"

The thought churned like acid in his gut, but he ignored the burn and focused on keeping his hands relaxed at his sides. What did he care about her games, anyway? The answer: He *didn't* care about them.

She brushed her hair off her forehead. "You really don't have a very high opinion of me, do you?"

"The truth is not going to get you out of answering the question."

She laughed, and damn it, he liked it. Despite himself and everything he could tell about her by just looking at that perfect face and bombshell figure, there were these moments when he actually liked her, too.

"Here's the deal with Nino," she finally answered. "If I was alone or didn't look . . . involved, he would have come over to the bar and made it difficult for me to leave."

Nash wasn't sure she was being honest with him. "You could have just said so. I would have been happy to escort you out of there without all the dramatics."

"Ah, but then it would have been much more like rescuing me, wouldn't it?" She smiled, full-on and sexy. "And we would have missed out on *this*."

Then the delectable witch twined her arms around his neck, again. Then she kissed him, again.

She was trying to distract him from his questions. He knew that. He should put a stop to this.

For God's sake, he was bigger, stronger, meaner than she was, but she was so damn wily, with those soft breasts and soft mouth and sweet scent. They overpowered his caution, sucker-punched his common sense, made him forget his own damn name. She tried to stick her tongue between his lips again, but he didn't want to make it easy for her, so he cupped her face in his palms and slid his mouth over her chin and down her neck. There were a few things he didn't want to miss out on either.

"Nash—" she started to protest, but it petered out when he found the scented spot behind her ear. The oversized gold hoop in her lobe brushed coolly against his cheek, but her skin was hot beneath his lips. He traced her ear with his tongue and savored the little shimmy she made against his chest.

Once again, he cupped that incredible ass and tucked her hips more firmly to his. She'd already commented on his "equipment," so there was no reason to think he'd scare her off with his raging erection.

He figured nothing could scare this woman.

When he made it back to her mouth, she proved to him that a beauty contest wasn't the only place she could come up a winner. She slid her tongue along the insides of his lips as if she wanted to taste him. Her mouth opened to welcome his heavy return thrust. You could tell that some women objected to the intimacy of a soul kiss—and wasn't that a big ol' hint as to what other pleasures they'd object to—but Eve Caruso was born to French. He settled in for the long haul, sliding his fingers into her back pockets as he sucked gently on her bottom lip.

He was going to take his time. She didn't appear to realize that, because she tried taking over, her hands sliding from around his neck to head south. He warned her off by taking a little nip of that plump lower lip, at the same time tugging upward on those skintight jeans. Eve gasped and he smiled to himself, knowing just where he'd caused the knot of seams to press between her legs.

Maybe she thought it had been an accident, because she tried her takeover move again and again Nash "punished" her with that small sting of a kiss and another little upward jerk on her jeans. She gasped again, her head falling back, and he took the opportunity to slide his mouth down her neck. Her breasts heaved against his chest.

Not ready to move there yet, not when it was so obvious that she was accustomed to having things all her way, he ignored the obvious to stroke his whiskery cheek against the side of her throat. Then he soothed the spot with the slide of his hair. She choked off a sound, and he rubbed against her again.

He wanted her scent all over him. He wanted his all over her.

Uh-oh. Wrong thought. Wrong woman. The warning pierced his consciousness just as something else pierced the back of his left calf.

His head jerked up. "Ow!" Craning his head over his shoulder, he peered down at his lower leg. "What the hell?"

In the dim glow of a landscape light, Nash could see a shadowy creature behind him, its back feet on the ground, its forepaws—fore*claws*—sunk into his leg, right through his jeans.

He gave his calf a shake. "Scat. Shoo. God damn it, go away." But the beast hung on.

"Don't!" Eve broke free of Nash's grip. "Don't hurt him!"

The cat's claws dug deeper, and Nash grimaced. "Instead of talking to the ugly thing, do you think you could disengage it or something?"

"I'm talking to *you*, you oaf. Don't hurt Adam." She kneeled down and petted the ugly bugger, even as it stabbed harder into Nash's flesh. "Let go, my baby," she crooned. "I won't let the big man hurt either one of us."

"I won't let the big man hurt either one of us."

Nash frowned over the odd remark, then it flew from his head as the damn cat flexed once more, forcing him to bite back another curse. Finally the tom released him, slowly though, first delicately lifting one paw, then the other. Nash peered over his shoulder at the new holes in his jeans, then at Eve. "Has that thing had its rabies shot?"

She was standing now, cuddling the tattered beast close to her chest. It stared at Nash with a satisfied cat-smile on its hideous mug. "Don't be such a sissy," she said, toying with the creature's stump of an ear.

"I'm not kidding." Beneath his pants, he could feel blood rolling from the wound and into his sock. "When did that thing last see a vet?"

"I don't know. We've just sort of met."

He rolled his eyes. "Leave it to the Party Girl to pick up any stray male that wanders by."

Whoops. Her nostrils flared, her back stiffened, and Nash knew he'd just shoved one of his size 15s into the enormous cavern that was his mouth. But damn it, he'd been in the middle of the hottest make-out session of his life with the hottest woman of his life when he'd been rudely interrupted by a cat—an ugly cat—whom she appeared to like a hell of a lot better than she liked him.

Don't you suppose she might at least try to look as if she regretted the interruption? Instead, she looked as if she regretted the fact that Nash was alive.

Which reminded him that she just might get what that implied. "Look, Eve, you've got to understand. We're talking about a fatal disease. You might not give a hoot about my hide, but I happen to—"

"You get rabies from an animal *bite*, Nash."

"—feel—" He took a breath. Grimaced. "Like a total ass."

"Which makes it oh-so-much-easier for me to say good night." She was all icy superbeauty, and he couldn't think of one more remark to make as she turned away. But wasn't it better this way? He'd already decided she was dangerous to him. Those spectacular kisses? She probably doled those out the way a Mexican restaurant served up tortilla chips—anytime and as many as you wanted. He should be glad she was moving away from him.

Except he didn't feel happy. He felt frustrated and irritated and still aroused. As she sauntered off, the cat snuggled closer to her neck so it could silently laugh at Nash over her shoulder as he stood there alone in the dark.

His calf started stinging like a bitch and he felt more blood roll. *Good*, he told himself, *you deserve it. Maybe then you won't forget that taking pleasure with the superbeauty can only end in pain.*

Chapter Eight

"You Should Have Seen the Way
   He Looked at Me"
The Dixie Cups
"A" side, single (1964)

Only her younger sister showed up for their wedding-planners' breakfast the next morning. Since it was rare that Téa would be late for any obligation, let alone miss it altogether, Eve expressed concern.

Joey lowered her latte cup to one of the small tables set up outside the spa dining room. The rain appeared gone for good, and it was a typical winter day in the desert—which was like early summer most anywhere else in the Northern Hemisphere. "You're kidding, right? Don't you remember that Johnny's been out of town for a week? Last night was his and Téa's first chance for catch-up nookie. I imagine they're sleeping in."

Eve frowned. After yesterday's disturbing meeting with the SEC, she wanted as much normality as possible. "Still, she could have dragged herself out of bed."

Rolling her eyes, Joey picked up her coffee again. "Have you forgotten the morning after a lover's absence? When was the last time you had sex, Eve?"

She wondered what her sister would say if she told her last night, on the grounds of the Kona Kai, with all her clothes on.

Her hand moved up to touch the collar of the sleeveless turtleneck she was wearing with an old linen skirt and embroidered espadrilles. Goose bumps prickled there, just thinking about the beard burn Nash had left behind. She'd tried calling all the shots, but he'd turned the tables and controlled *her* instead. What he could do by just tugging on her jeans should be outlawed.

That was another reason why she wished Téa were here this morning. One glimpse of her overorganized, über-punctual older sister and perhaps Eve would wake up to find that the world hadn't taken yet another wild left turn and that yesterday was only a bad dream.

Last night, she hadn't nearly orgasmed from the simple sensation of a man's stubbled chin against the side of her neck.

Yesterday afternoon, she hadn't agreed to cooperate with the SEC by getting close to Vince Standish again.

"Hey, no need to look so freaked out," Joey said. "If you want to see Téa so bad, why don't you go over to her office after breakfast? She'll show up there eventually."

"No!" If Eve wasn't waking up from this nightmare, then she was going to manage it the best way she could think of—by staying safe within the confines of the Kona Kai.

Closing her eyes, she drew in a deep breath of the warm, dry air, scented by green and gardenia and a faint tinge of chlorine from one of the many pools. The soothing trickle of water from a wall fountain sounded in the distance, and she thought she could even make out the light drone of a blue-winged dragonfly flitting over the surface of a birdbath. She'd be sheltered here. If she played sick and didn't venture beyond these walls, then she couldn't be faulted for not following the SEC's plan for her to make contact with Vince Standish.

That was the deal Eve had made with Sandy. The SEC wouldn't prosecute her for insider trading—no jail time!—if she would get a taped admission from him. Their strategy was for her to first gain his trust during the many social occasions they both routinely attended.

But she was going to have to skip the parties.

Sure, it would make it harder to do her work as a society columnist, but she figured that for the balance of the social season she could find plenty of people to dish about the events she missed. If not, then hell, she'd make up the details. Maybe it went against her journalistic ethics, but those were trumped by the single most important ethic her father had always emphasized: Look out for #1.

Joey set down her coffee cup again. "Hey, I heard stuff about your monster truck man."

Eve's gaze shot toward her little sister. "My what? Who?"

"I asked one of the guys I golfed with yesterday. Knew all about him."

From the sly smile her sister was giving her, Eve realized she was expected to pump for the information. So instead, she picked up her latte and blew across the frothy top.

Obviously annoyed, Joey narrowed her eyes but kept her lips firmly closed.

Eve sipped at her drink, then used her napkin to blot her upper lip.

Joey's eyes became mere slits. She was fifteen seconds, max, away from bursting.

Fifteen . . . fourteen . . . thir—

"Don't you want to know what I found out?"

Eve shrugged. "If you want to tell me." Of course Joey wanted to tell her. That was the secret to getting whatever one wished out of the youngest Caruso. She had absolutely zero supply of patience, so it usually took less than half-a-minute's worth of cool nerve and the ability to hide a smile.

"Bitch," Joey said, without heat.

Now Eve did smile. "Amateur bitch."

It was just as well Téa wasn't there. Calling each other names always agitated her. Which made Eve smile again, as she propped her elbow on the tabletop. "So tell me everything."

"He wasn't raised with little Miss Hollywood. She's his half sister. When their father and the girl's mom divorced, Dad took Nash, and Mom took the baby starlet."

Interesting. Some men might look upon the circumstances as a reason to break ties with the other side of his family, but it was obvious that Nash took his brotherly obligations seriously. "The Preacher," she murmured to herself.

"Yep, that's what they call him on the circuit," Joey confirmed. "Not because he's holding Sunday services or anything, but because unlike many others, he keeps out of jail on Saturday nights and does his best to keep the younger guys out along with him. For a man in a high-octane sport, he likes to keep things low-key."

Well. The good ol' boy was actually *good*. Now why did that make her positively itch to break some commandments with him? Which was so *not* a smart idea when she'd just decided to barricade herself inside the Kona Kai thanks to a "sudden illness." Nash Cargill was barricaded on her same side of the fence, and it wasn't the time for any manly distractions.

And as if that thought had conjured up its own evidence, a voice sounded from behind her. "Ladies."

Eve froze. If she didn't know any better, she'd say the birds had stopped singing, clouds had passed over the sun, nearby blades of grass had flattened themselves against the earth.

Joey's gaze flicked over Eve's head, then back to her coffee. "Wow, Nino. I didn't know they opened the coffins this early in the morning."

Nino Farelle. Eve should have known he wouldn't let her have the last—if unspoken—word last night by running out on him at the bar. Yesterday, he'd come to the Kona Kai expressly to see her, she'd known that. Expected it, actually, since the day she'd given up her condo and moved into the spa.

Though Nino hadn't been her boyfriend for almost a decade, whenever there was some change in her life—from a new haircut to a new lover to a new residence—he always managed to show up not long after to let her know he'd noticed. To let her know he was watching.

"Good morning to you, too, Giuseppina."

No one called Joey by her full name, their late grandmother's name, except Nino. Perhaps that's why her little sister disliked him so. Joey didn't know about the beating Nino had given Eve when she'd broken up with him—that was a secret from all but Téa.

"And Eve," he said. He was closer now, but she refused to turn and look at him. "How are you this beautiful morning?"

The words *after last night* hung in the air beside the question. "I'm well, Nino," Eve replied.

"Well-satisfied?" His olive-skinned fingers grazed her shoulder.

She fought her revulsion as she fought to remain still. From the corner of her eye she could see the thick scars on his knuckles and wondered if any of those had come from the punch he'd thrown against the wall right before the punches he'd thrown at her face.

"What do you want, Nino?" Joey barked out.

His hand fell away and Eve breathed, blessing her brusque little sister at the same time. As part of the management team at La Vita Buona, their grandfather Cosimo's legitimate business, Joey had more dealings than the other Caruso girls with their grandfather's illegitimate side—and associates. But by and large she turned a blind eye to what she heard and saw. It was Joey who claimed all the crime business was a lot more talk than action, even though it was Joey who visited the various "uncles" and "cousins" who wound up doing stints in county jail or federal prison.

Eve knew her little sister had a soft spot for men, especially those who had a dark and dangerous edge. Nino should have been right up her alley—he was as male, as gorgeous, and as deadly as they came—but Joey was smarter than her older sister, who had once imagined herself in love with him. Joey didn't even try to hide her dislike of the man.

"We'd offer you something to drink," she apologized

in an insincere voice, "but we don't have any blood suitable for a vampire on the menu."

"Then I'll just settle for Eve's coffee," he replied, seating himself between them at the table and pulling her cup his way.

A flush rushed up Joey's golden skin, and her brown eyes snapped.

Eve had left Joey to her own devices once before and still hated herself for it, so she forced herself to turn toward Nino. The sooner he got down to business, the sooner he would get out and leave her safely behind at the Kona Kai. "Is there something we can do for you?"

"Turn on your fucking cell phone." He lifted her coffee and took a long swallow.

She frowned. Nino liked to conduct his harassment in person. "Have you . . . have you been trying to call me?"

"Your grandfather has."

Eve's spine relaxed against her chair, the notion that Nino was on an errand for her grandfather making it that much easier to breathe. The fact that he wanted to move up in the ranks of her grandfather's organization was what had kept him away from her after that beating, and it was what had kept him in check all these years. He knew that if she told Cosimo about those punches, the same would happen to him . . . or much, much worse.

But she hadn't been silent out of pity for Nino. She'd kept quiet because the inconvenient bastard Caruso daughter hadn't wanted to bring more trouble to the family. It wouldn't have been easy for her grandfather to hurt the young man he'd taken under his wing when he was in his teens. She hadn't—didn't—want to be the cause of that pain.

Eve clasped her hands together in her lap to make sure they wouldn't tremble. Even knowing why Nino was here didn't make her any less wary of him. "What does Grandfather want?" she asked.

"He was going to come himself, but I talked him out of it," Nino said. "It's not safe for him to be moving about town right now."

Another reason she'd never ratted on the wiseguy. She believed he was truly loyal to her grandfather, an even more valuable commodity since an arsonist had recently sent Cosimo a threatening message by burning down the original venue for his eightieth birthday party.

"I'll try to get over to his house for a visit . . ." If Eve was serious about keeping to the Kona Kai—and she was—then she couldn't promise a particular date. ". . . soon."

Nino brought her coffee to his mouth again. "That will be too late."

"What?" Joey interjected. "What the hell are you talking about? Too late for what?"

"Calm down, *bambina*." Nino was smiling, obviously pleased with metaphorically pulling on Joey's pigtails.

Eve's upper lip started to throb. He'd smiled in just that way after the blood had gushed in her mouth. "Stop messing around," she said coldly. "Either spit out what you have to say or else—"

"Or else what?" Nino turned his evil smile on her. "You'll let your latest bull loose from between your thighs to turn on me instead? I think I can handle Nash Cargill, *cara*, just fine."

Nash. She didn't even want Nino knowing the other man's name. And yet now that Nino had said it aloud, Nash was all that she could think of. Big, strong, good ol' boy Nash, the straightforward Preacher who could sweep in and save her from all this. From Nino, from Vince Standish, from the SEC and their threat to put her in prison.

From all this ugliness of her own making. Nino had been her first bad choice when it had come to men, and Vince Standish had been her last. And didn't Sandy Dailey's ex—Scott Chambers—figure in there somewhere too?

More than once she'd wondered if that snake in Paradise her daddy had warned her about so long ago was none other than herself.

She wanted to set her forehead on the glass tabletop and weep, but crying hadn't gotten her anywhere since her father had disappeared. "Nino, what did my grandfather want you to tell me?"

He seemed to sense she was at the end of her rope. "That the official word is being sent out today. His retirement will go down May first."

Eve didn't ask if there was going to be a press release. The official word about his retirement from his "official" business had gone out two weeks before. He was stepping down as president of La Vita Buona on that same date. What Nino was talking about was Cosimo's unofficial—illegitimate—businesses run by the California Mafia. There had been speculation that while leaving the food company, he would retain his power within La Cosa Nostra. But it wasn't to be.

Now everyone would know, from New Jersey to Miami, from Palm Springs to Seattle, and all points criminal in between, that leadership would be changing on the West Coast.

"Any word on his successor?" she asked.

"Not yet." Nino's answer was short, but long enough

for her to be sure that he hoped it was he who would be named boss of bosses.

They were all silent for a moment, all acknowledging, Eve suspected, that whoever was named as the new leader would face in-fighting and out-fighting, from rival families, from rivals within their family, from the federal authorities. The whole California Mafia structure, the Carusos themselves, were going to be at risk.

"You'll take good care of him?" she whispered, unable to help herself. When their father had disappeared, Cosimo had stepped in, as much as he'd been able, to take care of his granddaughters. Even though he'd been preoccupied with regaining the mob boss's powers that he'd given over to his missing son. Even though Bianca had wanted little to do with her husband's family. "Promise me."

Nino hesitated. "If there was anyone I'd make a promise to, Eve . . ." There was an expression in his eyes that made him almost seem human. "But not that promise. I can't guarantee it. Not even for you."

She looked away.

"Cosimo has a promise he wants you to make, though," Nino continued.

Her gaze jerked back. "Me?"

Nino nodded. "Do what you can on the social circuit, he says. Make it clear that all is under control and all is well."

"What? Outside of family occasions, I don't generally party with the Mafia." And she wasn't planning on partying at all.

"You party with all kinds of people who have all kinds of friends," Nino returned. "And word gets around. The word Cosimo wants you to spread at every lunch, dinner, and fancy dance you attend is that there will be a smooth transition of command within the California Mafia. That power plays are out . . . or else."

She stared at him. "But . . . but . . ." Her plan to live like a recluse, like a nun behind the safe walls of the Kona Kai, was disintegrating before her very eyes. She might be able to ignore what the SEC wanted, but she couldn't ignore Cosimo. "I can't go traipsing around Palm Springs delivering threats."

"Then figure out a more charming method in which to get the point across." Nino was already rising from his chair, as if that was all there was to it.

"Good-bye, Giuseppina," he said. Then he leaned down to Eve. His mouth brushed her cheek. His whisper slithered into her ear. "And I'll be watching—you *and* Nash Cargill."

Nash. An image of him burst in her mind again. Big, strong, his arms reassuring, his voice a laidback rumble, his mouth so hot and hard on hers. So right. But oh, so wrong.

The only good thing about her grandfather's request was that stepping outside the Kona Kai's "convent" walls meant she'd have less opportunity to run into him.

Her hand moved to that sensitive spot on her neck again. One of the many bad things about her grandfather's request was how much the idea of not seeing Nash seemed to matter so much.

Chapter Nine

"Angel Baby"
Rosie & The Originals
"A" side, single (1961)

J emima Cargill threw herself onto the second cushioned lounger in the shade of the poolside, private
cabana. Her purple-casted wrist clunked against the
aluminum arm, and the sound caused the occupant of
the other lounger to shift his head toward her.

"Good God, you're going to hurt yourself with all
that pent-up energy," he said in his Aussie-accented
voice.

It wasn't energy but pure nerves, Jemima thought,
slanting a glance at the man she knew simply as "Charlie." As usual, his long body was covered by a white
spa robe. He wore a wide-brimmed khaki-colored
bush hat, wraparound Ray-Bans, and a thin white silk
scarf covering him from nose to throat.

"If I didn't see your big bony hands and feet, you
could make me believe you're the Invisible Man."

"1933 movie with Claude Rains, 1940 with Vincent Price, the TV show in the late fifties or the SciFi Channel version in the late 1990s?"

It was this kind of remark that made Jemima close to certain that her newfound friend was a veteran of the TV and movie biz like she was. "Or else you're a hopeless geek," she said out loud, "and that could be true as well."

"What are you talking about?"

She shook her head, not wanting to let on that she'd been thinking about his past or his profession—though it was becoming something of an obsession of hers. She only knew his first name and that he'd had some major facial surgery approximately four weeks before. Thanks to their side-by-side bungalows and shared suffering of insomnia, they'd struck up a friendship during the three weeks she'd been staying at the Kona Kai. But that didn't mean she could comfortably pry for anything beyond what he offered. Her agent, Larry Michaels, had recommended this spa precisely because the privacy of the guests was held sacrosanct.

"What exactly is *sacrosanct*?" she mused aloud again.

Charlie settled his wide shoulders against the cushion. "Sacred, you ignorant teenage Yank."

"Hey, maybe we could take a meeting and pitch that as a sitcom idea, you know? There was Sabrina the Teenage Witch, ours could be Jemima the Teenage Yank."

"You left out the ignorant part. And what would you do episode after episode? Instant Messenger your posse? Crib term papers off the Internet? Have sex with your boyfriend in the backseat of his parents' Hummer?"

She frowned at him. "You've either been watching

reruns of *The OC* again or you missed a dose of your meds."

Charlie shook his head. "Never mind."

Jemima swiveled on the chair so that she could face him, sitting tailor-style. Her gaze brushed across his long fingered hands, linked over his flat belly. When the recovery pain got to him he'd massage them to distract himself. "I'm too old, anyway," she said absently. "Almost twenty-one."

"Don't talk to me about too old," Charlie muttered. His right thumb stroked along his left forefinger. "You're a baby."

And that remark was just another reason she suspected Charlie was a player in the entertainment industry. Not necessarily an actor, because she thought she'd recognize the accented voice—if he was an A- or B-lister anyway—and she couldn't place his. But even producers and directors and agents liked to keep up a youthful appearance. Men included.

His right thumb went to work on his index finger, and with a sigh, Jemima reached over and grabbed his left hand between hers.

"Hey!" He tried to jerk away from her grasp.

"Relax. I give the best hand massage in Hollywood." The truth was, she had a thing for Charlie's hands. They'd begun their acquaintance by playing gin rummy, and her admiration for his card-handling abilities—he could do an in-air riffle shuffle and another that he called the Mulholland Bridge—had morphed into an undeniable fascination for his long, mobile fingers and wide palms.

She placed the back of his knuckles against her knee and began kneading the tips of his thumb and his pinkie. His skin was warm and rougher than hers. Masculine.

Male.

From beneath her lashes, she glanced over at Charlie, but she couldn't tell a thing he was thinking with those dark glasses covering half his face. "What color are your eyes?"

"At the moment? Somewhere between purple, green, and yellow."

"Not your bruises, your irises." She moved to his forefinger and ringman, massaging them with the same kneading action from tip to palm.

"Blue." He crossed one ankle over the other, and she verified that the curling hair she could see on them was a dark gold. Charlie was blonde, then. Blue-eyed. Old enough to warrant plastic surgery. Though, come to think of it, that could be to rectify some horrible facial defect or accidental injury.

Finished with his index finger, she began to work his palm with both of her thumbs, her cast only a minor hindrance. "What was that Mel Gibson film where he played the strange recluse with all the scars?"

"*The Man Without a Face*. Oversentimental story line, but Mel gets points for choosing something so challenging for his directorial debut."

Definitely face-lift for Charlie then, Jemima decided. He wouldn't be so matter-of-fact if the movie's premise mirrored his own situation. Not to mention that casual "Mel." It definitely sounded as if Charlie knew him.

And she wanted to know Charlie. More and more as the days—and nights—went on. "Have you ever been married?"

He tried pulling his hand away again, but she held fast. "What's this all about?" he asked.

"Just curious about your love life," she said lightly. "You tell me about yours, and I'll tell you about mine."

"You're too young to have had a love life. A love event maybe. Possibly a love weekend. No life."

She thought his skin had grown warmer. "You're starting to sound like my brother, Nash. I'm not your typical twenty-year-old, you know."

"I know," he muttered, tugging at his hand again.

She let him have it back, only to pull the other into her lap. "When I was eleven I played a runaway-turned-prostitute. I was a college student with a gambling addiction at sixteen and the opportunistic mistress of a drug lord last year. Not to mention the mental ward patient, the daughter of an international terrorist, and the teenage environmentalist who went head-to-head with a sleazy senator and the EPA."

Charlie's fingers closed over her hands, startling her. "Playing roles isn't living them, sweetheart. Acting out experiences isn't actually having them."

Her heart seized. "You've seen me on the screen, then. You think I'm lousy." She didn't want that to matter so much.

He released her hands and drew his own back. "I don't think you're lousy. Didn't you tell me you're making a movie with Mack Chandler next month?"

That was one reason why she wanted Charlie to think she was good. She'd settle for halfway decent. The idea of making a movie with American icon Mack Chandler had her shaking in her rubber-wedged sandals. Her apprehension had caused her agent to suggest this Palm Springs getaway. "Take some time to relax," he'd said. "Get your head ready for the next project. You won't miss the L.A. scene that much."

She didn't miss the L.A. scene at all. She'd been hanging around that scene as long as she could remember. Once you'd been let through a velvet rope by a bouncer who recognized your face only to have your feet barfed on by the "famous" contestant of the latest reality television show, you realized there had to be dimmer lights and better odors elsewhere.

With Jemima's mother now focused on her new husband, it was Jemima's first ever opportunity to run her career and her life on her own. Though she'd been itching for independence for years, now that it was actually upon her, she felt as unsteady as a California fault line.

She'd lived her life guided by others—a script telling her what to say, a director telling her how to move, her mother telling her what to do. Now, how did she know what she really felt?

"What do you think about him, Charlie? Mack Chandler, I mean?" Would he see right through to her insecurities?

Charlie sat straighter to reach for the tall glass of iced tea to his right. "Why would you ask my opinion?"

"You seem to know movies. And you don't pull any punches when giving your opinions about us Yanks."

He set the glass back on the small table beside him. Jemima realized he couldn't have taken a drink from it without moving the scarf he wore and exposing some of his face to her. "I think it'll be a great movie. What did you say it's about?"

"Mack Chandler plays Peter, a tough, seen-it-all vet of the war on terrorism. I play his neighbor, Deborah, who reminds him what it's like to live and love again."

Not only did the script call for on-screen kisses, easy work for a girl who'd exchanged spit with a narcotics kingpin in her last film, but this time she'd agreed to do more.

"There's a real love scene, Charlie," she confessed, her face going hot. "Full nudity."

He shrugged. Easy for him to be nonchalant.

"You'll wear a body stocking," he said. "Or those little stick-on things."

"You think that will make it any easier? The last time I was naked on film, I was eighteen months old and running through a living room in a diaper commercial."

Charlie shrugged again. "Mack Chandler will make you comfortable."

Would he? Could he? Suddenly, men were such an enigma to her. Just as was her reaction to them. For example, did it make sense that she was so attracted to a man whose business she didn't know and whose face she'd never seen? No. Yet Charlie made her laugh, and even in those long hours of the night when she couldn't sleep, he made her feel both rested and restless. They talked about nothing, but it seemed like everything.

What was she supposed to make of that?

This male-female weirdness didn't give her confidence about her first face-to-face with Mack Chandler. And if Eve was right, it could very well happen that night.

"There's a rumor MC's going to be at the party I'm invited to this evening," she blurted out. Her nerves had been jittering about it all afternoon.

Charlie stilled. Then his head turned away. "You know better than to listen to rumors, unless it's true you *are* the secret love child of Warren Beatty and Katie Couric."

She laughed, then flopped back against the cushioned lounger, thrusting out her legs. "I *knew* you could make me feel better. I'm really, really hoping you're right and that he'll be a no-show. You see, I have this terrible premonition that I'm going to make a fool of myself in front of him."

"Maybe MC should be worried about making a fool of himself in front of you."

She rolled her eyes. "Yeah, right. I don't think MC has ever crushed on me." Now why had she said that? But it was out and . . . and she wouldn't miss Charlie's reaction for the world.

Charlie was directing those enigmatic dark glasses her way again. "When have you met Chandler?"

She flung out a hand. "I've never met him. I've just always had the hots for him, that's all."

Charlie was silent a moment, then he cleared his throat. "You should have the hots for someone closer to your own age. One of those young up-and-comers on the cover of *Us* or *Entertainment Weekly*."

"Nah. Guys like that, they're dazzled by stuff that doesn't interest me. I told you, I'm not your typical almost-twenty-one-year-old." Jemima traced an aimless pattern on the hard surface of her cast. "I've been in this business for more than nineteen years. I've attended dozens of premieres and walked miles of red carpet. I've been to enough perfume launches to fill an ocean and to more than my share of bashes hosted by stoned runway models and their high, rock star husbands."

"So world weary."

There was wry amusement in his voice, and his

hand reached out as if to stroke her cheek. It stalled, though, then dropped to his lap.

Her stomach dipped, uncertain. Did she want him to touch her?

God, *yes*, she wanted him to touch her. But she couldn't be sure why. She'd played so many emotions over the years that she wasn't entirely certain she knew when she genuinely felt any of them.

To cover up her awkwardness, she shot Charlie a grin. "So, do you think I have a chance with Mack—outside of the movie script, that is?"

He shoved out of his chair, his movements abrupt. He stared down at her from his full height. "You're a little girl playing at things you don't know about."

It was so close to what she'd been thinking herself that she had to swallow a sudden lump in her throat. "Wh-what?"

"How can you want a chance with a man you don't even know?"

She didn't answer. Because she wasn't ready to tell the truth. She didn't know if she'd ever be ready. Without the words laid out for her on a page, scripted by someone else, how could she say that the stranger she really wanted a chance with was the stranger standing just two feet away?

Chapter Ten

"Party Lights"
Claudine Clark
"B" side, single (1962)

It was the recipe for a party Eve had attended a hundred times before. The expansive desert estate of some Hollywood exec, a five-piece combo playing everything from the Beatles to Bono to Beyoncé, an ask-for-it-we-have-it bar, a lush buffet catered by one of Palm Springs's poshest restaurants, and two hundred people with nowhere they'd rather be unless it was a different party with a more influential host, a more trendy caterer, or a more interesting guest list.

The fact was, reporting on scenes like this one was an almost scandalously delightful way to make a living. She loved Palm Springs, she loved the successful, entertaining, philanthropical—sometimes all three in one!—people whom she met during the social season's various celebrations and fund-raising events. She loved the chat, the flash of sequins, the tinkle of ice, and the rustle of silk that was the sound track of the good life and a good time.

She never apologized for her enjoyment of it—not even to The Preacher, Nash Cargill. It still surprised her that he'd seemed to understand that day in the parking lot. She would have guessed he expected all women to be nurses or teachers. Or nuns.

Strolling through the front entry, Eve booted the man out of her mind. She didn't have time for him tonight because she had a job to do. Make that three jobs. Collect info for her "Party Girl" column. Pass along the Caruso-transition-is-under-control message.

And then, last but not least, while smiling, while looking prosperous, not desperate, she must approach that SOB Vince Standish. Approach him and work on getting him to relax enough, to trust her enough, that at some later date he would spill the way he'd been screwing the SEC, not to mention helping his friends and hurting his enemies.

"Eve!" She was hailed by silver-haired Douglas Darnell, who hurried toward her, carrying two champagne glasses.

She winked at him and drew out her handheld mini–tape recorder from her jeweled purse. "The host looks dazzling," she said, holding it close to her mouth. "Very cosmopolitan in white slacks topped by a jacket with Japanese-inspired characters embroidered on the lapels and a pair of ruby suede loafers. Pliner?"

Grinning, Doug nodded. "You know your shoe designers."

Eve thumbed off her recorder and slipped it back in her purse, then took one of the proffered champagnes. They clicked glasses. "To—?"

"Our hearts' desires," Doug said. "What else?"

Two months ago Eve might have said she was living it. Now she didn't know what was in her heart.

Another group of guests came in behind her, and Eve moved on to allow Doug to greet them. The beautiful octogenarian who had written the society column for forty years before handing it over to Eve had trained her in the art of the party reporter. *Talk to as many people as possible. Never linger too long with any one guest.*

If you spent too much time with a man consoling his bruised ego with scotch after losing a skins game on the golf course that afternoon, or if you listened too long to a woman who was sucking down Cosmos after not eating for three days so she could fit into her cocktail dress, well, that's when you found out the kind of things you didn't want to know. Eve's column reported on new business partnerships, new romantic partnerships, new hairstyles. Her task was to get prominent names in print. Those she talked about welcomed her in order to start a buzz going or keep a buzz humming along.

Téa had once remarked that she figured Eve evaded being the target of gossip herself by becoming the one who talked about others. Smart woman, her sister. Nobody asked Eve about being a mob boss's bastard daughter when they wanted to tell her all about themselves instead.

Realizing she'd wandered onto the deserted poolside terrace, Eve forced herself to turn around and head back toward the action. Overcrowded rooms could bring on the claustrophobia that plagued her, but she couldn't afford to let that bother her tonight. She gazed across the large screening room that was serving as the dance floor and through the archway leading to the living room, taking in the faces of the newly arrived guests. And suddenly, there he was—Vince Standish.

The man whose secrets would keep her out of jail.

His gaze flicked to hers, and an odd dread clamped around the back of her neck like a frozen hand. She frowned, quickly dismissing the sensation as nothing more than craven cowardice.

Go. Move toward Vince.

With a breath, she stepped in his direction. Then a hand at her elbow halted her movement.

Gasping, Eve jumped, champagne sloshing down her fingers and onto her wrist. Her head whipped left. "Jemima." She transferred the glass and tried shaking her hand dry. "You startled me."

Leaning against a dark wall, the waif-actress, dressed in gauzy layers of violet chiffon punctuated with sequined flowers, grimaced. "Sorry. I didn't realize you were so—"

"Focused on someone across the room," a deep voice filled in.

Eve lifted her gaze. The darkness she'd registered as a wall behind Jemima was no wall at all but Nash Cargill, looking seven feet tall and solid and almost domesticated in a dark suit and a matching dark shirt, open at the throat. He looked . . . good.

Her mind flashed to that night in the bar. He'd looked good then, too, in a pair of faded jeans, a white knit sweater, his cowboy boots. She thought of him carrying her out the French doors, his lean hips between her thighs, his muscled arms around her waist, her hands resting on his heavy, wide shoulders.

Now her gaze focused on his mouth, and she remembered him nipping her bottom lip with his strong white teeth. The cold hand on her neck turned hot, and she tried tonguing away the memory of his kiss.

Except then he smiled, as if he knew what she was attempting to do, and she felt that delicious hurt all over again.

"Great dress," Jemima said. Tonight she was trying out yet another accent. German, maybe? "Where'd you get it, *mein freund*?"

Eve couldn't look away from Nash's face. "At a c—" Dear God. She'd almost said consignment shop, which was the truth. She'd traded three of her own dresses from last season for this one, which she could only hope hadn't first belonged to another of the party's guests. "At a cute little boutique. I'll take you there sometime."

"If I ever catch you wearing something like that, Jem, I'll tan your fanny."

Jemima gave a dramatic eye-roll. "Not again. First you wouldn't let me come to this party by myself and now this. I'm not a baby, Nash." And as if to prove it, she pivoted and strode off after a white-coated waiter carrying a sterling platter of champagne flutes.

Leaving Eve alone with Nash. If she thought— hoped—he'd hie after his sister to make sure the waiter carded her before handing over a drink, she was disappointed. Or maybe not, because he was still looking at her dress. More specifically, her body in her dress. She glanced in the direction of Vince. She should march over to him right this instant, but then she'd surrender this delicious moment with Nash.

Kisses she couldn't forget weren't within her comfort zone, but a man admiring her assets was her turf, and here she knew the rules to all the games and just exactly how to play him—*uh-hem*—them. She couldn't walk away just yet.

Lifting the heel of one strappy silver sandal, she tucked her right knee against her left. It was a subtle, sexy pose, one she'd learned from a runway model acquaintance, and it worked as she knew it would. Nash's gaze traveled down to her nude legs and then back up to her just-above-the-knees champagne-satin dress. It had a subtle flare at the hem, then was fitted close to her thighs, hips, and waist. The bodice was simple matching triangles held up by thin straps that ran over her shoulders. Another pair of straps ran from the point of the vee between her breasts then up to meet those at the shoulder, creating a frame for the swell of flesh above the semi-modest décolletage.

Nestled at her throat on a triple strand of delicate, white-gold chains was a pavé diamond heart. It was pure girl-candy, a treat she'd once bought herself from Baby Doll Gems, and something she couldn't bear to part with, no matter what. She touched it with her fingertips and gave Nash a smile. "From the Mafia Princess collection, of course."

His gaze lingered on the sweet piece of bling, then made another slow perusal of her barely-there dress. In a flashier color, or with an inch less bodice, or with a less-classy piece of jewelry, the whole presentation would have been pure nastiness.

Nash took his time checking it out anyway. "How in blazes does that scrap of fabric stay on you anyway?" he inquired in a mild voice.

"It's not about how it's on, it's all about what's under," Eve said, then sipped at her champagne, looking up at him through her lashes.

He had the nerve to laugh. "You want me to ask the

obvious, when what's obvious is that you're buck naked beneath that dress."

She was better than naked. And she knew telling him the details would drive him nuts. "Really, Nash. Do those Farrahs only go commando underneath their 501s and Hooter tees?"

His eyes narrowed. "How'd you guess?"

"Because you're obviously ignorant of the finer points of female occasion dressing."

" 'Occasion' dressing?"

She cocked her head toward the throng of well-heeled in the living room. "*This* is an occasion."

"Well, ma'am," his soft drawl made a long shivery path down the back of her spine. "I'd say any place you're in a dress like that is an occasion. So what are these finer points a simple country boy like me is missing?"

Once she told him he'd be unable to put them from his mind, giving her a smug satisfaction that would keep her warm all evening long. "Under something as slinky as this, it comes down to three simple things. One, a flesh-colored microfiber thong. Two, a La Perla strapless bra, and three . . ." She dipped her finger in the champagne and then drew it from the notch at her throat to the low vee between her breasts.

"Three?"

"Three is . . ." Once again, she moistened her fingertip in her drink.

Before she could touch her flesh, he captured it in his huge fist. "Stop teasing. Three?"

God, his hand was so big. Big and hot and firm. "Hairpiece—" Her voice squeaked, so she had to swallow and try again. "Hairpiece tape."

Blinking, he dropped her finger. "What?"

She cleared her throat, sent him her best cat smile. "Two-sided tape that keeps the dress in place so that all the naughty bits don't get too . . . naughty."

He shook his head. "*You're* naughty."

Another sidelong look through her lashes. "Oh, Nash, do you want to spank me too?"

"Damn straight I do. And it might surprise you, Party Girl, to find out just how much you like it."

Cretin. Caveman. Cowboy.

He was teasing her again, of course. Calling her bluff, so she resisted taking a hasty step away. And instead, she found herself remembering the feel of his wide, *firm* hand and felt a very un-PC little tingle rush up the back of her legs. Of *course* she didn't want to be spanked, she hated violence toward women from men, had a firsthand hatred of it as a matter of fact, but the fantasy of being draped over Nash's lap . . .

Without a by-your-leave, he plucked her glass out of her hand and chugged the remainder of her champagne. Then he cleared his throat and surveyed the crowd around them. "I'm losing my focus, thanks to you. I'm supposed to be here to keep an eye on Jem. Anybody liable to cause her trouble?"

Eve slammed the bedroom door on the unwelcome mental image inside her head and quickly drew around herself an air of insouciance. "You can't be serious. This is a private party. I don't think some villain is on the guest list."

Except Vince Standish. Oh, God, she'd almost forgotten Vince. Her gaze flicked to where he'd last been standing, but he was gone. Her stomach clenched. "I've known most of the people here for years."

"Is that right? Why don't you fill me in on who some of them are?"

She used the opportunity to search the vicinity. "In the corner over there, that's Steve Sanchez, he's retired now, but made a bundle in real estate before his forty-fifth birthday. By the archway is Earl Adamcyzk, he owns a PR firm in L.A. And Dr. Stanley Greenburg is one of the most notable plastic surgeons in the Valley. He's the one with the salt-and-pepper crew cut and the cigar. All perfectly respectable. Completely nonthreatening." None of them Vince.

"All wealthy."

Eve shrugged. "Yes."

"They all look alike too. They're short. Slight almost."

Eve shrugged again. "I suppose you're right."

"There's something else they have in common." As a waiter came by, Nash dropped off her empty champagne glass and picked up two others, handing over one.

"What's that?" She sipped at hers.

"They've all dated you."

She managed to swallow her champagne instead of spitting it out. "What makes you think that?" He was right.

"Am I wrong?" A knot of people moved through the crowd around them, and Nash sidled closer to Eve to give them room. His voice lowered, slowed to that thick drawl that poured like syrup through the air. "Or don't small, rich men turn you on?"

Small men made her feel secure. Without fear. Rich men . . .

"Here's a dollar, just for being pretty." Her father's voice, her father's roguish smile. Her father's love. He gave Téa a rose every Friday afternoon as reward for doing well in school. For Eve . . .

Here's a dollar, just for being pretty.

But Nash was looming over her, so she ignored the old memory and looked up at him, straight in the eye. "You know what kind of woman I am." She knew what kind of woman he thought she was, and maybe he was right. There was a reason she'd taken Vince Standish's insider tip and run with it.

"I know what kind of woman you *look* like," Nash corrected, "but appearances can be deceiving."

She thought of the night they'd met, when he'd plowed past her, the pouring rain unable to quench the fire and brimstone in his eyes. "You look like what you are," she replied. The righteous Preacher, out to protect the lambs of the world. His gaze had gone right past her.

"I look like a Bubba in a monster truck, you mean?" He grinned, obviously proud of it.

He looked different than any man she'd ever dated. Not wealthy, she supposed, because how much could a guy who drove a gas-guzzling mega-machine make? Not civilized, either. Not safe. Too attractive.

A pair of men moved past them, but then one hitched his step and circled back. "Nash? Nash Cargill?"

Eve blinked, then was forced to move out of the Bubba's range as a group gathered around him. At first she thought he'd been recognized by some old acquaintance, but then it became clear that the men were perfect strangers.

"I was there when you made the record jump at the Coliseum in 2002."

"I saw you last year in Sacramento."

Eve realized she should take the moment and run. With Nash otherwise occupied, she was free to find Vince and get on with her real party purpose. But she hesitated, surprised by the admiration in the voices of the men speaking to Nash.

Then Jemima was at her side again, wearing a little grin of her own as she watched her brother. "You know, I believe his fan club has more members in it than mine."

Eve turned her head to stare at the younger woman. "He has a *fan* club? Other than the Farrahs, I mean?"

"*Ja.*" Jemima nodded. "People love what he does. Most monster-truck events are a mix of races, jumps, and freestyle stunts, but the crowd really goes nuts for the car crushes. In rural areas, the monster-truck drivers are the equivalent of rock stars."

"Are you going to be opening any more garages?" another man was saying. "My teenager is about to turn sixteen and is wild for a custom truck, but the nearest Nash's is forty miles away."

Nash smiled. "As a matter of fact . . ."

Eve turned to Jemima again. "What's that all about?"

"Nash's Garages, *liebling.*" Jemima crossed her arms, tapping the fingertips of one hand against her purple cast. "It's a chain of stores that specialize in truck customization. They trick out people's rides, you know?"

A chain of stores. *Hmm.* Not such an uncomplicated good ol' boy, after all, Eve thought. "Is it . . . successful?"

"It's nationwide, with a new Nash's Garage or two opening every month. He'd be feeling out an expansion into Europe if he wasn't here babysitting me." Jemima made a disgusted face, as if that "babysitting" left a bad taste in her mouth. "He'll tell anybody who listens that he has a master's in Bad Ass, but the truth is he has a real honest-to-goodness MBA. He graduated at the top of his class in business school."

Eve took another step back as more people joined the small throng around The Preacher. Monster-truck driver. MBA. Wealthy entrepreneur. Complete, scary surprise.

She shuffled back again, bumping into someone. "I'm sor—"

As she turned, she realized it was Vince Standish's toes she'd stepped on. She should be grateful he'd found her, yes? After all, he was her most important item on tonight's agenda. But that odd feeling of a cold hand gripping her neck was back, with a vengeance.

If Nash hadn't distracted her, damn it, she'd have approached Vince on *her* terms. Now she felt flustered.

The older man smiled. "Eve Caruso, looking as beautiful as ever. Long time no see."

Chapter Eleven

"One Hurt Deserves Another"
The Raelettes
"A" side, single (1967)

In four-inch sandals, Eve stood taller than Vince Standish. Though short and long-distance-runner lean, he was a distinguished presence in linen trousers, collarless shirt, and Armani jacket. Recalling what he'd done to her life and realizing her left foot was still on his toes, she ground her stiletto heel against his slick European leather.

He winced, and she immediately faked an expression of contrition—then resisted the urge to grind away again and moved off his foot. She was supposed to be gaining his trust, not revealing how much she wanted to slap the traitorous rat-bastard to kingdom come.

"I'm sorry, Vince." Leaning down, she pressed her cheek against his. She hoped the SEC didn't expect her to bed him for the information they wanted, because just the thought of kissing him made her gag. But she'd been smiling at men all her life, so that part came easy. "How've you been?"

"More to the point," he said, taking her hand and drawing her away from the loud knot of men gathered about Nash, "is how are *you*?"

Eve glanced around for Jemima as Vince steered her toward an open corner, but the young woman had disappeared into the crowd. So she let the rat-bastard have her hand and all the venom she could spew at his back until he turned to face her again.

"Now," he said, releasing her fingers. "We can talk."

"About what?" she asked, setting her champagne on a nearby ledge. It was too much to hope that he'd admit his many sins right off the bat, but the way his gaze was cataloging her body parts made her wonder if he was checking her for a wire. *Not this time, buddy,* she thought, pinning a puzzled smile in place. *Not in this dress.*

"You've been on my mind so often the past few weeks," he said. "I wondered how you've handled it."

She swallowed. He knew she'd taken his stock tip? But how? Her broker wouldn't have talked, and she hadn't told a soul herself. Damn. This wasn't the way she wanted to play this. "I—"

"It had to be tough, finding your father's remains that way."

Eve's mouth shut. So he was talking about her father. And tough? It had been a total shock. In October, during Cosimo's eightieth birthday celebration, Téa and Johnny had stumbled upon what was left of Salvatore Caruso entombed in the crumbling wall of a man-made lagoon on Johnny's estate. Within an hour, a sixteen-year-old mystery had been solved. Her father's disappearance, which they'd always been certain had been mob related, had turned out instead to be a case of an accidental death covered up by her father's best friend.

"Why didn't you tell me about it the night of the party?" Vince asked, reaching for her hand again.

She put it behind her back. "We decided not to discuss it with anyone until we were certain. They took DNA from Téa, Joey, and me. Once the test results were in, we went public with the story."

"And by then I was on business in Mexico City. I tried to call you."

"Oh. I . . ." *I was busy selling off all my assets to cover the losses you stuck me with, Rat-Bastard.* "I've been leaving my cell off a lot since then."

"Poor Eve." This time when he went for her hand she had to let him have it. "I'm sorry. I know how much you adored him."

He did? Had she revealed so much to Vince? They'd casually dated for several months before his out-of-the-blue marriage proposal. That had been nearly a year ago. She shrugged. "No doubt about it, my father was a larger-than-life personality."

Vince gave what she supposed he thought was a self-deprecating smile. "That none of us other SOBs can quite live up to, is that it?"

Well, certainly not if you sabotage me with evil stock tips.

He squeezed her hand. "I still regret you refused my proposal."

"Oh, Vince." This was *not* where she wanted this conversation to go. "You would have tired of me before the ink on the pre-nup was dry."

"Not for us," Vince said, shaking his head at her as if she were a silly little girl. "We wouldn't have needed a pre-nup."

Eve struggled to hide her surprise. He had to be kidding, right? No pre-nup? The man was worth mega-millions, so of course he was kidding. She smiled at him again, because though she didn't want to rehash their dead-end romance, she still had to keep herself out of jail. Which meant keeping herself on his good side. "Don't we make better friends?"

"What if I said I don't want to be your friend?" As she opened her mouth to protest, he put the fingers of his other hand across her lips. "Now I'm not going to pressure you about marriage again . . . at least not yet, but I find I can't stop thinking about you, Eve."

Oh-kay. But what he'd said was good, right? It sounded as if it wouldn't be hard to get close to him again. Still, she glanced over her shoulder, looking for— For some reason, she was looking for Nash. But he'd disappeared too.

"Because things have changed for you now, haven't they?"

Her head whipped back toward Vince. "What? What do you mean?"

"Since you found out your father is dead. I'm sure you feel that your connection to your stepmother and stepsisters is more tenuous than ever before."

Half sisters, she thought to herself. Not *step*sisters.

But Vince was still talking, his words infiltrating her mind like smoke. "I bet now that your father is truly gone you wonder whether you're really a Caruso at all."

She stared at him. "Of course I'm a Caruso!"

"Shh. Shh. I know that." He rubbed his thumb across her knuckles. "But, well, what do you know about your mother?"

"My mother?"

"What did you say was her name?"

Had she ever? Had she talked to Vince about her mother at all? Eve cast her mind back to when they'd been together. So much had happened since then.

"Didn't you say she called herself Ingrid Nordstrom?"

That struck a chord. She could remember laughing as she'd told him. *"It might as well have been Ingrid Neiman Marcus or Ingrid Saks Fifth Avenue."* Those would have been just as real as Ingrid Nordstrom. When Eve was a teenager, Bianca had sat her down and explained they didn't know any more about her mother than the made-up name and the fact that it had been her twenty-third birthday the night she'd been hit by a car as she'd jaywalked across a dark street.

Criminals on both sides of the family tree, Eve thought, an inappropriate giggle bubbling up in her throat.

"I could help you find out who she really was, Eve. Together we could locate your family. Your grandparents."

Oh, fabulous. Wouldn't that be a happy reunion. What would her maternal relations see when they saw Eve? The bastard offspring of the mob boss's mistress their daughter had become. They wouldn't want her. "I *have* a family."

Téa and Joey, her dark-haired, dark-eyed siblings. If they knew what Vince had done to her, Téa would hold him down while Joey kicked his ass. And Bianca. Eve had Bianca too. Téa claimed not to remember a time when Eve hadn't been in her life, but Eve clearly recalled the day her father had taken her by the hand and led her into the house that was brighter and noisier than the apartment she'd shared with the pale ghost that was her only memory of her mother.

There'd been tears in the eyes of the beautiful brunette lady who had knelt in front of Eve to welcome her. That's when she'd known that she'd brought unhappiness with her into that bright, noisy house. And every day after, she'd tried her best to be pretty and charming to make up for it.

"I can see I've upset you."

Vince's voice. Vince.

Eve blinked, becoming aware of the party going on around her and the distinguished-looking man still holding her hand, a concerned expression on his face. Distinguished-looking, rat-bastard Vince, who had ruined her life.

Because she'd been greedy.

Because she'd thought she'd deserved the windfall he'd whispered about in her ear.

"Here's a dollar, just for being pretty."

Eve stumbled back, freeing herself from Vince's possessive hold.

He stepped forward, his gaze sharp. "What's wrong, love? What's the matter?"

You.

Me.

The cursed SEC.

And remembering them, Eve forced herself to plant her feet on the polished marble and pretend that there was nothing wrong that another glass of champagne and more time in Vince's company couldn't fix. "Let's talk about something more pleasant," she said, slouching a little so it wouldn't seem as if she was looking down at him. "Let's talk about you. You can tell me all about Mexico City, and what we don't get to, perhaps you can fill in at a lunch later this week."

Vince smiled. "That sounds perfect."

Eve linked her arm with his. "Perfection would be your company and another drink. Can you escort a thirsty woman to the bar, kind sir?"

"With pleasure—"

"That pleasure's gonna have to wait," a voice rumbled over her head.

Nash. She whirled. "What are you doing?" she asked as he yanked on her other arm, pulling her away from Vince, the man she was supposed to be spending time with tonight.

"Excuse us, friend," Nash said to the older man. To her, he showed his teeth in a dazzling smile. "They're playing my favorite song and you promised me a dance, Party Girl."

Chapter Twelve

"Walkin' and Talkin'"
The Marshall Tucker Band
Searchin' for a Rainbow (1975)

E ve was spitting mad, Nash could tell, which was strange, since the little guy she'd been talking to had a smarmy cast to his eye. "He must be stinkin' rich," he told her.

She blinked at him even as he continued hustling her away from the living room. *"Excuse me?"*

"I can't think of another reason for you to be wasting time with that dude. As a matter of fact, you didn't look too sure that you liked him yourself."

"I like him fine. Just fine."

Nash shook his head. "Honey, you can put your boots in the oven, but that don't make 'em biscuits."

Her beautiful face went blank. Then she shook her head. "I am *so* glad I don't understand a word you just said."

"Oh, yeah. Now why's that?"

"It confirms my belief in my own intelligence."

He chuckled as he tugged her onto the terrace. It was crowded out there too, though not as bad as inside the house. "I never thought for a moment you were stupid, darlin'. Now keep your eyes peeled."

"Peeled for *what*? I thought you wanted to dance."

"Sorry, two left feet. We're looking for Jemima. I can't find her."

Eve halted. "You're kidding. You can't locate your sister at a jam-packed party so you grab me in order to join the actress patrol?"

"Two sets of eyes are better than one." He ran his gaze along the knots of people standing beneath the umbrellalike patio heaters. None of the shadowy shapes looked like Jem.

"Why don't we ask Doug if you can use his intercom system? Then you can make an announcement like they do at those big box stores. 'Jemima Cargill, meet your brother in the condom aisle.'"

He tilted his head to take in her beautiful face and sarcastic mouth. "What's this thing you have about me and sex?"

Sputters came out of those valentine lips. "I have no 'thing' about you and sex."

"'Condom aisle'? Why not 'hair care' aisle or, better yet, 'auto parts' aisle? Honey, you think about me and apparently you immediately think about sex."

Eve made a sound that normally accompanied the stamp of a pretty foot. "I'm going back inside."

He captured her elbow as she spun. "Don't. Please. I need help finding Jem."

"She's at a party. Having fun."

He frowned. "What if she gets into some kind of trouble?"

"Nash." Eve sighed. "You've got to get control of these rescuer impulses of yours. Jemima doesn't need a nanny, a guardian, or even a super-solver. Let me explain this to you. Most women want a man who doesn't try to fix their problems, but one who only *listens* to them."

"A man who listens."

"Right. She doesn't want someone who says, 'Here, sweetie-pie, this is what you should do.' Instead, she wants a man who will provide sympathy, a second glass of chilled wine, and a supportive shoulder rub. She can figure out the solutions on her own."

Nash smiled. "You've just described the woman of my dreams, darlin', and I'd be eternally grateful if you introduce me to such a creature ASAP. I pour a mean glass of grigio, and I give great shoulder rubs." To prove it to her, he cupped her shoulders in his hands and prepared for a bracing demonstration of his skills.

But the sensation of her satiny skin beneath his hands derailed him. Instead of massaging her trapezius muscles with his thumbs, he found himself stroking the calloused edges over her sleek flesh with just the lightest of caresses. Her hair swished against the tops of his hands and he smelled soap bubbles.

"Well, well, well," she said in a sultry whisper. "Who's thinking about sex now?"

Damn bratty woman. He jerked his hands away and swatted her lightly on her sassy ass. "Come on, help me find Jem and then I'll take your advice and take up with a woman who wants tea and sympathy and not just my big sexy body like you."

She made that foot-stamp sound again, but he ignored it and grabbed her hand in his so she couldn't get away. Then he strolled about the terrace, doing doughnuts around the groups of people to make sure his sister wasn't among them.

Satisfied she wasn't on the terrace, he went back inside and walked through the crowded rooms again, with Eve at his side. He couldn't help noticing the assessing looks sent their way. "Know what everyone's thinking when they look at us, darlin'?" he asked, leaning close to her sweet-scented hair.

"There goes Beauty and the Beast?"

"Well, sure. But they can see that our story takes a different turn. This time the Beast tames Beauty."

Her dark lashes were a thousand miles long, but he could still see the sparkle in those blue-diamond eyes of hers. "When this is all over, we'll compare scratches and then decide who has come out on top."

"Either way I'm a winner," Nash murmured, then gave her a grin and changed the topic to something less dangerous. "This place is really something. I like this house."

"You're interested in home design?"

"I don't know about that." He wound down a wide hallway and into something that appeared to be a study. There were people in here, too, though no Jemima, and a wall of windows that looked out over the valley. "I appreciate the views. I like the idea of having a big sprawling house with plenty of room to spread out in."

"Where do you live now?"

"Do storage units count? Because then I have a place in L.A. and Arkansas, two in Texas and one more in Ohio."

The study had French doors that led to yet another patio, and he tried there next.

"Ah, but settling down would keep you out of the driver's seat of your big, badass truck, Nash."

They were alone on this terrace except for the clean night air and the carpet of twinkling lights spread along the desert floor. "I don't compete much anymore, anyway."

"Why not? Too old?"

He shrugged. "There are plenty of guys my age. And younger ones and older, too. But I've been on the circuit for almost ten years. Maybe I'm burned out. I like the families, though, who come out to see us. And the kids. You should see 'em. Cute as bugs. And they look the size of bugs up against the trucks. They're so funny. They want autographs and photos and they bring me stuffed animals."

He realized he was smiling again, which made him laugh at himself a little. "What can I say? I get a kick out of the kids. So I don't really know why I'm thinking of leaving the circuit."

"I do."

"Hmm?" He looked down at her, surprised. "Why?"

"Because it's obvious you want to settle down and have a family, Preacher-man. Your very own cute Cargill bugs."

Oh. No. He wouldn't put some kid through a childhood like his, not when he couldn't guarantee that he could keep his Mr. Hyde in hiding forever. "Nah. Not gonna happen."

"Oh, how the mighty will fall. Mark my words."

Instead of arguing with her, he towed her back through the study and through the house again, still without sighting the slight figure in a purple dress that he was looking for. His belly fisted. "Okay, now I'm officially worried."

"What would you call what you were before?"

He slanted her a glance. "A moderate concern exacerbated by a strange desire to hang out with you." If only to prove to himself he could be around the superbeauty and not lose his head.

When she took an annoyed breath, her breasts almost popped free of that dress and the double-sided tape. He tried not to look, but she caught him. "Told you about that sex-fixation," she said, a knowing smirk on her face.

Ignoring the comment, he moved his gaze off Eve and around the party guests, still not seeing that purple dress and dark hair. "Seriously, I'm worried."

"Nash—"

"Come on, you've got sisters. Haven't you ever felt the need to watch out for them?"

Eve was quiet for so long that he looked back down at her. She was toying with a set of thin gold bangles on her wrist. "Téa can take care of herself. And she has Johnny on her side now, too. But Joey . . . when it comes to Joey I have a protective streak a mile wide."

"Then you understand why I want to find Jem."

She surprised him by not offering any more protest and instead headed off in a new direction. "Follow me. I know some places in this house you've missed."

With Jemima now out of sight for more than half an hour, Nash took a harder look at the guests and the catering staff as he trailed Eve. Not one resembled beanpole Ricky Becker. As a matter of fact, the most threatening person he'd seen had been the silver-haired weasel Eve had been speaking to with that forced smile on her face. The other guests he'd met were a friendly mix of successful businessfolk and celebrity types. In the past, he'd attended a couple of Hollywood bashes with Jemima and had been turned off by the red carpet trappings, not to mention the way the partygoers automatically worked for the print media flashbulbs and the entertainment channel video cams. By contrast, this seemed like a real party, instead of a professional event.

"Where's the paparazzi?" he asked, catching up with Eve.

She glanced up. "This is Palm Springs. The first movie people came to the desert in the 1920s to get away from prying eyes, and that remains the town's prevailing attitude. I'm in attendance as a society reporter tonight, of course, and a photographer will show up from my paper sometime later, but we don't feed off the famous here. There's thick walls around many estates and resorts like the Kona Kai, but it's a long-standing tradition to respect each other's privacy even without them."

"What happens in the desert stays in the desert?"

She nodded. "Las Vegas took that attitude from us."

They weaved their way through the dining room, a butler's pantry, then the kitchen. Through another door was an entire wing of the house he'd missed. There was a media room, a library, and then a game room. At the far end of that large space, Jemima was with a small group gathered around a billiards table. With a pool cue in hand, she was laughing at something another young woman was saying.

Relief washed through him, unraveling the knot of tension in his gut. Nash caught Eve's hand as she started forward.

"Let's not," he said, answering her inquiring gaze. "She'll be happier without knowing I was shadowing her."

Eve pulled back from the entry and leaned her delicate shoulders and the back of her blonde head against the hallway wall. "So you're satisfied now?"

Oh yeah, right. Six inches away from the temptation of Eve's pouty mouth, full breasts, and those long legs that he'd already had wrapped around his waist once before. "I'm nowhere near satisfied," he admitted, putting a hand on either side of her head. "But I've got a feeling that's going to need a long night, a big bed, and your full cooperation."

And just like that, he discovered that the ol' black magic was stronger than he was tonight. Ceding the fight, just like that too, his lips covered hers. Her mouth softened beneath his, and he heard her make a breathy little moan. It jacked his desire up another ten degrees, taking his cock along with it, but he dug his fingertips into the plaster wall and kept the contact light. Her lashes drifted down yet he didn't follow suit, because she was so damn beautiful and because he still thought she was dangerous. It was better to be going into this kiss with both eyes open.

He pressed his tongue against her bottom lip and she opened for him. Oh, shit, it was going to be hard to remember caution when she was so melted-candy hot and sweet.

She made another moan and her foot slid around his calf.

His arm muscles turned to steel. *Keep your head clear!* he admonished himself. *Keep this light!* Stripping a woman down and screwing her in a public hallway wasn't The Preacher's way. But then he remembered. *Flesh-colored microfiber thong. La Perla strapless bra. Double-sided tape.*

Those three little items wouldn't take him ten

seconds to yank aside, push down, strip away. He was a breath-and-a-half from the Promised Land.

His fingertips went from nubby plaster to satiny Eve-skin. He slid his palms down her arms and broke the kiss as he circled her wrists. A shadowy doorway was behind them, and his cock throbbed as he pulled her into the semidarkness. Laughter from the game room floated through the doorway and Nash glanced behind him, noting another door.

Farther distance from the crowd. More privacy. Good, he was still capable of thinking.

"Nash?" His hand fumbled with the doorknob as he kissed the question away. This time he slid inside her lips immediately, rubbing his tongue against the velvet surface of hers. Heat flared out from his groin, and he stepped back behind the door he'd opened. A bathroom, he registered, shutting the door. He pressed Eve against its cool painted surface and lifted his mouth to breathe. No point in dying before he had her at least once.

A dozen times.

A hundred.

She was a woman made for endless, unforgettable sex.

But that was too dangerous. He'd settle for having her now, this once, so he could resist the next time she tried to get her teeth into him.

"Nash, touch me." In the darkness, he could see that her eyes were closed, but she grasped his hand in hers and brought it up to cover her breast.

He groaned as the warm, sexy weight nestled in his palm. His thumb stroked over the bare, hot skin rising over the top of the decadent dress. His other hand moved to cover her other breast. Her breath caught, and she set her top teeth against her bottom lip.

He rubbed his thumbs over the top of her breasts and her palms flattened against the door. She was his, he thought, pliant and aroused and anticipating his next touch. *His.*

His muscles clenched. His fingers tightened in possession. He bent his head to have her mouth. Her breath sighed out, sweet and hot against his lips.

Oh, God, they were gonna be good together.

Then, behind them, sudden laughter.

They both froze.

Then it came again, on the other side of the door, more laughter. A scuffle. Giggles. The wood panel behind Eve vibrated as the door to the room behind them slammed.

Two voices—not theirs—moaned in passionate abandon.

Nash took a moment to consider. Did he have a chance of distracting Eve from their unwelcome neighbors with another kiss, or had the mood cooled?

She shoved at his chest.

Cooled.

She shoved again, harder.

Okay. The mood was definitely dead.

Cursing in silence, Nash stepped back. He saw the whites of her eyes as she put her finger across her lips. He nodded, then followed her as she did a tiptoe dash away from the door, her high heels soundless against the tiled floor. They withdrew to the far side of the bathroom, putting the maximum possible distance between themselves and the couple in the adjacent room.

When she dropped to the ledge of the sunken tub, he took a seat opposite, on the commode. *Hell.* He had to shift his weight and adjust his damn pants for comfort, since his cock had yet to catch up to its unpleasant change in circumstance. He glanced over at Eve.

"Sorry," he whispered, trying to sound pleasant. Comically chagrined instead of flat-out still frickin' horny. No point in letting her know how high she'd driven his lust.

She shook her head in . . . bemusement? Anger? Frustration? It was too dark to make out the expression on her face. Then he heard her take in a short breath, let it out. An irritated huff. "I don't suppose we could sneak out unnoticed," she said.

A muffled giggle floated through the door. "I don't suppose," he answered.

"Meaning we're stuck here until they're done." Now there was a distinct snap in her voice.

Obviously, she wasn't taking the situation with good humor. Well, he wasn't happy either. This was supposed to have been his one-time, superbeauty stand. Crossing his arms over his chest, he swallowed another curse. " 'Stuck'? Gee, darlin', you could at least try to hold back your enthusiasm."

"Well, it's all your fault." Her toe began a silent *tap-tap-tap*.

She was pissed. Definitely pissed. As if he'd dragged her in without her full compliance. Frustration rose from that uncomfortable place in his lap, and he gritted his teeth. "Next time you put your tongue in my mouth I'll be sure to remember that means 'no.' "

The comment shut her up for thirty seconds or so. Then she slid her palms down her thighs as if they were damp and popped to her feet. "This"—her whisper had an icy edge to it—"is *really* all your fault."

His fingers curled into fists, but then he forced

himself to relax them. There was no reason to feel a sudden urge to hit something. The superbeauty was as hot as they came, but missing a chance for some stand-out sex was not a good reason to get all worked up. He stretched his legs in front of him and reminded himself that he could use his fist to quell his frustration later tonight . . . alone in a lukewarm shower.

She paced silently to the door, then spun around and came back toward him. As she neared, he could hear her shallow, fast breaths.

Wait a minute. Too shallow, too fast.

Narrowing his eyes, he leaned forward, trying to figure out what was fueling her agitation. It could just be desire thwarted, he supposed. Or simply a bad girl in a bad mood. But as Eve took another jerky turn around the small room, his belly knotted, like it had done when he'd been worried about Jem. When she approached him again, he caught her hand.

"*Jesus!*" Her skin felt frozen and her fingers trembled within the cage of his. "Eve, what's wrong?"

"Nothing." She tried tugging, but he wouldn't let her get away. "Let me go."

He shifted his hand to feel her pulse. It raced against his fingertips. Was she having a heart attack or something? Had he found Jem only to lose Eve? His belly knot jerked tight.

"Are you sick?" he whispered urgently.

"No," she whispered back, then he heard her take in a long, shuddering breath. "I'm claustrophobic. And if you don't let go of me right now, I'll scream."

Chapter Thirteen

"Yes, I'm Lonesome Tonight"
Dodie Stevens
Pink Shoelaces (1961)

Claustrophobic?" Nash repeated, rising. He kept hold of Eve's hand. "Then let's get out of here."

"*No.*" They were both still whispering, but she said the word as loud as she dared. If they left the bathroom, not only would they interrupt the couple making use of the room next door but the couple making use of the room next door would also know they'd interrupted her and Nash. "I can wait it out."

She'd have to. Beyond the fact that she didn't care for others to know her business, there was Vince to consider. Restarting their romantic relationship was out of the question, but he might become suspicious of those lunch dates she was promoting if it became public she was seeing someone else.

Her mind tripped over the thought. She wasn't thinking of "seeing" Nash . . . was she?

Yanking her hand out of his, she took another silent turn about the room, trying to calm her rabbity heartbeat even though the walls were crawling toward her. "I can handle this," she mouthed. She was strong, independent. A Caruso. "I can handle this."

She could. She would. No matter that instinct was urging her to run straight through the closed door like a cartoon character, leaving an Eve-sized hole behind.

Her shoulder brushed Nash's chest on her next lap around the room. "Do you have to loom?" she asked from between her teeth. Now the ceiling had lowered, she was sure of it.

"Testy, are we?"

She could feel the weight of his gaze, just something else making it hard to breathe. Her fingertips brushed the closed door at the other end of the growing-smaller space, and she did her best to sound casual. "A little aftereffect from an unpleasant childhood experience."

He was still watching her as she made another few trips around the room. "Have you considered talking to someone about it?" There was a note in his voice that might have been judgment or maybe even disdain. The perfect Preacher thinking the flock wasn't entitled to its neuroses.

"I don't need a shrink to tell me that I panic in confined spaces," she retorted. "Or why, for that matter."

"So why do you?"

She wiped her sweaty palms on her dress. "What would compel me to tell you?"

"Confession is good for the soul," he offered.

"Curiosity killed the cat," she countered.

"Your cat almost killed *me*."

Her feet halted and a laugh bubbled up. Eve clapped her hands over her mouth. The walls moved out a fraction and she found herself able to inhale a decent breath. Then the memories dropped back like a shroud. Darkness. Hide. Quiet. *Don't let anyone know you're here.*

Look out for #1.

Halfway into her lungs, her breath hitched and she felt herself hyperventilating again. Despite the dots of dizziness flying around the edges of her vision, she restarted her pacing, desperate to distance herself from the feeling that she was being buried alive.

"Can you tell me just one thing, darlin'?" Nash's drawl was thicker than the suffocating air. "Am I safe? Because right now I'm a tad bit worried that you're Glen Close and I'm Michael Landon's family bunny."

She saw red in the dark room and stopped in front of him to whisper furiously. "So you're saying you think I'm nuts? Or that I'm acting a part here? I was traumatized, I'll have you know. By our very own federal government."

"What, they confiscated your hot rollers?"

She was outraged into a full breath. "They broke into our house and stole all our money!"

"Who?" He sounded as if he didn't believe her.

"The FBI, that's who. My father's missing for a few days and they come in with crowbars and flashlights and hands . . . all their damn hands. Joey and I had to get away from them."

Her little sister had dived beneath her bed.

"Where'd you go, Eve?"

"The closet." It was still there in her head, that dark, coffinlike space. Clothes brushing against her face. Her back to the farthest corner, her butt on the cold hard floor. Already she'd been taller than Bianca and Téa, so she'd folded her long legs close to her chest and wrapped her long arms over her head as the gravel-voiced agents yanked open drawers and tore into walls.

The sound of her whole world coming apart.

"They found Joey first," she heard herself say. "Pulled her out by her ankles. She was yelling at them to leave her alone. Crying, sobbing." Eve's hands crept over her ears as they'd done that day sixteen years ago. "I should have done something to save her."

"Did they hurt her?"

It was like a movie playing in her head. "They smashed her piggy bank and then they threw her out of the room."

Quiet. Quiet. Don't let anyone know you're here, ordered the cowardly voice in Eve's head.

"And then they found you."

"After tearing our bedroom apart. After dumping out every drawer and separating the mattresses from the box springs. They sliced them open, looking for money." Then the closet door had flung open, she'd heard the screech of hangers against the wooden pole, seen the big hand in a surgical glove—making her feel dirty, tainted—that yanked her through the clothes to stand under the bright overhead light.

In the hall on the other side of the doorway had sat a white plastic hamper—their plastic hamper—piled high with green bills. Some of those dollars her daddy would have given her just for being pretty. All gone, just like him. All gone.

She swayed.

"Eve." The voice sounded from a far distance.

"Eve." Nash's voice. "Breathe."

But air couldn't make it past her tight throat.

He pushed her down on the bathtub ledge and lowered himself to the commode across from her. "Inhale,

Eve. Through your nose. Then breathe it out through your mouth."

"Can't."

His hands found hers. "Close your eyes."

"Nash—"

He squeezed her fingers. "Close your eyes."

She was too dizzy to disobey him. His grip was warm and firm, and this time it felt secure, not imprisoning. Her lashes fell.

"Imagine a wide-open field with tall grass," he murmured, leaning close to her ear. "There are dandelions. Butterflies. Take a long breath of the warm air and let it out slow."

Her frantic heart felt too big for her chest. There wasn't room for her lungs, let alone for air inside of them.

"Take the breath, Party Girl, or I'll spank you like a doctor delivering a baby."

The image pierced the dizziness. Nash and his spanking fixation made her want to laugh. She gasped in a breath.

"Now let it out slow."

She managed to do that, too.

"Good. That's good. There's a blanket on the grass, Eve. See it? Now keep breathing and stretch out on it. Let the sun warm your skin."

But Eve was shivering. "Cold," she murmured. "I'm so cold."

"I'll fix that." His knees bumped hers as he leaned closer. "Long breath in, long breath out. That's right. Keep breathing."

She felt him gather her in his arms. That wasn't right. She could handle this all by herself. "Nash—"

"Breathe in, breathe out," he instructed, pulling her onto his lap. "Now keep using your imagination. You've wrapped the blanket around your shoulders."

It was his arms that were around her. "You're toasty, Eve. Comfortable. Snug as a bug in a rug."

And she was beginning to be. His slow Southern voice was calming her pulse, his body heat was seeping into her frozen bones, melting her icy panic.

"This is why you ran out of the supply closet that day," Nash said.

It had been part of the reason. She'd been uncomfortable in the enclosed space and nervous about his big size . . . and then spooked by that sound of flesh hitting flesh. Without opening her eyes, she leaned the back of her head against his chest. "Uh-huh."

"Yet tonight you let me pull you into a dark bathroom."

"I was distracted at the time." There was no point in denying it. She could feel his chest rising and falling behind her, and she synced her breathing with his. She was calm now. The grass in the field smelled like Nash and the snuggly blanket surrounding her was more muscular than she usually liked, but she'd fought the phobia and won!

Or Nash had fought it for her.

No. *No.* She could save herself. She only ever had herself to rely on. Her body struggled against him, trying to get up, get away. Be independent.

He tightened his hold on her and growled in her ear. "Do I have to distract you again?"

She turned her head toward his to tell him exactly what he could do with his distraction—

And he covered her mouth with his lips.

She made a sound from the back of her throat. It was a protest, of course. But a quiet one, because there was still a reason to be silent . . .

. . . some reason . . .

But the details of it fled as he hitched her closer and kissed her harder. Her mouth opened beneath the pressure and he slid his tongue along the edges of her lips, painting the insides of them with a gentle touch. Heat flushed over her body and she reached out with her own tongue to meet his. They slid against each other like reunited lovers. Wet and warm. Wanting.

Turning on his lap, she twined her arms around his neck. It was so good to breathe again. Feel. Taste. Feel and taste Nash.

She'd worry later about showing him her weakness.

His tongue moved deeper into her mouth. She wiggled, and beneath her bottom, Nash was aroused.

Okay. Good. They were equal then, because she was aroused too. His hand slid from her waist to cup her breast, and her nipple beaded to an almost painful tightness. He brushed his thumb over it, and over and over, until she pressed her breast into his hand. He tightened his fingers on the hard bud, pinching her through her clothes until she moaned how right it felt into his mouth.

His other hand tightened on her hip, then he dropped the teasing fingers from her breast to her knees, bared by her rucked-up skirt. His hot flesh palmed her skin, stroking her from knee to thigh.

Alarmed voices started chattering somewhere in the far recesses of her mind. Rational voices. *He doesn't approve of you. He doesn't like you. He's The Preacher and you're the Party Girl. Right now you've got big problems and you don't need to add a man like this one to the mix.*

But that wasn't going to happen. He wasn't going to intrude on the mess that she'd made of things. Because he didn't approve of her, because he didn't like her, he wasn't entering her life. He was just the hot tongue in her mouth, the fast thrum of her heart, that firm, caressing hand on her skin. She could have just this. This moment.

It was so, so much better than being alone in the dark.

She pressed close to his chest.

No one would know. There was just the two of them in the room, and Nash wouldn't be telling. He might pray for their souls later, but he wouldn't confess to anyone what they'd been doing.

"Open your legs for me, Party Girl," he murmured against her mouth, sliding his forefinger along the seam between her clenched knees. He drew it upward, opening her thighs. When he reached their juncture, he cupped her.

Her body clenched, and she jerked against him. He murmured soothing nonsense, kissing her chin, her cheeks, her ear, as he pushed her microfiber panties into the swollen folds of her sex. "You feel so hot, so soft, here," he said. He rubbed his cheek against hers, and the sandpaper sensation of his whiskers prickled more heat across her flesh.

Everywhere.

"Eve . . ." He drew his finger along the triangle of the panties, to the hipline, and then back down the crease of her thighs. Her legs opened wider and his fingers teased across the damp fabric. "Eve," he murmured again. "I want in."

She squeezed her eyes tighter.

"Please, darlin'," he said again. "I want in."

And apparently someone else did too, because there was a sudden thud against the bathroom door. They both jerked toward it.

Oh, no!

"I can get it," a man's voice muttered from the other room. "It's probably just stuck." There was another thump, and then the door popped open. Light flooded the small space.

Oh, God. No.

Dazzled by the light, Eve rapidly blinked at whoever had discovered them. Nash had already hot-potatoed his hands from their illicit location, but one arm was curled about her waist and the palm of the other hand rested on her knee.

Eve shoved it off her skin and shot up from Nash's lap, staring, aghast, as she finally took in the man standing in the doorway. "Johnny?"

There was a sparkle in the man's blue eyes and a sheepish smile on his face. "That's me. Téa and I have been apart for a week, and, uh, well, you know. Then she wanted to fix her makeup in the mirror. I didn't realize . . ."

A disheveled Téa peered at them from behind her fiancé's shoulder. "Eve? And . . . Nash?"

Eve sighed, ignoring a sudden throbbing in her head, as well as the residual throbbing . . . elsewhere. "Nash, you know my sister, of course, but this is my almost brother-in-law, Johnny Magee."

She didn't like the unholy grin overtaking Johnny's face as he stepped into the room and held out his hand to the other man. She hadn't wanted anyone to find them together, but at least it was only Johnny and Téa. Though she was still an idiot for getting herself in this position with Nash, at least it was family. That had to make it okay, right?

Except Nash didn't look as if it was okay with him as he rose to shake Johnny's hand. He looked wary. "Pleased to meet you."

And maybe he had reason for that wariness, because Johnny's grin only grew bigger. "Likewise. And as Eve's closest male almost-relative on the premises, I think I now get to ask . . . exactly what are your intentions?"

Chapter Fourteen

"Cold and Lonesome"
The Outlaws
Hurry Sundown (1977)

Middle age sucks, Charlie thought, staring at the television screen and trying to ignore the throbbing bass line that was his face. The damn thing seemed to start up drum practice the same minute the moon came up.

That explained why he was in a bad mood and had been in a bad mood nearly to the day since he'd moved into the Kona Kai while recuperating from his facelift. When he was healed, he'd be better.

Back to his old self.

Shit. The thing was, "old" was the operative word. He had to face facts: He'd never be better. Plastic surgery could only do so much. His knees would still crunch when he squatted to tie his shoes. Too many hairs would show up on his pillow every morning. At his Hollywood rec league basketball games, he couldn't stop his buddy and agent, Larry, from going baseline any more.

Middle age really *sucks,* he thought, flipping the channel selector on the remote. His thumb quickly clicked past an old movie he recognized from the late 1980s. *Honey Hunt* was a classic guy movie, heavy with sophomoric humor, gratuitous nudity, and a loud rock score. The inflatable breasts on the women who traipsed through its scenes could have been used to raise a shipwreck.

The piece of crap had banked 39 million gross in U.S. box office sales and made Mack Chandler a household name.

Sometimes Charlie despised Mack Chandler. While the movie star was the source of Charlie's own wealth, it was the demands of Mack's career that had led Charlie to Dr. Ajmil Singh, a reputed wizard with a scalpel. "I'll take a decade plus off your face," the surgeon had promised.

But though you could erase the age from a man's expression, you couldn't erase it from his body or his mind or his heart.

Charlie was getting too damn old for this business.

He flipped the channels again, past an old rerun of his friend Tom in a *Bosom Buddies* episode and then to one of Bruce's *Die Hards.* Willis shaved his balding head now. With his free hand, Charlie ruffled his hair, wincing when even that gentle action made his healing sutures twinge. At least there was still plenty there to run his fingers through. He could spare the world a Kojack 'do for a few years yet.

With luck, by the time he had more hair coming out of his ears than remained on his head, he'd be long retired to his ranch in Montana. Hell, if he wanted, he could get out of the business today. God knows he could afford it. He had more money than Harrison Ford and everyone knew Harrison Ford had more money than God. Charlie could walk away this moment and leave the field open to all the slick youngsters who were still secretly thrilled every time they were photographed—cuffs of dress shirt stylishly unfastened—strolling through a field of paparazzi beside six feet of skinny legs and implants who smelled like cigarettes and hair spray and whom they'd met a mere ten minutes before.

Maybe that was the answer. Chalk up the face-lift as a final stupid mistake and then make a few phone calls to clear his schedule for good. Back in Montana, he could use real high-country snow instead of ice packs of cocktail cubes to ease his aching face.

Yeah, that's just what I'll do, Charlie decided. That was the solution to his problems. The old guy was going to give up the game.

He dropped the remote and rose from the couch to locate his cell and call Larry. And then, from outside his bungalow, he heard the scrape of chair legs against concrete.

"Damn," he murmured to himself. "Jemima." Back from her party. Apparently sleepless. Again. It was how they'd struck up their acquaintance, through their mutual insomnia. First it had been just an occasional comment or two through the wooden partition that separated their private patios. Then he'd invited her over for a game of gin rummy one night, and from there they'd developed a . . . friendship of sorts. Now when she couldn't sleep, she'd just as often choose to stretch out on his lounge furniture as her own.

When that happened, he'd never failed to join her.

But tonight . . . tonight he dropped back down on the couch, his gaze flicking toward the nearby sliding glass doors to ensure the curtains were completely covering them. Jemima couldn't see in, Charlie couldn't see her. Good. Because tonight, his ass was going to stay glued to the cushions. Jemima was just something else it was time to give up.

Over the past weeks he'd enjoyed her company too much. His near-jealous reaction to her confession about having the "hots" for Mack Chandler proved that.

He focused his attention on the TV and resumed surfing through the channels. Celebrity poker, one of the four dozen incarnations of *Law & Order*, *South Park*'s Kenny dying yet again. Nothing captured his attention, at least not enough to stop him from thinking of Jemima Cargill reclining on the lounge chair on his patio. He wasn't going out there, but he could see her as if he had, he could see her pale skin in the moonlight, baby-clear and baby-soft, her big eyes darker and deeper than the desert night.

Gritting his teeth, he thumbed to the next channel. On the screen, a boomer-dude trying to throw a football through a tire. Thunk.

Great, Charlie thought. Something else he had to look forward to—erectile dysfunction. Maybe if things got too quiet in Montana he'd come out of retirement to do a Bob Dole or a Mike Ditka. Just another spokes-oldie for ED.

Damn, that idea was depressing. His gaze wandered toward the glass doors again, but he forced it back to the TV. Getting old sucked, but hanging with twenty-nothing Jemima wouldn't stop the hands of time either. She didn't need his midlife crisis in her young-thing, rising-star world.

Then he heard a quiet sob.

The sound froze him. But it didn't come again, meaning he must have imagined it. Despite that, he muted the television sound, in silence watching the boomer-dude—thanks to a medical miracle you should ask your doctor about—now throwing touchdowns through that hanging tire. Jesus, could the pharmaceutical company get any more obvious with their imagery? Even *Honey Hunt* had thirty seconds' more subtlety than this.

Then he heard it again. Another choked-back noise. Jemima. Jemima crying.

As the trademark Levitra flame flared, he grabbed up his hat, sunglasses, and scarf and was out the sliding glass doors.

"What's the matter?" he demanded, staring at her through dark lenses from the foot of her lounge chair.

Her head lifted. "What?"

He remembered to add an Aussie inflection. "What happened at that party? Why are you crying?"

A pleased smile broke across her pretty, young face. "That sounded real?"

Charlie closed his eyes. "You're acting?"

"I was practicing. But I thought you were asleep. I'm sorry if I bothered you."

You're always bothering me. Your pretty smile and pretty hair and pretty laugh. Your baby face and your sometimes cynical attitude. "I was just going to bed."

She tilted her head. "That's good to hear, Charlie," she said, her voice soft. "You need your rest."

"Because I'm an old man?" It came out more bitter than he intended.

"That's not what I said."

"Mack Chandler is old too, you know. Too old to be playing your love interest, if you ask me." Costarring with an actress less than half his age would make Chandler look like a fool.

Certainly the women he'd acted with during the last twenty years would see that. Likely they'd send Chandler hate mail for landing a leading role in a love story when they were now relegated to stage plays or mother-in-law parts. But Mack Chandler would pay for the privilege by being the butt of late-night jokes. Playing a much younger woman's lover was the punch line of a Leno monologue if Charlie had ever heard one.

So? Chandler would deserve it.

"You were right, by the way," she said. "Mack Chandler wasn't at the party tonight."

"I'm a goddamn psychic."

"Maybe so."

"I'm sure you found some young stud to dance with you anyway," Charlie muttered, taking in Jemima's dress, a pretty thing in a color that matched her cast. Gauzy. It looked vintage, maybe.

Shit. Vintage, like him.

"I didn't dance, but I did think about the film."

After Jemima took the role to Oscar level, Charlie would be in Montana, his satellite dish pulling in the Academy Awards ceremony, and as he watched her on his big-screen TV he would feel . . .

As if he'd done the right thing.

No regrets, no looking back. He'd decided retiring

was the prescription for his bad, middle-aged mood, and he was going to swallow it down.

"I'm thinking about quitting," Jemima said.

Charlie stared. "What did you say?"

"Mack Chandler—"

"Is an egotistical has-been."

"—cares more about this movie, this business than I do. I'm thinking of leaving it to him."

Wasn't the aging process a vicious thing? Now his hearing was going. "What did you say?"

"I'm pretty certain I'm going to quit."

"This film?"

Jemima shook her head. "The business."

He dropped to the end of her lounge chair, her small bare feet just inches away from his thighs. He put his hand over her cold toes. "What the hell are you talking about?"

She shivered, and he gentled his voice. "Jemima, I don't understand."

"This is not what I want."

Thinking she meant his touch, he jerked his fingers away. "Sorry—"

"No! I don't mean you. You, I want ... I mean ... I don't ..." Her voice trailed off, and though he couldn't detect a blush through his sunglasses, he could feel her embarrassment in the air.

He drew her feet onto his lap and curled his big hands around them. She gave a tiny flinch, but he continued to hold them, warm them. "What's going on, Jem? A minute ago you were practicing your tears and now you're talking about quitting."

"Okay, I admit I'm confused. About a lot of things. But I never chose this profession. My mother took me to auditions before I could talk or walk. She managed my career, she managed *me*. In interviews she says it was my ambitions she supported, but a nine-month-old doesn't have ambitions, a nineteen-month-old doesn't, a nine-year-old doesn't have an ambition to not go to regular school, to not play with regular kids, to not *be* regular."

"But . . . you're good. You know that you're better than good at acting."

She shrugged delicate shoulders that glowed like pearls in the darkness. "It seems to me I'm good at being something I'm not, Charlie. But now that my mother is looking the other way for the first time in twenty years, perhaps I should do what I want instead."

Did that really mean quitting the film? Charlie felt an upsurge of optimism that he hadn't experienced in weeks. With Jemima out of the picture—literally—he could go back to Hollywood. For some reason he didn't want to think about, it wouldn't bother him to go back to the business if it meant no potential run-ins with Jemima.

He could forget about this hellish slide toward middle age.

Though he loved his place in Montana and could imagine himself happy there for the rest of his life, it would seem so lonely now. No friends . . . no Jem . . .

So back in Hollywood, his forty-something body now wearing his former thirty-something face, he'd also be back to those good ol' days when his only future plan was the next party and his only worry was remembering said party's address.

"Aren't you going to ask me what it is I want, Charlie?"

His head turned toward Jemima. She was sitting up now, her silky hair tousled about her bare shoulders, the cut of her dress just revealing the slightest hint of young, unenhanced breasts. She looked fresh and near-ripe and untouchable, all at the same time.

And maybe he wasn't so old after all, because his body reacted to the sight in a way that made Viagra, Levitra, and Cialis completely unnecessary. He decided this was stupendous news. Hurray. Hoo-wah. It showed he was still young. It meant middle-age crisis was just a term made up to sell magazines and self-help books.

His mood had been just a temporary, very temporary, aberration. And though her lithe body was turning him on, his interest in Jemima herself had been a temporary aberration too. Any second it would go away.

Beneath his scarf, he smiled at her in great relief. "What is it you want?"

She leaned closer. Thinking she wanted to whisper it to him, he leaned toward her, too.

"This," she said, and then her mouth found his, right over the thin covering of the silk scarf he wore.

Stunned, Charlie didn't bolt away. He meant to. He should have. Instead, his hands left her bare feet to cover her bare shoulders. They gripped her, hard, in preparation for pushing her away.

But he didn't do that either.

Instead, he let her kiss him, her mouth warm and mobile and incredibly arousing even from behind that veil between them.

His pulse thudded in his ears, louder and faster than the ache in his face that he couldn't even remember now.

Jemima Cargill was kissing him. Young, twenty-nothing Jemima Cargill.

And God, if that didn't prove that he was definitely sliding into the second half of his life after all. Because he liked her kiss. More than liked it.

The truth of that had him rocketing back, shooting to his feet, running for the sliding glass doors to his bungalow and locking himself behind them. It wasn't a mature reaction, but, damn it all, it was a certainty that he was.

Because, cliché of all clichés, Charlie had just proved himself to be most decidedly middle-aged—by falling in love with a much, much younger woman.

Chapter Fifteen

"Girls Can Tell"
The Dixie Cups
Chapel of Love (1964)

Hinged screens were set up in three corners of the dressmaker's large workroom. Joey and Téa were already behind two of them, changing into their gowns when Eve walked in. She smiled to herself. The excitement of this final fitting was likely to blow out of the water any talk of what had happened at the party the night before.

Téa would be too preoccupied to tell Joey about catching Nash and Eve in the bathroom. She wouldn't have to defend, pretend, or explain it away.

Which was good, because she didn't have any idea how to rationalize to her sisters, let alone herself, how she'd gotten into such a potentially compromising position. She'd only been thinking of how quickly he could distract her from her fear. How easy it was to lean on him. How strong his arms felt around her. But that had been her stupid panic talking. No man was reliable. The only one she could depend on was herself.

"Come in, come in," Mrs. Diaz said, gesturing Eve further into the room with a hand holding a tomato-shaped pincushion. "Your dress is hanging right behind that screen over there."

"Is that you, Eve?" Joey's head popped around the edge of the screen in the opposite corner. "We thought you might be avoiding us."

"Avoiding you why? I wouldn't miss the unveiling of the dresses for anything."

Joey grinned. "Unless you didn't want to talk about your private prayer session in the bathroom with The Preacher last night."

Eve groaned. "Téa . . ."

"Sorry," her sister called back, sounding not the least bit repentant. "It wasn't me, it was Johnny who spilled the beans."

Joey shook her finger at Eve and slipped into her Ricky Ricardo imitation. "Lucy, you have some 'splaining to do."

Instead, Eve rolled her eyes and escaped to her own corner of the room. "So, uh, Joe, why don't you tell me about your latest visit to prison and Uncle Benny."

"Oh, yeah, as if I'd fall for that," Joey retorted. "I want details, everything from 'hello' to how you ended up on his lap. For a man you said thought you were the devil incarnate, he sure isn't afraid to get singed."

Except Nash singed me, Eve thought, recalling how she'd melted in his hands. Maybe he was right. Maybe she did have a thing about him and sex.

She pushed the idea away by turning her attention to the bridesmaid's dress hanging behind the screen. Her forefinger ran down the cool pale satin of the full-length skirt. Téa was having a formal evening wedding, but she'd opted to wear black and carry red roses, while her two attendants would be dressed in bridal ivory and carry bouquets of creamy gardenias.

"Do you remember how we used to plan our weddings before going to sleep?" Eve asked her sisters. The three of them had shared a room, and after attending a cousin's nuptials one June Saturday, they'd spent an entire set of summer nights imagining their own big events.

Téa laughed. "I sure do. Joey was eleven and didn't see anything wrong with marrying both Siegfried *and* Roy."

"I really just wanted those tigers," Joey admitted.

"Well, you've always liked your men with a dangerous edge," Téa said. "But I don't recall anything about your groom, Eve."

"Because she didn't want one," Joey put in. "She only wanted the fancy dress and the big party. Even then she didn't think there was any guy good enough for her. Already wedded to her ego."

"Joe?" Eve asked pleasantly, as she loosened the tie of the wrap dress she'd put on that morning.

"What?"

"Just so you know, later today I'm going to staple your earlobes to your shoulder blades."

"All the better to hear your explanation about doing the naughty with the monster-truck man."

Téa laughed.

Eve hung her dress on a hook and carefully lifted the satin bridesmaid's gown off the padded hanger. "Don't encourage her, big sister. It's bad karma and you'll end up gaining five pounds and getting a big zit on the day before the wedding."

"Now that is plain cruel," Téa complained. "Just for mentioning weight and blemishes in the same sentence, I'm going to tell Joey something Johnny didn't."

Eve paused in the process of sliding the dress over her head. "Fine. Except don't forget the only reason you know about me and Nash in the first place is that you were making whoopee in the middle of the party yourself."

Téa didn't respond to that. "She looked dreamy, Joe," she said instead. "Not just flushed and tousled, but dreamy."

The white satin gown fell around Eve just as Téa finished. She met her own eyes in the long mirror propped against the screen. Dreamy? No way. She hadn't had a dream involving a man that wasn't a nightmare since she was twelve years old. It was the same with the wedding fantasies. Like any normal girl she'd loved thinking about the fairy-tale dress and the glittery presents, but she'd never fooled herself into believing that some man would stay.

That some groom would love her forever.

She didn't want to love anyone that way herself. It left too much room for heartache and disappointment. Look where loving had gotten Bianca—married to a man who cheated and who expected his wife to raise his lover's daughter. Face it, relying on a man—for his fidelity or his love—didn't make good sense.

Sucking in a breath, she slid up the invisible zipper on the side of the dress and then appraised her appearance in the mirror.

Eggshell-colored satin made tiny sleeves that fell coyly over her shoulders. The bodice was a wide U-shape that revealed just a hint of the top rise of her breasts. Then the dress fit snugly around her waist and hips, to pool at her ankles in a slight, elegant train. Eve rose on her tiptoes to simulate the height of the matching pumps they'd ordered.

"Hey, Eve, how does yours look?" Joey called out.

It looked . . .

It looked . . .

"Oh, no." Téa's voice had an anxious edge. "Is it bad? How bad? I thought the style would flatter both of you, but if it doesn't, you've got to be honest, Eve. I'm counting on you to tell the truth, because we both know Joey will lie through her teeth if she thinks she's being loyal to the family."

"I resemble that remark," Joey said cheerfully. "But really, I think I look pretty darn decent."

"Eve?" Téa prompted.

Eve gazed at herself in the mirror, at the gleam of the satin and the faint tinge of warmth on her cheekbones. Her eyes looked very pure, very blue.

"Eve?" Téa said again, her voice edging higher.

"I—" A startling thought came out of nowhere. *I want Nash to see me in this dress.*

And it *was* startling, because it wasn't the kind of dress a woman wore for a man. It wasn't a dress made to knock his intellect out cold while tickling his libido— the only kind of dress she should want to wear around Nash Cargill. That kind of dress would give her the power. This kind of dress . . .

Made her look like a bride. Someone a man would want to spend his life being faithful to. Someone a man would want to be the mother of his children. *I get a kick out of the kids,* he'd said. And she'd pictured him with some of his own cute Cargill bugs.

Which immediately squashed that silly little notion about Nash and her brideful self. The Party Girl would certainly never be The Preacher's idea of mother material.

Sending herself a brittle smile, she swept her hair over her shoulders, then stepped out from behind the screen. "I think it's lovely, Téa. I think it's perfect for your big day."

Joey was already standing in the middle of the room, admiring herself in another set of mirrors. The gown worked just as well for her much more petite figure. Against the ivory, her golden skin gleamed, and her velvet-dark eyes looked full of mysterious fire. "You're the angel, Joe," Eve said. "You look as if you're just about to unfold your wings and head off for heaven."

Joey met her eyes in the mirror. "We look good, but I bet Téa will look even better."

They both turned to watch their big sister step from behind her screen.

Eve's heart jumped to her throat. Téa didn't look bridelike at all. She looked . . . "Royal," she heard herself say. "Powerful." Her older sister had the same apricot-gold skin as Joey, but her body had more height and more curves. The color of her dress was deeper than black, it was a primitive, primeval color, that ran along the lines of Téa's body like a dark river.

"You're going to be a terrific foil for Johnny's blonde looks," Joey said.

Téa burst out laughing. "You brat. How'd you know I chose it with just that in mind?"

"Because you're an interior designer. You're not just dressing your body, you're setting a scene."

"The golden boy and the pagan queen," Eve agreed. "You're going to slay him."

Téa's smile turned sly. "Just what I had in mind. Have to keep him in line every chance I get."

That's where Eve had gone wrong with Nash, she realized. Controlling men came second nature to her, but he shattered every hold she had on him. He was attracted to her, he desired her, that was obvious, but instead of her using that against him, he . . .

Used her attraction, her desire for him against *her*.

That's what had gone wrong at the party. She'd let him use sex to get a hold on her—a move that was usually hers.

"Oh, my God!" Joey exclaimed.

Eve started, then shot her sister a glance. "What is it? What's the matter?"

Joey pointed a finger at her. "I saw it! Téa's right! You were looking dreamy."

"I was not." Eve curled her lip and tried looking whatever the opposite of "dreamy" was. "You have me mixed up with someone else."

"I do not. Nobody knows you better than me . . . except maybe Téa, and she's already caught you looking dreamy-eyed. That Nash Cargill has really gotten under your skin."

"He has not." Eve shot a look of appeal at her older sister. "No man gets to me. You tell her, Téa."

"I'd like him to get to you, Eve."

"What?" She took an involuntary step back. "That's because you've gone all the way gooey since you fell for Johnny. But some of us don't need to fall in love to enjoy men and to enjoy sex."

"I know you've enjoyed the sex, Eve. But have you honestly ever enjoyed the men?"

Licking her lips, Eve darted a glance at Joey. No help there. Her little sister was looking at her with narrowed eyes, an assessing Italian angel. Joey had a legion of guy-pals. There was no doubt she enjoyed the men in her life.

But Eve had never had one male friend. She'd never told a single man about her claustrophobia, let alone the incident with the FBI that was its cause. Her heart jumped into her throat again. "Maybe you should mind your own business," she said. "Maybe you don't know one thing about me."

Téa's expression froze. The back of Eve's neck burned hot, and she didn't dare look at Joey. Though the two youngest traded insults on a regular basis, neither of them ever attacked their oldest sister. Téa was too serious, too responsible, too caring to shrug off the usual sibling barbs.

And that hadn't been a usual sibling barb. It had been a poison-tipped arrow wrapped in Eve's own fear of Téa's question. *"Have you honestly ever enjoyed the men?"*

No. Not once. Never.

Until Nash. She enjoyed the way he teased her. She enjoyed the way he treated his sister. She enjoyed the way he looked and the way he touched her. The way she wanted to touch him.

Oh, God.

She swallowed. "I'm sorry, Téa. I didn't mean that to come out the way it sounded."

Her older sister spun away to stare at her reflection in the mirror. "Don't worry about it."

Eve's neck burned hotter, and her stomach shriveled to the size of a walnut. "No. Really. It's just that . . ."

I've lost everything.

I'm in trouble with the SEC.

I don't know what Nash is doing to me.

Téa's spine was ramrod-straight, and Eve had to grip her fingers together so she wouldn't grab her sister's shoulders and cry all over the back of her brand-new bridal gown. She hated the idea that she'd hurt someone who'd only been generous with their father, her family, and her love all these years. But Eve couldn't excuse herself without confessing to all the things she didn't want the Carusos to know.

She didn't want to be more trouble for the family that had done so much for her.

"I'm sorry, Téa," she mumbled, staring down at her bare feet and wishing she could take back so much of the last months of her life.

"I'll forgive you," her sister said, "on one condition."

Eve looked up. "What condition?"

"Johnny bought a table for the hospital auxiliary's masquerade ball at the end of next week. You have to sit with us. Joey's coming."

"No problem." It had been on the Party Girl's calendar in any case.

"Invite Nash Cargill, too."

"No!" Good Lord. Her big sister obviously wanted to play matchmaker. "Come on, it was fifteen minutes in a bathroom, not a sign of true love."

Joey sidled closer. "Afraid you'll get dreamy again?"

Eve shook her head. "You two are sad."

Téa turned. "Then make us happy. Invite Nash."

Eve hesitated. It was a ridiculous request, of course. But Téa had never treated her as less than a one-hundred-percent sister, and she gave far more than she ever asked for. Then there was that sense that she herself was spinning out of control. If she invited Nash and he agreed to come, she could prove to herself at the masquerade that at least one thing in her life was stable.

That she still held all the cards when it came to men.

Chapter Sixteen

"Feelin' Good"
Blackfoot
Flyin' High (1976)

A shaman was chanting softly through speakers, there was the green scent of sage curling in the air, and a butt-naked Nash was lying facedown on a cushy tabletop, covered in nothing more than a soft white towel.

His sister had insisted on the massage, claiming it would relax him, but there was nothing relaxing about more inactivity. Obviously Jemima was trying to bore the big brother right out of him.

There wasn't a chance of that happening. Not that he wasn't itching for something to do besides observe Pilates classes, eat mandarin orange, avocado, and almond salads, and shop for teeny girlie clothes in Skittle colors—his sole occupations since becoming his sister's self-appointed bodyguard—but Nash had a hunch. Blame it on all the nuts he'd been eating or the

New Age flute tones wafting through the air, but he couldn't shake the feeling that he had a real purpose here in Palm Springs.

And a man nicknamed The Preacher couldn't ignore that sense of a Higher Power at work in the universe. The best Nash could figure was that he was still supposed to be protecting Jemima.

The door to the massage room opened, then snicked softly shut. With his face buried in the horseshoe-shaped pillow at the head of the massage table, Nash couldn't see the massage therapist as she approached the table. But he knew what she looked like already. He'd shaken hands with Helga, not realizing until he heard the feminine name that the five-foot-ten-inch, slender figure with the long fingers and silver brush cut was a woman. Dressed in no-nonsense hospital scrubs, she'd already worked over the front of his body and had given him a few minutes alone to turn to his stomach and rearrange the towel across his buttocks.

He heard her move toward the small countertop and sink in the room. The oil she used was sage-scented too, and he imagined she was coating her hands with it again before getting about her business on his back.

Her footsteps now took her toward the massage table, and he consciously loosened his muscles. Helga had already commented on the coiled tension in his body as she'd kneaded his front side. It seemed insulting to the woman that he was unable to relax under her professional touch. Her hands had been pleasantly warm and competent, and if he could just let go a little, he probably would enjoy it.

Helga said it wasn't uncommon for someone to fall asleep during their massage. Since he'd been sleeping like shit since he'd ended up in a dark bathroom with

Eve Caruso a couple of nights before, he could use the extra Zs.

Clothing rustled beside him, then something ruffled the hair at his nape, sending goose bumps sprinting down his spine. Nash forced himself not to squirm. Okay, he knew he was overdue a visit to the barber, but why the hell was Helga-the-masseuse blowing on the back of his neck? It was embarrassing. The goose bumps for damn sure were.

Helga had to be twenty years older than he was and probably disinterested in men to boot, and he was reacting as if she'd laid her tongue on him.

She blew again, and he gritted his teeth against a second round of that skittering sensation against his skin. *Calm yourself, Cargill,* he told himself. His too-long hair would get in the way of her massage, that was all. She was trying to spare him from getting the ends of it greasy with her hands.

Then she put them on him.

His body jerked, shocked by their chill.

Christ! What had happened to that "pleasant warmth" he'd experienced before? He frowned, his forehead bunching up against the circular pillow. Thumbs dug in and edged down the muscles of his neck, then pushed out along his shoulders. More goose bumps flagged out across his flesh. Feminine fingers feathered against his deltoids.

His cock stirred.

And then he knew who was touching him.

"Hey there, Eve."

Her hands whisked away from his body. "How'd you know it's me?"

"Well, when it wasn't Helga's clinical touch, I could

think of only one woman who can't keep her hands off me."

"You wish."

"Every minute, darlin', and I'm paying at least a couple of bucks for each one spent on this table, so get back to work."

She laughed. "I took a couple of classes. You'll get your money's worth." Her fingers returned to his skin.

He flinched again. "Jesus, your hands are colder than a well-digger's butt in winter."

"Then you'll have to warm them up for me, handsome."

He didn't need to see her face to imagine that saucy tilt to her lips and that sassy gleam in her eyes. "The heat's all on the other side, baby."

Eve kneaded his trapezius muscles with both hands. "I don't know about that. I find you're pretty hot all over."

That shut him up. She'd been teasing before, but there was something new in her voice now. Something . . . husky.

And damned if pressed against the massage table was not where his hard-on was aching to be. He squeezed his eyes tight and tried to pretend it was Helga who was stroking his skin.

It didn't work.

"What do you want, Eve?" he asked, aware he sounded surly.

"I thought you had that all figured out."

He'd said she couldn't keep her hands off him. That she had a "thing" about him and sex. That was true. But he didn't expect it was a rare occurrence for a woman with Eve's air of experience, so he wasn't going to feel bad about stomping out all the little fires she managed to set inside of him.

Let her go and play with matches around someone else. One look and he'd known she was trouble for him, and despite previous lapses he was re-determined not to succumb to temptation again. He had no wish to let the man-trap eat him alive.

Her hands stilled, each cupping one of his shoulders. "Uh, thanks, by the way."

Thanks? Was she reading minds? Did she *want* him to keep his distance?

"For helping me out with my little . . . problem the other night," she clarified.

Her claustrophobia, brought on by small, enclosed spaces. He remembered the feel of her, thrumming with tension in his arms. "You're okay now? This room isn't very big."

"I'm all right. The skylight helps."

In his mind's eye, Nash replayed those minutes in the darkness all over again, the pale shape of her face and the fear in her eyes that turned their blue into black pools of anxiety. "I'm a flag-waving, law-and-order type of man myself. I never thought I could consider the FBI sons of bitches."

"Joey calls them the Federal Bureau of Ignoramuses. They take a particular pleasure in hounding her."

Startled, Nash lifted his head and craned it over his shoulder to stare at Eve. She looked as shockingly beautiful as usual, in a simple pair of straight leg jeans, sneakers, and a white, long-sleeved T-shirt pushed up to her elbows. "The feds are still after you?" he asked.

She shook her head. "Not me. But Joey works with my grandfather in the family's gourmet food business.

He recently announced he's going to retire, and so they're keeping their eye on him and those associated with him."

"What?"

"You'll get a crick in your neck." She pressed the back of his head so that he was forced, facedown, into the horseshoe pillow. "My grandfather, Cosimo, is retiring from La Vita Buona and the other . . . businesses he's involved in. The FBI is interested in those other businesses. So they give the Carusos a goose every once in a while to see if they can shake anything free."

Nash tried imagining the kind of sangfroid it took to be able to talk about a federal shakedown with such equanimity. A self-assurance built on years of practice? Yes, but a self-assurance that fell apart when a door closed behind her and a light turned off.

"Joey strikes me as a woman who can handle it, I guess," he murmured. But *Eve*, Eve didn't handle the demons in her life so easily. He knew it. He'd embraced her as she'd struggled against her vulnerability.

And damn, if vulnerable was just the way he didn't want to think of her. He didn't want to be anyone's white knight anymore.

"You're right. If anyone can handle it, Joey can. It's Téa who gets the most upset." Eve was making long strokes down the sides of his spine, from the base of his neck to that line of the towel across his hips.

The touch seemed to wrap around his groin and tug at his balls. He cleared his throat. "Téa? Did you say something about Téa?"

"She's the edgy one. Particularly right now, with the wedding coming up. We're all trying to keep her calm and happy."

Nash was trying to focus on her words. He was, honest he was, but she must have really taken some massage classes, because she *was* good at touching him. She was taking her time, rolling his muscles with her thumbs and working at the kinks. Except instead of loosening him up, he was just getting harder and harder.

"That's why I agreed to ask you to the masquerade ball," Eve said. "I know you'll want to go along with it."

Some part of that "I know you'll want to go along with it" got through the haze of sexual pleasure starting to fog his brain. "Huh?"

"Johnny bought a ten-seat table for this upcoming charity thing. Téa would like you—and Jemima, too—to join us." Her magic fingers worked back toward his traps, and he almost groaned aloud in bliss. "So will you do it?"

"Sure," he murmured, thinking only of Eve's blue eyes and her heart-shaped mouth and her hands, stroking, touching, taking him—

"Wait. What? What did I just say?" He craned his head to stare at her again.

"You said you and Jemima will attend that party. We'll all be there." Her smile was way too innocent, when her fingers were still engaged in their carnal activity, working at his hips now, under the towel.

" 'We' as in that brother-in-law of yours, right?"

"Brother-in-law-to-be."

Someone should tell her that a woman with her looks didn't have a prayer of pulling off the sinless act. "What, he wants another chance at giving me the third degree? Is he going to have his shotgun this time?"

A blush rose up her cheeks. "He did that just to be funny. Johnny knows I can take care of myself."

He frowned. "Then why is he insisting I attend this party?"

A flicker of expression crossed her face. It dismissed the last of the lingering sexual fog in his brain and put him back on full Eve-alert. With a swift movement, he rolled over and sat upright on the massage table, bunching the towel in his lap.

"What aren't you telling me?" he demanded. And he'd thought her vulnerable! He should have known something was up when she'd barged into his massage session. She'd wanted him where she could have the upper hand. With her fingers on him she'd figured she could get him to agree to anything. Wily witch.

Her little pout didn't move him.

"Out with it, Eve."

She shrugged. "It's just that Téa . . . Téa's in full-blown bride mode. Discovering the two of us in the bathroom together gave her this romantic idea about us."

"Romance is the last thing on my mind when I'm around you." It was either screw her or strangle her, that was it.

"I tried telling her that, but she has this idea in her head about you attending the masquerade ball with us, and I'd like to make her happy."

"You want me to fake a romantic interest in you?"

"No!" She shuffled back. "I just want you to go to the party. That's it, I promise."

Nash shook his head. Because that might not be "it" when it came to the two of them. "Look, you and I are both too old and too experienced to pretend there isn't some fairly combustible chemistry between us."

She raised that damn eyebrow.

He didn't let it deter him. "More than fairly combustible, and don't bother denying it."

"So? I'm not in the market for any explosions at the moment."

"Me neither." He'd said that too quickly, hadn't he? But it was true. He'd tried considering sex as a workout or as an itch that needed scratching, but it rarely failed that he didn't end up with some lovely yet needy woman whom he couldn't walk away from until he'd paid off her charge cards or married her off to one of his buddies or both. He'd vowed to take a break from that—at least until he made some more single friends.

The next woman he went to bed with would be strong, secure, and absolutely average in every way.

He narrowed his eyes at the ball-breakingly beautiful woman standing before him, who hadn't had an average day since being born a mob boss's daughter. "So let me get this straight. You don't want sex."

"I'm not against pleasure, but I've got a pretty full plate at the moment."

It was as if she could take it or leave it. "You don't like being with men?"

She frowned, and her voice rose. "Why is everyone asking me that lately? I've never been with a girl, if that's your question."

He laughed. "Don't encourage my imagination to go there, please. But seriously, we get close and lips will lock."

Her smile didn't look the least bit uncertain. "I'm convinced I can resist your oh-so-many charms."

The confident tone struck him like a bolt of lightning.

Epiphany.

Revelation.

That was it! That Higher Power wasn't telling him he was here just for Jemima's protection. Nash was also here to take the superbeauty down a peg or two as well. Eve Caruso needed to be taught the lesson that sexual chemistry could be stronger than her control of it, and Nash Cargill was the one appointed teacher.

The Lord worked in mysterious ways after all, he decided, because he now realized he was in Palm Springs to get laid.

But then his cock started to make its opinion on the idea known in rigorous fashion, and reason resurfaced.

Whoa. Wait just a minute.

Wasn't it more than a tad too convenient that the good Lord and his lust were on the same side?

Not to mention that by his agreeing to Eve's invitation, she had him just where she wanted him. *You're an idiot, Cargill. A led-around-by-your-dick idiot.*

"It isn't going to work, Party Girl," he said. His cock was still hard, and it was damn difficult to ignore while gazing on the woman who'd fueled a dozen of his most recent fantasies. "The fact is, Jemima's getting fed up with me and there've been no further problems regarding her. I'm on my way outta here."

Chapter Seventeen

"Tell Him"
The Exciters
"A" side, single (1962)

Eve rushed back into Nash's massage room. He was standing beside the table, shrugging into one of the white spa robes. In a different mood, she could have had a jolly old time ogling his full-frontal nudity.

He looked over but didn't bother rushing to cover himself up as he grinned. "Well, well, well. Gonna try to change my mind? I admit, darlin', spending more time with you would be easy on the eyes—okay, and hard on the rest of me—but I've got my own life to get back to."

Mute, she held out the fax in her hand.

His gaze flicked to it, then back to her face, and his smile died. "Now you have me as nervous as a hound dog pissing peach pits."

Eve swallowed. "This just came through on the

machine in the front office. Maybe it doesn't mean anything, but I thought you should see it right away."

He pulled it from her hand. It was addressed to him, care of the spa, but the return number had one of those bogus 555 prefixes they used in the movies. The single line of text was typed onto a blank page, and Nash read it aloud. " 'You can't watch her every minute.' "

There was no name in the From line, and no signature either.

Nash's fingers tightened on the single sheet. "I've got to see Jemima."

"I called her already," Eve said. "I didn't tell her anything about the fax, just found out that she's in her room and not planning on leaving it anytime soon."

"Thanks." He'd already belted the robe and was shoving his cell phone and his card key into one of the wide patch pockets on the front. "I'll head over there and make sure she stays put until I figure this out."

Passing by Eve on his way out the door, he paused. She smelled the Kona Kai's special blend of sage and citrus oil on his skin. Beneath that she could still smell Nash's own particular scent. She'd washed it off her hands after leaving the massage room and before finding the fax.

His thumb stroked over her bottom lip. "Thank you."

Without thinking about it, she followed him out the door. His long strides ate up the gleaming marble floor, then he disappeared into the men's changing room. Before she could decide what to do with herself next, he came out, carrying his clothes and still wearing the knee-length robe along with his beat-up cowboy boots.

Another man would have looked silly. Not Nash.

Eve found herself hurrying behind him again, through the spa building's doors and out into the sunshine, as if walking in his shadow could protect her from the memories that fax had yanked to the surface. Nino had stalked her for weeks after their breakup and before the beating he'd given her. Remembering that, the ugly, dark tickle of someone's gaze tracking her every movement feathered down her spine.

"You're good to her," she blurted out. She meant it, but she also meant to distract herself from thoughts of the past. "Jemima's lucky to have you."

Nash glanced at her over his shoulder. "With Allison—that's her mother—honeymooning, I'm the only relative Jem's got."

Shrubbery, pools, the other guests were passing by in a blur. "Your father—?"

"Dead. But he wouldn't have been a help anyway. He was a drunk, a mean one, which was why Allison took baby Jemima and scrammed in the first place."

Joey had told her something about this. "Leaving you behind?"

The guard manning the entrance to the residential part of the property held open the gate as they approached. Nash paused to let her pass through first. "I suppose she figured I was near big enough and mean enough to hold my own with him."

Near big enough? And where was a mean bone in Nash Cargill's big, muscled body? What kind of woman left her son—even a stepson—alone with an alcoholic? What kind of mother?

She'd fallen behind him again, and he cast back another glance. Then he stopped, a puzzled half smile on his face. "Eve? You're not getting weepy-eyed over a tough ol' *hombre* like me, are you?"

Of course not, because despite the creepy fax, she was in a good mood. Really. Nash had refused the invitation she'd been forced to extend. Any time now he was going to be walking out of her world, leaving one less distraction from the job of getting her life back on track. Eve had been relieved to hear him say he was leaving, though it had taken a moment to sink in. Staring at Nash and all his long, strong muscles, she'd still been remembering how much she enjoyed feeling his strength beneath her hands.

More than she'd ever enjoyed touching any other man, because it was the first time she'd enjoyed a man's body without first wondering what was in it for her.

Nash's smile turned to a frown. "You *are* crying." His thumb rubbed across her cheek and something skated across the hard, cold surface of her heart, startling her.

She jumped back.

"Eve?" Another male voice, not Nash's.

Her head whipped around and there was CEO, rat-bastard Vince Standish, standing on the path leading to her suite. Vince. A physical reminder of what was the #1 priority in her life and why she never cried over a man.

She was happy to see him. Really.

"I've been waiting for you," he called out.

Without giving in to the urge to take a backward look, she moved away from Nash and toward Vince. With only a quick swipe at the damp skin of her face.

"See you around, Party Girl," Nash called, and his retreating booted footsteps made it quite clear that he was moving away from her, too.

Ignoring the hollow sound, she smiled for Vince. Reconnecting with the CEO, gaining his trust, getting him to a place where he would spill all his dirty dark secrets was what the SEC wanted from her. And she wanted what they wanted, because that would keep her out of prison.

She held out her hands to him. "What a surprise! I wasn't expecting you."

"I had a free afternoon and thought I'd take you up on your lunch invitation." He was in Palm Springs business casual—linen slacks, dress shirt, no tie, a sports jacket that cost more than two times the used clunker she was forced to drive. "Unless you have other plans?"

Now she couldn't help glancing over her shoulder, but Nash had disappeared. "No. No plans."

"Good," Vince said, smiling. "Cargill's not your type."

Eve didn't bother asking how he knew who Nash was or how Vince had managed to breach the private, secure side of the Kona Kai. Vince could find out anything about anyone. Bianca knew that they had dated and would give him access to any part of the spa.

Eve tacked on another pleasant smile. "Shall we lunch on one of the poolside patios?"

"That's fine, as long as we'll have some privacy."

Together, they turned. As they retraced her and Nash's footsteps toward the public grounds of the spa, a movement in the bushes caught the corner of Eve's eye. The tomcat, Adam. He glowered at her, then skittered away, leaving her strangely bereft.

Fickle creature. She would have cheered him on for sinking his teeth into Vince as he'd done to Nash.

They settled at a small table by one of the pools, an umbrella shielding them from the interrogation-intense light of the sun. The muted clatter of cutlery and chatter rose around them, and Eve sat back in her chair and crossed her legs, willing herself to forget about faxes and Cargills and the feel of long, strong muscles beneath her palms.

This was her world. Vince, whose pose mirrored hers, was the kind of man who fit within it, who fit with her.

Okay, yeah, he was a petty louse who had screwed her over, too, but that was only due to her own weakness. *"Here's a dollar, just for being pretty."*

There was no "just" to anything, she knew that now. All good things came with strings attached.

The waitress brought their ice teas with lemon, and she and Vince chatted about mutual acquaintances, the upcoming concert season, about the renovations he was making to his house in Lake Arrowhead, a mountain resort in the San Bernardino mountains. More than one L.A. mover and shaker kept a couple of nearby getaways; in Vince's case it was Palms Springs for the cool Southern California months and Lake Arrowhead for the summers and occasional ski weekends.

Their matching salads were delivered. Eve smiled to herself, trying to imagine Nash Cargill sitting across from her, willingly spearing slices of a lowfat entrée of butter lettuce, chicken breast, and mango.

Weren't the two men polar opposites? And she could almost forgive herself for taking Vince's stock tip. The man was charming, urbane, amusing.

Not a man who would stomp through a public place in a bathrobe and cowboy boots. Not a man who would drive a monster truck as testament to his monumental ego.

Vince didn't tease her like Nash did. He didn't challenge her like Nash did.

Like all the other men she knew, Vince accepted Eve at face value.

He'd wanted her face, so he'd wanted *her*.

"Eve." Vince leaned forward and placed his hand over hers.

Instinct screamed to pull back, but she flattened her palm to the table. A man didn't trust a woman who flinched away in distaste.

"There's something I've been meaning to confess to you, Eve."

Her heart jumped. Was this it? Would he confess now, without wire or eavesdropper or any way to document the conversation to elevate it above the he-said-she-said level?

She tried to laugh. "Oh, well, Vince. Maybe now isn't the time—"

"It's exactly the time." His fingers gave hers a ruthless squeeze. "I'm not getting any younger."

"Okay." Her next laugh sounded as stilted as the first one. Was age an impetus to admitting his wrongs? But unless he gave concrete details that could be checked out, she didn't think the SEC could use her recollection of the conversation against him. She'd caught enough crime TV to know that repeated conversations were called hearsay. "But that goes for all of us."

"Precisely." He looked across the pool, then back at her. "So I'm hoping you'll understand my urgency, since we're both mature adults."

What? Vince was twenty-plus years older than she was. She was only twenty-eight! *"Going on twenty-nine,"* she remembered Nash pointing out. It made her want to smile, though, because he'd been needling her, of course. He'd been challenging her sex appeal, then he'd proven his own by morphing that do-it-for-Nino kiss into something hotter and realer and . . . more unforgettable than any other kiss she'd ever had in her life.

Nash Cargill wasn't the only man who'd ever touched her, but he was the only man she'd truly ever wanted to touch back, just for touching's sake.

"Eve?"

Her distracted gaze jerked across the table. Vince.

Her first priority, Vince.

Damn it, she shouldn't be letting her mind wander. Not when she was happy to be sitting here with him. Not when she was equally happy that Nash Cargill was taking his big body and his gentle hands and his look-beneath-her-looks self out of her life.

Everything was going to turn out fine. The way it was supposed to be.

"Did you hear what I said?" Vince asked, a frown creasing his forehead's perfect fairway tan.

"I'm sorry." She turned her hand to give his a little squeeze this time. Though a moment ago she'd been daydreaming about touching Nash, it was all about Vince now. Eve Caruso could, *would* do whatever was necessary to keep herself out of trouble. "I was distracted for a moment. What did you say?"

He was annoyed at having to repeat himself—that was obvious. "Did you think about what I said at Doug's party?" he asked.

"At Doug's party—?"

"About resuming our relationship," he explained impatiently. "You really owe me an answer about that, Eve."

She stared at him. Hadn't she already made it clear she wasn't interested in him romantically?

"Smiling, holding my hand, asking me to lunches," Vince continued. "You know what you're doing, you know what you do to me. So let's not play any more games."

Eve looked at her fingers entwined with his as if they were someone else's. She'd been friendly to him at the party. She'd mentioned a future lunch date. But it was he who had shown up uninvited. It was he who had brought up romance.

And yet the fact was, it was she who had wanted to get close to him again.

She took a breath. "Vince, what exactly are you saying?"

"That I'm ready to settle down, Eve. That I've had enough adventures and enough trials and errors. I know you, and you know me, and you've made it clear to both of us that we belong together."

She'd made it clear? *She'd* made it clear? How was that?

"The bottom line is I don't care for any more coy lunches or 'let's-just-be-friends' dinner engagements." He wore a relaxed smile on his face, but his words held a hard edge. "It's all or nothing now, Eve. You've brought it to that. So what's it going to be?"

Her mind rattled through possible ways to answer that question. "No, hell no," wasn't smart, not with the SEC breathing down her neck. But there was an odd light in Vince's eyes, and his insistence that she'd done something to bring the situation to a head frankly weirded her out. She didn't want another lunch, let alone a promise of a lifetime with him. So stalling was the only option.

"Vince, I haven't really thought . . . considered . . ." Her heartbeat revving, Eve struggled for the right tone, the right words.

His cell phone rang.

Vince released her hand to reach for it, and she pulled her fingers to her side of the table and then safely into her lap. What to do? Oh, God, what to do?

But maybe she was going to be rescued from making that decision, because even as he grunted into the phone, he was pushing his chair back and rising. When he flipped the phone shut and stared down at her, his slight size struck her as more menacing than Nash's larger proportions.

"I've got to leave immediately. We'll have to discuss this later."

"Great. No problem. Sure." Where did fugitives head for these days? Bogotá? Berlin? Belize?

"In two, maybe three days," Vince said. "I have to head to L.A. this afternoon, but I'll be back as soon as I can. Then we'll finish our talk."

She'd be on a plane tomorrow, if she could find her passport in the boxes she'd yet to unpack after her move from luxurious condo to one-bedroom family-owned suite. "Oh, well, I'm not sure—"

"Then we'll finish our talk."

And she *would* talk with him again, she thought, her heart sliding toward her lap. Though she'd let a man down easy a hundred times before, at the moment, she couldn't afford to let Vince down at all. The fact was, she had to spend more time with him to get what the SEC wanted. An hour ago, she'd been happy about that, right?

"And next week I need a date for the hospital's masquerade ball," she said. There was an open spot at Johnny's table now that Nash had refused her.

Remember? She'd been happy about that, too.

Chapter Eighteen

"Done Somebody Wrong"
The Allman Brothers Band
At Fillmore East (1971)

As day turned to darkness, Charlie reached for the bag of crushed ice on the table beside his patio lounge chair and placed it over his eyes. The blepharoplasty he'd undergone to remove his drooping upper lids and the puffy bags below his eyes seemed to be taking the longest to heal.

Or maybe it was just another excuse not to look at himself in the mirror. He'd had to trim his nose hair today.

Again.

And there were some gray whiskers mixed in with the blonde on his chin. He could shave them from his skin, but that didn't erase them from his memory, though hell, that would likely be going soon anyway.

Maybe then he'd forget about Jemima. About the touch of her mouth beneath his, about the scent and the warmth of her young, nubile body so close to his. He was goddamn in love with her, but how could he do anything about those feelings when he was going through this disgusting midlife, male willies thing? The losers in *Sideways* had depicted the dissatisfied, aimless feeling, and Bill, too, in *Lost in Translation*. Fine films, but a hell of a way to actually live your day.

He couldn't even suck down whiskey or pinot noir, thanks to the pain meds.

Here he was, successful and wealthy by anyone's standards, but still less than happy. Growing up, he'd figured he'd be married by the age he was now, with a kid or two to reexperience childhood with. Instead, he was forty-something with a face-lift, desperate to retain his muscular, twentyish physique. Where was everything he was supposed to have learned by now—prudence, patience, kindness, temperance, perspective?

Where the hell was wisdom?

Through the partition separating his bungalow's patio from Jemima's, he heard her sliding glass door open, shut. Then footsteps, light, quick, definitely Jemima's. A rustle as she settled herself into her own lounger.

Behind the ice, he squeezed his eyes shut tight. Pretend she isn't there, he told himself. You're an actor, this should be easy.

That's the way he'd decided to handle his unwelcome emotional state. It wasn't there. Just like Jemima wasn't there.

If he could pretend he was a Korean War–era submariner in *Over His Head*, which had garnered him a Golden Globe less than five years before, then he could act as if he'd never been attracted to Jemima Cargill. He could ignore her very presence.

The youngster-to-ignore's voice floated through the flimsy partition. "Who stars in *Ferris Bueller's Day Off*? Tom Cruise?"

He wasn't going to answer. Let her think he wasn't there, or asleep. But, Jesus. *Cruise?* How could she think Short Stuff had the comedy chops for that, despite his launching pad of *Risky Business*? Ever since, Tom had been overcompensating for his half-ling stature with Navy jets, race cars, and samurai swords, not laughs.

"Or is it Pee Wee Herman?"

Charlie bit his bottom lip, willing himself not to respond. But Pee Wee Herman! "Matthew Broderick," he bit out, not able to let another second of celluloid misinformation go unchallenged. "Son of the late James Broderick, who played Alice's husband in 1969's *Alice's Restaurant*, who was also in *The Group* and *Dog Day Afternoon*. He played the father in the TV series *Family* from 1976 through 1980."

"Ah! Matthew of *The Music Man* and *The Producers*, and husband of Sarah Jessica Parker."

"Right." Now that she wasn't wallowing in total ignorance, he could relax and return to pretending to be comatose.

"I met Sarah Jessica Parker at a *Vanity Fair* thing last year."

Whoop-de-do.

"She seemed really in love with her husband and their life with their son," Jemima said, her tone admiring. "And they say actors can't have it all."

"I thought you had decided to give up the acting life." He had to comment, didn't he? The last thing she'd told him was that she was going to quit the business. Not that he'd actually believed he'd get that lucky.

The trough that was midlife was full of waves that could lift a man up and then drop him down just as deep.

"At the moment, I don't feel like letting anything— or anyone—chase me away from what's already planned."

That sounded ominous. If there was one thing he'd learned in his years—middle age had to be good for *something*—was that flexibility was paramount. There were times to advance and times to retreat, and he wanted her—please God—to be retreating from him and any more ideas she had about touching him or kissing him.

He cleared his throat. "Listen, Jem, about the other night."

"I'm not talking about the other night."

Okay. Good. But it begged the question, and he was so effing lousy at playing half-dead bodies. Every director he'd ever had had whined that he couldn't hold his breath worth a damn. "So what *are* you talking about?"

"Oh, my brother Nash just stormed out. He's been haranguing me all afternoon, convinced my fan is stalking me again."

The sound that came out of Charlie's mouth sounded like a wounded seal. He took a deep breath and tossed the ice pack away from his eyes. "Jemima, please explain."

It wasn't sweet, but it was short. She had a teenage fan who, months ago, had started hanging out near the studio where she'd been working and then at her home. Her mother had gone ballistic, the kid had been taken into custody, evaluated, and set free. Except now, the young man was missing.

"I trip on the street, Nash gets a bizarro fax, and suddenly he sees the boogeyman behind every palm tree."

Charlie felt as if he were pushing through Jell-O as he rose from his lounger. She was young, he told himself, trying to think calmly through his panic. Inexperienced. Not well-versed in the wacko ways that Hollywood fame could warp people who wanted to grab a piece of it for themselves. Women sent him used lipsticks, worn panties, worse.

He had friends who'd found fans in their bushes, in their kitchens, in their beds. Models' faces had been slashed, actresses murdered.

He wrapped his fingers around the edge of the partitition and tried to sound calm. A mature man could sound calm, couldn't he, even when fear was squeezing the breath from his body?

"You've got to take these things seriously, Jem." His heart rate was seriously jacked up, that was certain. Where the hell was his buddy Larry in all this? As her agent, how could Larry possibly have let one of his most valuable clients gallivant around Southern California with a nutcase on her tail? Charlie was going to have to track the man down and kick his careless ass.

"I have taken it seriously. We've talked with the LAPD and the Palm Springs police, and today I contacted the most reputable threat management firm in Hollywood. I'm okay, Charlie. There are signs, a distinct set of signals, that point to potential problems. Their assessment is that my fan is not dangerous to me. He's just on a trip away from home."

"They told you that?"

"Obviously they don't know exactly where he is and

what he's doing, but yes, they told me in their opinion he isn't a threat to me. I believe it, they believe it, everyone believes it except Nash."

Without even meeting the guy, Charlie decided he loved Nash. "I think you should listen to your brother."

"He wants me to go away with him somewhere in Europe. Heidelberg, maybe? Krakow? I had to shove him out of my bungalow and lock the door."

"You should leave with him." Damn it! She had to take every precaution. She was too precious, too young, too . . . loved to lose.

"What? I can't just take off, not when I'm supposed to report to the set soon."

"Go to Europe. Trust Larry to track the kid down in time." He'd say anything he must to keep her safe.

"And maybe not. I have this movie I've agreed to do. I'm not giving that up."

Charlie hardened his jaw. "The movie with Mack Chandler."

"Yes, but— Wait a minute, how do you know about Larry?"

Tightening his fingers on the partition's post, Charlie took a breath. "You mentioned your agent's name one time or other."

"I did not."

Charlie tried thinking fast. But he was too old—or too worried. And anyway, he'd do *anything* he must to keep her safe. The decision was just that easy. That quick. He didn't even bother with a deep breath.

"Because," Charlie said, "as a matter of fact, Larry's my agent too." Sans hat, Ray-Bans, and scarf, he walked around the partition.

And presented Mack Chandler's new and improved face to the woman he'd tricked into intimacy.

As he'd expected, Jemima reared back in shock, her small hand rising to her throat.

He gave her Mack Chandler's *People* magazine's Most Beautiful People smile and dropped Charlie's put-on Aussie accent. "Hey, baby. Surprise."

She'd gone statue-still, so he marched forward to give her a better look at him. "I can't take credit for the idea. It was Larry who thought of us getting acquainted outside the set."

Her agent, Larry Michaels. Their mutual agent. Charlie had known the guy since he'd first come to Hollywood. Larry had been the bartender at the Beverly Hills hotel where Charlie had waited tables. They'd shared a house for a time. Charlie and Larry were the same exact age, the same temperament, and apparently, the samely stupid when it came to dealing with Jemima Cargill.

When she'd confessed to Larry her nervousness over working with Mack, the other man had come up with the "great" idea that the two of them could get to know each other off the set. "Strike up a friendship," Larry had advised. "Charm her before she knows who you really are."

So Charlie had covered his scars and bruises with hat and glasses and scarf and tacked on the Australian accent he'd developed for a straight-to-video flick he'd done before *Honey Hunt*. Then he'd gone out of his way to meet Jemima—which hadn't been too hard, since Larry had managed to make sure the two of them had been assigned neighboring bungalows.

It had all seemed like a good idea at the time.

But what a disaster.

Jemima was such a little thing that she took up less than two-thirds of her chaise. He dropped down to the empty cushion beside her slender thighs and put on another smile again. Most of the swelling was gone, and he was sure he was recognizable as Mack Chandler. As she continued to stare at him, though, a flutter of concern batted around his gut. "Uh, what do you think about the face?"

Her next action didn't quite answer the question about his features, though it made it perfectly clear what she thought about *him*. She slapped him, brisk and hard, across the left cheek.

He ran his tongue along the inside of his mouth, tasting blood. "Christ, you're strong," he complained.

But it was all talk. He welcomed the sting, as he welcomed the burning glare she was now training his way. Jemima Cargill would have other costars, other movies, other chances for Oscar fame. Her talent would not be hidden away. But *she* would be hidden away now. He was certain that unmasking himself as Mack Chandler would send a woman as young and tender as Jemima Cargill to Heidelberg or Krakow or wherever it was her big brother Nash wanted to take her.

As far as Charlie was concerned, it was a happily ever after. The reality equivalent of the hero on the horse cantering off into the sunset. Alone, naturally.

"I don't want to see you again," she said.

"Of course not," he murmured. "I completely understand." Okay, he'd miss her, but he'd worry about that some other time. Now Jemima was the one to focus on. Jemima who would be going far, far away.

Relief flooded him, lightening his heart. He was free in the knowledge that sweet, beautiful Jemima Cargill would stay safe. He was free of his costar, and now free to forget about this unfortunate attachment. He figured he'd never lay his eyes on her again.

She leaped off the lounger, in a move that reminded him just how much litheness he'd lost in the last twenty years. "I don't want to see you again," she hissed.

"Of course not," he repeated. "I completely understand."

"Until," Jemima continued, "the first day we report to the set."

Chapter Nineteen

"(When) I Get Scared"
The Lovelites
"A" side, single (1966)

With Vince Standish out of town for a few days, Eve was determined to enjoy her life, such as it was. You had to take your pleasures where you could find them when you were a flat-broke, mob boss's daughter with the SEC on your tail. She attended two charity luncheons on her newspaper's press pass, went to tea with a bunch of women with bright clothes and a kick-ass attitude from the Red Hat Society for an upcoming freelance piece for *Palm Springs Life* magazine, and strolled through the El Paseo shopping district, leaving quickly before being tempted to charge something at one of her favorite boutiques.

When you were a flat-broke mob boss's daughter with the SEC on your tail, you could take some pleasures, but you had to restrain your lust.

And wasn't that just plain damn depressing?

After her frustrating window-shopping trip, Eve returned to the Kona Kai as dusk settled into the Coachella Valley. Low-lying landscape lights glowed along the walkways, and she tried to brighten her mood along with them. *Come on, Eve*, she chided herself. *What happened to the happy-go-lucky Party Girl?*

Even an enthusiastic tomcat greeting from ragged-eared Adam couldn't lift her spirits. He trotted at her heels as she paused on the way to her suite and unlocked a storage closet that Bianca had given her access to. Though Eve had liquidated most of her furnishings at a high-end consignment store, there were boxes of personal items that she'd stowed away for that time when she once again really had a place to call her own.

Which, for all she knew, would be at Martha Stewart's former stomping grounds, Camp Cupcake.

Morose thoughts continued to flow like sludge through her head as she stacked two cartons into her arms and shoved two others out the door with her feet. It wasn't quick work to move them in that same manner toward her suite, but she had no plans for the rest of the evening anyhow. Nothing to distract her from feeling sorry for herself.

Oh, hurray.

A few feet from her door, long arms reached around her shoulders to pluck the boxes from her hands. Then they froze, leaving her in the circle of a strong, masculine embrace, a man's hands cupping hers.

A man. Hah! It was Nash, of course, as she'd known from the instant she'd felt his heat at her back. Against her breastbone, her heart took up an insistent beat.

"Call off your killer cat," he said into her ear, his breath hot too.

"Adam," she said pleasantly, glancing down at the vigilant tom. "Sick 'em."

Nash's biceps gave her a squeeze. "Bad, ungrateful girl," he murmured, lifting the boxes over her head as he took a cautious step back.

Relieved woman—until now. Though she'd known Nash had been around the spa the past few days, shadowing Jemima—okay, so she'd asked—Eve hadn't run directly into him. A piece of good luck, she'd thought, considering the fact that the last time she'd seen him she'd somehow ended up with tears—tears!—on her face.

But now he'd turned up again like the proverbial bad penny—just like the return of her own bad luck.

Without bothering to check that he was following, she shoved the boxes that were on the ground the remaining distance to her front door and unlocked it with her card key. Then she booted them across the threshold and held the door wide for Nash. He deposited the cartons he was carrying onto the coffee table in the living area, then cast a glance toward the door she still held open and the forbidding feline guardian that stood just outside of it.

Nash jerked a thumb in Adam's direction. "Sorry, darlin', but I'm not leaving until he does." And he plopped himself onto the corner of her couch.

Eve scowled at him. She scowled at Adam. Neither one seemed to care the least about getting into her good graces.

And to think that's what she'd once liked about the cat.

And Nash, too.

But the truth was, his company, as unwelcome as it might be, was preferable to that of her own dark thoughts. So, still wearing her scowl, she shut the door, then puttered about the room, turning on lamps, rearranging the boxes, then finally opening a bottle of sauvignon blanc in order to pour out two glasses.

Without a word, she handed one to Nash, though he probably would have preferred a Bud. She didn't want him getting that comfortable. He wasn't going to be here too long.

He stayed as silent as she was, which she tried to ignore as she settled on the carpeted floor beside the boxes and applied herself to opening the first. Not that she didn't take furtive glances at him through her lashes at the same time. Nash wasn't usually quiet—at least not around her.

But this time he sat back on her cushions, muscular, mile-long legs out in front of him, a thoughtful expression on his face as he gazed about the room. She'd kept a dozen crystal wineglasses in the hopes that one day she'd entertain again, and the delicate flute looked even more fragile than normal in his wide, tanned hand. Poor, defenseless glass, so easily crushed.

Except Nash would never be so careless or aggressive. She thought back to a few minutes ago on the Kona Kai path. He'd surrounded her with his maleness and with his heat, yet she hadn't spooked. She *should* have spooked, but since that night in the dark bathroom, it was impossible to see him as a physical threat. He'd encouraged her to visualize butterflies, for goodness' sake!

"What have you been doing the past few days?" she asked over the mild screech of tape pulling free of cardboard.

"Sticking close to Jem, natch. But she thinks I'm about as handy to have around as a back pocket on a dress shirt. Still, I've told her I won't leave until her 'fan' turns up back in his La-Z-Boy at his mama's house or until Jem reports to the set of her latest movie. The producers have promised top-notch security there. What with a costar as blazin' as Mack Chandler, they have to keep a close eye on things."

"In the meantime, the close eye on Jemima is you."

"You're not saying that with enough sympathy. Now she's locked up all right and tight for the night, studying her script, she says, but today she made me go with her on one of those celebrity home bus tours."

His disgusted tone made her laugh—and made her suspect that his disgust was exactly why Jemima had hauled her brother along on the tour in the first place. "What, you didn't enjoy the sites?"

"It's misnamed. It should be the dead celebrity and/or relocated celebrity home tour. I now know where Dinah Shore and Cary Grant once lived. Where Debbie Reynolds and Eddie Fisher honeymooned, where Eddie Fisher and Liz Taylor honeymooned, where Liz Taylor and Mike Todd honeymooned, where Liz Taylor and Mike Wilding honeymooned. I was holding my breath to find out where Liz Taylor and Kevin Bacon spent their bridal night, but apparently that was one degree of separation too many."

Eve choked back another snort of laughter. Admit it, she'd missed the big man. It had been her best idea all day to allow him inside. Feeling herself relax, she took a swallow of wine.

"So what's with the depersonalized zone?" Nash asked.

She looked up.

He made a circular gesture with his glass. "This

looks a lot like the room I have here. More hotel room than home."

She shrugged off the unsettling observation. Unsettling, because the sterility of the surroundings had begun to bother her, too, and was exactly why she'd retrieved the boxes from storage. A few photos and personal things would make it feel more homey—and make her feel it was less likely she'd be sent to prison sometime soon.

She shoved that last thought away. "I only moved in here about a month ago. Sold my condo and came here until I, uh, find something else."

The lie usually spilled easily from her lips, but now she had to force it out. Maybe fibbing to The Preacher gave it extra weight.

"But great minds think alike and all that," she continued. "Because I'm adding some personal touches as we speak." For a moment she dug around some folded fabric she'd added as cushion in the box. Then with a flourish, she pulled out a frame. It slid free of its spongy wrapping protector.

Oh, she thought, feeling her lips curve. *It's this one.* A framed 8 × 10 photograph of the family, circa six years old for Téa and Eve. They stood side by side in lace first communion dresses, with matching organza veils attached to white velvet headbands. Téa, wouldn't you know, looked properly pious, gloved hands folded at her waist, while Eve appeared ready to pinch Joey, who was grinning at the camera with a look that said, "I'm not wearing any itchy white lace and I'm never gonna!"

Behind the three girls, Bianca wore a serene expression and a jade green Chanel suit, while their father took up the rest of the photo with his dark good looks and the obvious force of his exuberant personality. He had one hand on Bianca's shoulder and the other on Eve's, and his smile seemed to embrace all of them. She remembered the warm glow of being with him, even as she wondered for the thousandth time how her pasty Nordic DNA had managed to overwhelm her brunette Mediterranean half.

"*He* looks like a movie star. Your father, obviously."

"Yes." With her finger, she traced Salvatore Caruso's arm from his shoulder to the fingers that rested on her pristine lace. Even now, she could almost feel his touch, their warmth, that secure feeling she'd had when he was around her. Her father had rescued her from the quiet apartment and the bewildering loss of her mother and brought his inconvenient daughter into the warm bosom of his real family. God, she loved that he'd brought her home and made her a full-fledged Caruso.

"I understand you thought he was missing until recently. I'm sorry."

Eve flashed back to the night her father's remains had been found, and the memory of the smell of the algae-choked lagoon invaded the room. Johnny had only let them see the moldy wallet that had been the initial piece of evidence that the remains found interred in the rock wall had been Salvatore's. The clammy leather had been sticky to the touch, and she'd wanted to throw it down . . . and hold it close.

Pressure built behind her eyes and she squeezed them shut. She wasn't going to cry. She hadn't cried over that loss or any other in sixteen years, and there was no point in weeping about it now, especially not when she'd rather smile thinking about Salvatore. "It wasn't such a shock," she said lightly. "When a member of the mob goes missing, right away you're pretty sure he's not merely wandering around with amnesia."

"Still . . ."

Shrugging, she looked back down at the photo instead of Nash's sympathetic face.

"Tell me something about him."

Like what? "He learned to shoot by taking target practice on bats in the summertime." It was the first thing that popped into her head. "When he was a kid, he and his friends would sit on the curb of Palm Canyon Drive, right across from the Desert Inn, and hone their skills."

She wondered what had made her tell him that. Was her subconscious trying to shock The Preacher with her father's mobster ways?

It didn't seem to faze Nash, though. "Yeah? My old man took target practice on the neighbor's windshields when the spirits moved him."

Meaning his father was a drunk. A mean drunk, but one his son could still pun about. Trying not to be intrigued or impressed by the contradiction, Eve set the photo on the coffee table and shoved her hand back in the box.

Nash picked up the frame to study it more closely. "You look good in white," he said. "How come you've never married?"

Who could love me? Shocked by her inner voice's automatic question, she went cold all over. *Who could really love me?* And just like that, tears stung her eyes again.

"Eve?"

She didn't dare look up at him. Damn Nash. Damn him. How did he manage to do that? He was making her weak once more. Shutting some doors and then asking questions that opened up others.

There were emotions, doubts, that were better locked tight in the cold box that was her heart. She didn't want to examine what she kept in there—the fear that on the inside, she wasn't the pretty, charming Eve she'd perfected to please the Carusos. And that she also wasn't really the sexy, beautiful Eve who had control of the men in her life.

"Darlin', are you all right?"

"I'm fine."

"No you're not." He sounded kind. Caring. And then he said the most dangerous words of all. "Let me help."

But she couldn't let him do that. Her fingers flexed, squeezing the fabric she'd packed around the items in the box. *Buck up, girl! Look out for #1!* No man, not Nash, not anyone, could help her. That would mean they would have power to hurt her as well. The only way to win, to stay strong, was to retain the control on *her* side of the line.

"Sweetheart, you're crying again."

She had to stop him from focusing on that. Keeping her eyes cast down, she blinked rapidly, willing the excess moisture away. As her vision cleared, she noted what she was clutching in her hand. Blue-and-green plaid, a crisp white blouse.

"Come on, Eve, talk to me." It was a beguiling voice, as old as time. Was he then, indeed, the snake in the garden? A voice that promised so much but would only pay out in heartache? "Why the tears? Just talk to me."

Eve shut out the temptation and directed her thoughts heavenward. *Forgive me Father, for I will sin.*

But what else could one expect from a Caruso?

Now she looked up at Nash, lifting the clothes from

the box. There was always one certain way for her to remain in charge. "Just feeling nostalgic, is all. I've had some good times in this school uniform."

His eyes narrowed, then flicked from the garments in her hands to her face, then to her mouth. Even from across the table she felt the heat leap to the surface of his skin. Was she good or what?

Or make that very, very bad.

Because a man as dogged as Nash Cargill, a man who couldn't stop himself from wanting to "help," was only going to be stopped from trying to look inside of her by one thing.

Sex. She was going to have sex with him.

And what was wrong with that? Hadn't she been telling herself to take her pleasures where she could find them?

Rising to her feet, Eve held the old uniform against her body. Nash was watching her with brimstone kindling a fire in his silvery eyes. Still, it was heat, and she felt it lick along her flesh as his gaze dragged over her. Her throat tightened, turning her voice husky. "Would you like to see how it looks on me?"

His nostrils flared. The heat in the room jumped another fifteen degrees. But then his arms crossed over his wide chest. "You're bluffing."

Shaking her head, Eve smiled at Nash. "My daddy didn't believe in gambling, which means he also taught us never to bluff." Never, ever, ever.

Chapter Twenty

"Keep it Cool"
Elvin Bishop
Hometown Boy Makes Good (1976)

Nash watched Eve disappear into her bedroom, hips swaying in a confident, seductive dance. Then he quaffed the remainder of his wine and refilled the glass from the bottle she'd left on the table, trying to ignore the bead of sweat rolling down his spine. She was out to break him.

Damn woman.

Damn sexy, seductive woman. He'd done something or said something that had touched a tender spot, and now she wanted to make him pay.

After more fruitless days of trailing behind his little sister, after more days of catching maddening glimpses of oh-so-erotic Eve around the Kona Kai, days that gave him nothing else to think about but how frustrated he was and how horny she made him, he was going to let her try.

But all the points were not going to Eve in this match, as much as it was obvious she expected them to. She thought he would fall at her feet and give her the balm or the entertainment or whatever it was that she considered sex, but he wasn't going down on his knees that easy.

Then she sashayed back through the bedroom door, and he had to bite his tongue to hold back his groan of surrender. She'd done it. She'd really put on that cursed school uniform. Eve had grown some since last she'd worn the thing. Plain white cotton strained across her breasts, and the plaid skirt's hemline was a scandal all by itself. He wasn't going to think about what was underneath it.

White cotton panties? Black silk thong? Nothing at all?

Oh, my God. His cock got into a shoving match with the zipper of his jeans. The fact was, she was going to kill him.

And the knowledge of it was in the sultry lowering of her lashes. In her confident stroll that was taking her closer to him. In the fact that her toenails were painted cotton candy pink.

It was the same shade as the color she'd painted her heart-shaped mouth. Her tongue sneaked out to touch the deep bow of her upper lip. "So what do you think of my outfit, Nash?"

He remembered the first occasion they'd met, that night in the bar. She'd stepped between him and Jemima then, offering herself as sacrifice to his libido, just as she was doing now. Distracting him from Jemima, that time. This time, distracting him from . . . what?

Standing before him, just an arm's length away, she drew her big toe along the back calf of her other leg.

The shy, yet still seductive movement only made his palm itch to spank her in an all-woman way.

"Well, Nash?" she purred.

Careful, careful. He sucked in a breath and pointed to a spot on her blouse with a finger he prayed wasn't trembling. "You have a stain, right there, where the sleeve meets the shoulder."

Her eyes flared open, lashes flying high. Her gaze darted down to the place he'd indicated, and she frowned.

With that, he'd changed the rhythm of the play, and she narrowed her eyes as she looked back up at him. The party girl was feeling a tinge impatient, but she was trying not to show it. "That doesn't really matter, does it, Nash? The uniform and I, well, we haven't gotten . . . out . . . in quite a while."

He almost laughed aloud at the implication. The idea that Eve Caruso hadn't gotten "out" recently was like trying to believe that he didn't give his truck a good wax job on a regular basis.

"I thought you might want to know," he replied, straight-faced. "Aren't you planning on wearing it to that masquerade event you told me about? I figured that's why you tried it on."

She blinked again. "No. Well . . . maybe . . ." Her hand reached down for the glass of wine she'd left on the table, and she took a healthy sip. Then she set the glass back and toyed with the top button of her blouse, the one that was barely containing her cleavage. A woman redoubling her seductive efforts. "Do you think that would be a good idea?"

He thought a good idea would be locking them both in a room without any clothes on at all, but that was the thought she wanted him to have. With a jerk, he lifted his gaze off the teeny-tiny button that looked close to popping. "Me, I never tell a lady what she should wear."

A smile played around the corners of her mouth. "But Nash, we both know I'm no lady."

Good God, how much was a man supposed to take? As much as her lines sounded like canned seduction, they were overpowering when coupled with her classy, superbeauty self. It was like Miss America starring in a raunchy porn movie.

The stuff of every man's fantasies.

But he steeled his spine and started thinking about ice cream, ice sculptures, ice machines, ice hockey. Yeah. Red-faced men with big long sticks.

Which made him think of himself and the damn pole that was jutting up between his legs. "Darlin'," he managed to grind out. "To a man like me, all women are ladies from the day they're born until the day they die."

A mulish expression crossed her face, and she looked more like the little girl she was pretending to be. "Don't you want to touch me, Nash?"

With every muscle, tendon, and cell of his being. But that was what she expected from him, from any man, from every man. It was obvious to him that somewhere along the way she'd learned to consider her beauty a value, she'd learned to use it as a weapon, she'd learned to make it a buffer between herself and other people. Men.

Who would look inside her head and her heart if they could get inside her stupendous body instead?

She asked the sixty-four-thousand-dollar question again, with just a tad more edge. "Really, Nash, don't you want to touch me?"

His palms gripped his thighs as he gave her his

best Bubba grin. He knew a surefire way to shake her off, and he drawled it all out for her, in his best Southern-speak. "Well sure I want to touch you, darlin', but why don't you come over here and touch me first?"

She stepped back, looked taken aback. Looked almost shocked by the idea of it.

Exactly what I wanted, thought that mature, sensible, rational part of him that didn't like a woman just because she had a cotton-candy mouth, big breasts, long legs, and blonde hair. Of course, somewhere inside there was a randy teenager jumping up and down, a teenager who was yelling that he would come from just touching his tongue to Eve's kneecap and it would be the best come of his life, but Nash figured that was just big talk. In reality, it would take his tongue to her upper thigh, at least.

Then he made the biggest mistake of the evening yet. As he watched her back away, he heard himself murmur out loud, "After all, one good dare deserves another."

Instantly, her gaze turned crafty. How could he have been so stupid? Guessing he was playing his own game with her would only egg on her competitive spirit. No doubt Eve was accustomed to coming out on top when it came to sensual sports. And not that he didn't think he could hold his own with her in a purely sexual sense, but he worried that—

The thought was lost as she landed in his lap. That clean, bare-flesh-and-bubbles scent of her rose around his head, and he was just inches from that cotton-candy pink mouth. "Eve . . ."

His good sense was stumbling around in his brain, waving its arms like Robot on reruns of the TV classic

Lost in Space. Danger Will Robinson! Danger Will Robinson!

His hands gripped his thighs tighter, and he willed them not to lift and touch her silky thighs, her round ass, the curves of those womanly breasts that were bursting out of that damn bad-girl blouse. But he couldn't avert his gaze as she brought one forefinger to her tongue and licked the pad. He nearly went cross-eyed as he watched her inch that glistening tip to his mouth.

She painted his upper lip with wet heat.

His fingernails bit through his jeans as she repeated the process on his bottom lip.

Then her gaze met his, pondering, assessing, deciding, and he held firm. Oh, God, all of him held so rock-hard firm. She took no pity on his erection as she ground her cute little butt against it and went for the buttons on his shirt. Her breaths came easy, softly, and he knew she was still toying with him, those easy breaths signaling this was not for herself but to make him lose control and give her what she wanted.

Worship, not sex.

Sex, not intimacy.

And Nash was determined not to let her get away with it, because sometime in the last few years he'd gotten tired of tab-A-into-slot-B sex. He wasn't interested in being the manner in which Eve released her tensions or covered up her emotions, even if he had to ultimately push her off his lap and stalk out of her place with the longest flagpole of a hard-on he'd ever had in his life.

Shifting to straddle his knees, she pushed the edges of his unfastened shirt apart. As the cotton rasped across his pecs, the muscles twitched, and his nipples contracted to stiff nubs.

Eve froze.

She was staring down at his chest as if she'd never seen one before. And maybe she hadn't, considering the weasely little runner types she seemed to prefer in her bed. Then one of her fingers finally moved, making a slow trail from his throat, over his slamming heart, and then around the lower curve of his right pectoral. Her other hand mirrored the movement, and hot chills rushed down his spine with the good news.

Oh, but there were more hallelujahs to follow. She pushed his shirt off his shoulders and pulled it down to his elbows. He had to leave it there unless he wanted to risk lifting his hands—which he didn't. He didn't want to risk any kind of move at all, because what Eve was doing to him was so damn arousing that he didn't trust himself to touch her flesh and then not take over.

This time, with this woman, giving her the lead was the only chance he had to make it equal. So he held fast as she explored his chest with the lightest of fingertips, circling, circling, but never touching the small points at the center. He would have thought it was more practiced seduction on her part, but he could hear her breath coming faster now, he could feel the new warmth of her skin and the avidness of her gaze as she explored his body.

Then she bent her head and sucked his nipple.

His hips bucked. He closed his eyes and ground his teeth, the pleasure rippling, rippling down his back then shooting through his bloodstream.

A feminine sound of appreciation buzzed against his breastbone and his lashes lifted. The ends of her silky blonde hair brushed against his chest as she lifted her lips. He stared down at the brand of cotton-candy pink ringing his nipple and fought another surge of his hips.

And then lost the fight when her mouth latched onto his other nipple. His right hand jerked free of his thigh, in one move yanking the tails of her blouse from her skirt. His palm found the sleek small of her back and she flinched, goose bumps rising against his callouses.

Now he believed she was turned on too.

His other hand found the hem of her skirt and snaked underneath. As her teeth nipped down on him, he curled his fingers around her ass. Her bare, naked ass.

Oh, bad girl.

Naughty, no-panties woman.

The Preacher was going to have to punish her with pleasure.

Chapter Twenty-one

"Long After Tonight is All Over"
The Paris Sisters
"B" side, single (1967)

She'd won. Triumph flooded her as Nash's long fingers caressed the bare skin of her back and her behind. He was going to give her what she wanted.

Then his big palm lifted off her butt and landed again, giving her naked flesh a mild slap. Her head popped up and her gaze jerked to his as glittery heat fanned across her skin. Desire sizzled in her blood.

"Don't think this is the end of the game, darlin'," he said, his eyes molten silver. "It's not over until the beautiful lady sings."

But before she could snicker or tease or take back control, he shifted his hand from her butt to the back of her head. His other emerged to get a firm grip on her chin.

He tilted it just so, then moved in for the kiss.

As his tongue sank into her mouth, she sank onto

his lap, indulging herself in a greedy wiggle against his erection. His hand fell back to her hip. He flipped up her skirt and squeezed her right cheek in warning. "No cheating," he said against her mouth.

But she called the rules here. This was her game. To make sure he understood that, she thrust her tongue in his mouth and wiggled again.

The second spank was just as playful but delicious as the first, igniting sparklers across her skin, tightening her nipples, contracting her womb.

It was hard to kiss and swallow her little cat smile at the same time.

Nash must have discerned her struggle, because he lifted his head and sighed. "You like that too much, don't you?" He sighed again. "Have it your way, then. I'll take mine the next time around."

But there wouldn't be a next time around, so Eve wasn't worried. In fact, she was elated. The small pop that was her usual sexual release might be just enough to snap her out of her present funk. By Jon Stewart time, she'd be alone in bed with the TV and Comedy Central, and perhaps relaxed enough for sleep.

Winding her arms around Nash's neck, she kissed him, hard. The world tilted. It took a moment to realize he'd lifted her and was carrying her away from the couch. "Hey," she said, spearing her fingers in the too-long hair at the back of his neck and pulling his lips from hers. "Did I give you permission to head to the bedroom?"

His footsteps halted and he looked down at her, his eyes and his smile lazy. Confident. "Didn't your daddy teach you that might makes right?"

Oh, but Nash would never use his strength against her, and the certainty of that thought sent a strange frisson of—security? pleasure?—down her back. Something of that little quiver must have shown on her face, because his smile died.

"Oh, darlin'. That was a stupid thing to say, wasn't it? I'm sorry. I was just mouthing off."

She didn't want his apologies. Though she trusted him in how he used his strength, she didn't want him to be so considerate of her moods. He was supposed to scratch an itch, not *care*. So she leaned in to kiss his bottom lip. "That's what happens when you should have been mouthing *on*," she teased.

He laughed and hitched her higher to bring them once again lip-to-lip, tongue-to-tongue, breath-to-breath. His strides ate up the last of the distance to the bed as the heat between them evaporated any further thoughts.

Or doubts. She'd never been one for self-sacrifice, anyway, and Nash was here, hot, and making her hot too.

The mattress met her back. She'd left one low-wattage lamp on by the bed, and its light turned Nash's shoulder to gold as he sat down beside her. His gaze ran over her body, from disheveled hair to hiked-up skirt. "You're ahead of me in the bare-naked department," he said, reaching down to pull off his boots. "I'd better hurry up."

Yes. Still, as he went about undressing, she tortured him by rubbing her thumb over his nipples, massaging her lipstick prints into the tanned skin of his chest. And what a chest. It had taken her breath away at first, all that rippling muscle and smooth flesh. She'd never considered herself a chest woman; she'd never considered, really, what body parts of a man she liked, until now. She definitely liked Nash's chest.

Then he stood, half-turning to shuck his jeans and boxers.

Oh, she liked his butt too.

Then he turned back to face her.

And she wasn't sure what she thought about *that*.

He glanced down at himself, then rubbed a casual palm along his length and grinned. "You're inspiring me to great heights."

"And breadth." She liked seeing him touch himself, she realized. It proved how comfortable he was with his own sexuality. How comfortable he was within his own skin. What a turn-on.

Another flush of heat washed across her body. As if he could read her mind, he palmed himself again. "All for you, darlin'."

All for me. Oh, now she liked the idea of that too. Reaching out a hand, she stroked her nails along his thigh. "Then I must have been a *very* good girl."

He laughed. "Not exactly what I've been thinking, but we can compromise on that point." The mattress dipped as he stretched out beside her and reached for the buttons of her blouse. "This, however, has got to go."

He bared her in seconds. Her nipples puckered as he tossed away her bra, too, and then he bent his head to take one in his mouth. Suction. Heat. The rasp of his tongue. Her back arched and she went wet between her thighs. Nash moved to her other breast, and desire burned inside of her.

She cradled his head in her hands, caressing his silky hair. "Oh, yeah," she whispered as he swirled his tongue around the point and then tugged gently with his teeth. "Oh, this is really good."

Better than good when he lifted his head and looked

down on her, his gaze intense. He watched his hand slowly unfasten the button and zipper on her skirt, then push it down her thighs.

As she kicked it away, he froze. "Pretty." His voice was thick. "Pretty. Naked."

"I get a deep discount on bikini waxes." He was still staring, and she had to resist the urge to reach down and do a Venus de Milo. "Haven't you ever seen a Brazilian?"

When he still didn't say anything, she felt a trill of nerves edge along her spine. "Nash?" Despite herself, her hand crept down.

Catching it, he lifted his gaze to hers. "I thought I'd seen it all. Initials, lightning bolts, you-are-here arrows, Xs to mark the spot."

Not sure whether he was serious or not, she fought the urge to laugh.

Until he squeezed her fingers. Until he said, "But you, Eve, I've never seen *you*."

There was now nothing to laugh about, not when her chest tightened, not when goose bumps broke out across her skin, not when his free hand moved to cup her mons.

His eyes closed. "Ah, Eve. I thought it might be like this."

Like what? Like what?

The question flew away, though, as he stroked his long middle finger along the seam between her swollen folds. Her legs parted, her folds parted, and then Nash was there, circling her clitoris and then sliding lower to play at the wet entrance to her body.

Her thigh muscles clenched, her womb contracted, she closed her eyes against the delicious, sweet intrusion. He was gentle, soft, insistent. His tongue was back on her hard nipple as a second finger sank inside of her.

Eve gasped. Her hands found his body, and she ran them over the thick muscles of his shoulders, arms, chest. Her desire was rising higher, flying now, the promise of that pop of release hovering over her like those butterflies he'd once made her imagine. Her palm slid lower and she felt his hard belly twitch as her fingers found him, circled him, gave him the message that it was time. Now. Right now.

His hand withdrew from her body. Okay, good, he'd replace it with that other part of him any second. As soon as he took care of that condom he'd taken from his wallet and placed on the bedside table.

But instead, instead, he trailed his mouth down her torso. Heading she-knew-where.

"No." Her body jackknifed up. She was breathing hard, the noise loud in the room. "Not that."

He blinked at her. "What?"

"I don't want that."

"You'll like it. I'm good, because *I* like it." He gave her a silly-girl pat on her hip.

She pushed his hand away. "I don't want that and I don't do that."

"Darlin'—"

"If intercourse isn't enough . . ."

Now he was frowning at her. "Intercourse?"

She huffed, hunching her shoulders and crossing her arms over her breasts. "It's not the wrong word."

"It's precise, I'll grant you that. But prissy. I think *you're* prissy."

There was still heat between them, desire was still bubbling through her blood, but she was also considering shoving him off the bed so that he would land on his judgmental ass. She could always finish this with the convenient little appliance in her bedside table.

"Do you want sex or not?" she demanded.

He shrugged. How could one man be naked and beautiful and so maddeningly confident all at once? "I wanted it all, but..."

"But?"

He rubbed his chin. "But I guess I can compromise once again—"

She tugged him down on top of her before he could change his mind.

"—as long as you beg." He reached for the condom.

"Right," she scoffed, closing her eyes to hide her delight in his surrender and the sensation of his hard, hot skin rubbing against hers. Her knees widened to make room for him.

And then had to widen some more.

Nash was a big man, she knew that, but she hadn't taken into account how much room his hips and thighs required. With his knees and gentle hands, he nudged her lower limbs outward, spreading her, opening her to him.

When he came down on his elbows, his big hands cradling her face, she felt like a butterfly, wings pinned to the mattress. But it was her heart that fluttered against her chest as the head of his erection briefly grazed the knot of nerves made so vulnerable by her wide-open position. His mouth came down on hers and he soul-kissed Eve, his tongue and lips taking . . . giving . . . taking.

He caressed her clitoris with the silky head of his penis again, and she tilted her hips to lure him lower. It was a shallow thrust he returned. Not enough. She wrapped her legs around his hips, barely managing to lock her ankles so she could bring him where she wanted him. So she could demand the sensation she wanted.

Nash thrusting. Hard. Nash inside her. Hard.

He slid into her wet heat, stretching her. They both groaned.

"Good," she whispered against his mouth. "Nice," she said as he bent his head to lick the side of her neck.

But then he pulled out and went back to that gentle outside, upward stroke.

"Nash."

Deep slide.

"Yes."

Back out.

"*Nash*."

Gentle stroke.

Deep slide. Gentle stroke. Deep slide.

It was maddening. Frustrating. Not quite enough and he knew it.

She was going to kill him. She was definitely going to kill him, toss his body to the floor, then finish this off herself, with her non-demanding, non-frustrating, no-ego appliance.

But though it didn't have Nash's ego, it didn't have his muscles or heated skin or arousing, masculine scent either. She lifted her head and bit the edge of his whiskered jaw in retaliation. He grunted. Slid deeper.

Oh, yes, yes, yes.

Only to slide back out. All the way out.

"Nash."

He reared back, breaking her ankle lock, the muscles in his arms bulging. "You need somethin', darlin'?"

His drawl was heavier, sultrier, like a hot humid night that the desert had never, ever experienced.

"You know what I need," she gasped out, as his erection teased her swollen nerve endings.

"Then you know what you need to do." His eyes were intense, but he was smiling at her, a gentle smile that set those butterflies tumbling inside her chest again.

He sat back onto his knees and slid his hands to her inner thighs, holding her open, wide, vulnerable.

Except Nash would never hurt her.

He slowly ran his shaft along her folds, up and down, but never inside her, never enough. "Oh, Eve, you feel so good. You feel so right."

Hot goose bumps prickled her skin. She was close. He was getting her so close.

Except Nash was holding out. He would never give her what she wanted until she gave him what *he* wanted first.

Fine, fine. It didn't matter. She would put him back in his place later. In a minute. As soon as he got the job done. "Please, Nash. Please, I'm begging you."

His eyes glittered as he looked down at her, but there was still such tenderness on his face. How could that be? "You're beggin' for what, Eve?"

Was there a word for it? The ordinary ones didn't seem quite right. "I'm begging for you."

Where had that come from? But there wasn't time to worry about it, because he covered her again, sliding down, sliding deep. They groaned together again.

But even then he didn't follow the usual game plan. While he gave her those lovely deep thrusts, he punctuated them with those wet, caressing slides. Stroke, slide, stroke, slide. His hips kept her thighs pushed wide, and every movement stretched her tighter, took her higher, coiled the desire tighter, until, until . . .

"Nash, *please.*"

He sank fast and deep, deeper than ever before, the base of his shaft pressing against her clitoris in small, insistent pulses, one, two thr—

And she climaxed, her arms and legs splayed wide on the mattress as pleasure exploded through her body. She trembled and trembled and trembled, and inside her those butterflies broke free.

Chapter Twenty-two

"All I Want to Do is Run"
The Elektras
"A" side, single (1963)

E ve, you're in charge of the chat," Téa said.

It was morning, and Eve stared out the window of the breakfast room at the Kona Kai. Blue sky, more sunshine, green shrubbery, and clear water. Something flitted through the periphery of her vision, and she turned her head. Butterflies.

You could blame it all on them, couldn't you? She was usually wary of large men, and her look-out-for-#1 life philosophy made her heed her hunches. From the first, she'd been afraid Nash was the snake in her personal paradise. But he was as tricky as the devil, wasn't he, because he'd made himself appear all sweet and safe and manageable by bringing up butterflies. There in that dark bathroom, he'd whispered of them, allaying her anxiety.

Setting her up for a fall.

"Eve. *Eve.*"

She started. "What?"

Téa frowned at her. "Weren't you listening? You're in charge of the chat at the rehearsal dinner next week. I know everything went fine at the bridal shower, but I need you to be on alert at the dinner too. You know, ready to jump in and redirect the conversation or smooth over any awkward pauses."

Eve closed her eyes. That's exactly what she'd done last night. Jumped into bed with Nash, because she'd wanted to smooth over the awkwardness of their too-personal conversation. And while she'd managed to redirect their energies, she'd failed to follow through with the plan.

I didn't make it clear it was a one-night stand.

"You can't plan everything, Téa," Joey said, rolling her eyes. "People are going to have their own agendas . . ."

Eve stopped listening. Agendas. What was Nash's? She'd wanted to shut him up and scratch an itch, but why had *he* gone to bed with *her*? The Preacher certainly hadn't been thinking romance—he'd made that clear in the massage room—so perhaps she was worrying for nothing. Perhaps he'd been looking for a quick lay and nothing more.

She hated him for that. Of course it would be hypocritical to find fault in the intent, since it was hers as well, but still—

Joey's voice cut into her thoughts. "Eve, tell her to reconsider."

She blinked. "Reconsider what?"

Now it was Joey who frowned at her. "Haven't you been listening? I think Téa should change her mind about giving herself away on her wedding day."

Give herself away, Eve thought. That's exactly what it felt like she'd done last night. Given herself away during sex and then not managed to get herself back.

"I think she should have *Nonno* do it," her younger sister continued.

That recaptured Eve's attention. She sighed. "Oh, Joe—"

"He was not responsible for the groom's father's death, if that's where you're going. Grandpa said he didn't order the killing of Johnny's dad, and I thought we all agreed we believed him."

The legs of Téa's chair screeched against the tile floor. "I'm going for a refill," she said and hurried away with her coffee cup in hand.

Eve let out another sigh and narrowed her eyes at Joey. "You've been neglecting your tact exercises again, haven't you?"

"Who do I need to be tactful for? It's just the three of us, and we all know what happened. Johnny's dad was whacked"—she made a slashing motion with her hand—"to curry favor with Cosimo, since the rumor was that he'd killed *our* father. However, it wasn't true. End of story."

But the story hadn't ended there. Sixteen years later, Johnny had come to town to find out the answers to his father's death, and he'd fallen in love with Téa. Then the two of them had discovered what had happened to both their fathers. Despite the unpleasant truths that had wound their pasts together, Johnny and Téa were determined to have their happy-ever-after future.

Still, it could make for some awkward pauses and uncomfortable conversations amongst the relatives.

Sighing, Eve propped her elbow on the table and her

chin in her hand. "Do you sometimes wonder about other families' lives? What planning a wedding might be like when one-half of the guest list isn't wanted by the FBI?"

"Nobody is wanted by the FBI . . . well, not half the guest list, anyway," Joey amended. "But I don't waste my time wondering about stuff like that. We can't choose our family."

"If I could I would have chosen you, Joe." The words came from nowhere, even as their older sister returned to the table and sat down. What would have happened to her if Salvatore Caruso hadn't taken responsibility for his paternity and brought Eve home to his wife and other little girls? "I would have chosen you and Téa every time."

Her sisters exchanged a glance. "Eve?" Téa said. She reached out a hand and covered Eve's cold fingers. "What's going on? What's the matter?"

The matter was that she seemed to have misplaced her customary sangfroid. At unexpected times, and despite her best efforts to keep them down, emotions kept welling up. They would pop free and fill her chest, tighten her throat, sting the backs of her eyes like tears. Maybe even cause her to go to bed with a dangerously wrong man. "Not enough sleep," she whispered.

Joey shook her head. "Come on, spill. It's got to be more than lack of sleep prompting you to express devotion to Bridezilla, here. Johnny said one more list and he's going to throw her in a plane and take her to Vegas where they'll say yes with only Elvis and Priscilla impersonators as witnesses."

"Ignore the idiot," Téa said, "God knows the rest of us do. Except for the part where you spill, Eve."

And, telling herself not to, she did. "I went to bed with Nash Cargill."

"Cool," Joey said, a grin breaking over her face. "He looks competent."

Téa glared at their younger sister. "What planet do you come from, Joe? If he was competent, would Eve be crying about it?"

"Well, she might, since he didn't stay the whole night. I know, because when I pounded on her door at o'dark-hundred this morning, she answered it wearing that ratty old robe she has and a pillow crease on her cheek. I woke her up, and when I woke her up she was all alone, else she'd have been wearing one of those scratchy-looking sexy numbers she buys."

Used to buy. Tears stung Eve's eyes again. The man hadn't even stayed the whole night, and she didn't have a single credit card with enough life left in it to buy something with which to entice him back.

She froze. Is that really what this drama was all about? That Nash had walked out on her?

That Nash hadn't waited for her to show him the door first?

There was no denying that she was accustomed to being on a pedestal when it came to men. She called the shots, from the first kiss to the first sex to the last good-bye. That had been her intention last night. From the safe distance of her marble footing, she had planned to bid him good-bye, arrivederci, adieu. With a thank-you, of course. It would have only been polite.

Instead, after the big moment, she hadn't even disengaged! She'd let him turn her in his arms, and then she'd fallen asleep with Nash still half-hard inside of her. When she'd woken to Joey's banging on her door, he'd been gone and she'd been all alone except for the drool on her pillow.

Maybe because she didn't recall disengaging from his body, she couldn't disengage from the memories of the night before either. Or maybe he'd taken part of her with him when he'd left.

Téa's hand squeezed hers. "Don't look now, but Nash Competent-Or-Not Cargill is on the path outside and approaching the building."

Oh, God. Eve hastily swiped under her eyes with the backs of her hands. "Of all the times and all the places in the world, why is he *here*?"

Joey glanced over Eve's shoulder, then glanced back at her face. "Uh, because he's staying at the Kona Kai? Because it's morning and the coffee's free?"

"Joe!" Téa scolded. "You're not helping."

"Don't blame me, okay?" their younger sister said. "I'm in a state of shock. Have you ever seen Eve ruffled? Over a man? I'm thinking it must be chilly in hell today."

The truth of that had Eve sucking in a calming breath. She disengaged her hand from Téa's and wrapped her fingers around her latte cup instead. "Tell me I look okay." She kept her voice low and resisted the urge to smooth her hair. "And let me know if it seems like he's coming over."

"You look like heartbreak as usual, and he's walking in the door," Joey said. "Now he's spotted you. Now he's heading this way."

"Oh, great." Eve felt the back of her neck burn and wondered how she'd managed to swallow the butterflies that had been floating around outside. Was this . . . this . . . uncertainty what other women meant when they talked about the morning after? She didn't know, because she'd never let a man spend the night in her bed. And she'd never let a man in her bed and then out of it without being the first to say good-bye.

The hair rising on her arms, she could feel Nash approaching. "Don't you guys dare leave me," she said between clenched teeth.

Joey laughed. "Are you kidding? I wouldn't miss this for the world."

Eve vowed to put Vaseline on her little sister's toilet seat at the very next opportunity.

Then he was there. "Good morning, ladies." His hand slid up her spine, then underneath her hair, to cup the back of her neck as if he knew it was burning there. And at the touch of his calloused palm on her naked skin it burned even more.

Oh, God. Images, memories, sensation rushed like goose bumps through her and over her. She was almost grateful for the hold he had on her because she had the distinct, primitive urge to run. But she couldn't let him know he affected her that much. She had to take this opportunity to regain the upper hand.

Pressing her knees and ankles together, she glanced up, hoping she expressed total surprise. "Who? . . . Oh, it's you. Good morning."

He looked down at her with his eerie, almost-clear, almost-gray eyes. She thought that if she looked hard enough she might find herself reflected in their silvery mirror and see . . . what?

A woman who'd been swindled into giving up her place on top.

Worse, somehow, he'd sweet-talked her into giving up some of herself.

He leaned over and kissed her mouth. She tried

pulling away, but his hand was against her nape and there was nowhere to go. His head lifted, and he should have looked silly with her berry-colored lipstick smeared on his masculine mouth, but instead it only reminded her of the night before.

Her lipstick prints on his chest.

His chest. Wide, heavy with muscle, the skin hot against her hands, her mouth, her tongue.

"Damn," he murmured, and then swooped back in.

Again, it was he who managed to pull back. He laughed as he straightened, rubbing his thumb over his lips. "You taste like coffee," he said. "And I need some. Don't go anywhere."

He moved so quickly he probably didn't hear her scoff. "Why would I go anywhere?" she said anyway. *I'm not afraid of you.*

She glanced at Téa and Joey's faces. They were both looking at her with sympathy. Her little sister shook her head in pity. "You are so, so gone."

And then Eve was. It wasn't a conscious thought. It was her feet pushing against the polished marble floor. Her hands shoving away her cup. Her legs, striding out of the breakfast room in order to find some place where she would be safe. Some place where she could come to grips with having lost part of herself to Nash. Someplace where she could figure out a way to get it back.

Chapter Twenty-three

"No Big Thing"
The Royalettes
"A" side, single (1962)

Jemima aimlessly followed the maze of paths that led around and between the mini-suites, bungalows, and cottages of the Kona Kai's residential area. Ordering a room service breakfast had been her original plan, but she couldn't stand another minute between the walls that were too close to those of Charlie.

Correction: Mack Chandler.

Her face burned, and she hugged her casted arm tighter against her body. For two days and two nights she hadn't been able to get that image of his face out of her mind. His beautiful face that she'd seen on the covers of a hundred celebrity magazines and tabloids. His rangy body that she'd admired on large screens, small screens, the teeny screen of her portable DVD player. Mack Chandler's irrepressible smile and bright eyes that softened the knees of a million-plus women, worldwide. But it was the image of his face as he'd stood on her patio that she couldn't erase from her memory, Mack Chandler's face looking down at her with such—what?—pity?

Because Mack Chandler was one and the same with her amusing, ironic, sympathetic, card-shuffling Charlie. What an idiot he must think she was. He'd been playing her while she'd been falling in love with him.

She made an abrupt halt and replayed that last line in her head.

While she'd been falling in love with him.

No! No. It wasn't true.

This feeling wasn't love. That . . . knowing, that recognition she'd experienced the first night she'd talked to masked-man Charlie and every time since, was likely just loneliness talking. All by herself in Palm Springs, on her own for the first time in forever, it wasn't surprising that she'd latched onto someone—especially someone as funny, yet rock-solid, as Charlie. She'd wanted to be with him in the dark hours of the night not because this soul-mate-sense was something real but because he'd been the only other person awake nearby.

That had to be it. Because surely it wasn't love.

She would recognize that, wouldn't she? And she didn't find anything familiar about this odd mix of calm and turmoil and security and trembling and happiness and tragedy swirling like a funnel cloud inside of her.

It had to be humiliation or something very like it, since she'd gone ahead and fulfilled her own prophecy. She'd made a fool of herself in front of Mack Chandler.

Now all she could do was regather her pride. Jemima

stared down at her feet, expecting to see the tatters.

But they weren't there, nor was any evidence of how she was to go about the regathering. With a sigh, she squared her shoulders, looked up, and gazed right on the door to Eve Caruso's suite.

Eve! Eve, with all her sophistication and her experience, would know how Jemima could regain her dignity and be able to face Mack Chandler, cool, calm, and collected, once again.

Following her brisk knock on Eve's door, it swung open to reveal the blonde looking half-wary and half-harried. "Oh, it's you," she said with obvious relief.

"You're expecting someone?"

"Not exactly," Eve replied, her gaze darting over Jemima's shoulder. "Come on in."

Jemima frowned, eying Eve's strained expression. "I have a better idea. It looks like we both could use some time away. Do you have a favorite hideout we could disappear to for a few hours?"

The other woman smiled. "Now there's a plan."

They arrived in the spa's parking lot quickly enough, and Jemima suggested they take Eve's nondescript car instead of her pink SUV. "That way," she explained, "Nash will think I'm around the premises somewhere and not worry."

That made Eve hesitate. "Wait a minute. Are you positive you should be leaving the Kona Kai without him?"

"If I tell him, he'll insist on coming with us. Do you want to risk that?"

"God, no." Eve was already sliding into the driver's seat of her Hyundai.

Jemima made her way to the passenger side, seated

herself, then slammed shut the door. "Despite what I'm sure he's told you, I'm not a child. As a matter of fact, I came to see you about a very adult problem."

"Oh?" Eve glanced over, her hand stilling on the ignition. "What's that?"

Jemima squirmed on the seat. For her, friends were rare. Not only had her mother hovered at her side for years but Jemima had also gone to studio schools with a minuscule number of pupils; either that, or she'd had special one-on-one tutors. The occasional feeling of connection with another person of a particular cast or crew was only destined to last as long as it took to shoot the movie.

But with time usually so short, Jemima had a knack for quickly assessing the people around her. It was what had given her the confidence to strike up that friendship with Charlie—and look how that had turned out.

But Eve was a woman and Jemima was desperate, to boot. So she inhaled a quick breath. "I need help with a man," she said, "and I think you're just the one who can give me the best advice."

Eve blinked. "On men?"

"One in particular."

Eve was silent as she turned the ignition. The little car coughed to three-packs-a-day life, and then Eve started to reverse. "Well—" Her voice broke off as she slammed on the brakes. "Oh, *hell.*"

At that, one of the back doors opened and Nash wedged his big body into the car. "Just the women I wanted to see." He was wearing that aw-shucks, shit-eating grin of his, but there was a dangerous glint in his narrowed eyes.

Still, Jemima might have been ticked off by the interruption if Eve hadn't been handling that emotion all by herself. Over her shoulder, she glared at Jemima's brother. "This is a private excursion. Do you *mind*?"

"Nope." Nash couldn't angle his long legs enough to fit behind either passenger or driver, so he half-reclined along the blue vinyl. "I seem to have this odd hankerin' for a private excursion with you."

The temperature inside the car soared as Jemima's gaze jumped between the two. Now wasn't this interesting? Her brother, the unmovable force that he always was, butting heads with Eve Caruso, who had her ice-queen act down to a science. Jemima had witnessed her shatter men and their attendant egos with just a dismissive flick of her eyelashes.

It was a skill Jemima envied and one that she'd hoped to acquire from the other woman during their getaway.

Nash looked at Jemima and raised an eyebrow. "You have a problem with a third wheel?"

Suddenly, she didn't. Not that she really expected her self-appointed bodyguard to let her escape with Eve now that he'd caught them, but here was her chance to see an accomplished Woman in action. She shook her head and settled back to watch the show.

Except as they headed out of town on a near-empty stretch of road that led them toward the dun-colored, rubble-strewn hills, the only action inside the car was the flow of the air-conditioning fluttering the ends of Eve's blonde hair. The only sound was the hitch in Eve's breath every time Nash shifted in the backseat.

Jemima finally cracked under the pressure, angling her legs toward the driver's seat. Since she couldn't bring herself to straight out ask how to cut a man off at his knees, she settled for the next thing she'd been dying to know from Eve. "So, what's it like to grow up in the mob?"

Nash choked. "*Jesus*, Jem—"

Eve held up her hand. "She can ask. I'm not ashamed of it."

"No?" Jemima waved the fingers of her casted arm. "I mean, not that you *should* be—I certainly don't expect everyone to have the soul of a saint like Nash here does—it's just that—"

"Eve isn't her family," Nash put in.

"I wouldn't be so sure of that," Eve murmured. "But the fact is, Jemima, when I was a kid, I didn't know any different. Then, later . . . well, later you could say it had its uses. It was a convenient way to keep my dates toeing the line, for instance."

From the backseat came Nash's voice. Soft. "You can't always count on that, darlin'."

Eve glanced up at the rearview mirror, and her voice mimicked his gentle drawl. "Now I don't have to, Nash. Now I can make men toe the line all by my little bitty lonesome."

"Careful, now. Because then *lonesome* might be the operative word." His fingers skimmed her shoulder.

And sophisticated, experienced Eve Caruso jumped at the simple touch. Jemima blinked, wondering at the intense reaction, but Eve whipped a quick left and Jemima couldn't be sure if it had been Nash or almost missing the turn that had caused their driver to jolt.

As the back end of the car fishtailed, Jem braced against the dash and Nash swore. "Are you trying to kill us?"

"It's an idea," Eve bit out.

This new road was narrower than the one they'd left, and the layer of undisturbed, chalky dust on the pavement ahead made clear it wasn't a well-used route. "This looks like the perfect dumping ground for a badass body," Jemima told her brother. "If she really has something against you, big bro, I'd be worried if I were you."

The ensuing silence was thicker than the grime settling on the car. "So much for my chances at hosting *Saturday Night Live*," Jemima said with a little laugh. "I was joking."

"I'm sorry," Nash suddenly said. "I should have left a note or something."

Jemima turned to look at him, but he was looking at Eve.

"I didn't want a note," she replied, her unblinking gaze trained out the windshield.

"Then if you'd stayed at the breakfast table with your sisters, I would have explained—"

"I don't want an explanation!"

"Well, hell, woman, what *do* you want?"

Eve's nostrils flared. Jemima could only stare, unsure what was going on but unwilling to miss a second of the surprising drama. If she had to guess, though, this looked like the good part—the part where Eve would cut her big badass brother down to size, just as Jemima longed to do to Mack Chandler.

But instead of a showdown, Eve slowed down. Braked. Jemima looked out the window and realized they'd stopped at the bottom of a steep, winding driveway in the middle of honest-to-God nowhere.

Eve opened her car door. "Jemima wanted a hideaway, " she said. "This is mine."

They trudged in a single-file line uphill. "I'm surprised your piece of junk vehicle made it this far,"

Nash grumbled. "Smart thinking on deciding against tackling this incline."

"Where are we going?" Jemima asked. It was summer-hot, and though she was appropriately dressed in shorts and flip-flops, the skin beneath her cast was starting to sweat. The makeup artist on the movie set was going to give her hell if she showed up with a weird tan line.

"A friend's house," Eve said, sounding as right as rain now, as cool as rain, too, as if she'd never sweated a moment in her life. Her sunflower yellow cotton sundress had yet to wilt. "She's in Toronto at the moment, so I check on it from time to time for her."

And then, out of the rugged boulders and sandy dirt around them, they saw a turquoise door. A door? Shielding her eyes with her hand, Jemima blinked, and the structure around the doorway became visible. It was a house, made of materials and colors that blended into the environment.

Eve skirted the doorway to a small shaded front terrace. She grabbed two twig armchairs that were tucked in the shadows and drew them forward. "Sit," she said, then turned to sweep her arm in the direction they'd come, "and take a look at this."

"This" was an amazing, eye-popping view. Jemima sank onto one of the chairs and tried to take in the desolate expanse of desert spread out in front of them. Perched on a rocky outcropping of a rocky hill, the house was positioned with its back turned on civilization. It had to be around somewhere—Jemima knew they hadn't traveled all that far—but from here they might as well have been a thousand miles from other people, and from the Starbucks and the Jiffy Lubes and the multiplex theaters of the nearby communities.

There was a weird beauty in the barrenness. Without the massive, bright, look-at-me! markers of a big, or even a small, city, at first your gaze discerned nothing, and then . . . a cactus . . . the scuttle of a sunning lizard . . . a rock shaped like the profile of the director of her last movie.

Jemima looked at Nash to gauge his reaction only to realize he hadn't followed Eve's order. He wasn't sitting. He hadn't turned his attention to the vista she'd indicated either. Instead, he remained where he was. And now, his gaze focused on Eve's face, he drifted toward her, joining her as she sat down on the terrace's low wall.

Jemima narrowed her eyes, now way less interested in the scenery than the scene happening right in front of her nose. What the heck was going on between The Preacher and the Party Girl?

Her eyes straight ahead, her elbows propped on her knees, Eve leaned over her legs, her perfect blonde hair half-hanging over her face. Nash caught a few strands with his forefinger and tucked them behind her ear.

"Beautiful," he murmured.

"I think so," Eve replied, unaware he was still looking at her face. "It's . . . comforting."

For the first time, Nash glanced at the view, then back at Eve's face. He frowned. "Comforting. How?"

Jemima swallowed, now feeling like an eavesdropper instead of an audience. But she didn't want to interrupt the moment. There was something important in the air.

"How is it comforting?" Nash prodded again, looking back out at the desert.

"It reminds me I'm not the only insignificant thing in the world."

Jemima saw her brother's big body stiffen. Then he turned his head toward Eve slowly, very, very slowly, as if he was afraid of disturbing a butterfly perched on his massive forearm. His voice was husky, yet barely above a whisper. "You . . . feel insignificant?"

"Mmmm. Don't you?"

"I . . ." He ran his hand over his hair.

As if monster-tamer Nash could ever feel less than the vital, larger-than-life man that he was!

"I think I could," he finally said, his gaze never leaving Eve's face. "I think maybe I could."

Jemima stared as the truth of what she was seeing dawned upon her. What Nash had just communicated, not in so many words, but in that strange huskiness in his voice, in that odd stillness of his body, in the way he was looking at Eve, was that size and vitality were no guarantee. He was vulnerable.

Her big, brash, overbearing brother was at risk. His heart could be broken. He could be made insignificant if the right person didn't offer her heart back. *He's on the verge of falling in love and he doesn't even know it.*

She watched him reach over and take Eve's hand. All those Farrahs, whom he'd grumbled about for leaving him, Jemima thought. The truth was that he'd never cared enough to hold onto a single one of them.

But now, she could tell, he never wanted to let Eve go.

A certainty started in the soles of her feet and moved up her legs, straightening her knees so she had to rise from her chair.

So this was what love looked like. She hadn't recognized it, because though she'd played dozens of roles, she'd never played someone in love. But now she knew its appearance. And she already knew what it felt like.

She'd been right from the first. She was in love with the SOB next door.

But Charlie—pardon, Mack Chandler—talented actor that he was, had just been acting when he'd seduced her heart.

Jemima drew in a deep, calming breath. She couldn't let him trample her to desert dust by not loving her back! She still had to work with him, and she was going to work with him. She *was*.

But how could she even the obscenely tipped scales?

Only one thought came to mind: By taking revenge.

Chapter Twenty-four

"Take Me Back"
.38 Special
Special Delivery (1978)

As they passed through the gate leading to the Kona Kai's residential area after their return to the spa, Nash watched Jemima pick up speed, leaving him and Eve in the dust. "She's worrying me," he said out loud.

"And that's news?"

"I'm counting down the hours until she goes onto the set."

"So you can get back to your life."

He nodded. "Back to business." His hand found hers, squeezed. "That's why I left your room so early this morning. I had to make a call to my team, and I didn't want to disturb you."

She lifted an eyebrow. "So considerate."

He grinned. "I thought so, until you looked ready to

bite my head off and then spit it into your latte this morning."

"I didn't look anything of the kind!"

"Remember, I know you have this thing about me and sex. Admit it, when you woke up you were itching for round two and got mad because I wasn't there to satisfy it."

She tried to sneer. "I don't need a man, even a big strong one like you, Nash. I can satisfy myself any time I feel like it."

"Not when I stole the batteries out of your vibrator."

Her jaw dropped. "You did not."

"Little blue gadget? Works underwater? But guess what, darlin'?" He leaned close to her outraged face and lowered his voice. "So do I."

She wrenched her hand from his to stab her finger at his chest. "I don't believe you went into my drawer, and if you did, *your* gadget is going to be blue."

"I was just lookin' for a mint. For you. You've got yourself some mean morning breath, Party Girl."

Slamming her luscious lips together, she made that little foot-stamp sound again. God, it delighted him to push her buttons. And confronting an outraged Eve was far easier than confronting what he'd felt out at that desert house.

What he'd seen. Eve, so damn vulnerable.

He didn't think she'd even realized that she'd said "I feel insignificant," and he knew she hadn't realized what it had done to him.

He didn't want any more weak women in his life.

Except Eve wasn't weak. Good Lord, she wasn't weak. But there were tender places inside of her. The fact that she didn't know about them, didn't see them or even acknowledge them, made her only that much more compelling. Trouble was, uncovering those hidden tender spots inside of her opened up hidden spots inside of him. Made him feel things in a way he hadn't felt in a long while, things which he didn't want to feel now. Those kinds of feelings could be dangerous.

They were closing in on her front door, and he slid an arm around her waist. He could keep what was bubbling between them on a superficial level, though. He knew he could. "I'm at your service for round two now."

She slid a look at him from her ice-blue eyes. "Is that right?"

"Uh-hmm." He pictured that Brazilian bikini wax in his mind. "Hard and aching."

"That's such a shame." She held up one hand and wiggled her fingers. "I have a nail appointment in ten minutes."

"I'm sorry the manicurist is going to lose out on the appointment, but something tells me you're not much of a tipper."

Red brightened her cheeks, and he had to hold back another laugh. She really had no experience getting razzed by a guy. Before she could slap him or stomp off, he grabbed her hand and kissed her knuckles. "Come on, Party Girl, let's celebrate the day."

Walking backward, he tugged her toward her door.

"I'm going to celebrate getting rid of you," she said, dragging her feet. "Last night was it, Nash. You took off before I could make that clear."

"So that's what all that snoring was supposed to mean." Her feet stopped altogether, and the horrified expression crossing her face made him take it all back. "Okay, okay, you don't *really* snore. Just heavy breathing punctuated by the occasional snort."

But she still appeared horrified, and he realized she wasn't gazing at him but over his shoulder. He turned his head.

On the mat in front of her doorstep lay a limp, dirty pile of something furry. Something lifeless.

He swung his body around, but Eve caught his elbow before he could move toward the door. "What is it?" she cried. Her fingers dug into his skin. "Is it Adam?"

Her personality-challenged cat? The orangeish color was right. "I'll see." In four strides he was bent over the mat, then he relaxed and plucked the thing between two fingers and held it up.

Rearing back, Eve gasped.

"It's a stuffed animal," he reassured her. A dirty and neglected-looking stuffed animal, though yes, a cat, and with one missing ear. "Some kid must have dropped it." Stuffing dribbled out of a tear across its neck.

"Sure," she said, edging closer. "A stuffed animal. Some kid must have dropped it."

She didn't seem convinced, though, so he shook it, more stuffing drifting through the air like snow. "It's not your cat, Eve."

But her strained expression and brittle posture were giving him the willies. He tossed the drooping toy away and pulled her into his arms. Her body shivered.

"What's the matter, darlin'?"

She burrowed her cold nose against the warm skin at the side of his throat, and now he shivered. "Darlin'?"

"Hold me, Nash."

His arms tightened. "I am holding you. Can't you feel me?"

"Not yet," she whispered. "Not yet."

He managed to get her inside, and she managed a

little smile once the door was locked behind them. "Would you think I'm crazy if I changed my mind?"

"If this is about that nail appointment, I'll think you're crazy if you don't."

She rubbed her fingertips over his mouth, and he caught one, nipped. Her body trembled against his, yet still she shook her head. "Arrogant man."

"One of my best qualities." He backstepped her toward the bedroom, unwilling to let her out of his embrace.

"You remember the rules?"

He rolled his eyes.

"And you're going away."

It wasn't a rebuke, he knew, or a wish for more. It was reassurance she was looking for.

Isn't that special? he thought. A woman he was about to bed wanted to be certain he would be moving along. A bubble of primitive, violent heat rose inside him, and he drew his hands into fists to fight the feeling off.

Hell, he should be glad about that, though. Eve Caruso, party girl, superbeauty, was too much trouble, was too many contradictions for a man who needed to take the emotional low road for everyone's sake.

"I'm only here for Jem," he reassured them both. "As soon as she's settled, I'll be saddling up my horse and heading straight out of town."

Leaving Eve behind and nothing, he vowed, else.

Chapter Twenty-five

"As the Years Go Passing By"
Elvin Bishop
Feel It! (1970)

Charlie shuffled the cards and laid out yet another hand of solitaire. A single-person game. Perfect for a solitary man.

Not that he was feeling sorry for himself or anything.

It wouldn't be so bad if he weren't stuck here in Palm Springs. A few more days and he would have his last follow-up with the plastic surgeon. By then the scars would be faded enough for him to leave the seclusion of the Kona Kai. But God, what wouldn't he give to be back in Hollywood right now, on Tuesday, midnight basketball night.

They'd been keeping it secret for years, a minor miracle in Tinseltown, but testament to how much the men in the league enjoyed—no, needed—the activity. The youngest son of the president of one of the biggest talent agencies in town ran a community gym, and for a hefty annual donation, once a week he made the basketball courts accessible to the movie industry's upper echelon—from actors to agents, producers to screenwriters.

They'd talked about building some courts for their exclusive use somewhere, but they'd decided it wouldn't be the same. Midnight basketball league needed a gym that was still warm from other bodies. Real basketball needed layers of both old and fresh sweat and walls that never seemed to stop echoing high fives and curses and referee whistles.

Next week he'd be back though, ready to kick Larry Michaels's ass as thanks for coming up with the idiotic idea of meeting Jemima under false pretenses.

Okay, fine, he probably could have called a halt to it himself, on the first or second night of their acquaintance. And certainly by the third or fourth, when he was sure there was more chemistry between them than could be blamed on the painkillers. But he hadn't been that smart.

It was the kind of chemistry that would play well on the big screen between two actors, but in real life it could wreak havoc in the lives of two people who were twenty years apart.

One fresh and beautiful. The second tired and aging and old enough to know that what starts out as fun and games could lead to aches and pain.

From the other side of the partition, he heard the screen to Jemima's sliding glass door open with a long *scri-i-itch*.

And to this tired and aging dude, who by rights should have been contemplating a second career in commercials for Metamucil and arthritis medication, it sounded exactly like the opening of a zipper.

Holding his breath, Charlie strained to hear what Jemima was doing next door. With luck, she wanted a mere taste of the fresh air or a quick turn on her patio. Then she'd go back inside and do whatever she'd been doing for the past few days since he'd revealed his Mack Chandler alter ego. He hadn't caught a single glimpse of her after that, though he'd been assured by the maid who came in every day that Jemima was still living next door.

Living next door, still untouched by her stalker—and probably still hating his guts for his deception.

Her footsteps rang clearly in the night air, then he heard her scrape the legs of her lounge chair against the pavement. She was dragging it closer to the partition!

He considered jumping up and running back inside, but he was a mature man, wasn't he? Wasn't that the goddamn problem, after all? So instead he'd sit right where he was and pretend not to be here.

He was supposed to be good at that pretending stuff. He had two Oscars to prove it.

Jemima settled onto the cushions of her lounge chair. He heard the rustle of clothes, the crinkle of paper—she must be reading a book? a magazine?—her little sigh, like Goldilocks finding just the right bed.

Oh, Christ, why was he thinking of beds?

Then he heard the rustle of clothes again. A dress, one of those flimsy, vintage-y things Jemima sometimes wore. In his mind's eye he could see it, could see the hemline of the flowered fabric being drawn up her creamy leg, over her knee, toward her thigh.

Charlie bit the inside of his cheek to wake his stupid self up. He couldn't hear all that! He could hear clothes, granted, but not what they looked like, and certainly not the flesh they might or might not be revealing.

There was that crinkle of paper again.

Another little sigh.

The tiny creak of the lounge chair as she settled deeper into its cushions.

There couldn't be more than four feet and a two-by-four separating them, so that *was* a sweet, feminine little moan.

"Peter," she whispered. "Oh, Peter."

Charlie's mouth went dry.

"I can't go on like this."

She was unbuttoning the buttons of her dress, one of dozens of buttons that marched down its center. "I want you, Peter."

Her fingers brushed the tops of a pristine white bra, the same bra Peter had watched her fold in the laundry room. Her slim fingers had moved over it with practical intent, but he'd been fascinated by the way she'd maneuvered it into a small dome by turning the cups one into the other, inside out.

Turning him inside out.

You can't want me.

And as if she heard the words in his head, she responded aloud. "Don't you want to touch me, too? Feel my warmth?"

I can get that from a hundred women.

"I don't mean that kind of warmth." With a twist of her fingers, she unlatched that white bra that looked so new, so clean, that would smell of every good thing Peter had forgotten about America and women and soldiering while he'd been fighting for his life in that mercy-forsaken country. "This kind."

Pushing aside the bra, she placed her palm over her heart. He pretended to stare at her hand, pledging allegiance to—what? Not to him. Not to what could be—but it was really her breasts that he was looking at, their slight rise and tight, puckered nipples. Girlish breasts too sweet and too innocent for a man like him, who'd touched so much dirt and death.

His breath and his pulse sounded loud in his head, louder than when he'd stepped into that dark hut in the mountains and faced the feral gleam in the eyes of other frightened men who, by a stroke of birth and fate, fought for the opposite side.

Just frightened men like himself, that's all he saw, even as he tried to remember the towers, and young girls, and the scent and feel of clean clothes that were the reasons he was about to pull the trigger. Because to do that, he needed something more than the vague notion that he should want to stay alive for some vague place he barely remembered as home.

"You deserve me, Peter. I deserve you."

Peter. Peter. *Peter.* Charlie shook his head, shaking himself out of the skin of the character that Jemima's reading of the script had draped over him. She'd been reading the part of Deborah, who put everything on the line to pull war veteran Peter out of the ugly abyss where he'd been wallowing since his tour in Afghanistan.

For weeks Peter watched his neighbor Deborah go through the motions of life—washing windows, doing laundry, pleasing herself with sex—and through that relearned how to live himself. How to find a reason to go on. Joy.

"I feel like a fraud," Charlie said out loud. "I'm going to be making a movie about a man scarred from battle when the closest I've come to that is confronting a scalpel on a Palm Springs hospital bed."

He walked around the partition to face Jemima.

She was stretched out on the lounge chair, wearing cropped jeans and a sweatshirt, the script tossed on the ground beside her. "Don't feel bad," she said. "I've never washed any windows."

His gaze flicked from her face to the ruffled papers, then back to her face. "What was that reading of yours all about?"

She shrugged. "My way of doing a Deborah on you."

"You wanted to provoke a reaction."

"I wanted to see if you were like self-indulgent Peter, who merely pretends he doesn't want Deborah."

"That's for her. Peter pretends he doesn't want Deborah because he's thinking—"

"Only of himself. And despite that, the script calls for Deborah to be ever-understanding, ever-loving, no matter how little he gives back to her."

"He believes he's doing her a favor. He knows she could get so much more from someone else. Someone younger." Charlie touched the small suture-bumps behind his ear. "Not so scarred."

"Well, FYI." Jemima crossed her arms over her waist and tapped the fingers of one hand against her cast. "Deborah would love to be interested in someone else, but that's not in the cards. Or in this case, the script."

Charlie smiled a little. "You're going to bring some feistiness to her?"

"Face it, Charlie, right now Deborah's a doormat."

"Young."

"Doormat." She sang it out.

Charlie smiled again. "So what would she really say to Peter?"

In one graceful move, Jemima stood, her bare feet balancing on the cushions of her chair. She threw her arms wide. "That I'm young and juicy and if you knew what was good for you, you'd stop all your boring self-sacrifice and give me what I want!"

Was that Deborah talking to Peter, or Jemima talking to him? "Jem. Really. You can't—"

"I can. I do. You, Charlie. I'm giving you one last chance. I want you."

He stepped back. "Jem . . ."

"I had this plan. I was going to accept your disinterest in my heart but make you want my body anyway and then leave you flat in revenge, but that's not what adults do."

He tried laughing. "You're no adult."

"Turned twenty-one yesterday."

He frowned. "I missed your birthday."

"You're going to miss a lot."

With a sigh, he dragged over a chair and sat down. Both knees crunched, reminding him of all the life he'd lived in the twenty years that was between them. How could he explain this to her?

Movies, he thought. They always talked about movies.

"Look, you want this out adult-to-adult? Then, fine. The truth is, I'm not disinterested in one thing about you, but . . . it's better this way, okay? It's like . . ." He ran his hand through his hair. "Remember? Bill never touched Scarlett."

Jemima plopped down on the cushions again, her expression curious. "Is that what he told you?"

Charlie shook his head. "I'm talking about the *film*, about *Lost in Translation*. Everyone loved that movie because the hero had sex with the singer and not with the starlet."

"I think she was a philosophy student. And I don't

think the audience liked him having sex with the singer. I didn't."

Frustration edged his voice. "You know what I mean."

"I think everyone loved that movie because when the character of Bob whispered in the ear of the character Charlotte, they could make up their own ending."

"Yeah? Well I'm guessing Bill murmured. 'Admit it, Scarlett, sushi pizza blows.'"

"And *I* think Bob said, 'Mack Chandler better not use me as a rationale for his own middle-aged fears.'"

"It's you who could really get hurt!" She was twenty-one years old. He was twice that, and twice smarter when it came to sidestepping potential disaster.

Which meant he had no reason to stop Jemima from rolling off the lounger and padding toward her sliding door. She glanced back at him, the light from the outdoor fixture washing down, washing any sign of age from her face. Except her eyes looked old, dark, and too cold. Too distant already.

"Then I guess, Charlie," she said, and her voice creaked like his knees, "all we'll ever have is Palm Springs."

Chapter Twenty-six

"I Can Only Think of You"
Pure Prairie League
If the Shoe Fits (1976)

Charlie called Larry instead of going after Jemima, like every midlife hormone he had was urging. "Hey," he said, trying to sound casual. "How was basketball tonight?"

He could picture his old friend in his mind's eye—receding hairline, slight paunch, his face still red from the evening's game. "That damn Orlando has elbows like ice picks," Larry grumbled. "His inside game sucks, though. George shut him down."

"The Brits can't shoot for shit." Charlie settled back into the cushions of his sofa and propped his feet onto the coffee table. "Next week I'll be back to show 'em how it's done."

"Now that sounds like the real Charlie," Larry said, chuckling. "I was beginning to think the surgeon had cut something more significant than a few years off your pretty face."

"Fuck you." Charlie frowned. "What's that supposed to mean, anyway?"

"It means I haven't heard anyone whine so much about a little pain since Levy hit the floor from that knee injury."

"Next time a doctor drags your face up by the roots of your hair and staples your cheeks behind your ears, we'll talk about whining and pain."

"That's one benefit of working my side of the business. I can look as ugly as I want. Speaking of business . . . how's my beautiful girl?"

Charlie cleared his throat. "Your beautiful girl. What girl is that?"

"Jemima Cargill, dumbass. Did she like the bouquet I sent her for her birthday?"

The birthday Charlie had ignored. But not Larry. Larry had remembered and had probably sent her some extravagant arrangement. Roses, Charlie would bet. God, that just pissed him off.

His hand tightened on the phone. "What are you thinking, Larry?"

The other man sounded puzzled. "About what?"

"You're married," Charlie bit out. "To a woman I introduced you to fifteen years ago. What the hell are you hitting on Jemima for? You having some sort of midlife crisis and now you're running around after teenagers?"

There was a long silence on the other end of the phone.

"Well?" Charlie practically shouted the word.

"Well," Larry finally said. "I sent Jemima flowers on

her birthday because she's my client. You know I would never betray Natalie by going after another woman."

"Jemima Cargill is a *girl*," Charlie grumbled. "You said it yourself."

"Right now she seems a hell of a lot more mature than you. What's going on? Those sutures still hurting?"

His balls were aching, that's what was wrong. And his head. And his heart. He was lusting after a much younger woman, and the stupid truth was he'd been unable to talk himself into believing it was merely that. It wasn't just physical. He was in love with her. From the top of her twenty-one-year-old head to the bottom of her twenty-one-year-old toes.

Shit.

"Let's talk about something else," he said. "What's up with poor old Levy? Has he seen a doctor?"

"Oh, yeah. The diagnosis is that he tore the meniscus cartilage in his knee."

"Damn. Levy lives for basketball. Guess that means we'll have to find a replacement for him in the league. Maybe Orlando can recommend another Brit with a bad shot. If we let the young guys in, they've gotta be lousy to make up for it."

"Oh, Levy's not out."

"You're kidding." Charlie ran his hand over his left knee. "The meniscus—"

"Levy's getting it fixed. He went to see one of the orthopedic guys for the Lakers, and he said if Levy was still playing full-court basketball he was much too young to be letting a bum knee put a stop to it."

"Yeah?" Charlie rubbed his own knee again. "But Levy's older than we are, and after Tuesday nights it takes *me* three days to recover."

"But on the fourth day you're eager to do it all over again, right?"

"Right." As much as he hurt Wednesday mornings, it was a good kind of hurt, an I've-still-got-it kind of hurt. "You don't just lie down and quit because there might be some pain involved."

"Nope," Larry concurred. "The game's too fun, hell, too important, for that."

But it didn't seem too mature either. "Does that mean we're fools, Lar?"

"Are you kidding? That means we're *wise*. We know what matters, and it's not the year on our driver's licenses or the strained muscles in the offing. It's good for us. Gotta keep the ol' heart working, right?"

We know what matters.

It's not the year on our driver's licenses.

Larry had been talking about basketball, but . . .

"Right," Charlie said slowly. His headache eased, and so did the frustration that had been plaguing him for days. He found himself standing up. Striding toward his sliding glass door. "You're right. Gotta keep the ol' heart working."

He didn't remember ending the call or walking onto his patio and then around the partition. But suddenly he was on Jemima's patio. Standing by her back door. The curtains were drawn, but the lights were on.

She wasn't sleeping.

But she was dressed for sleep, he noticed when she slid open the door to his light knock. He stood there, hypnotized by the sight of her in a pair of filmy pink bikini panties and a powder blue T-shirt that skimmed her belly button.

His eyebrows rose as he took in the text stretched across her breasts. " 'Mack's my man,' " he read aloud.

She stepped back, then turned around. He followed her inside, shutting the door behind him. Now in better light, her panties appeared even more transparent, the shadow of the cleft between her cheeks drawing his gaze. Sweat popped out on his skin, and his sutures started to itch.

He jerked his focus upward. There was text across the back of the shirt too. "If Mack can't do it, no one can."

Maybe he said it out loud, because she glanced at him over her shoulder. "You don't recognize it? Comes standard with every Mack Chandler Fan Club membership."

He made a vague gesture at the shirt. "What is this?" he asked, his voice hoarse. "A taunt?"

She spun around and crossed her arms over her chest so that Mack was no longer her man. "I could ask you the same question, Charlie. Why are you here? Is this a taunt?"

"I . . ." He closed his eyes, wondering what the hell it exactly was. "A hope," he finally said. "It's a hope."

She was silent, so he was forced to open his eyes.

Her beautiful dark eyes were narrowed.

"What?" he asked.

"Just trying to figure out if that's a line you're throwing me, Charlie. Something from one of your old movies, like that Aussie accent you put on."

"Ah, Jem." He ran his hand over his refreshed face. Here he was, the older one, but he'd acted like a bone-headed boy. "I'm concerned that . . ."

Her eyebrows rose. "I'm waiting."

He didn't know what to say.

She tapped her twenty-one-year-old toes. "I'm still waiting."

"Damn it, Jem!" He wanted to tear out his hair. He wanted to turn off his feelings. He wanted Jemima Cargill.

All his frustration and fear sounded in his voice. "Young hearts bounce. Old hearts break."

And there, finally, was the truth. The truth about why he'd been resisting her.

It wasn't that she was too young or that she might get hurt. It was that *he* might get hurt. *Old hearts break.*

She stepped up to him. The palms she cupped around his face were gentle. "Then I guess I'll have to take very good care of yours."

He sighed, his hands coming around her, his fingers linking loosely at the warm small of her back. "So now you know."

Looking up, she smiled at him, and he thought of all the nights she'd smiled just like that while he'd kept himself hidden from her. It hadn't saved him from this. From her.

Thank God.

"Now I know what?"

"Now you know I'm not a hero," he said. "I've just played one on TV."

Her smile deepened, and she moved back to strip off that appalling Mack Chandler T-shirt. "I can get a hero any time for the price of a movie ticket. What I want forever is you, Charlie. Just you."

And thank God for that, too. He took the shirt from her hand and flung it across the room. Then he reached for the woman he had decided to marry. He hoped it wouldn't take long to convince her.

It was time to get off the bench and live—and love—for all he was worth.

Chapter Twenty-seven

"A Thing of the Past"
The Shirelles
"A" side, single (1961)

E ve took advantage of the near-deserted state of the Kona Kai bar—it was the last shift, and most of the resort's guests were early birds, not owls—to give herself a critical once-over in the mirror behind the call liquors. In the past few days since the impromptu run to Diane's house in the desert, she hadn't been feeling like herself. With all the time she'd been spending in Nash's company, she wondered if she'd caught something from him.

There was a definite flush along her cheekbones, which made sense, considering the perpetually heated state of her skin. And her stomach had been so jumpy lately! *She'd* been jumpy, and every time she'd tried inhaling a deep breath it had gotten caught at half-lung level, instead of the relaxing belly-breathing she practiced in yoga.

She hadn't been eating either, because she'd had too much revved-up energy to do anything detailed like make a meal, let alone eat one. With Nash still watching over Jemima, he'd often eaten with her. The few times Eve and Nash had met over a table, she'd played the shell game with whatever she'd ordered: asparagus tucked behind the baked potato, baked potato bites pushed beneath the ribs of a chicken breast.

With the tips of her right-hand fingers pushed together, she lifted her hair where the part met her forehead. Her pinky brushed something—

She held back her hair to bare the skin. A zit! Her pinky had brushed a zit!

Eve Caruso had never had a blemish in her life.

With a quick glance around the room, she hurriedly feathered the hair back over the reddened spot. This is what she got for not following her rules. With Nash in her bed every night, she wasn't getting enough sleep. He was following *her* rules, that was good, though he rolled his eyes every time she dragged him upward by his shoulders, but she wasn't following her own. No men were supposed to stay the night in her bed.

Up that close, you might start believing you could rely on them.

For Nash, she'd made an exception. . . . She saw the dreamy smile tilt the corners of her lips, and although she knew it was goofy of her, she couldn't help herself. Nash, with his heavy, rounded muscles. Nash, who'd led her to the discovery that she was a glutes woman.

And a hamstrings woman.

And a biceps woman.

And a washboard abs woman.

You named one of his hard, bulging muscles and she loved it.

A snort of laughter bubbled up, and she clapped her hand over her mouth. Not only was she getting goofy but she was getting sex-obsessed as well.

What Nash could do to her body had totally revised her opinion of orgasms. What in the past had always been a healthy half hour of exercise culminating in a little *ta-da* toot delivered by kazoo was now hours of greedy touching, sinuous writhing, and soul kisses climaxing in a whole symphonic crescendo, complete with kettledrum and cascading chimes.

Last night, when she'd happened to mention it to Nash—in an unguarded moment when sated satisfaction had overruled good sense—he'd suggested she write letters of apology to all her previous lovers. He'd blamed the lackluster events on her!

"Face it, Party Girl," he'd said. "It sounds as if you've never lived up to the ballyhoo of your beautiful face and centerfold body."

"So, I've never lived up to my advertising," she'd retorted, "until now? Until you?"

He didn't even bother hiding his smugness. "Damn straight. Until now. Until me."

Annoying, arrogant, luscious man.

How did he know just how to make her smile?

Movement in the corner of her eye made her body still, even as her belly jumped and her nerves stretched tight in welcome anticipation. She couldn't tell without turning her head, but it was probably Nash. He'd had calls to make, he'd said, but it would be just like him to show up near closing time and help her break down the bar. She drew her fingers along her throat toward her breasts, unfastening the next two buttons of her tailored white shirt.

A game of try-to-pick-up-the-bartender sounded like a fun way to end the evening.

Prepared to saunter over to the new patron with her sex appeal set on Oooze, Eve licked her lips, then turned.

Her hand hastily refastened her buttons. Playful disappeared from her smile. "Uncle Tuna!"

Tony Pesce, known as The Fish to her grandfather's crew, called Uncle Tuna by Eve and her sisters all their lives, hitched himself onto one of the barstools. He smoothed his hand over the front of his pearl-colored silk dress shirt. *"Buona sera,* Eve."

Knowing him to be a friend of Bill W., Eve picked up a cup and saucer. "Decaf or the hard stuff?"

"Decaf. *Grazie.*"

She served the coffee along with a kiss to each of his lean, olive-skinned cheeks, stretching across the cold marble to make the deliveries. "Mmm. Acqua Di Gio," she said, naming the Armani cologne. Nash smelled of nothing fancier than shaving cream—and sometimes her. Uncle Tuna, though, perhaps because of his malodorous nickname, always made it a point of pride to smell like the best at the men's fragrance counter.

"You like it?" Uncle Tuna covered her fingers with his.

"I adore it." She turned her palm to squeeze his hand. It felt too dry, and the skin was thin, she realized. The hand of an old man.

A pang squeezed her heart. Uncle Tuna was edging up there in years, yet he was still younger than her grandfather, Cosimo, the only male blood relative Eve had left in the world. "Is everything all right?" she said. "Nothing's happened?"

With the announcement of Cosimo's retirement, something *would* happen, that was sure. Maybe not tonight, or next week or even next month, but the shuffle in the Caruso leadership would shake everyone up, from within the family and without. She suddenly remembered the lifeless figures of the canary and that pitiful stuffed cat on her doorstep. As far-fetched as it sounded, was the mob trying to send messages through her?

"Nothing's happened," the older man reassured her, lifting his cup between both hands. "This is a courtesy visit, that's all."

Relieved, and telling herself that nothing had happened at her place either, she let him sip his coffee, then watched him return the cup to its saucer. "What kind of 'courtesy'? Nino passed along Grandpa's last message." That she was supposed to lay to rest any rumors about family discord as she went about the social circuit. "I've been doing what I can."

Uncle Tuna waved his hand through the steam rising from his cup. "Just checking in. Cosimo is hoping you're not starting to avoid him like your big sister, Téa."

She relaxed. Téa had issues with their Mafia ties, but Eve didn't want—couldn't afford—to turn her back on the meager amount of family she had. And a Caruso was what she was damn grateful to be. "You tell Cosimo I'll get by and see him just as soon as I can."

"You're not answering your cell phone."

"Well. You know how it is." Trying to avoid the SEC and Vince Standish made it imperative that she rarely picked the thing up, but of course she didn't want to get into that. "How have you been, Uncle Tuna? Any new lady in your life?"

"No, no." He looked down at his coffee, sighed. "No time for women, not with all the *disordine* caused by Cosimo's retirement. And my brother, the one in Chicago? He was indicted last week."

"Oh." Eve reached for the pot to top off his coffee. "I'm sorry to hear that."

Uncle Tuna shook his head. His tone was morose. "Conspiracy to commit."

Murder, Eve finished for him in her head.

"Goes back to 1986. Two of his guys turned on him. They were helping the feds build a case." He shrugged his shoulders in a whatcha-gonna-do? way.

Eve mimicked his sigh, his shrug.

Uncle Tuna continued glumly. "He's got the prostate, you know. I heard they've got good health care in those prisons, but I worry. They say the mob kills, but the cancer—it does more than its share."

"You're right. But I'm certain the doctors in prison will take good care of your brother." She patted Uncle Tuna's hand, then couldn't help but wonder what Nash would think if he actually did choose this moment to come into the bar.

Would The Preacher understand or be appalled by her commiserating with Tony "The Fish" Pesce?

She whirled away, busying herself with the pot of decaf. What did it matter what Nash would think? That was the whole point of her rules. If she didn't let a man too close, she didn't have to deal with his judgment, his disappointment.

His defection.

Though of course they now knew that her father, Salvatore, *hadn't* left his family willingly. He'd been killed accidentally. Still, during his life he'd never given his wife his whole heart. As much as Eve had loved her father, life with Salvatore and Bianca had proved the danger of giving a man emotional mastery. Salvatore's unfaithfulness with Eve's mother and others had brought unbearable hurt to his wife.

Eve never wanted to be in the position of needing a man's love. Her rules were to ensure that never happened.

Swallowing hard, she met her eyes in the mirror. If Nash Cargill walked into the bar right this minute, the smartest thing for her to do would be to tell him their affair was O-V-E-R. She'd let him know up front, right away, that she held the reins on this . . . relationship—for lack of a better term—and that she'd decided to pull back and get off the ride.

She glanced over her shoulder. Maybe an introduction to Uncle Tuna would do all that for her.

Except she could see that her aging mobster "uncle" was rising off his stool. Turning to him again, she tried pasting on a smile. "Leaving already?"

"*Sí*. I have to go now, *cara*. I'll be sure to tell your *nonno* that you're doing fine."

But she wasn't doing fine! No matter how smart it was, the idea of breaking up with Nash was making her stomach churn instead of jitter. Her skin was cold, instead of hot.

But Eve forced her expression smooth and took hold of both of Uncle Tuna's old, thin hands. "You take care of yourself."

His eyes began to twinkle, and his head gave a little tilt in the direction of the far end of the bar. "You have a new customer. And it looks to me like he's the one who wants to take care of you. *Ciao*."

Eve looked after Uncle Tuna instead of looking at

the bar's latest patron. It was Nash, of course. It had to be Nash.

And she had to break things off with him.

Taking a deep breath, she squared her shoulders. Reminding herself it had been destined to end when Jemima left Palm Springs anyway, she turned to tell him that instead it was ending now.

But it wasn't Nash who was sitting on a stool, wearing a small smile, his avid gaze focused on Eve.

It was a stranger.

Chapter Twenty-eight

"Sweet Talking Guy"
The Chiffons
"B" side, single (1966)

Not until she stood across from the new man seated at the bar did she recognize him. The Boy Scout SEC agent who had accompanied Sandy Dailey that day at Denny's. She couldn't remember his name.

Maybe it would be better to pretend she didn't remember him at all, she decided. She put on a polite smile and placed a cocktail napkin in front of him. "What can I get for you?"

His pale skin, thin dark hair, and slight physique hadn't changed in the days since they'd first met. But he smiled with a confidence he hadn't revealed that afternoon. "Hello, Eve. I'll take a whiskey-and-Seven and some of your time."

A little chill tickled the base of her spine as she busied herself making the drink. She didn't like this guy. She didn't like the way he was looking at her.

But the rocks glass was steady as she set it on his napkin without spilling a drop.

As she made to move off, though, SEC-Boy caught her wrist. Eve didn't jerk away; instead, she stared down at his hand and then back up at his face.

"Excuse me?" Her voice was icier than the cubes she'd dumped in his drink.

"You forgot what else I asked for."

That cold tickle grew stronger. She raised her brow, giving him her pointed me-Amazon, you-peon look. It had felled bigger men than this one.

"That time I wanted," the peon said.

"I'm busy."

He let go of her wrist as he took a deliberate glance around the deserted room. "You don't look all that busy to me."

"We close in ten minutes. I have a list of things that need to be done."

"Apparently cooperating with the SEC isn't one of them."

Eve crossed her arms over her chest. Obviously a bad memory wasn't going to get her off the hook. "Did Sandy send you?"

His thin smile came and went. "She doesn't know I'm here."

"Well then maybe *you* don't know that I phoned her a few days ago and explained that Vince Standish made an unexpected business trip out of the country. His secretary called with the news and didn't say when he might return. There's nothing I can do about that."

"You seem like the kind of woman he'd be rushing back to see."

Eve pretended she didn't want to smack the

presumptuous blockhead right across the face. Instead, she smiled with as much saccharine as she could muster. "Thank you, a girl always likes to hear a compliment."

She didn't. She much preferred Nash's brand of outrageous insults. Her gaze flicked to the French doors that he would come through if he did decide to visit tonight. *Please God, he won't.* Minutes ago she'd been looking forward to breaking off with him in a neutral location, but now she didn't want to risk his running into SEC-Boy.

Nash, let me introduce you to the federal agent trying to shake me down as payback for my little felonious lapse a few weeks ago. Something told her The Preacher—a self-avowed, flag-waving, law-and-order man—wouldn't shrug off her illegal activity just because she had that genetic excuse for her crime.

"You're a beautiful woman," SEC-Boy said, drawing her attention back to him. He patted the seat of the stool beside his. "Why don't you join me in a drink?"

Eve didn't want to. She didn't want to make nice to the blockhead, she didn't want to spend another second in his company, she didn't want to do anything but go back to her bedroom and pull the covers over her head.

Better yet, pull the covers over her head and Nash's.

But no! She was going to end that, she was, and the blockhead being here made that just more imperative.

She smiled at him again, because she had to. "I'm sorry, but I'm not supposed to imbibe on the job."

He took a sip of his drink. "That's right. You wouldn't want to get fired, now that you're flat broke."

How kind of you to point that out. "I'm watching my pennies." *Saving up for that attorney that I can't afford and would do just about anything not to need.*

"Just as closely as we're watching you, I'm sure."

"I'm sure." She gave him the last polite smile she had and half-turned to go about her business.

But again, SEC-Boy stopped her, catching hold of her hand this time. "I could ease things for you."

"Ease things?" Her heartbeat thumped against her breastbone. "You'd do that?" *And why?*

"If you cooperated with *me*."

There was the catch. There always was one when it came to men, even boy-men, like the blockhead still holding her hand. But while she'd love to give the twit a piece of her mind and dump his drink in his lap, that wouldn't help her case with the SEC. She was going to have to let him down the nice and easy way.

Eve searched her memory for his name. Jerry? Tim? No. Terry. His name was Terry.

She widened her eyes like the dumb blonde he most likely considered her. "I'm not sure what you're getting at, Terry." Often men couldn't bring themselves to flat-out proposition her in plain English. If she acted as if she didn't understand their innuendo, they'd slink away before coming straight out with it.

"I want sex. You and me, in bed." Terry rubbed his middle finger against her palm.

Yuck. Ick. Bleah. Eve pictured her sister Joey's repulsed response as behind her back she used her free hand to give him *her* middle finger. She wished her purse weren't so far away, under the counter beneath the cash register. If she could reach it, she'd switch on her mini-recorder and get this little weasel's blackmail on tape.

Then she'd use it to get him off her case and maybe even out of a job.

Without that, though, she couldn't afford to make an

enemy out of him. "Oh, I'm sorry, Terry." How did one look contrite when one really wanted to kick? "I have a boyfriend."

She didn't let herself think of Nash. He wasn't her boyfriend. He never would be.

"I don't mind sharing," SEC-Boy said, smiling again. "I'm not looking for a future, Eve, just some fun."

No duh.

"Well, um, Terry . . . I don't think that will, um, work." She fumbled around, going for dumb again even as her mind was racing. She needed to wrap this up before she lost her patience and her chance to extricate herself from this mess with the SEC. "I hope I haven't led you on in any way."

"But you have, Eve."

She blinked. "I have?"

He did that revolting finger-to-palm rub again. "A woman who looks like you . . ."

"Here's a dollar, just for being pretty."

"What a pretty girl. I'd never hurt you."

Red edged Eve's vision. Her looks weren't anything she'd asked for. And yes, at times she enjoyed the power they gave her. But they weren't an open invitation. And she was sick, damn sick, of people seeing them as that, or worse, as a commodity to be bought or bargained for.

She narrowed her eyes at the little weasel. "Listen, S—"

An unexpected movement cut her off. Not through the French doors, where she'd expected him, but through the doorway to the Kona Kai's small lobby came Nash. He halted, his gaze taking in Eve, the back of SEC-Boy, their linked hands.

She couldn't tell what he thought about any of it.

And then she thought that this might be the perfect way to break things off between them.

It came to her in the single *ka-thump* of an unsteady heartbeat. If she could make Nash believe that she had solicited or was encouraging this . . . this flirtation with weasel Terry, then he'd back away from her. For good. She knew it.

SEC-Boy remained unaware of Nash's presence and she pretended she was too, even as she flicked a final glance at him from under her lashes. His big body was still, his expression unreadable. All she had to do was play up to the federal agent who was holding her hand and she'd rid herself of the man who was holding her—no, not her heart. Not that. The man who was holding her interest.

"Well, Eve?" Terry-the-weasel asked.

"I . . ." This wouldn't be hard. Nash would stride away, disgusted with her, and after that she'd find some way to put off SEC-Boy. It was a sensible plan. "I . . ."

But then she couldn't go through with it. Eve Caruso, who'd been taught from childhood to look out for #1, who had done just that many times, from the day she'd let her little sister be dragged away by federal agents, to the day she'd taken an insider stock tip and run with it, couldn't push out the words that would save her from Nash Cargill.

Their time together would end, and soon, but she didn't want his last memory of her to be the sight of her coming on to another man.

"I want you to let go of me," she told SEC-Boy.

"Now, Eve." There was a *tsk-tsk* in the agent's voice,

and he walked the fingers of the hand not holding hers across her shoulder to the button at her throat.

She jerked back, but his hold tightened and the button popped free.

"I want to see all that you're hiding underneath there."

Her breath was coming fast, and her heart seemed to be ricocheting around her chest. There was something ugly, something ugly and dirty, in Terry's eyes, and she felt the skin along her spine go damp.

"No." Her voice sounded too high. Almost afraid. "Please let go of me."

The agent didn't loosen his grip. "I want to see," he insisted.

"The lady said let go of her."

Nash. For a second she'd forgotten him in that nasty light in SEC-Boy's eyes. "I'm all right, Nash," she hurried to say. "I can handle it."

"Tell him to leave us alone, Eve." SEC-Boy was smiling now. Apparently his little federal badge lent him a lot of confidence, because he didn't even glance at the much bigger man behind him. "Tell him we have a date tonight."

"We don't have a date, tonight or any other time." She tried to tug away from him again, but his grip was like a vise.

Then he pulled her forward, and her hip bones thunked against the bar. She cried out, more surprised than hurt, and then cried out with more surprise as SEC-Boy's drink was suddenly knocked to the ground, shattering the glass.

By Nash.

"*Get your hands off Eve.*" Her monster-truck driver loomed over the other man like an avenging angel, his face hard, sparks shooting from his all-seeing, almost-clear eyes.

Whether in shock, fear, or just plain stupidity, the blockhead didn't let go, even as he stared up at Nash.

"Don't make me ask again." Nash spit out each word like a bullet. "Don't make me hurt you."

Terry's hand dropped. Eve stumbled back, and her elbow knocked into a bottle on the counter. It fell to the floor with another crash.

His hands curled into fists at his sides, Nash stepped closer to Terry. Eve almost felt sorry for the little weasel, who went pale. "Leave," Nash ordered.

Terry slid off his stool, though his knees must have been rubbery, because he swayed. His hand clutched the stool.

Nash's expression tightened, his eyes emitting more sparks. "*Leave!*" he roared.

And Terry did, scuttling off without another word or glance behind him.

The sound of the shattered glass and Nash's furious voice seemed to linger in the empty confines of the bar. His breathing heavy, he glanced at her, then glanced away. "Are you okay?" His voice sounded as if it had been grated.

"I'm fine." There was a short broom and a dustpan tucked in a corner at the end of the bar and she walked toward them, the soles of her shoes crunching over the broken bottle. She didn't know where to look or what else to do. "Thank you."

"Don't thank me," he snapped. The fury was back in his voice, and it froze her in her tracks.

What was making him so angry now? Was he mad at *her*? She stared at him. "Nash?"

"Don't goddamn thank me!" His steps jerky, he

strode toward the French doors. As he passed one of the small cocktail tables, he lashed out at it with his foot. It screeched across the marble floor, and one of the pair of used wine goblets sitting on top of it toppled. With a rough swipe of his hand, Nash sent the other dashing to the floor.

He exited to the sound of more breaking glass.

Chapter Twenty-nine

"Desperado"
The Eagles
Desperado (1973)

Fifteen minutes after the scene in the bar, Nash swung open the door of his suite to find Eve on his doorstep. It was late, and though he couldn't think of anyone else who would come knocking at one in the morning, it was still a surprise. After all those angry voices—correction, *his* angry voice—and shattered glass, he'd figured she would stay well clear of him.

He'd been glad about that.

"Can I come in?" she asked.

"Not a good idea," he said, forking his hand through his hair. His blood was still hot and his heart heavily pounding. Why the hell was she here? She should be running the other way as fast as her long legs could carry her.

"Look," he said, forking his hand through his hair again, even as he guessed now that he looked as much like a beast as he'd acted. "I don't think we should see each other any more."

She froze, then nodded. "All right."

Cowabunga. He swung the door to shut it, but her foot was in the way. His gaze jerked to hers.

"Well, you don't think I'm going to take it just at that, do you?" she asked, pushing the rest of her inside the suite and closing the door behind her. "This is a first for me."

Now frustrated and still no calmer than a few minutes before, he followed her into the living area. The couch was littered with reports and industry magazines, the day's newspaper and his cell phone. Unlike hers, his place wasn't two actual rooms but a small sitting area unseparated from a bedroom. So she plopped down on the bed, the white comforter poufing up around her like a cloud.

He crossed his arms and tucked his hands underneath them so he wouldn't give in to temptation and touch her. "A first for you how?"

"No one has ever broken up with me before."

He raised an eyebrow, going for that cool that she always did so well, even though his pulse was still pumping too fast and his skin was still heated by anger. "Were we going steady or something?"

"'Or something' will do. And I've always been the one who does the brushing off. So in honor of this inaugural event, you need to give me a little more about your reasoning."

Jesus Christ, why? She'd been witness to the scene he'd just made in the bar. She'd had a firsthand view of his explosive temper, which, until tonight, he'd mistakenly thought was under better control. "I want to break things off." *Before someone gets hurt.*

She didn't move.

Dropping his clenched fists to his sides, Nash tried again to hold in his frustration. She wanted an explanation. A breakup excuse. Fine. What did men usually say? "Babe, I'm afraid I'm one of those clichéd commitment-phobes."

She shrugged. "I'm not looking for a commitment."

Oh, shit. There was that.

And there was Eve, still waiting for him to say the right words before she would go away and leave him and his uncivilized tendencies be.

"Maybe I can make it easier for you," she said, crossing one leg over the other and letting her foot swing. "What did you tell the final Farrah?"

He stared Eve straight in the eyes. "Now that I've paid your outstanding Visa bill, booted your ex out of the apartment over the garage, and fixed your kid's bicycle, I think it's time I move on."

"Oh. Guess that one won't suffice either," she said. "Anything more appropriate?"

"Damn it, Eve." He curled his fingers tighter, done with playing around. It was time to get her out, get him back alone. "Why are you being deliberately obtuse? You know you'd be better away from me, better away from someone who . . ." Shit, he hated thinking of himself like this, but there was no way around it.

"I'm listening. Someone who? . . ."

He dug his fingernails into his palms. "Someone who went crazy when he saw that sonofabitch manhandling you. Someone who heard you cry out in pain and then wanted to pummel the one who caused it."

"Nash—"

"It was fucking ugly, all right?" He stalked to the couch and shoved a pile of papers to the floor, then slammed his ass onto the emptied space. "*I'm* fucking ugly!"

"Nash—"

He pressed the heels of his hands into his eyes. "I saw the way you looked at me, Eve." That had been the final straw. The instant he'd known that Mr. Hyde was loose again and he'd lost the power to hold him back.

"And how was that?"

"The same way I used to look at my old man."

"I was startled—"

"You were *scared*. I know how that is. Watching the rage explode and the glassware hit the ground and wondering if the next flying fist is going to hit you."

"Your father was violent."

"Yeah." Nash choked out a laugh. There was no question about that. "On a good day. On a bad day, a drinking day, he was homicidal."

"What are you saying?" Hers was a soft, quiet voice that only made the echo of his own bellow in the bar seem louder, more shameful. "Are you saying your father killed someone?"

"Himself." He let his head drop back, clunking against the wall, and the beefy, brutal man who had been Stu Cargill stomped across the black screen of Nash's closed eyelids. "He killed himself with the booze, with the anger. You can imagine."

"Nash." Suddenly she was there, beside him. He smelled her fresh, clean scent and opened his eyes to watch her transfer a stack of reports to the coffee table so she could take a seat on the cushions beside him. Her eyes were so big and blue and her mouth a soft, warm pink. "I'm imagining he hurt you. Am I right?"

Party girl. Good-time girl. She was so effing beautiful to look at that his chest ached with it.

"Did he hurt you, Nash?"

Her beauty was still mesmerizing him. "Only until I got big enough to hurt back." He hadn't been ashamed of standing up to his father, though. "The first time I caught that swinging fist of his, he stopped going after me."

"But when you were not yet big enough?"

He gave her a ghost of a grin. "I was quick. I had to stay home from school only a few times."

Now she closed *her* eyes.

"Ah, Party Girl." His hand reached for her face, but he forced it back to his thigh. "I told you it was ugly."

"But you're not, Nash." She opened her eyes, and in their true blue he knew she believed every word that she was saying with such sudden fierceness. But she was wrong. "You can't believe that his actions tainted you. You're not like him."

"Oh, Eve." He wished she would leave, but the adrenaline in his blood was seeping away and he was suddenly too tired to pick her up and push her out the door, so he would have to do the next best thing. "I'm very much like him."

He hesitated and called himself a coward for it. It was time for the truth. "Ten years ago I put a man in the ER."

She opened those very blue eyes very wide.

Yeah, honey, see me clearly now.

"Broke his collarbone, his arm, his jaw."

Her body twitched. "Were you drunk?"

"I was enraged. One of the Farrahs had a kid, a little kid with long blonde hair." His hand reached toward hers, but again he dropped it. "I walked in on a visitation with her daddy to find him slapping his child around. One eye was swollen, and her mouth was bleeding." And then he'd seen more red. "I pulled the guy off her, slammed him into a wall, and the rest is a rap sheet with the Dallas P.D."

"You were arrested?"

"Taken into custody. Not a proud moment for a man like me who believes to the bone in respecting the law. They let me go because the guy I whupped had a restraining order to keep him away from another ex-wife and kid."

Her hands were clasped together in her lap. "Any, uh, incidents since then?"

"No. I've been doing okay at keeping things light and easy. Been keeping myself under control—until tonight." It had been her little gasp of pain that had snapped his leash.

"Then Nash—"

"I don't like the man who sends people to the hospital, okay? I don't like my emotions taking over. Making me do things"—*feel things*—"that cause trouble."

"You didn't cause me any trouble." She put her hand on his thigh, but he jerked away from her touch.

"Look, Eve, something—the situation with Jemima, maybe—has put me on edge. I'm not a good person to be around right now."

"Why don't you let me be the judge of that?"

Because he wanted her to go away. He wanted his old pre–Party Girl life back, when he could resist blonde superbeauties with one hand tied behind his back. When he didn't remember the vulnerable look on her face when she'd looked out onto that endless desert vista that had made his heart twist, and then twist again as it had tonight at the idea that she was vulnerable to some man.

Some other man.

He didn't want to care about Eve that much.

"Nash." She slid off the couch and onto her knees, gathering his too-big hands in her slender ones. "Listen."

He looked down at their combined fingers and saw his knuckles as they'd looked ten years ago, swollen and scraped and dirtied with another man's blood and his own. With a yank, he jerked away from her. "Don't touch me." She was too clean, too fresh, too vulnerable to be this close to his savage tendencies.

Instead of obeying, she pressed closer, coming between his bent legs to grab his hands again and hold on. She sat back on her heels and looked him straight in the eye. "I know men. I'm the daughter and the granddaughter of a Mafia boss, so believe me, I know violent men. And you, Nash Cargill, you are not one of them."

He pulled away from her grasp, and her hands fell to his thighs. "You don't know me."

"Maybe I know you best of all." She rose onto her knees and moved in, so that her belly was pressed against the cushions of the couch. His legs were on either side of her arms, and he told himself to move. *Get up*, he commanded himself. *Walk past her. Get away from the warmth of her hands and that warm look in her eyes.*

"And I trust you, Nash." Her hands moved to mold the half-erection beneath them.

He groaned and pressed back against the cushions. "What the hell are you doing? Eve . . . Damn it, Eve. No fair."

Her hot palms traced his length, half-hard going to

whole-hard in that single stroke. "Let me show you what a good man you are. Let me show you how much I trust you."

The new, sultry purr in her voice sent a shiver down his back. And, God help him, he couldn't look away as her nimble fingers unsnapped his jeans and loosened his fly.

What kind of man would let her do this now? But he seemed stapled to the couch, unable to do anything but watch her next move. The skin of her palms was hot, hotter than even his, as she pulled him free.

Get up, he commanded himself again. *Walk past her. Get away from the warmth of her hands and that warm look in her eyes and—*

Her thumb rolled over the crown, massaging into his skin the drop of moisture already waiting there. Groaning, he dropped his head back again and watched her through half-closed eyes, weakened by her touch, weakened by the sight of Eve Caruso on her knees, his flesh in her hands.

He was a strong man. He had a violent streak. But the sight, the sensation of Eve's ministrations, weakened his resolve. He was at her mercy.

And then she bent her mouth to him.

His hand shot out, tangled in her hair. Her breath blew against his wet tip as she looked up. "I want this, Nash."

"You don't do this." At first, he'd thought it was a coy game on her part, but as he'd spent more time in her bed, he'd learned she hadn't been playing around about that. "You don't *need* to do this."

"Oh, but I think I do."

He shook his head. "Not for me, damn it."

"Not for you," she agreed. "But you said it yourself more than once, I have a thing about you and sex."

"No."

Her mouth closed over him.

And if she knew men, then she knew that he was no longer capable of protesting. A man could only be noble for so long when there was blonde hair drifting against his thighs and a valentine of a mouth servicing his cock. His hand slid out of her hair. He was weak. So damn weak when it came to her.

Teeth clenched, Nash sucked in a breath of air. His fingers drew into fists again as he forced his hips to stay down, to let her do what she wanted and not what instinct wanted him to demand. Her tongue swirled around him, and she looked up at his face through her lashes.

Miss America starring in XXX-porn.

Except it wasn't porn, it was Eve, sending him a message, telling him something with the heat and wet of her mouth. He lifted his hand to her hair and held it away from her face, watching as color infused her cheeks. Even her lips were rosier as she continued pleasuring him.

His breath was tight in his chest. Eve, going against her rules. Eve going against her rules for him. To make him feel good and to forget what had happened that night.

But . . . but he didn't think it was just for him—or maybe that's what all men wanted to think. Except then her hands circled the base, he jerked at the new contact, and she hummed in satisfaction.

"You make me so hot. You always make me so hot," he murmured, tucking her hair behind her ear.

The flat of her tongue trailed from head to her hand.

She looked up. "Making you hot makes me hot too." Her free hand slid beneath his shirt. "I never knew . . ." Her fingernails bit into his ab muscles, kitten claws kneading his skin.

Again, he fought the urge to lift his hips to that wet and waiting mouth. "You never knew what, honey?"

A little cat smile tilted the corners of that pink mouth hovering over him. "I never knew that it only took touching you to make *my* honey."

That was it. There was no fight left in him. His hips lifted. His cock—he couldn't help it!—tapped on her lower lip, demanding entrance again. And with a last little smile, she opened and took him in. Deep.

Desire flashed like lightning through his blood. Somehow she had his shirt unbuttoned now, her hands were all over his chest, and she was taking him deeper, sucking harder.

Showing her inexperience, because as she moved down the shaft her teeth scraped along the sensitive flesh. He swallowed his moan and pushed his shoulders back against the cushions. Eve had never done this before, he could tell.

She'd really never done this before.

But it didn't matter, because whatever she *did* do was so damn good, every scrape, every shift of unpracticed lips made it so much more special, because it was Eve who was touching him.

And she was so damn, damn special.

"Eve. Honey. You're so pretty. Beautiful. Your mouth feels so good." A litany of say-anything blow-job praise tumbled from his mouth. But he wanted more. He wanted to feel her, naked against him, him, hard inside of her.

The climax was coming fast and hard on him. "Eve."

He tugged at her hair, but she ignored him, running the flat of her tongue in barbershop stripes down his pole. It was such a crazy turn-on that he wanted her to do it for the rest of the night. For forever.

But heat was pulsing up from his heels and pulling his balls up tight against his body. They needed a bed. They needed to make it to the bed.

He put his hands under her arms to lift her away.

"No," she said, shaking her head so the ends of her golden hair swirled around the juncture of his thighs.

"Eve. Honey. You've got to stop."

"No."

His laugh was breathless. "Seriously. If you trust me, then believe me when I say you've got to stop."

She looked up. Lifted her mouth. Smiled. "Oh, Nash. That's the whole point. When we trust each other, we don't have to stop. I want everything you have to give. No holding back, no holding out. Right now I want the man who drops everything to rescue his sister and the man who drives a big, silly truck and I want the man who makes me want to do this."

And then she took him again, took him toward her heart, and he lost everything to her. He gave everything to her. He lost it all.

He won it all.

When he could think again, breathe, remember his name, he looked down to find her collapsed onto her knees, her head pillowed on his thighs. She'd fallen asleep.

God, how long had his post-orgasm coma lasted?

But he was calm, now. Almost content.

He stroked her hair, pushed it away from her face. How young she looked. Still flushed. The superbeauty had finally lost her supercool. Sitting up, he slid his hands under her arms. As he stood, he lifted her against his chest.

She protested in a drowsy voice but turned her face into his neck.

Turnabout was fair play, but she looked too tired for more sex tonight. He carried her over to the bed, pulled off her shoes, then rolled her in that cloudlike comforter. Without her eyes opening, her cheek burrowed into one of the six pillows.

Nash walked slowly about, turning off the lights. Then, remembering her claustrophobia, he returned to the bathroom, flipped the switch, and half-closed the door.

His gaze trained on her dimly illuminated, sleeping face, he shed his clothes, then crawled into that burrow of covers with her to spoon her body. Hadn't he wanted her to go away? Yet here she was, closer to him than ever. She'd rejected his claim of being like his father, he suddenly recalled, because she claimed to know violent men.

A thought suddenly struck. *Good God.*

Oh, good God. He didn't know where the idea had come from, but he knew . . . he knew . . .

His arms tightened around her. He put his mouth beside her ear, feeling her silky blonde hair against his face. "Who hurt you, Eve?" he whispered. "Who beat you?"

Her body stiffened, the questions penetrating her sleep. Would she trust him? Did she really trust him?

Nash held his breath.

"Nino," she finally said. "It was Nino."

Nash left it at that, only tucking her more closely against him. It didn't take long for her body to relax again and for her breathing to even out. He held her there, against his pounding heart, and though he knew she wouldn't want it, didn't need it, would never ask for it or be grateful for it, he stood guard over her sleep until it was light.

Chapter Thirty

"I'll Be Seeing You"
The Poni-Tails
"A" side, single (1959)

A re you running away from me again?" Nash asked
as he ducked under the canopy and slid into the
passenger seat of one of the Kona Kai golf carts.

Eve's fingers stilled on the ignition key and her belly
fluttered, but she turned her head to send him a cool
glance. "I've never run from a man in my life."

She'd never been at a man's feet—and why had that
made her feel both powerful and vulnerable?—either.
It was that wild, hot, poignant memory of last night
that she was trying to distance herself from. He'd been
asleep when she'd rolled silently out of his bed this
morning, but apparently in the time it had taken to
shower and change, figure out that her crummy Hyundai wouldn't start, and snag the golf-cart keys, he'd
managed to wake up, shower, and go looking for her.

His hair was damp, but there was a sexy, gritty

shadow of whiskers against his chin. He hadn't taken the time to shave.

Resisting a little shiver, she cleared her throat. "You're not spending the morning with Jemima? You usually do."

Nash pulled his cell phone out of the front pocket of his jeans, checked that it was on, then shoved it back inside. "She's sleeping in, she said, and then she has some aromatherapy thing booked." He gave her a pointed look. "Which means I'm all yours."

But he wasn't. He never would be.

Instead of directly answering, she turned the key. "I'm going for coffee."

His eyebrows rose. "The Kona Kai out of beans?"

The Kona Kai was gated, walled, completely enclosed. And today, instead of seeming like a safe haven, it had seemed dangerous. Too fenced in.

"Widening my horizons." She glanced around at the surrounding mountains. Distances were so odd in the desert. The San Gorgonio Mountains were far across the valley, yet thanks to the dry air and the unrelenting azure blue of the sky, their details were stark to the eye. Taking in deep gulps of oxygen, she drove the cart out of the parking lot and into the street, heading for "the Village," as the downtown area of Palm Springs was known.

"Eve."

When she didn't respond, he touched her cheek. "Eve, *darlin'*."

Those distant mountains seemed to move in now, locking her breath in her lungs. She knew what he wanted to know. It was something she never talked about, but just those two words in that slow, low voice of his were so hard to hold out against.

She joined the busy four-lane traffic on one of the main thoroughfares. Being crowded by Caddies and Mercedes and elegant SUVs gave her an excuse not to look at him. "I guess it wasn't a dream last night, then."

"Some of it was pure fantasy for me, but no, none of it was a dream."

When she'd gone to his room the night before, she'd been surprised, then distressed by his reaction to the events in the bar. He'd thought they'd made him ugly, when instead what she'd seen, what she'd *known*, was that he was a man good from the soles of his feet to the crown of his head.

It was all she could do not to weep about what he'd told her, and she never cried over a man. Instead, it had been her great pleasure to show him how beautiful she found him. How trustworthy. Even now, her skin prickled at the memory, and a shiver danced down her spine. Nash, heavy and hot in her mouth, his enjoyment her delight, his gratification her titillation, his satisfaction her bliss.

Well, if he'd thought his life experiences had tainted him, then maybe he would believe this one of hers tainted her, too. That would be okay. Good. Exactly what she needed. Because putting space between her and The Preacher became more of a necessity with every passing minute.

She braked at a red light. "At eighteen, I thought I already knew everything there was to know about men."

"But you didn't know Nino."

"I didn't know enough about Nino, anyway." She tried to sound matter-of-fact. "He was older, very possessive. I found that exciting at first, and then I found it stifling. When I broke it off, he—"

"Hurt you." Nash's neutral tone mirrored her own. "How bad?"

"Bruises here and there. Two black eyes. A split lip."

In her peripheral vision, she saw Nash's fingers tighten on his thighs, but his voice remained oh-so-calm. "Did you press charges?"

She shook her head. "I didn't tell anyone but Téa, for several reasons. Political reasons. Family reasons." *Mafia* reasons, but she figured he could read that between the lines.

"But—"

"He's never hurt me again. He wouldn't." She didn't think so, anyway. But Nino never stopped watching, she knew that.

"You were just eighteen? How the hell did you keep the beating a secret?"

The light changed, and she carefully pressed down on the accelerator, not letting her emotions get the best of her. Nash was sure to find this whole account repellent. He was sure to find *her* repellent, which was all to the good. "I excel at keeping things to myself."

There was a long silence. The Preacher was taking it all in, she figured, cataloging who she was and what the Party Girl had been a party to in her past. *She* wasn't ashamed of it—her experiences and her family made up the whole cloth of who she was—but now he would certainly take those steps back that she needed.

There was a lot about the Carusos and about her that a man like Nash Cargill would find too dark—and he didn't even know the half of it.

Still, his quiet was stretching her nerves taut. Maybe she should slow down so he could jump out at the intersection, thus removing himself from her offensive presence.

At the next red light, she glanced over at him.

His head turned toward her, and his words exploded into the air. "Jesus Hayseed Christ, Eve!"

It was so not what she'd expected—*Let me out, Eve, this is way too weird for me,* or *The Mafia connection is getting a might too close for comfort*—that a laugh was startled out of her. "Jesus *Hayseed* Christ?"

His big hand reached out and cupped her cheek with a gentle touch. "Oh, darlin'," he whispered, then his mouth pressed a soft kiss onto hers. And then another. "What else could the 'H' stand for?"

She could only stare at him, and at that half-frustrated, half-bemused light in his eyes. This man, who worried he was violent, touched her in a million tender ways. Her skin heated, her stomach fluttered with nerves, her hand went to her forehead, and she swore she could feel another pimple forming.

Oh God, oh God. He'd asked what else could the "H" stand for.

How about, How could this be happening?

How about, How come he wasn't running the other way as fast as he could?

How about, How could she say good-bye to a man who said "Jesus Hayseed Christ"?

Instead, Nash chucked her under the chin. "Light's changed, Party Girl."

She started, then faced forward again and pressed the accelerator. These physical symptoms had to be some sort of illness. She'd thought that before. It was something she'd caught in the days since she'd met Nash, she decided again, with a heavy feeling of dread. Because no man ever—

The thought jumped out of her head as a black limo knifed over from the lane beside hers. Its red rear lights flared. Eve gasped, then stomped on the golf-cart's brakes and instinctively threw her arm over Nash's chest.

He shoved her hand aside. "Is somebody trying to kill us?"

"No." She hauled on his elbow as he tried climbing out of the cart. "It's my grandfather." Her mood lifting, she jerked the wheel right to edge over to the curb. "I'll be back in a second."

The limo had parked at the side of the road as well. Eve ran to the rear door and pulled it open. This was exactly what she needed. A quick dose of her grandfather Cosimo, who would remind her of the woman she was. Strong, ruthless even, no pushover for anyone, including Nash Cargill.

"Grandpa!" As she slid onto the wide backseat, a shadow darkened the car's doorway. Then Nash was stepping inside the car too, his long, muscular leg pressing against hers so she was forced further along the slick leather.

"*Cara.*" Her grandfather shot a quick, assessing look at Nash, then turned his attention back to her. "I hope I didn't startle you and your friend, but I couldn't pass up the opportunity to say *buon giorno.*"

She smiled at him, then leaned forward to kiss both his cheeks. "You made Nash nervous, but I'm so glad to see you."

"Nash doesn't look like a nervous man to me." He raised his silvery eyebrows at Eve. "An introduction, *per favore*?"

"Of course." She half-turned on the seat. "Nash, this

is my grandfather, Cosimo Caruso. Grandpa, meet Nash Cargill. He's a guest at the spa."

"Is that right? And a businessman, I think? You drive those enormous trucks too, *sí*?"

"Yes."

The two men shook hands, Nash frowning. Eve guessed it didn't sit well with him that Cosimo was already familiar with his resumé. She smiled, glad again. "That's my grandfather."

She'd intended to visit with Cosimo alone, but this was better. Much better. Just in case Nash was romanticizing or minimizing the idea of the California Mafia, one look at her grandfather should clear that up. In a European-cut suit colored something between rose and taupe, with a matching silk shirt and tie, he appeared wealthy and powerful. But the power wasn't in the clothes, it was in the watchful glint in his dark eyes and the fierce aura that surrounded him. This man was the real deal.

Once meeting Cosimo Caruso, one couldn't forget he was California's *capo di tutti cappi*.

And the boss of bosses never wasted a moment. "So, you're spending time with my granddaughter?" he asked Nash.

Leaning back against the cushions, Eve hid her smile. The honed steel behind the words should scare even a monster-truck driver away. Of course he would deny it.

Nash crossed his arms over his chest and sat back beside her. "Yes."

Eve jolted upright. "No, we're not."

He flicked her a glance. "Yes, we are."

"No."

"Yes."

"No!"

"*Cara,*" Cosimo interjected. "As your sister Joey would say, cut the gentleman some slack. You're here, he's here, the two of you are spending time together, at least *this* moment in time."

Nash shot her a grin. "Exactly."

Eve sighed. "Fine. But 'for the moment' is the operative phrase."

Cosimo laughed. "I don't envy you," he told Nash.

"Hey—"

The sound of a cell ringtone interrupted her protest. Nash pulled out his phone and frowned down at the screen. "Excuse me," he said. "I have to take this, it's my sister." He stepped out of the car and onto the sidewalk.

"Nice young man," Cosimo remarked.

"He's not nice . . . well, he's *very* nice, but I don't want you or anyone else getting the wrong idea."

"I heard he helped out with an unpleasant situation in the Kona Kai bar last night."

Cosimo had spies—or maybe just Nino—everywhere. She shrugged. "I could have handled it."

"Ah, *cara*. But you don't always have to handle things alone. You need to learn that. All you have to do is ask for help."

He couldn't know about the SEC situation, could he? He didn't. "I'm fine, Grandpa." But suddenly she was nervous again, and she wanted out of the car before she blurted out *her* troubles, making trouble for the family that had taken her in. "Just fine."

"You're certain?"

"Of course. Yes. Really." And before her babble could reveal any more, she slid toward the door. "I'll see you again soon."

Without giving herself a chance to give any more away, she was standing on the sidewalk beside Nash, and the limo was pulling back into traffic. She watched it cut through the other cars and turn a corner. Then she glanced over at Nash.

He was staring down at his phone, a new frown on his face. Her belly fluttered again. "What is it?"

"Jemima."

"Something's happened to Jemima?" Oh, God. The stalker. Images flashed through Eve's mind. The car coming toward them. Jemima falling. The threatening fax. Then, oddly enough, the dead canary and that mangled stuffed animal.

But Nash was shaking his head. "Something happened to her, all right, but not what you're thinking. She got a call from the L.A. police this morning. Ricky Becker showed up at his mother's, and he has an iron-clad alibi for the past few weeks."

Air whooshed out of Eve's lungs. "That's good." Except Nash still had a funny look on his face. "Isn't it?"

"Of course. It means she doesn't need a bodyguard any more."

Oh. Right. She waited for the relief she should feel. Nash was definitely going to distance himself from her now, because he was going to leave Palm Springs. She wanted that. It was what they'd both been waiting for.

"But . . . but she'd probably like your company a little longer." Eve couldn't believe what she heard herself suggest in that rational, I-don't-care-either-way voice. "She doesn't report for the new film for a few more days, right?"

"Right. Except she had even more interesting news. She's marrying Mack Chandler. Today. As a matter of fact, they're on their way to Vegas right now, and then they'll be honeymooning at Chandler's ranch in Montana."

He repeated what Jemima had told him. Mack Chandler had been staying in the bungalow next to hers. They'd fallen in love, and nobody—including Nash—was going to stop her from becoming Chandler's bride. Nash had spoken to the actor too and had found himself reassured that the other man was looking out for Jem's welfare. "My little sister," he said, shaking his head. "The Hollywood wife."

"Wow. Okay. Right. Whoo." She was babbling again, just as she'd done in Cosimo's car, and she *never* babbled. Jemima marrying. Jemima marrying Mack Chandler. There was a juicy item for her "Party Girl" column, but that wasn't at the top of her mind. "This means you're really free. You could go. Tomorrow. Tonight. This afternoon. Now . . ."

"Yeah, I could." Nash shoved his phone in his pocket, then shoved both of his hands through his hair. "I could get back to business."

"You were only staying here until Jemima was safe."

"Uh-huh."

And it was time for them to part. Past time.

"Or you could stay until after Téa and Johnny's wedding," she heard herself say. A flush rushed over her skin. Had she just asked him to stay? Oh, God. She'd just asked him to stay. She never, ever asked a man to stay. There had to be some reason why she would break another rule. "I . . . uh . . . I could use a date. It could be fun."

Nash stilled, and Eve wished back her words. They had to be on account of that sickness she was suffering from. Would he buy that as an excuse?

But then a grin slowly dawned over his face. "Well, well, well. There's an offer that's hard to refuse."

She held her breath.

"You want more fun, huh? When you put it like that, I sure can't leave a lady like you in the lurch."

Chapter Thirty-one

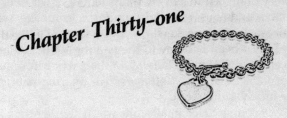

"Fooled Around and Fell in Love"
Elvin Bishop
Struttin' My Stuff (1975)

Nash had told himself that staying longer in Palm Springs was for what Eve had said—fun. Indulging longer in his affair with her was his reward for playing unnecessary bodyguard to Jemima—and for not punching a wall after hearing the details of Eve's beating, like he'd wanted to. But the wedding he'd agreed to attend with her was still a couple of days away, so tonight he'd said yes to escorting her to that masquerade party she'd once mentioned too.

It had sounded like more fun.

Except it was really torture, and he'd only been in the ballroom of the Desert Stars resort for a mere twenty minutes.

It had started back at the Kona Kai. He'd thought himself oh-so-clever by wearing all black accented by a white collar he'd folded from a handkerchief—The

Preacher going as a preacher. Then Eve had turned his every brain cell to jelly by traipsing out of her door in that scandalous schoolgirl uniform, complete with kneesocks and sneakers.

They'd been halfway to the parking lot before he'd been able to think. Halfway to the party before he'd been able to speak. "Tell me you're wearing panties," he finally ground out.

"Of course." Her small smile was naughtier than his prurient thoughts. "Little white cotton ones."

Making those little white cotton panties an image he couldn't get out of his head.

Torture, pure torture.

So, arms folded over his chest and teeth clenched, he sat at an empty table, watching Eve circulate about the party with a tiny tape recorder in her hand when all he wanted to do was take her somewhere private, flip up that saucy skirt, and—

A tall body dropped into the chair next to Nash's. Johnny Magee, dressed like a riverboat gambler in a white ruffly shirt and shiny jacket. On another guy it would have looked too pretty, because Johnny Magee, with his golden hair and toothpaste smile, *was* pretty, but he carried it off with an air of cool that made clear he was all guy.

"Glad you could join us, Cargill," he said, putting out his hand to deliver a firm shake. "Sorry Téa and I weren't here when you arrived. The photographer captured us for some photos."

"Yeah. He got Eve and me, too." The pictures were supposed to be developed and delivered to the tables before the party ended, and Nash figured he'd snag one for future days when he wanted to remember the party girl who had once tried so hard to wrap him around her pinky finger.

His gaze found her again in the crowd of two hundred or so costumed guests. Another flashbulb popped, blazing her already-bright hair. As if he could ever forget her.

Johnny's gaze followed his. "Quite a woman, our Eve." Then he looked at Nash, obvious speculation in his eyes. "Don't you think?"

"Yeah. Sure. A lot of fun," Nash replied, then hastily diverted the conversation. Magee had already shown his propensity for awkward questions. "And you're marrying into the Caruso family in a few days."

Johnny turned his head, and Nash saw him looking toward a nearby table where Téa stood talking, wearing a pink bunny outfit, complete with fluffy tail pinned to her own very excellent one. "Yeah." How he managed to look both suave and besotted at the same time, Nash didn't know, but he did feel sorry for the guy. Besotted had to hurt. "She's the best gamble I ever made."

"Gamble?"

Johnny turned back to Nash. "Long story. Old history. Upshot: happy ending."

Nash appreciated men of few words, but he couldn't help being curious about Cosimo Caruso and the California Mafia. Despite what Nash's VP of Finance had imparted to Nash on his first morning at the Kona Kai, Nash might have been able to dismiss the organized crime connection if he hadn't met the boss of bosses in the flesh. Eve's silver-haired grandfather radiated more potentially lethal power than a high-octane hemi-engine. "You don't have any qualms about marrying into . . . uh . . ."

"The mob?" Johnny shrugged. "We keep our distance from that side of the family. When I look at Téa, her mother, her sisters, I tell myself I'm marrying into a mob of gorgeous women."

Which made Nash look the superbeauty's way once more.

"Eve said you'll be her date at the wedding." Johnny sounded speculative again.

Nash shrugged. "Should be fun."

"Fun?" the other man echoed, and the way he studied Nash's face reminded Nash that Johnny Magee was a professional gambler. He probably read volumes into the slightest tic.

But Nash could be as stony as they come. "Fun."

That's all it was between him and Eve.

Johnny ran a hand over his hair. "Maybe I should warn you—" Whatever he'd been about to impart was lost as something over Nash's shoulder caught his attention. He frowned. "Oh, damn. Damn, damn, _damn_."

Nash turned to see little sister Joey Caruso come striding into the party, heading their way. Along with a mulish expression, she wore a skimpy, glittery costume that made her look like an Italian Tinkerbell. Then Nash's attention shifted to what—who—he figured Johnny was swearing about. Eve had said only Téa knew what had happened to Eve ten years before, but it seemed that circle had widened to Johnny as well as Nash. Because walking a pace or two behind Joey, but definitely tagging along with her, was Nino Farelle.

The man was dressed in pinstripes, like the gangster he was. As Nash watched the dark, slick-haired figure stride into the room, his muscles clenched and his stomach tightened into a knot of fire. On each hand, his fingers slowly contracted toward his palm.

This was the man who had hurt Eve. Blackened her eyes. Split her lip.

A high whine buzzed in Nash's ears as his anger gathered force.

Nino and Joey were still a few tables away when the mobster bent down and murmured something to the small woman, then peeled off toward the bar. Nash followed him with his gaze, never looking away until Joey reached the table. She yanked out the chair beside Johnny's and threw herself into it, squishing the sheer wings that were somehow attached to her shoulders.

Johnny cleared his throat, then leaned over to kiss her cheek. "Hey, there." He hesitated. "What's up with your, uh, date?"

"Don't ask." She tucked her dark hair behind her ears and rolled her eyes. "I'm sorry, but we're stuck with him for the evening."

Not if Nash had anything to do about it. As much as he wished to control the Mr. Hyde inside himself, he wouldn't—just *would not*—sit here with that man, knowing—

"What's the thundercloud on your face all about?" Suddenly his favorite schoolgirl plopped into his lap and put her arms around his neck.

Without thinking, he relaxed one of his fists so he could palm the small of Eve's back. But his gaze shot back to Nino, still in line at the bar. The anger burned in his belly. "Nothing you need to worry about."

She grabbed his chin and turned his face toward hers. "It's nothing *you* need to worry about."

"Eve—"

"Nash." She jumped to her feet and pulled him up by the hand. "Come dance with me."

There must have been steel in her superbeauty body,

because she yanked him away from the table, then pushed him onto the polished hardwood floor, where a few couples were moving together. She draped herself over his stiff body, her arms once again around his neck. He found his own already at her back.

"For God's sake, Eve," he muttered. "I told you I have two left feet." The band was playing an old Styx ballad, but his simmering mood wasn't sailing away with the tune.

She pressed her body harder against his. "I have two right ones. Together we make a couple."

His hands tightened on her warm waist. *Together we make a couple.* He shook his head to get the words out of his mind and glanced over again to monitor the man who'd just reached the white-coated bartender. "I have something I need to do besides dance."

"I picked up on that from across the room," she said. "And you're wrong."

"You were watching me?"

"More like feeling you." Her valentine mouth curved into a smile. "You glower with power."

He didn't laugh at her rhyme as she'd meant him to. "Eve—"

"I don't need your help."

She didn't need him, is what she meant.

"I took care of it years ago."

She could take care of herself.

And for some reason, those messages made the flames of anger inside of him flare higher. "Can't you let me—"

Her cool fingers moved over his mouth. "No, Nash. I can't let you. You don't want to hurt anyone again. You'd hate that."

His gaze shifted from her face to Nino, who was

weaving through the crowd with drinks in his hands. The hands that had dared to touch, to *injure*, Nash's Eve.

His Eve.

A wild thought knifed through his hot mood, stunning him.

"We're supposed to be having fun, remember?" Her fingers moved to tangle in the hair at the back of his neck.

Nash clenched his back teeth. That's right, that's right. Fun. She was a selfish, hedonistic party girl. One who was good with men. All men. How she made him feel, how she felt to him, that was just part and parcel of the superbeauty power she had over any poor dope with an XY chromosome combination.

He stared down at her, trying to see her as nothing more than that mouth, those breasts, that blonde hair, those legs. No one who needed his protection. No one to get worked up over.

"I can't let you do what you're thinking of for me, and then despise yourself afterward," she said, all earnestness and sincere eyes. Her fingers caressed his nape. "I just can't let you, Nash."

Proving that she, Eve Caruso—not a puppet with the body and face of a goddess but a complex, warm, crazy-making woman—was concerned about him. Cared about him.

Wanted to safeguard *him*.

As no woman ever had.

That wild thought rushed into his consciousness again, smothering his anger.

Oh, God, no.

Would he despise himself afterward if he beat the crap out of Nino Farelle? It was hard to know, Nash decided, when everything else in his mind was being trampled by that one reckless thought that he couldn't ignore. That one terrible, tragic thought.

He was in love with her.

Oh, shit. Oh, fuck. I am so, so screwed.

He was in love with Eve Caruso.

And that wasn't any kind of fun at all.

Nino Farelle made it through the next couple of hours without confrontation or punishment for two reasons. One, he didn't spend any time at the Magee-Caruso table, and two, Nash was so knocked on his ass by the revelation of his feelings for Eve that *he* spent most of his time in his chair, staring off into space or staring at her.

What the hell was he supposed to do now?

She must have extracted some kind of promise from him on the dance floor, because though she checked back every so often, she left him mostly alone to work the room with that tape recorder of hers. There were "Party Girl" column inches to fill, he supposed, and her job required that she chat and smile and circulate.

She was so damn good at being sparkling, he acknowledged, and he watched her as if he'd been thirsting for sparkle his entire life. Nash closed his eyes and held his head in his hand. *Christ, how had this happened?*

And what was he going to do about it?

Then, suddenly, it was as if the bubbles had gone from the room. Nash's eyes snapped open, and he sat up straighter in his chair. He couldn't see Eve anywhere. At his last glimpse of her, she'd been talking to a skinny dude dressed in a toga—one of those

Napoleon-sized men she'd hung with at that first Palm Springs party he'd attended.

Nash shoved his chair back from the table. Téa looked up, mid-conversation with her soon-to-be groom.

"Do you see Eve?" he asked, still searching the crowd.

She scanned the room as well. "No."

Joey bounced over. "Something wrong?"

"Eve," was all he said.

Her fairy wings quivered, and she frowned. "Haven't seen her recently. I was just in the women's lounge and she wasn't there."

Nino was nowhere in sight either.

And Nash had a very, very bad feeling. He'd never put much store in intuition or hunches before, but he couldn't ignore the clamoring voice inside of him.

Go find her. Go find her now.

With that angry fire kindling back to life inside of him, he circled the dance floor, passed through the bar line, crisscrossed between the tables. No sign of Eve. She must have left the ballroom.

At a trot now, he exited through a carpeted hall-way and double glass doors to the wide sidewalk adjacent to the parking area. Small groups were congregated out here too, but none of the costumed people were dressed like a Catholic schoolgirl in trouble.

Because she *was* in trouble, damn it. When he found her he was really going to spank her this time. Even if she liked it.

"Looking for someone?"

Nash swung toward the male voice.

Nino. Nino Fucking Farelle, all alone, leaning against a pillar and sucking on a cancer stick, smoke rising around him like evil. Nash's hands fisted, and the flames in his belly shot high.

But Eve wasn't in Nino's clutches, Nash reminded himself quickly, and kicking the shit out of the guy would only waste time. *Find Eve. Find Eve first.*

Shoving his fists in his pockets, Nash advanced on the other man. "I'm looking for my date."

"*Your* date?" Nino took a drag on his cigarette. "She just left with somebody else."

"Yes?" Nash's voice could cut glass, and that bad feeling he'd had in the ballroom quadrupled. "Who?"

"Why do you want to know?" Nino tossed his butt to the cement.

Nash crushed it out with his heel. No sense in being subtle. "Just give me the name, asshole."

The gangster's eyes narrowed. "I've punched people for less than that."

"No doubt." If Nash let that be a trigger for a fight, though, locating Eve would only be delayed. "But I'm a lot harder to hit than a teenage girl."

Nino jerked back, and then he had the balls to look almost ashamed. "She told you."

"Yeah, she told me, but I don't have time to take it out on your face. Who the hell did she leave with? Something's going on."

Nino's gaze snapped to his. "What's going on? I have orders from Cosimo to keep an eye on the girls and—"

"It's a hunch I have. *Who was it?*"

"Vince Standish," Nino replied. "I heard him tell her that he wanted to show her a new piece of artwork he recently acquired."

The ball of fire in Nash's belly rolled. "She fell for the old etchings line?"

"Yeah. Which doesn't sound like Eve," Nino said slowly. "I think you're right. I think there's a problem."

Something insectlike skittered down Nash's back, and heat shot to his knuckles. *How could she do this to me?* he wanted to scream.

But it wasn't her fault he'd fallen so damn hard. It wasn't her fault that in a man like Nash, passion equaled violence. It wasn't her fault that after he found her tonight, the next one he'd have to save her from was himself.

His blood pumping hot and fast, he eyed Nino. "Do you know where this guy lives?"

Chapter Thirty-two

"You Got a Lot to Learn"
Henrietta & the Hairdooz
"B" side, single (1963)

Y ou invited me to the party. You should have known
I'd be back." Vince Standish frowned as he maneuvered his Jaguar through the quiet streets surrounding the Desert Stars.

"Oh, but I knew not to count on it," Eve replied.
"You're such a busy man." The fact was that in the past
days with Nash, she'd gone back to ostrich-mode when
it came to Vince and her deal with the SEC. Rather
than worrying about the future or obsessing on the
past, she'd been enjoying every present moment with
Nash Cargill.

He'd dressed up as a preacher tonight, and at first
sight of him she'd had the oddest compulsion to confess—

"Yes, I'm busy." Vince shot her a look. "But we have
things to discuss, remember?"

Oh, she knew they had things to discuss. When he'd first approached her tonight, from the instant he'd slid his palm from her shoulder to her wrist and kissed her cheek she'd known that she couldn't go on faking a friendship with the rat-bastard. She had to get the goods on him ASAP. To that end, she had a plan.

Eve Caruso was still looking out for #1.

Through her short plaid skirt, she fingered the thin mini-recorder resting in the hidden homemade pocket. In high school, she'd sewn it into her skirt herself under seamstress Téa's guilty supervision. Her big sister had been nervous about the alteration that Eve had been making so that she could squirrel away Catholic schoolgirl contraband—lipstick, bubble gum, a tiny handwritten list of conjugated French verbs.

Now it was holding her method of escape from under the thumb of the SEC. She didn't need or want to wait for a wire. She had her very own recording device.

"I'm looking forward to our talk, Vince," she said. "And to see that new piece of sculpture you have."

He smiled at her now, and she mentally rolled her eyes. Men were so easy to play.

Except Nash. Her stomach tumbled in one of those nervous somersaults that just thinking of him could bring on. She was still suffering from that Nash-virus— jittery stomach, hot skin, wild bursts of euphoria. She hoped he took the symptoms with him when he left.

And just like that, her mood swung down. It did that too, lately. She'd be high on life in his company, in his bed, only to plummet low with the realization that their time was running out.

That's what you get for forgetting your own rules, Eve.

At his house, Vince unlocked the front door and swung it open. The smell of stale air wafted out. He grimaced. "My apologies. The staff still has a couple more days off. I came here from the airport, threw on my costume, and immediately headed back out."

She smiled up at him, trying to look appealing. Trustworthy. "My, you *were* anxious to see me."

He gave her a puzzled look. "But of course. It's time we settled things between us and set a date."

Eve's stomach reacted again, but this wasn't the exciting, weightless roll she felt at thoughts of Nash. She touched her tape recorder as reassurance and let Vince guide her through the foyer, past a massive, ornately framed mirror and doors that she remembered led to a powder room and a coat closet. From there they walked into the spacious living room with windows overlooking one of the Desert Stars golf courses. Athlete Joey would know its particular name. Eve only knew that all that empty grass laid out in front of her made her feel particularly alone with Vince.

"Sit down, sit down." He urged her onto one of the massive couches, then took his own seat on an otto- man placed near her knees.

She edged further along the sand-colored velvet. "So, where's this new sculpture?" Her gaze circled the room, but no piece popped out at her.

He waved a hand. "We'll get to that." His hands rubbed along his toga, as if his palms were sweaty.

A little frisson edged down Eve's spine. She was the one who should be nervous. But she covered up the feeling with a bright smile. "Then tell me how your business trip went. Any exciting new plans or accom- plishments?"

Her fingers hovered over the hidden recorder, not yet ready to turn it on. She didn't want to waste tape or battery power on irrelevant chitchat.

"I told my team in South Africa that I'm getting married."

Whoa. Whoa whoa whoa.

Another shiver shot down Eve's spine. She tried laughing it away. "Married? Wait a minute. What's that all about?" Surely, surely—

"I know we haven't ironed out all the details, but I was shopping for diamonds, and in my enthusiasm I let it slip."

" 'We' haven't ironed out all the details?" Eve echoed, sliding further down the couch.

Vince rubbed his palms on his toga again. "I haven't felt this nervous since I was fourteen years old."

Eve didn't want to think of the other time she'd felt this nervous. If she did, she'd want to run away, run out of Vince's stale house and into fresh air and sunlight and Nash's arms. But she was Salvatore Caruso's daughter, and the ability to fake confidence was bred in her genes.

Doing her best to be mob-daughter strong, she eyed Vince and refused to back away another inch. "What are you nervous about?"

"I'll feel much better when I hear you say yes." He popped up from the ottoman, the hem of his toga swirling around his calves.

She gave her voice a steely edge. "Yes to what, exactly?"

"Say yes you'll marry me."

"You're kidding."

He smiled, apparently relieved now that he'd gotten it out. "Of course I'm not. I thought I made it clear before this last business trip that when I returned we'd come to an understanding. I'm sure I made it clear."

Her brain scrambled to think back to the last occasion

they'd met. She'd been so preoccupied with Nash, before and since, that the meeting had made little lasting impression on her. And then, she'd been aiming to please. Trying to win Vince over. Gain his trust.

All of which she still had to do if she wanted to get that information for the SEC. And she *had* to get that information for them, or Sandy would prosecute her—and perhaps put her behind bars.

"Vince, I didn't realize . . . I didn't take seriously . . ." She spread her hands in mute appeal. "I thought we'd been through all this last year."

His smile didn't drop. "Yes, but now you've had time to reconsider. Wouldn't you find your life more pleasant with me?"

"I don't find it unpleasant as it is."

"But things have happened to you. Things that made you feel vulnerable. In need of someone." That weird smile on his face didn't die.

"I don't know what kind of things you mean," she said slowly.

"I would never have really hurt you, you know. When I saw you with that girl on the street, well, it was just an impulse. I didn't think it through."

Oh, my God.

"It was my temper. My damnable temper. You made me want you so much and then, because you wouldn't let me have you, it got the best of me." Vince was still grinning at her, but his normally bland face suddenly looked frightening and ugly.

Nash had thought of himself like that. But this . . . this was the real face of someone scary. A monster.

Eve rose to her feet. *Don't show any fear.* "Well, um, no harm done. But I think we should save the rest of this conversation for another time. Another day." *The one where you're locked behind bars in a loony bin.* "I have to get back to the party."

"We're not finished," Vince protested.

"Everyone will wonder where I am." Wouldn't they? Her sisters were accustomed to the Party Girl partying on her own, but certainly Nash would be concerned about her absence.

Or he'd learn that she'd gone off with some other man and decide good riddance.

She took a step in the direction of the front door, but Vince blocked her way. "You want me to apologize," he said. "But it's your own fault for playing so hard to get. And I'm only really responsible for the bird and the fax. That stupid cat trick was dreamed up by this incompetent fool on my payroll."

Eve froze. Her muscles, her brain, her breath. "What?" her voice sounded faint.

"The canary was after you confessed to the SEC and before I decided I could forgive you for it. The fax was just a warning to that hulk who was shadowing you." Vince's eyes narrowed. "Who is still shadowing you. That's your fault too. You need to tell him you're taken."

Near-miss of the car. SEC, canary. Nash, fax. It was all starting to make sense in a twisted, sick sort of way.

"It was *your* bad tip that set the SEC after me," she murmured. Somehow Vince had learned of her talking with them.

He nodded. "I know. I've got to be more careful. The Exchanges have new computer systems that cross-reference trades and company announcements. Much more sophisticated than years past. They pass along the information to the SEC."

Not that she'd tell him, but the SEC had already had their eye on Vince. They'd told her they'd been on the lookout for suspicious trades made by names in the same ZIP code as his and even on the same country club rosters.

"It's too bad you took my advice, though, Eve. I wasn't sure you would, you know. It was vindictive of me, but if you hadn't lost your values, you wouldn't have lost all your money, now, would you?"

She almost wanted to laugh, because this vengeful bastard was right. As much as she would like to blame him for being dirt poor, the only one to blame was herself. And the only one who could get her out of this mess was herself, too.

"So you set me up on purpose," she said, sliding her hand into her hidden pocket.

"Of course. I actually thought it was quite a brilliant revenge at the time." He reached up to pat himself on the back. "I've let slip information to other friends and lovers at other times, but I always made *them* money."

"Like who?"

He laughed. "Jealous, my darling Eve?"

Yuck. "Well, yes."

"You really want names?"

Oh, yeah. "Perhaps it will take the sting out of what you did to me. You know, if I could believe it might come out the other way some other time."

Even crazy men could be easy. He seemed eager to get back into her good graces and so spilled a surprising number of names, dates, and illegal trades that he'd been part of. When he wound down, he held up his hands. "Satisfied now?"

Eve hoped her old friend Sandy Dailey would be, anyway. "Very."

His smile widened. "Then about that wedding date . . ."

Which had her thinking of Nash again. He was supposed to be her date to Téa's wedding. Generous, strong, law-abiding Nash, who would sneer at what her greed and selfishness had led her to.

But with luck, he'd never know.

With luck, when she made it back to the party, he'd be there and she could dance with him again, laugh with him again, take him home and make—have sex with him again. Yes, he'd leave town, but without ever knowing what she was truly capable of. Without ever knowing the real Eve.

She shoved her hand in her hidden pocket and clicked off the recorder. "I want to go back now, Vince."

"Of course you don't. At least, not until you've seen the ring and we've set a date, and . . . well, I have champagne cooling in the fridge. We can discuss all this in bed."

Never. Never ever ever. She could barely suppress her shudder. "I want to go back to the party." To her family. To Nash.

Vince shook his head. "No, Eve."

She refused to acknowledge the uneasiness welling inside of her. Was she a mob boss's daughter or not? Taking a deep breath, she forced herself to start off again in the direction of the front door. When Vince put his hand on her arm, she gave him a narrow-eyed look and shook his hand away.

"Stay," he said.

"If you won't take me, I'll walk."

And she did. She refused to scurry away like a timid rabbit. Instead, she headed steadily for the exit, and freedom.

"You can't do this to me." Vince's voice sounded more bewildered than demanding. He was right behind her. She could almost feel his hot breath on the back of her neck. "You can't do this."

She glanced at him over her shoulder and sent him her most withering look. No more nice girl. "Of course I can. I'm a Caruso." Then she grabbed the doorknob in front of her and pulled it open. She stared, surprised at not finding the outdoors in front of her.

Oh. Coat closet, she thought.

She made to back away, but then she felt steely hands on her back. Vince shoved her inside, hard. With a stumble, her knees and palms hit plush carpeting. The door slammed behind her, and she heard it lock.

His voice sounded calm, not crazed, as now she figured him to be. "Eve, my love. You just need some time to reconsider."

Time. It had no meaning for Eve in that small, black room with its stale, heated air. She knew she had to get out, get away, but the heavy darkness kept her down.

Her lungs felt leaden too, holding her to the carpet like an anchor.

She pressed her cheek to the fibers and tried rising to her feet. Somewhere a party was going on, with music and dancing and laughter. She had to get back there. But the panic acted like a weight, pulling her back.

There were clothes brushing her cheeks. She gathered them around her, cowering further into the corner as she heard the people with the guns and the loud voices dump drawers and break toys in their eagerness to catch the Carusos doing something wrong.

But no! No. That was before. That had been sixteen

years ago, when she'd been a helpless little girl. She'd been yanked out of the closet that time, though she'd wanted to stay in the darkness forever, hiding from the fact that her father had disappeared, hiding from the cruel voices of the federal agents, hiding from her cowardice, which had meant she hadn't lifted a pinky to stop them from roughly pulling her little sister from under the bed. But then a hard hand had reached into her hiding place and latched onto her arm, leaving bruises that hadn't faded for weeks.

The next thing she'd known she'd been blinking against the dazzling light, and the hand had softened. "Look what we have here. A blonde this time. And such a pretty one."

"What a pretty girl," he'd whispered in her ear, his mouth too close. "I'd never hurt you."

When no one was looking, the federal agent who'd been holding her had grabbed a fistful of bills from the laundry basket the FBI was using to contain the money they'd found stashed around the house. He'd shoved them into the front pocket of her hot pink jeans. "You keep these, pretty girl. It'll be our secret."

Fast learner that she was, Eve had smiled at him.

And he'd given her another fistful of bills.

She'd turned them all over to Bianca after the agents had left—leaving holes in their walls and their floors and their box springs—and been proud of what she'd accomplished. Four hundred dollars just for being pretty. Another five hundred for the smile.

Ever since, she'd been getting what she'd wanted from men just for being pretty. Just for her smile.

But not now. Now all those smiles and prettiness and need for financial security had backfired. Vince had used her greed against her.

He'd said if she hadn't lost her values, she wouldn't have lost her money. But her values had always been of the easy-come, easy-go variety, right? There was that genetic excuse she had. She was a Caruso, after all.

But a Caruso wouldn't just lie here on the floor like a dead body, she reminded herself. A Caruso wouldn't be beaten down by her own phobias.

"Get up, Eve," she whispered.

She sucked in a shallow breath, forcing the air past her tight throat and rose once again to her hands and knees. Then she turned over to sit on the carpet. Her panting sounded loud in the cramped space.

"Get up and find some way out of here."

But the darkness and the sound of her panting were swirling around her and holding her down again. Her heart was six inches too high in her chest and beating sixty times too fast, and there were yellow dots darting about her vision.

Like those butterflies Nash had talked about.

Nash. *Nash.* She remembered that night in that other darkness, and she could hear his voice in her head, his slow drawl calming the frantic beat of her heart.

"Imagine a wide-open field with tall grass. There are dandelions. Butterflies. Take a long breath of the warm air and let it out slow."

With that full breath of air in her lungs, her panic subsided, and she could think more clearly. She had to get out of here.

Even if Nash didn't miss her, her sisters would. Though they were used to her making the rounds at social functions, they knew she wouldn't leave for the evening without saying good-bye. And her purse was on the table! They'd know she wouldn't leave without that.

So they'd ask around about her. Not just Joey and Téa, but Johnny too. Her almost brother-in-law took his familial responsibilities seriously.

The parking valet would likely remember her leaving with Vince. She hadn't been trying to hide it. And if Joey or Téa or Johnny called here or came by, what would Vince say? Certainly not that he'd locked her in his coat closet.

But he was so unpredictable, he just might.

Or he might tell them about the SEC and all the trouble she was in.

A new rush of panic swept over her. She didn't want anyone, especially the family, to know about that!

She had to get out of here.

If only Nash . . . Tears seeped out to run down her chin, those emotional, useless tears that Nash wrung out of her. Biting her bottom lip, she dashed them away.

She didn't need a man to rescue her. She could only rely on herself.

Stand, she commanded herself. *Move*. But she didn't, she couldn't, not with the cloying blackness around her and the dry-cotton taste of panic on her tongue. Her arms hugged her knees and she pulled herself into a tight little ball as the dark squeezed her, squeezed her, squeezed her to nothing. To insignificance.

Then, through the thick walls, she heard the doorbell sound. Someone was pounding on the entry door, then the deep bellow of Nash's voice vibrated through the wood and plaster and into her heart.

"Eve? Are you in there? Eve?"

Oh, God. Those stupid tears overflowed again. He'd come to the rescue! He'd come to rescue her after all.

She tightened her hands on her knees as relief

washed more tears down her cheeks. Nash. Nash would bring the sunlight and the fresh air and the butterflies. He'd find her here and—

Then do what to Vince?

And what would that do to Nash?

Galvanized by a new kind of distress, she found herself on her feet, at the closet door. She tried the knob, tried it again, her clammy-sweat hands sliding off. As more noise sounded from outside, she kicked out in frustration and panic.

Nash couldn't find out what Vince had done. Glad for her rubber-toed sneakers, she kicked again. Wood cracked. Heart pumping harder, she kicked once more, higher, and the wood cracked again.

"Eve? Eve!"

To the note of urgency in Nash's voice, she kicked out one more time. The door splintered away from the lock, and light and air rushed in as she swung it open. She shot into the entryway just as a heavy thump hit the front door and it burst open too, Nash and Johnny right behind it.

"I'm all right," she quickly assured them. In the enormous foyer mirror, she saw herself as they did, her hair in sweaty clumps, mascara raccooning her eyes, her lipstick smudged.

Maybe they wouldn't guess what happened.

Maybe they'd believe they'd gotten her and Vince out of bed.

Except Nash was already snarling at the older man, who stood frozen in the living room. "What the fuck were you doing to Eve?"

It didn't sound like "What were you doing fucking Eve?"

Movement in the mirror shifted her gaze. Her sisters, Téa and Joey, hovered in the doorway. Of course they were here, too. And upset.

Eve watched Nash's reflection glance at her, then at the splintered closet door, then back at Vince. "You bastard." His huge hands fisted, and he surged forward.

She swung around to catch his elbows, feeling the coiled tension in his arms. "No, Nash. Not for me. I'm okay. I'm all right."

Frowning, he paused.

Joey pushed Téa aside to leap over the threshold. "Why'd you leave?" Her gaze transferred to Vince. "What are you doing here with Eve?"

Vince lifted his palms. There was a smirk playing at the corners of his mouth. "Relax. There's no need to overreact. Your sister and I, we left the party because we had some things to discuss. You see, I have some information—"

"No." Eve's heart jerked in her chest, and she clutched Nash tighter. "Not that!"

"No," Vince agreed, turning to Eve. She didn't understand that odd look in his eyes. He had to know she wasn't going to marry him now, so why did he look so smug? "It's not that, Eve. It's something else."

What?

"What?" Nash demanded, echoing her thought. "Spit it out." He stepped forward again, and Eve had to use all her strength to haul him back.

"Yeah," Joey chimed in. "Why does my sister look like something the cat dragged in?"

Eve almost smiled. Count on Joey to always cut to the chase.

But then Vince was smiling too, and Eve felt another cold shiver roll down her spine. She'd thwarted his plans—as crazed as they'd been—and he wouldn't take that well.

"I have friends in all sorts of places," he said. "And one of them recently told me the most interesting piece of information. I was saving it for a special occasion."

Joey rolled her eyes. "What?" she demanded.

Téa walked inside the house, her gaze on the older man. "No, Joe. Shh."

"Oh, please," Joey started. "What's he—"

"My friend told me about the results of the DNA testing on your father's remains, Joey." He didn't take his gaze off Eve's face. "That's when the something fascinating came to light."

The DNA test? Eve's stomach clenched. Something fascinating? In October, Eve and Téa and Joey had given samples in order to positively identify the remains. Her heartbeat revved higher, and her head went dizzy.

Were the remains they'd found *not* their father? Could it be? . . . Oh, God, could it be that he was still alive somewhere, as she'd always hoped? "It wasn't him," she heard herself say aloud, her hands squeezing Nash's muscled arms. "It wasn't Salvatore."

"Oh, no," Vince said, his gaze on her face, his voice pleasant. "It was Salvatore Caruso's remains, all right. But you, Eve, this was about you."

"Me?"

Joey made a noise, and Téa grabbed on to their little sister's shoulder.

"Yes, Eve, you," Vince confirmed. "The tests prove that you're not Salvatore's daughter."

Cold flashed over Eve's flesh. What? *What?* She

stared at Vince, recognizing the sick pleasure and the absolute truth in his eyes.

He smiled as he delivered the ultimate revenge. "You're not a Caruso after all."

Chapter Thirty-three

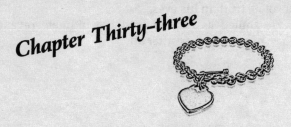

"Love Don't Come Easy"
Crazy Horse
Crazy Moon [One Way] (1978)

*T*hat's it. Now Nash was going to kill the smug, skinny son of a bitch. His mood, simmering since the ballroom and all the way to this ostentatious quasi-villa, had not been quieted by the sight of that broken door and Eve's bedraggled appearance. But now, now Nash could feel rage rocketing upward from the soles of his feet and radiating out from his chest, all ready to turn his fists into steel and Vince Standish's face into pulp.

Why would the bastard say such a thing?

He jerked his arms from Eve's grip, then took her shoulders in his hot hands, trying not to squeeze too tight. "You stay out of the way, honey," he said, holding his breath to check his anger as he propelled her backward to place her shoulders against the wall. "He's going to pay now."

His gaze took in that broken closet door beside her, as well as the tracks of dried tears on her face. "He's going to pay, big."

"No," Eve whispered. Under his hands he could feel her body begin to tremble. Her blue eyes stared into his face. "Don't. Don't do it."

"Darlin'." He tried to keep his voice patient though vengeful heat pumped through his blood with every pound of his heart. "I just can't let him lie to you like that. I can't let him try to hurt you like that."

"I'm not lying," Vince called out. Then he showed off the cell phone in his hand. "And the minute you come near me, I'm calling the police. You'll be up on assault charges before you can blink."

Nash spun toward him. "Before *you* can blink you'll be flat on your back with your head up your ass."

"Forget that." Joey threw herself forward. "*I'm* going to hurt him."

Johnny caught her around the waist, pinning her arms at her sides and holding her feet off the ground. The wildcat continued to thrash. "Little sister, calm down."

"Jesus Christ, Magee," Nash said. "Keep a hold of her. I don't want her in the way."

"I tell you." Joey thrashed harder. "I'm going to hurt him."

Nash threw Vince another furious glance. "Look what you've done now, you petty little shit."

"The truth isn't petty," he replied, a sneer on his face. "Salvatore Caruso probably did only one decent deed in his life and that was when he took in his *goumada*'s bastard and claimed she was his own. But do you know who she really is? Nobody. She's nobody."

Nash surged forward, instincts set on Destroy.

"*Nash.*" Téa's voice was sharp. "Eve."

He whipped his head her way. Eve was staring straight ahead, her blue eyes wide and dark, her body visibly shaking as silent tears ran down her cheeks. As he looked, her knees gave out and she started sinking down the wall to the floor. He leaped toward her, catching her when she was only inches from the ground. Breathing hard, he set her gently onto the floor, then hunkered beside her.

"Darlin'." He palmed the tears away with his hands. The rage redoubled, pumping adrenaline through his blood and coloring the edges of his vision black. He was having a hard time talking over that thick knot of rage in his throat. "You wait outside with your sisters."

"No!" Her fingers blindly clutched at him again, seeming to find his hands by accident. "Don't leave me."

Shit. He was in no mood to help her at the moment, except with his fists.

"Eve—"

"Please." Her fingers tightened on him. "Please don't leave me."

He'd never seen her like this. Tearful. Almost lost. But he had to leave her because he needed to crack the asshole's head. And he *did* have to; nothing else would satisfy the bloodlust that was clanging like a fireman's bell inside of him.

He could almost thank his daddy for giving him the size and the experience to make the weasel feel the error of his ways. His rage barely restrained now, he shot the other man a searing look. He was going to teach him not to mess with his woman.

"I need you, Nash."

His gaze jerked back to Eve's face, and the bell inside his head paused midring. "What?"

"I need you to take me away. I need you."

No! She couldn't. She couldn't need him. She couldn't ask that. Not now, when he had to give his boiling emotions an outlet. Right now Eve was needing quiet and tenderness, and right now he had only violence and fury to offer her. "In a little while . . . later . . ." When he had Vince laid out and Mr. Hyde locked away again, then he could give her what she asked for.

Her mouth moved, the plea soundless this time. I need you.

I need you.

And those three little words finally, fully penetrated.

Eve Caruso needed him. It was a confession of the highest order, he realized. A biggie. A first.

Nash swallowed, hard. His heart was thumping, his blood was bubbling in his veins, his fists were primed for that gratifying connection to someone's flesh. He couldn't just give that up!

And yet . . .

. . . he had to try. Whether it was because of maturity or love or just that damn desperate look on her face, Nash knew he had to find a release valve that wasn't broken glass or his fist on someone else's face.

Blowing out a long breath, he made his fingers relax as he shook his shoulders loose. "Okay, darlin'." His voice was croaky with the effort, but he found a way to make it relaxed too. "Okay. I'll take you away from here."

He cuddled her close in his arms. She buried her face in his neck and didn't look at anyone, didn't say anything, as he walked her out of Vince's house.

Glancing back, Nash saw Johnny set down a subdued Joey, even as big sister Téa started toward Vince.

"Now you and I have a few things to discuss," she said to him.

Nash ghosted a grin at the lethal sound of the words and wondered if he'd left the other man with the most dangerous of them all.

But the smile died as he settled Eve into the passenger seat of her car. She let him buckle her in as her head dropped to the back of the seat and her eyes closed.

His heart jolted, not with anger this time but with worry. "What is it? Did he hurt you after all? Should I take you to the hospital?"

"No. No hospital. Just take me away."

The junkmobile took three tries before it started, but Nash swallowed his curses and pulled away from the curb. "We've got to get you a better ride," he said.

She didn't answer. As a matter of fact, she remained silent until he took a familiar turn. "Not the Kona Kai," she said sharply. "Not there."

He glanced over at her. "Okay. Where? . . ."

"There." Her finger pointed out the windshield to a neon sign blinking M TEL and then VACAN Y.

Eyebrows raised, he turned in. It was one of those kitschy leftovers from the 1950s, with a cement pool in the center of the parking lot and drive-up to the doors. He stopped in at the office, where he was given a regular key on a ring with a plastic tag that read Swinger's Hideaway and an insulated ice container.

"Thirty bucks on your credit card if you steal the bucket," their friendly host said.

Nash considered asking him to make change for the Magic Fingers machine certain to be part of the bed, but the manager was already walking back to his recliner and rabbit-eared TV set. Eve, on the other hand, was right where he'd left her. Silent, on her side of the car.

"Look, we're number 1," he told her. She didn't even blink.

At their door, he helped her out of her seat. He wasn't certain she wouldn't have sat there all night if he hadn't. Inside the room, he grimaced, but after a quick inspection decided it looked clean enough. There was one of those paper strips across the toilet seat.

Eve stood in the middle of the barf-brown carpet like she didn't know what to do with herself. So Nash guided her to the bed and helped her out of her shoes, kneesocks, plaid skirt, and white blouse. Her plain white cotton panties and lacy bra should have given him carnal thoughts, but instead he could only focus on the frozen expression on her beautiful face.

His shirt and the white collar came off next, then he stripped his black T-shirt off and dropped it over her head. With the fabric hanging down her front for modesty, he unfastened her bra from underneath, then slipped it off her. She let him push her arms through the sleeves of the shirt as if she were a child.

Inside of him, fury sparked once more to life. He should have done something more! He should have made the bastard pay!

But he took a deep breath and tucked her into the bed with that same kind of parental care.

With the covers up to her chin, Eve spoke. "I figure he was right about the test."

Nash turned away. There was a slice of open window showing between the curtains, and he stared at it, watching M TEL change to VACAN Y, then back again. So she believed Vince was right about the DNA results. There had been something about the expression on his face and then on Johnny's, Téa's, and Joey's that made Nash believe it too.

He tried to sound neutral. "Do you think he has that kind of access?"

"I said I wouldn't marry him, so he paid for that kind of access. Oh, and he sent that fax to you. He was driving the car that almost hit Jemima and me, too."

Nash froze, the rage rising to fill him again. How could he have walked away from Vince? There was nothing to do but return to the villa. He spun back around, his gaze landing on Eve's golden hair spread across the pillow, her blue eyes, looking bruised from the mascara she'd cried off her lashes.

Eve, vulnerable. Eve needing him. There was no way he would leave her.

So instead of running out of the motel room, he strode to the bathroom instead. There, he wet a washrag with warm water and squeezed it several times, imagining it was Vince's neck, until he had himself under control again. Then, though it was so rough that it would likely take off a layer of skin, he went back into the other room and sat on the side of the bed. To remove makeup and lipstick and tears, he drew the damp cloth over her with long, slow strokes.

The tension growing inside of him eased once more. As he followed the contours of Eve's incredible face, the fire inside him sputtered out. He refolded the cloth and again drew it across her forehead, her eyes, her lips, with the gentle bath feeling as if he were cleansing himself.

Nash Cargill, finally erasing the violent streak on his soul.

Tonight he'd been tested, but he'd proven himself stronger than his past. Bigger than his father's memory. He might always be the sort of man who wanted to use his fists first, but now he trusted that he wouldn't use them without thinking.

When he tossed the rag on the bedside table, he felt clean for the first time in a decade.

The bedside light went out next, though he left the one in the bathroom burning. As he crossed to the window to draw the curtains more fully across the glass, he considered where he should sleep. On the stained carpet or the uncomfortable chair cushioned with wipeable plastic?

"Nash?"

"I'm here, darlin'." He seated himself beside her again and brushed back her hair. "I'm right here."

Her hands slid up his bare arms. "Take me away," she whispered.

"Eve . . ." He leaned over her with an elbow on each side of her head. He could guess what she meant, but this wasn't the time. "Darlin'—"

"Take me away." She lifted up and bit the pad of his bare pectoral.

He jumped, a new kind of fire immediately springing to life. "Eve."

"Now, Nash. *Now.*"

This was distraction sex and—

She nipped at his chest muscle again, and all his misgivings fled.

The residuals of the emotions of the past few hours poured into their first kiss. He could taste the heat of passion on his tongue and the sad flavor of confusion on hers. But he didn't want that. He didn't want her thinking of anything but him, of them, of how far away he could take her with the rub of his flesh against hers.

He shed his boots, socks, and pants, then crawled under the covers. She threw herself against him, twisting her upper body along his. He shoved his hands underneath her panties to cup her ass and keep her pressed close to his already-aching cock. Her mouth opened wide under the onslaught of his, and she let out a near-sob as he pushed his tongue deeper.

The vulnerable sound made him hotter. He took one hand and slid it under the T-shirt she wore. But that wasn't enough for her. She broke away to strip off the shirt, and as she threw it off the bed, her nipple brushed his lips.

He didn't decline the accidental invitation. The tip hardened against the roof of his mouth as he pressed it there. She moaned, her hand plumping the soft part of her breast to offer it up for his feast. Sucking harder, he drew in a breath through his nose, breathing in Eve's soap bubble scent and the unmistakable fragrance of aroused female. He shifted around the hand beneath her panties in order to smooth his fingers against her sweet, pretty pussy. Following the bare curve, he found the source of that wet, delicious heat.

His long finger slid easily inside her, making them both groan.

"Eve, sweetheart, baby." He moved to the other breast and circled it with his other palm to feed himself her nipple. This one was already hard, already distended, and he welcomed it with a tiny bite.

Eve jerked, her pussy taking more of his finger. They both moaned as he filled her with another.

"Nash. Please. Please."

He was pleased. He was effing ecstatic as he felt the

tension taking over her body. She wasn't thinking of anything but this.

"Do it now," she urged him. "Do it now."

He laughed, letting her breast go with a little pop. "To do it now is to do it too quick." He had more that he wanted. More of *her* that he wanted.

Flattening his tongue, he ran it up her slender neck. As he bit the lobe of her ear, he thrust a third finger into her body.

"Huh." She exhaled in a huff. "Nash, *now*." With urgent hands, she tried pulling him over on top of her, but he ignored her wishes. Instead he went back to kissing her mouth, pulling free of the heated glove of her body to shove off that cotton underwear.

She kicked it away with thrashing legs, then went back to trying to tug him over.

"Nuh-uh," he said against her mouth. "I want more."

"More later." Her hand slid down to his pole-hard cock. "This now."

He hissed in a breath of air, determined not to give in just yet. A man strong enough to resist plowing his fist into Vince's face could resist the lure of Eve's tight little pussy for a while more. It would be better to take the longer route. To let the desire build, higher and higher.

Or lower, as the case may be. Because suddenly Eve made another frustrated sound and ran her mouth down his body. To his navel, and beyond.

His back bowed. She chuckled as she hooked her fingers into his boxers, then shoved them down his legs. He feebly tried to kick them down as he held his breath . . .

. . . then felt her mouth take in the head.

Heat jolted to his balls. Her tongue swirled.

His brain spun.

"Eve, Eve, Eve, Eve." Closing his eyes, he was ready to promise her pancakes for breakfast, a brand-new car, hell, half his business. Up on her knees, she shifted closer to his thighs. He lifted his lashes and took in the curve of her beautiful, delectable bottom. Oh, God. This must be heaven.

Almost heaven.

As she practiced her new skills on him, he slid further down to flatten himself against the mattress. She followed his movements, her pretty ass twitching in a way that drove him crazy. Then, careful, careful, slow, slow, he slid his palm up the inside of her thigh, from her knee to her Brazilian. It was only another inch or two to find her sweet, hot place.

He filled it with his fingers.

Her mouth sucked him harder.

His thumb found her clitoris and circled in time with her tongue.

They both moaned.

He continued to work his fingers inside of her, his other hand rubbing against the pretty, full curve of her ass. Her flesh heated beneath his hand. The inside of her was wet, creamy. A place he wanted to know more intimately.

With little nudges, he urged her to straddle his body. That gave her more direct access to his cock, and she took advantage of it. He grunted, might have been derailed if not for the destination he had in mind, which was a few, few inches away. Nash shoved a doubled-up pillow beneath his neck.

And drew his tongue along Eve's bare pussy.

Her body jumped as if electrified. He kept one hand's heavy weight on the cheek of her bottom, left fingers deep inside of her, and gave all the attention of his tongue to the little nubbin that was standing up, begging for his favor.

For his pleasure.

She remained frozen, her mouth around him, as his mouth made love to her.

It would only take seconds, he guessed. So he took advantage of the brief moments, lapping at her flesh, savoring her taste, feeling the climax growing beneath the palm of his hand and the tip of his tongue.

Her back arched, that pretty curve that he'd never forget for his whole life. He caught her clitoris between his teeth. His fingers dove farther into her body.

She released his cock and shook with the power of her orgasm. He took in every shudder, then, oh, God, without warning his own came on. With just the beauty of Eve in his eyes and the taste of her in his mouth, he spurted against his belly.

With gentle hands, he lifted her back on the pillows, then he cleaned himself up in the bathroom. When he returned to the bed, she was staring up in the darkness.

Despite the tracks of tears running down her cheeks, he climbed into the bed and gathered her into his arms. She wasn't going to scare him.

"I love you, Eve," he said. All the vows he'd made to himself, all the profiles he'd concocted of the kind of woman he wanted had been swept away by this overpowering, God-so-right feeling that he had when he was with her. Her trust tempered his steel. Her tender places introduced him to his own. She was exactly the right woman for him, and he didn't want to hold the truth of that back from her any longer. "I'm so in love with you."

More tears flowed down her heart-stopping face. "What did you do to me?" she whispered.

He pressed a kiss to her wet temple. "Nothing to worry about. You let me be with all of you this time, nothing held back. I made love to the real Eve."

There was a long pause, then another whisper that sounded more like a plea. "Who is that? Because I don't know who she is anymore."

Nash held her closer, wiped out by the aftermath of adrenaline and the last incredible, unforgettable minutes. "We'll figure it out in the morning," he said.

But in the morning, she was gone.

Chapter Thirty-four

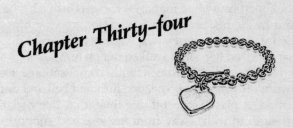

"Walkin' By Myself"
Wet Willie
The Wetter the Better (1976)

Nash waited twenty-four hours for Eve to return to him at their room in the Swinger's Hideaway.

She didn't.

She didn't call, either. They'd never found a need to exchange cell phone numbers, but she could have called the room. Several times he'd tried hers at the Kona Kai, but she hadn't picked up.

Flat on the mattress, his hands stacked beneath his head, he stared up at the water stain on the ceiling above the bed, studying it as if it might provide a clue to how he'd gotten to this place in his life. It was shaped like a boomerang.

Right back to where he'd started?

But that didn't make sense. He'd never been in love before. God damn, chest-aching, ball-breaking love. Just another black mark on Eve's side of the score card.

Besides having left him at a cheesy motel vehicle-less, the superbeauty had managed to crawl inside his head and inside his heart, not to mention making him go against his very own vows. And then, when he'd told her he loved her, she'd walked out on him.

He'd sworn off women with complications. He'd sworn off women who needed him. But hell and damnation, it pissed him off, big-time, that Eve had the strength to walk away from his love and support on arguably the most vulnerable day of her life.

Couldn't she give a single goddamn inch?

He swung his legs off the mattress and didn't cast one last look back at the bed. His eyes were closed as he stripped the case off Eve's pillow and, in case the guy at the checkout desk would be watching for contraband, folded it into a small square and stuffed it in his front pocket. It smelled like her.

The plan was that later he'd make a voodoo doll out of it or something.

Now the plan was to get the hell out of Palm Springs. Though tonight was Téa and Johnny's wedding, his date seemed to have disappeared.

As he waited on the curb for the taxi he'd called to show up, he noticed that clouds were gathering in the bowl of the valley. There was an undesertlike dampness that chilled both the air and his thoughts. Fine. He allowed himself another few minutes to worry again about how Eve was doing and what she was thinking. It had to be hell to suddenly doubt your identity. He could understand that. He sympathized. He'd sympathized so damn hard over the last twenty-four hours that the feeling had carved a deep, vicious hole in his belly.

But hell, you couldn't tell the man who loved you

that you needed him and then vanish before he did nothing more than lose himself a little more in your body.

Or maybe it wasn't her fault at all. Maybe it was that he wasn't cut out for this love shit and she'd recognized that. She'd moved on to get what she needed from someone else.

Damn it! And without giving him a chance first!

As the yellow taxicab pulled up, Nash reminded himself that loving Eve wasn't a mandate for action. Her leaving, when he thought about it, was actually a reprieve. Now, without a second thought, he could walk away and go on with his life.

No one was holding a gun to his head.

A thought that seemed incredibly ironic when a dark sedan pulled up beside him as he left the cab and crossed through the Kona Kai parking lot. The back door opened as the passenger side's front window slid down. Through it, Nash found himself staring at the barrel of a gun.

Nino Farelle poked his head out the open door. "We'd like to take you to a talk with Mr. Caruso."

Nash would have run like hell—only jackasses didn't have a healthy respect for metal implements that spit bullets—if the other man hadn't then added, "It's about Eve."

They drove quickly through the streets, a gun still trained on him, thanks to a wiry older man whom Nash recognized from that night in the Kona Kai bar when he'd first seen Nino. For his part, Nino did nothing but stare out the windows in silence. Nash decided he could be just as stone-faced. He crossed his arms over his chest and watched the world speed by. After pausing at a guardhouse peopled with three armed men, they came to a stop in the courtyard of a gray-stoned fortress.

There was another guard standing at the front door. Nash shot a look at Nino. "Is that an Uzi?"

The other man smirked. "What, you get your firearm facts from the movies?"

Well, uh, yeah. Believe it or not, some good ol' boys didn't like bad ol' guns. But Nash just shut up and let them usher him inside the cold house, the wiry guy still pointing that barrel his way. Their feet clattered loudly on marble floors, and as they reached the double doorway of what appeared to be a study, Joey Caruso jumped to her feet.

"Nash!" A frown pulled down her lips as her gaze shifted from him to the older guy with the gun. "Uncle Tuna, what are you doing?"

"This is the man you last saw with Eve," he replied, his brows lowering.

"Uncle Tuna, put the gun away." Joey cast a look at her grandfather, who was sitting behind a massive desk, his expression revealing nothing. "*Nonno*, do something."

"Put the gun away, Tony," Cosimo said calmly. "You're upsetting Joey."

"In case you were wondering," Nash felt compelled to put in, "I'm a little upset about it too."

Cosimo's gaze cut to him. "My apologies, then. We're all . . ." He held up his hands.

Joey materialized beside Nash. She had this rapid way of moving that seemed to take her from place to place in the blink of an eye. "So Eve's not with you?" she demanded.

Nino made a noise. "Obviously not, *bambina*."

Nash ignored him. "No, we were at a motel, and

then she left. You saw her. She was very upset after what Vince Standish said about the DNA test."

Joey's head whipped toward Cosimo again. "See? We should have told her. We should have told her the instant the results came back."

The old man acknowledged this with a nod. "Maybe, *cara*." Then he gave a very Italian shrug, the movement small and elegant. "We did what we thought was best."

Nash raised an eyebrow at Joey. "So what he said was true? She's not a Caruso?"

"No! Vince Standish was one-hundred-percent wrong. Eve most definitely *is* a Caruso." Then the starch seemed to leak out of her spine. "Just not by blood."

"And no one knew until this DNA test?"

Joey shook her head. "As far as we know, not even my father. One day he came home with this little girl and told my mother she was his. No one doubted him."

"Your mother didn't? She just raised this daughter without a word of complaint or need for any proof separate from your father's say-so?"

Joey cast another glance at her grandfather, who remained silent. "You have to understand, he had more personality, more confidence, than any ten men put together. And my mother had no reason not to believe Eve wasn't my father's daughter. His . . . extramarital affairs were well known. Then there was Eve herself. Imagine her at three years old. I was a baby of course, but the way my mother tells it, no one could resist taking her into their heart."

And Eve would have done what she'd had to, to be loved. Nash could imagine that. Thrust into a new family, she naturally would have used her beauty and her charm to make a place for herself. *Ah, Eve. Have you ever believed anyone loved you just for yourself?* "How long have you known the truth?"

Joey made a shrug identical to her grandfather's. "A few weeks. We decided that right before the wedding wasn't a good time to spring this on her. We were still debating whether to *ever* tell her."

Nash couldn't decide what he would do in the Carusos' shoes. He only knew one thing for certain. "That asshole Standish."

Cosimo lifted a lethal-looking letter opener off his desk and idly turned it over in his hands. "Don't worry about Vince Standish."

Nash tried to pretend that his blood wasn't running cold as light glinted off the letter opener's blade. Shit. This was the frickin' *Mafia*. He kept forgetting about that. In this case, it was almost a pleasant thought.

"I just wish Eve had picked up her dress for the wedding." Chewing on her bottom lip, Joey gestured toward a pale gown swathed in cellophane and hanging over a chair. "And that she hadn't missed the rehearsal dinner last night. There's only a few more hours until the wedding."

Nash shoved his hands in his pockets, his fingers finding the pillowcase. He didn't have any more wishes about Eve, except one—that she'd be easy to forget. She didn't want him. She was handling her problems on her own. "Look, I'm sorry about the situation, but I'm heading back to L.A. today. I'm going to go now, all right?"

The "Uncle Tuna" guy muttered something under his breath, but Nash pretended not to hear the rumbling.

"If someone could give me a ride back to the Kona Kai? Or I can call a cab."

Joey was drumming her fingertips against her thigh. He didn't think she'd heard a word he'd said. Her gaze lifted to meet his. "Did she mention anything about her plans for today? She's not answering her cell, she hasn't been at the spa. If I could just link up with her . . ."

Nash was already shaking his head. "I told you, I haven't seen her since the morning after the masquerade ball."

"*What?*" Joey's eyes rounded, and she clutched at his arm. "You haven't seen her in over *twenty-four* hours? I thought she was with you until *this* morning." She looked over at Cosimo, whose expression was suddenly grim.

The old man set down the letter opener, and his gaze shifted. "Nino?"

"I told you it was a possibility, Cosimo," the younger gangster said. "When she was missing, I told you one of the other families might have taken her as leverage."

Now it was Nash's turn to go bug-eyed. "What?"

Cosimo picked up the letter opener again. "I'm retiring, Mr. Cargill. The change in circumstances, it causes hotheads to want to grab power in any way they can, you understand?"

Uh, no, he didn't.

Joey moaned. "That's got to be it. Otherwise she would have come to the dinner last night, or at least phoned. Someone has Eve."

Nash's blood went icy.

Cosimo stood. "I need to make some calls."

"Are you sure?" Nino asked. "Unfounded accusations, violence, will only escalate tensions."

The boss of bosses' eyes flashed. "This is my granddaughter. If something happens to her, *my* tension will escalate."

"Wait a minute." Nash was trying to calm them and himself at the same time. "What if she just went to the mall or the movies?"

"Overnight?" Joey questioned.

"To a friend's house, then."

"We've called everyone we can think of."

Nash tried again. "Maybe she went out to her friend Diana's."

Joey blinked. "Who?"

"Her friend's house in the desert. She said it was her hideaway."

Cosimo and Joey, then Cosimo and Nino exchanged looks. "We don't know this Diana," the old man said.

Nash inhaled a breath. "She took my sister and me to a house in the desert, not more than an hour from here. She told us it was her special place. Her hideaway."

"Why wouldn't she tell me about her special place?" Joey asked. One of her small hands curled into a fist and she banged it against her thigh. "Damn it. She's been keeping secrets. Mom knew it, Téa knew it, I knew it, but we didn't press her, since we were keeping one ourselves."

"We should check this friend's house before we do anything else then," Nino said. "Where is it?"

"It's . . ." Nash realized he had no idea. And he also realized that though he would like nothing more than to give them directions and then take off for L.A., that wasn't going to happen. "I don't know the directions, but I can get there myself."

Joey nodded. "Okay, okay. This sounds good. I'll go with you."

"The wedding," Cosimo reminded her. "Your sister's expecting you to help her get ready. We can't take the chance that any more of the family won't make it back in time."

Joey put her hand over her eyes. "*Nonno*, you can't risk missing it either. What are we going to do?"

"I'll go with Cargill," Nino started. "We—"

"No!" The last person she'd want Nash to bring to her special place was Nino Farelle. "I'll go alone. The instant I spot her, I'll call on my cell phone."

Joey whirled to grab up the plastic-wrapped garment over the chair. "Bring the dress, too. Bring the dress and then bring her to the wedding wearing it. If you drive fast and you talk fast, you can make it."

Nash almost smiled. Joey Caruso could give orders as chilling as her grandfather's and with the same kind of implied muscle behind them.

"I'll do my best." He took hold of the hanger, but Joey didn't let go.

"Are you sure you'll find her there?" she asked, a wealth of worry in her eyes.

"I am." He couldn't say how he knew, but suddenly he did. That hunch thing again. Eve was definitely there.

But what would her reaction be to his intrusion?

And could he really get her to the church on time?

And then there was the question of his own plans. With his admission regretted (by him) and rejected (by Eve), he needed to be thinking of himself now, too. But later.

"I'll need some wheels," he said.

Cosimo nodded. "Nino, get him some keys. The Lexus, I think."

Nash shook his head. "No, I have a better idea." He looked out the windows. It was starting to rain, and he was going after a woman.

Boomerang.

Chapter Thirty-five

"Chapel of Love"
The Dixie Cups
"A" side, single (1964)

Eve sat on Diana's low terrace wall, staring out at the desert. She'd been doing that very same thing for hours, losing herself in the vastness that was spread before her. Clouds had moved in to blanket the tops of the mountains, and she let them weigh heavily upon her, too, making her smaller. Less.

So there would be less confusion. Less sadness.

Now she was one of the cactus. Or that hard boulder, there. Or that cold-blooded lizard, a creature without its own heat. No. She was less than the lizard, she was the lizard's tail, something without its own power.

Almost nothing at all.

"You know who she really is? Nobody. She's nobody."

In the distance, her gaze caught the movement of something big kicking up dust. Heading straight for her, the big thing wasn't bothering with the road; instead it churned through the sand on enormous tires.

Eve considered retreating to the house and locking herself behind the door, but she didn't have the energy. With luck, he wouldn't even see her. With luck, she was as insignificant and invisible as Vince had said and as much as she felt, and Nash would drive right up the driveway and then drive right back down again, unaware of the ghost that was Eve sitting on the terrace wall.

It had to be Nash, of course. Who else would be driving a truck the size of a moving van?

The huge thing took the steep driveway the way another vehicle might take a three-inch curb. He swung it around as he parked so that when he exited the car he was less than four feet away.

His clear eyes widened, and he shook his head. "Damn, Party Girl," he drawled. "You look like you fell out of the ugly tree and hit every branch on the way down."

Apparently she still looked substantial, though, even if she didn't feel it. Upon arriving at Diana's the day before, she'd borrowed some cropped-off sweatpants and a worn T-shirt. She hadn't changed out of them or showered or even washed her face or brushed her hair.

Ghosts didn't need to bother with that kind of thing.

But this ghost still had to get rid of Nash. "Go away."

"Now why am I not surprised to hear you say that? And I brought you something and everything."

She turned her face from him. "I don't want anything."

He stepped back to duck inside the enormous, dusty truck. "Well, this isn't a present you can refuse, darlin'. It's something that already belongs to you." In his arms was a cardboard box, holes punched in the sides.

He walked it toward her.

Eve scooted farther along the wall.

Nash halted. Sighed. "Look, I already went through a lot to get this for you. I even had to make a call to the doctor to see if my tetanus vaccination was up to date."

"What are you talking about?"

He set the box on the ground, placed his cowboy-booted foot on top of it, then turned his wrists to expose his inner forearms. Several bloody scratches marred the tanned flesh.

Eve dropped her gaze to the box, which was wiggling on its own now, as if it were alive. "You have that cat in there."

"Now don't you know how to ruin a surprise," Nash said. "But it's not 'that cat,' it's *your* cat."

"Not anymore." Adam had befriended the old Eve. The one who had sashayed through her world, chin-high, confident in being a Caruso. Now she didn't know who she was, only whom she didn't belong to anymore. "Take it back."

Instead of obeying, Nash bent down and opened the flaps of the box. With a yowl, the tom jumped out, looking ready for another brawl. Then it saw Eve. It got that familiar soft expression on its face and leaped onto the wall instead of on Nash's throat. Adam picked his way toward her, mewing in plaintive complaint.

She tried to ignore the creature when he bumped his big head against her shoulder. Despite herself, her fingers moved to caress the fur between his ears. "You shouldn't have brought him," she said. "Cats don't like change."

He shrugged. "He's your cat," he said again.

"Stop saying that!"

"Well, it's true. You gave that thing your affection and your time, and now he belongs to you. You can't make that go away. I don't get why you'd want to."

She shook her head. Though the cat climbed into her lap, she directed her attention away from both him and Nash. *I'm that twig of scrub brush tumbling across the dirt. That piece of broken glass.*

"What if I told you his real name is Pumpernickel?"

Eve started and looked over at Nash, who seated himself on the wall a few feet away from her. "What are you talking about now?"

He stretched his legs out in front of him. Those long, muscular legs that the old Eve had stolen peeks at whenever she could. "What if I told you that I found out the cat's real name is something like Pumpernickel or . . . or . . . Puddin' Head?"

"I'd say you must have fallen out of your truck onto *your* puddin' head."

"What I'm trying to tell you, Eve darlin', is that you care about that cat, no matter what its name is."

Oh, I get it. Her eyes closed. "Just so you know, that's an incredibly simplistic response to a complicated situation."

"Hey, I'm a simple, Southern country boy." His drawl flowed through the words, heavier than molasses. "What can you expect?"

She opened one eye. "Exactly where in the South are you from?"

"Deep South, darlin'." He rubbed his chin with the back of his hand. "Deep, deep South."

Something made her press harder. "Exactly where in the deep, deep South?"

"Um . . ." Then he shrugged. "San Diego. Deep, deep in Southern California."

She stared at him. "You fraud."

"Only my accent. And I can't help it. I hang out with a lot of good ol' boys, and it rubs right off them and onto me."

Shaking her head, she turned back to the view.

"Since I'm comin' clean, I might as well tell you that I'm here to take you back to the wedding."

Her gaze jerked toward him again. "The wedding." She'd forgotten about the wedding.

"Téa and Joey have been trying to reach you for more than twenty-four hours. You didn't think you should let them know where you are?"

"There's no phone line out here. And my cell died." Same with her car. The battery had finally gone kaput. "But anyway, I'm not . . . I can't go to the wedding, Nash. I just can't."

"I know you think so. But you gotta, Party Girl. It's a matter of life and death."

"Yeah, right."

"Really. I promised Cosimo I'd bring you back. He and his men were ready to go to war with some other mob families, thinking you'd been abducted, but I convinced them to hold off until I checked for you out here."

Eve's mouth went dry. With her grand— With *Cosimo's* impending retirement, the California Mafia was really on edge. She knew that. There'd been arson in

October, just ahead of his birthday party, so she could see him worrying that something worse might happen before the big Caruso wedding. "You have a cell phone. Call and tell them I'm okay."

He shrugged. "I already tried that, on the way up the driveway. This is the middle of nowhere, darlin', and apparently that means no cell service either."

"Oh, God. Nash—"

"I know, I know. But I doubt they'll be satisfied until they see you in the flesh anyway." He hesitated, then plunged ahead. "Joey gave me your bridesmaid's dress. I have it in the truck."

Aghast, Eve shrank back. "I can't *be* in the wedding. Not now."

"Well, you can't leave your sister without one of her attendants, can you? It won't be, uh . . . even."

Good ol' Nash was really grasping at straws now. She could tell he didn't know if "even" was important. But it would be important to Téa, Eve thought, her stomach turning to lead. Interior designer Téa, with all her lists and her meticulous overmanagement of every detail, deserved this day to go off as perfectly as planned. Could Eve's final act as a Caruso sister be to screw that up?

She squeezed shut her eyes, feeling that wet sting behind them. What she needed was distance. *I'm that piece of scrub brush tumbling across the dirt . . . I'm that piece of broken glass.*

The mental imagery didn't work. She was broken, all right, but she knew she couldn't stay here and damage Téa's big day. "You win," she said wearily, getting to her feet. The cat purred in her arms. "Let's go."

She'd think about facing the Carusos later. For now

she just had to get into that humongous truck. One step at a time.

"Um . . ." Nash was hesitating again, rubbing his big hand against his chin. "I know there's no phone out here, Party Girl, but what about hot water and a blow-dryer? You, uh, wouldn't want to scare the wedding guests, now, would you?"

It was lucky she was a ghost, Eve decided, because otherwise he might have hurt her flesh-and-blood ego.

Once she saw herself in the bathroom mirror, however, it was hard to blame Nash. She didn't look like Eve Caruso, not with the dark smudges underneath her eyes, her hair snarled and her lips chapped. A hot shower and a hair dryer could only do so much, but she did the best she could with them and the few cosmetics Diana had left behind.

The dress and the shoes still fit, though she didn't look in the mirror once she put them on. Instead, she swathed herself in a sheet from Diana's linen closet. A trek back across the desert could add a layer of dirt to the pearl-colored satin if she wasn't careful. Nash had already reloaded Adam back into his box and into the backseat of the big truck by the time she shuffled out the front door.

Thanks to the height of the truck and the protective sheet, he had to bundle Eve into her place as well.

For a moment he held her against his chest. She lowered her gaze and watched his steady pulse beating against his neck. Two nights ago he'd told her something she hadn't wanted to hear. In situations such as this, the old Eve would have made some flirtatious remark, confident that her sex appeal would deflect the awkwardness of the memory.

This Eve just wanted to cry.

He drove back toward Palm Springs in the manner in which he'd arrived—without regard to roads. Instead, he drove directly across the desert, and she appreciated the virile hum of the big engine. It was like Nash, straightforward and strong, knowing where it wanted to go and then just going there.

She could remember a time when she'd been so certain about things, but it seemed like a long time ago. Before the SEC debacle, before Salvatore's remains had been found. A lifetime ago. Another life ago.

Some other woman's life.

As they neared Palm Springs, it was almost dark, and traffic choked the streets. Johnny and Téa were marrying in a chapel near the center of town, and it seemed as if everyone in the valley was traveling in that direction. Eve wiped her palms on the sheet, almost as nervous about not making it to the wedding on time as she was about making it at all.

And then they were there, with only minutes to spare. The parking lot and the streets were crowded with cars. The guests had to be already seated inside. Three hundred people whom Eve was supposed to walk past, though she didn't know who Eve really was.

Nash pulled up to the loading zone, stopped the truck. Neither one of them moved.

"I have a secret to tell you," he finally said.

"What?" She was staring at the stained-glass window over the entrance. It glowed with color. *I'm that triangle of green glass. No, that small curve of blue.*

"It's something I've never told anyone."

Eve blinked, then turned her head to look at him. "What?"

"Jemima's mother had an affair while she was married to my father."

From the corner of her eye, through the open double doors leading into the vestibule, Eve saw movement. It would be the wedding party, she guessed. Joey, the two groomsmen, Téa herself. Johnny would already be waiting for his bride at the front of the church. "Why are you telling me this?"

"I'm pretty sure Jemima's not my father's daughter." Eve shook her head. *"What?"*

"I'm pretty sure Jemima's not my half sister, biologically speaking. A couple of years ago, her mother, Allison, let slip a hint or two." Nash got out of the truck before she could think of an appropriate response.

She watched him through the dusty windshield. He came around to her side and helped her out. With her feet on the sidewalk, she found she couldn't move. Nash unwound the sheet and tossed it back into the truck.

He cleared his throat.

She couldn't look at him. "I don't think I can do this." She'd always been a coward, but as a mob boss's daughter she'd most often managed to fake her confidence. Now without that identity behind her, she couldn't even pretend anymore.

Then Nash touched the small of her back, somehow propelling her stiff body forward. With his help, she made it slowly across the sidewalk and up the steps. At the threshold to the church, though, she froze again. Trying to stay out of sight, she peered inside the open doors. The vestibule was lit by pillared candles in all shapes and sizes. It smelled of smoke, warm wax, and promises.

Just as she'd supposed, there were the two groomsmen—Johnny's brother and a friend of his, both in black tuxedoes. And she saw Joey, too, looking just as wonderful as she had that day of the fitting. Then across the vestibule, another door opened. It framed Téa, breathtaking in her pagan-queen wedding dress. Her expression both nervous and elated, she searched the room with her eyes.

Her gaze found Joey's, who shook her head.

Téa had been searching for Eve.

Nash bent to her ear. "What I told you about Jemima . . . what I was trying to say . . . you weren't born their sister, or even their half sister, that's true. But to Téa and Joey and Bianca and Cosimo, it doesn't matter. It doesn't matter if your name is Eve or Pumpernickel or Puddin' Head. They care, and always will care, for you. They've known about the results of that DNA test for weeks and didn't want to tell you because it didn't matter to them. You're you, no matter what. No matter what, you're their family. Now go join them."

"It's not that easy."

"It's better than easy. This time, you get to choose to love them, not because you have to, not because you're three years old and alone in the world. But because you want to. You get to choose to love them back with everything you have."

Without moving, Eve continued staring at her older sister. Then Bianca appeared at Téa's elbow. Bianca, sleek and lovely in a nubby silk suit the color of café au lait, a small bouquet of gardenias in her hand. Twenty-five years ago, Bianca Caruso had faced just such a moment of soul-wrenching shock and confusion as Eve was facing now. Twenty-five years ago, her identity as beloved wife had been shaken when her husband had brought home his mistress's daughter.

Twenty-five years ago, Bianca had bent down to the

little girl who'd looked so different from her own daughters and had hugged her to her heart.

Bianca had chosen to love Eve then.

So how could Eve do any less now?

"You get to choose to love them back with everything you have."

She took a step inside.

The small group in the vestibule glanced her way. The women froze, then expressions of relief and joy overtook their faces. Trying on her own tentative smile, she took another step.

"Good job, Eve," Nash whispered from behind her. "Good job, good luck, and good-bye."

What? Without thinking twice, she whirled around. "No! You can't go now."

For the first time that day, she noticed he was wearing jeans, a chambray shirt, his beat-up cowboy boots. He looked tired and his eyes were shadowed, his chin gritty with whiskers.

For the second time in her life she went against everything she'd always believed would be the safest path. "Please, Nash. Please stay."

And then Bianca and Joey and Téa were there, their arms encompassing her, and she lost sight of him as she blinked away her tears.

Chapter Thirty-six

"The Kind of Boy You Can't Forget"
The Raindrops
"A" side, single (1963)

E ve." Nash touched her shoulder, and she looked up, grateful for the excuse to wrap up yet another conversation. She murmured an apology, then turned to give him her attention.

Though the wedding ceremony had gone off without a hitch and the reception was in full swing now, she didn't have her feet under her yet. To take in this new turn in her life would require time, time that didn't include a gazillion guests and a nine-piece band in attendance. Not to mention the distracting, sophisticated beauty of the setting Téa had designed. The ballroom was dressed in black and white, accented with elegant floral displays of white and blood red roses. Stones that glittered like diamonds were strewn across the tables.

"Eve," Nash said again, shoving his hands in his front pockets. "I'm going now."

Going? Her knees went woozy with that just-hit-dry-land feeling they'd been fighting since she'd stepped out of his truck. She clutched his arm. "No—"

"Yes," he interjected, cutting her off. A faint yet grim smile turned up the corners of his mouth. "Look, it's been a big day for me. I rode my mighty steed across the desert. I rescued the fair maiden from the empty castle. Finally, I returned her to her royal family."

"Nash—"

"Since then, I've been acting like some kind of knight waiting around for his reward, but now I think I'll just demand it. Give me a grateful peck on the cheek and release me to go on to my next adventure."

"You can't—"

"I've had my time at the party, Party Girl. I'm done."

Her fingers tightened on his arm. He meant he was done with her. Two nights ago he'd told her he was in love with her, but she'd known not to believe it, even as much as she'd wanted to. From the beginning, he'd been clear about leaving, just as he'd been clear that what he really wanted in a woman was all the things Eve was not. The Law-and-Order Preacher wanted a secure, uncomplicated woman. Instead he'd dabbled with her—a woman with a mistaken past and a misbegotten present that he didn't even know about.

Well, fine. That was just fine. She didn't need him. She didn't need any man. Anyone.

Though she'd learned she wasn't really a mob boss's daughter, she hadn't forgotten that men were still inherently unreliable.

"All right." She dropped her hand from his sleeve, promising herself she'd be pleasant and dignified as she walked him to the door of the ballroom. "Let's go—"

"No one's going anywhere." This was Joey, grabbing both her elbow and Nash's and pushing them into vacant chairs at a nearby table. "The fun's just about to begin," she declared, dropping into the seat on the other side of Eve.

Bewildered, Eve looked about the ballroom. Though the cake had been cut and consumed, no one looked in any hurry to leave, including Johnny and Téa. Eve watched them also being urged to take seats.

"What kind of 'fun' do you mean?" she asked Joey. But the younger woman had popped up again and was filling clean stemware with champagne for the three of them and then the others settling into chairs around the table.

Toying with her champagne glass, Eve studied Nash from beneath the protection of her eyelashes. He didn't look very happy to be sitting beside her, she thought, which reminded her of all his annoying, irritating, arrogant ways. She should be glad to be rid of him.

But she still didn't want him to go.

One of the groomsmen came by and dropped a pair of dice on the tabletop. "What's this?" she asked. It was Johnny's brother, Michael, wearing his customary reckless grin.

"We call it Tossing for Toasts," he said. "A game in honor of our gambling groom. Each table will roll the dice, and whoever is seated at the corresponding numbered chair has to get up and say something. Tell a funny story, tell a serious story, give the bride and groom your good wishes. Then we all drink. The game ends when the first person slides to the floor."

As Michael moved on, Nash pushed his champagne away. "I really do have to be heading out, Eve."

No. It was the only thought she had as dice were

tossed on the other side of the room and a cousin of
Johnny's got to his feet. "Don't go quite yet." Leaning
close to rub her shoulder against his, she also managed to brush her fingertips across his thigh beneath
the cover of the tablecloth. "I haven't given you that
thank-you you've been waiting for," she said, automatically using her practiced purr. Anything to get him to
stay.

"Damn it, Eve—"

Joey was back, whirling into her chair and cutting
off what Nash had been about to say. She burst into
laughter along with the crowd at the end of Johnny's
cousin's soliloquy about his dissatisfaction with the
single life. Champagne glasses were lifted.

Eve took only a tiny sip.

Joey slanted her a glance. "You can do better than
that."

Eve shook her head as more noise erupted when
someone at the next table rolled their dice. "I better
not. I haven't eaten much tonight, and I didn't eat all
day yesterday. There wasn't any food at Diana's."

"What?" Joey frowned. "Your car battery was dead,
your cell phone battery was dead, and you didn't have
any food. What did you think you were going to do?"

Across the room, an older woman stood up. One of
Téa's favorite clients. As she started a tipsy ramble
about interior design that was somehow related to
a good marriage, Eve stared at the woman's eye-
bugging hat. It seemed to be trimmed with yards of
orange ribbon and a real bird-of-paradise flower. "I
didn't worry about it. I knew Nash would come for
me."

Startled, she replayed the words in her head. *"I knew
Nash would come for me."* They'd popped out of her

mouth without thought, but they were nonetheless true, she realized, her hand squeezing the stem of her glass. Somewhere, in the secret center of her guarded heart, she'd known that Nash would come.

Lucky for her she was seated, because her knees went wobbly again and the lights in the room started a slow spin.

Nash looked over at her, apparently unaware of her now thudding, frantic pulse. "I'm leaving."

"No." She grabbed for his thigh again and thought of what she could say to get him to stay. What she could do. She needed more time to figure out what was going on here! *"I knew Nash would come for me."* "Not yet. You can't leave yet."

"Why not?" he asked, his voice flat, his eyes watchful.

Why not? Why not? She couldn't think. She didn't know. She didn't know anything beyond the fact that she couldn't let him go. There was that feeling fluttering in her belly again and something tugging at her heart, but she ignored the sensations. She still had to be careful, didn't she? There was no one but herself to protect her from making any big mistakes. No one who would pick her up if she fell.

"Why do you want me to stay, Eve?" Nash insisted.

Her mouth opened, some unknown confession ready to trip off her tongue. Pulse pounding, she yanked it safely back. Then, using the tools she'd always had at her disposal, she ran her hand up toward his groin, looked him boldly in the eyes, and licked her lips. This was how she mastered men. "Because I still have that 'thing,' Nash." She set her voice to Sultry and left it there. "That 'thing' about you and sex."

Beneath her hand, his thigh tightened to iron. He

shifted closer, his eyes snapping cold sparks. Fire and brimstone, but the cold kind. The cold, cold kind. She shivered, and his breath felt icy too as he breathed against her cheek.

"Don't play me like that, Party Girl. Don't play me like that ever again." He lifted her hand off his leg and set it on the table. "It's been fun. Real fun, but I'm sorry to say that I finally realize it was never real."

Her skin chill-bumped. Air refused to move into her lungs. The sound around them was hushed to muffled whispers.

She'd blown it. She'd fallen on old, superficial habits and turned Nash away from her.

Her gaze followed him as he rose from the chair. Then she saw him start, turn, and look at Michael Magee, who was gesturing at him and then at the dice. She could read Michael's lips, though she couldn't hear his voice. Toss the dice. Toss the dice.

With an impatient gesture, Nash did. Then all eyes at the table turned to Eve. Joey was elbowing her in the side. Téa and Johnny were looking at her too, expectant smiles on their faces.

She had to make a toast. Tell a story.

But weeks ago she and Joey had drawn straws for the maid-of-honor position and the toast-making duties. She'd lost, gladly. Now she had nothing to say.

Years of party-going, a lifetime of trying to be pretty and charming, made her unable to stay in her seat, however. Someone ran over with a cordless microphone as she came to her feet and looked out upon all the people who'd come to witness Téa and Johnny's wedding.

Time slowed as she studied those she considered friends, as well as those the old Eve Caruso had believed were family. They were still that—she'd made that choice back at the church—but she didn't yet know exactly who *she* was.

Her gaze landed on the bride and groom, looking as happy as they both deserved.

Nearby sat Uncle Tuna, along with a handful of her grandfather's aging mobsters even Téa couldn't leave off the guest list, men who had watched Salvatore Caruso's fatherless daughters grow up, treating them with a kindness and indulgence they didn't bring to their day jobs. At the next table was Cosimo himself, his posture as straight as any soldier's. Then Bianca, with an encouraging smile on her face, sitting with Johnny's relatives.

Also ringing the room were more friends who had grown up in the Coachella Valley as she had. All looking at her. Nanette O'Riley, who had held Eve's hand on the first day of second grade when she'd found out she hadn't been assigned the same classroom as Téa. Buzz Tyler, the public high school quarterback who'd come out before most of them had understood what "out" was. And there, on his other side, was . . .

Sandy Dailey.

Eve's mouth went dry with guilt. Though she had that tape of Vince Standish's confession to pass along, she no longer had that genetic excuse for her own crime, did she? Her gaze darted in Nash's direction, hoping he couldn't detect her anxiety, but his place was empty. She could see him threading his way between the tables in the direction of the exit.

All right. If she made a fool of herself, he wouldn't be there to see. If the truth about the illegal insider trading ever came out, The Preacher wouldn't be there to know.

Whew.

Eve, still keeping her secrets.

Eve's heart safe.

Suddenly, Téa was beside her. "Are you crazy?" she whispered furiously. "Look what's happening. You can't let Nash walk out."

"But—"

"Eve, that man is in love with you. Don't mess this up."

"This is your wedding day," she whispered back, her gaze never straying from the tall, strong figure leaving her behind. Did he really love her? A man like Nash, *could* he love her? He'd said so, but . . . "I'm supposed to say something."

"Then say the right thing, little sister. You have the microphone. Say the thing that will make him stay."

Oh, God, Eve thought. That was it. That was the truth.

She wanted him to stay, didn't she? This man she trusted. This man she was certain she could rely on. She *so* wanted him to stay because she was so in love with him. It was symptoms of that she'd been suffering from for days and days.

And if Eve didn't let the truth of that free, it would be smothered in the darkness of her heart forever.

Except she was nobody. Vince had said that. *"She's nobody."* Nothing beyond the looks she'd used all her life. Why would Nash want her?

"Watch out for the snake in Paradise," she heard Salvatore whisper in her ear again. But that snake wasn't Vince, it wasn't anyone or anything except her own self-doubt, she knew that. She only needed to stop listening to that hissing voice. Though her outside beauty was only skin deep, what she had inside was worth something too.

Nash had made her believe that.

An idea formed in her mind.

Her heart thudding, she squeezed the microphone tight as she spoke into it. "To the bride and groom— you two know how thrilled I am for you. But, uh, I have more to say than that. Téa, I hope you won't regret giving me this moment."

"I don't regret anything I've ever given you," her big sister replied.

Téa meant love. Eve had almost turned away from it, but not any longer. She looked over at Cosimo. *"You don't always have to handle things alone,"* he'd said.

"Um, Grandpa? If you could give me some of that help you offered?" She nodded toward the entrance, where two of his bodyguards stood, solid and alert in sand-colored suits and silk ties.

Without a smile, the California Mafia's boss of bosses made a small gesture with a finger. The two men blocked the exit to the room, just as Nash reached it. He halted, then glanced over his shoulder at Eve and frowned.

She wouldn't let it stop her. "Joe," she said, holding out her hand, "I need you too. Get me up on this table."

Joey jumped to her feet and steadied Eve as she climbed onto her chair and then onto the tabletop. The soles of her shoes crunched on the diamond decorations as she stepped over the fallen dice. From this new height, she looked across the heads of the bewildered wedding guests at Nash. It wasn't enough. "A chair, Joe. I need a chair."

Grinning, Joey lifted a chair on top of the table. Eve pushed it into position, then, with a deep breath, gathered the hem of her dress in one hand. She stepped out of her bridesmaid pumps, then stepped up onto the chair.

The room went dead silent. Her pulse started racing as she saw Nash turn fully around and cross his arms over his chest. He did not look amused.

That was all right. It wasn't funny to her, either.

It was terrifying.

She glanced down at Téa again, who was smiling. "If this goes bad . . ."

"I'll still be here," her big sister assured her. "Always."

Eve forced in another deep breath. Then she looked past the beautifully dressed guests and the sparkling champagne and the sophisticated floral arrangements to the man in blue jeans and cowboy boots. A real man. The real thing.

"Nash Cargill," she said from her position on the pedestal she'd created from table and chair, the pedestal that had always kept her safe from heartbreak. And away from the real thing. "Nash Cargill, in front of all these witnesses I'm telling you that I . . . I . . . I love you."

The walls of the room seemed to revolve crazily, but she focused hard on his face and saw his eyes narrow. The crowd spun away too now, and it was just the two of them, Nash and Eve. "You're in love with me?" he echoed.

She swallowed. "Uh-huh. Yes. Absolutely."

"So what does that mean you want from me, Eve?" He gestured at the table and chair setup. "To be another worshiper at your feet?"

He didn't believe her. But she was prepared for that. It was why she was on top of the table to begin with. "I don't want your worship. I just want you to love me back. And . . . and I think you do." Oh, God, she hoped he did. He'd said so and she was strong enough to believe him now. Ready to be vulnerable enough to act open to the idea.

"I trust you, Nash, with everything, but most of all with my heart. To prove it to you I'm going to close my eyes and jump off this table and trust that you'll be there for me." Nash would catch her when she fell.

His mouth dropped. She didn't let his incredulity deter her. Instead, she looked over at the bandleader, who seemed almost as surprised as Nash. "Drumroll, please."

Then she dropped the microphone and closed her eyes. *Okay, Party Girl, you can do this.* Drumsticks started a rolling rhythm. She inhaled a final deep breath in preparation for her leap.

A pair of strong arms wrapped around her thighs and hauled her off the table. The steady drumroll petered out to an embarrassed trickle, then died altogether. "Jesus Christ, Eve," a voice growled in her ear. "Are you nuts?"

It was Nash, his expression furious. He let her slide down his body until they were face-to-face, her feet dangling.

Now it was her turn to frown. "You ruined my grand gesture."

"You ruined my fucking day." He dropped her to the floor.

"But—"

"Grand gestures are just like your beautiful face, Party Girl," he said, his light gray eyes as hard as mirrors. He was angrier that she'd ever seen him, but this was an icy, controlled passion. "All style and no substance. I don't want that."

Was he saying he didn't want her now?

This wasn't right! This wasn't the way it was supposed to go! She'd climbed on top of a table for him, willingly making a fool of herself to make a point to him. He was supposed to want her forever!

"I love you, Eve, but I wish like hell I didn't, because I don't want just your surface." Stepping back, he crossed his arms over his chest again. "If you love me, if you want me, you have to prove it by showing me what's on the *inside*."

Eve swallowed, hard. So he did love her. Fine. But maybe she didn't love a man who was so damn picky. Maybe she wanted someone who was a little more appreciative of grand gestures and beautiful appearances. Maybe . . .

. . . maybe she was still that coward, shrinking in the darkness of her closet.

"Nash . . ." she heard herself whisper.

His expression didn't soften. "I don't want just the pretty, polished parts you show everyone else, Eve. I want the whole, real you."

Oh, God, he was still challenging her. He was still the only man who had ever insisted on seeing more than her face value. It was what she loved about him the most. It was what she never wanted to do without.

It was the most exciting, yet frightening, thing she'd ever confronted in her life.

She flattened her damp palms against the sides of her dress. "I cheated through four years of high-school French," she said quickly, before she lost her nerve.

A little gasp off to her right reminded her that their high-school languages instructor had been invited to the wedding.

"I write poetry and have an accordion file folder of rejections from publishers across the country."

Now it was Joey who gasped. Or maybe it was a giggle. Brat.

Nash wasn't laughing, though. Nash was still staring down at her with those mirror-clear eyes of his. He wanted more. He wanted everything.

Her nervous gaze darted away from him and around the room, stopping on one particular face that wouldn't let her forget the widest crack in her beauty. The ugliest secret she held. Sharing it would show Nash the real Eve Caruso—and probably drive him away from her too.

But she'd come this far. In the past months her life had been shattered, then her identity had been shattered, but now it felt as if she was on the verge of putting the pieces back together. Ironic, that by breaking her silence she was going to make herself whole. She might lose Nash over it, but it had to be done if she was ever going to be more than what people saw on the outside.

Looking down, she took a breath. "Three months ago I invested every dollar I had based on an illegal insider stock tip. A bad stock tip. As it stands, I have no money left, I'm being investigated by the SEC, and my next known address could very well be federal prison."

Instead of assessing how Nash was handling the news, she glanced over at Téa, then Joey, then Bianca, then Cosimo. Her family. The ones who had always loved her, no matter what. She needed them now, and she could finally let it show.

"I need help." The tight locks on her heart burst open with the words, filling up all her lonely, empty spaces with warmth. "I need all of you."

The four of them started toward her.

But Nash already had her. His arms closed around Eve, and she shut her eyes tight as tears leaked out against his chest. He was always squeezing the emotions out of her, wasn't he? Always getting to her insides.

"Here I am, Nash," she said. "This is me, warts and all."

"And they say you can't make a pillbox hat out of a possum's hide."

She looked up at him, her one man, her real thing. If he thought he could get away now, he didn't know how ruthless and determined this whole, new woman could be. This Caruso. This mob boss's daughter. "Once again, I have no idea what you're talking about."

"It means I'm relieved, grateful, happier than a moth in a mitten." He gave her his slow, country boy grin, and in it Eve saw the brightness of their future. "It means I love you and I want you, darlin' Eve. Warts and all."

Why Do Women Love Inappropriate Men?

*Y*ou know who you are, but perhaps you won't admit to it. You're the wild child drawn to the quiet, bookish guy reading *The Economist;* or maybe you're the reserved society lady who secretly loves nothing better than a ride on a Harley clutching a leather clad biker; or perhaps you're human and he's a vampire . . . But any way you look at it, there's no greater thrill or challenge for you than being with someone you know you shouldn't.

Well you're not the only one . . .

In these four upcoming Avon Romance Superleaders, the old adage that opposites attract never rang more true. Enjoy!

Coming May 2006 ♥

THE
Care and Feeding
OF
UNMARRIED MEN

♥ ♥

By Christie Ridgway

Palm Springs's "Party Girl" Eve Caruso has finally met her match. "The Preacher," aka Nash Cargill, is in town to protect his starlet sister from a stalker, only to realize that he'd rather "stalk" Eve! But can this granddaughter of a notorious mobster be tamed?

The rain was pouring down on the Palm Springs desert in biblical proportions the night he stalked into the spa's small bar. He was a big man, tall, brawny, the harsh planes of his face unsoftened by his wet, dark hair. Clint Eastwood minus forty years and plus forty pounds of pure muscle. Water dripped from the hem of his ankle-length black slicker to puddle on the polished marble floor beside his reptilian-skinned cowboy boots.

She flashed on one of the lessons her father had drilled into her. *A girl as beautiful as you and with a name like yours should always be on guard for the snake in Paradise.*

And as the stranger took another step forward, Eve Caruso heard a distinctive hiss.

The sound had come from her, though, the hiss of a quick, indrawn breath, because the big man put every one of her instincts on alert. But she'd also been taught at the school of Never Showing Fear, so she pressed her damp palms against the thighs of her tight white jeans, then scooted around the bar.

"Can I help you?" she asked, positioning her body between him and the lone figure seated on the eighth and last stool.

The stranger's gaze flicked to Eve.

She'd attended a casual dinner party earlier that evening—escorted by her trusty tape recorder so she wouldn't forget a detail of the meal or the guest list, which would appear in her society column—and hadn't bothered to change before taking on the late shift in the Kona Kai's tiny lounge. Her jeans were topped with a honey-beige silk T-shirt she'd belted at her hips. Around her neck was a tangle of turquoise-and-silver necklaces, some of which she'd owned since junior high. Her cowboy boots were turquoise too, and hand-tooled. Due to pressing financial concerns, she'd recently considered selling them on eBay—and maybe she still would, she thought, as his gaze fell to the pointy tips and her toes flexed into involuntary fetal curls.

He took in her flashy boots, then moved on to her long legs, her demi-bra-ed breasts, her shoulder-blade-length blonde hair and blue eyes. She'd been assessed by a thousand men, assessed, admired, de-sired, and since she was twelve-and-a-half years old, she'd been unfazed by all of them. Her looks were her gift, her luck, her tool, and tonight, a useful distraction in keeping the dark man from noticing the less showy but more famous face of the younger woman sitting by herself at the bar.

Eve placed a hand on an empty stool and gestured with the other behind her back. *Get out, get away,* she signaled, all the while keeping her gaze on the stranger and letting a slow smile break over her face. "What would you like?" she asked, softly releasing the words one by one into the silence, like lingerie dropping onto plush carpeting.

"Sorry, darlin', I'm not here for you," he said, then he and his Southern drawl brushed past her, leaving only the scent of rain and rejection in their wake.

Eve froze in—shock? dismay? fear? *"I'm not here for you."*

What the hell was up with that?

Coming June 2006

Her Officer and Gentleman

By Karen Hawkins

Christian Llevanth isn't your average highwayman—he's inherited a title and a fortune. But he's unable to enjoy his newfound status as he continues to seek revenge and close in on the Duke of Massingale, the man Christian believes murdered his mother—if only he wasn't so drawn to the duke's beguiling granddaughter Lady Elizabeth.

♥

"I have no wish to fall in love." Beth declared.

"Which is exactly why you are so vulnerable to it."

"Nonsense. That will never happen to me. Beatrice, you seem to forget that I am far too pragmatic—"

"May I have this dance?" came a deep voice from behind Beth.

She started to answer, but caught sight of Beatrice's face. Her cousin stood, mouth open, eyes wide.

Beth turned her head . . . and found herself looking up into the face of the most incredibly handsome man she'd ever seen. He was a full head taller than her, his shoulders broad, but it was his face that caused her to flush head to toe. Black hair spilled over his forehead, his jaw firm, his mouth masculine and yet sensual. His eyes called the most attention; they were the palest green, thickly lashed, and decidedly masculine.

Her heart thudded, her palms grew damp, and her stomach tightened in the most irksome way. Her entire body felt laden. What on earth was the matter with her? Had she eaten something ill for dinner that evening? Perchance a scallop, for they never failed to make her feel poorly.

Unaware his effect was being explained away on a shellfish, he smiled, his eyes sparkling down at her with wicked humor. "I believe I have forgotten to introduce myself. Allow me." He bowed. "I am Viscount Westerville."

"Ah!" Beatrice said, breaking into movement as if she'd been shoved from behind. "Westerville! One of Rochester's—ah—"

"Yes," the viscount said smoothly. He bowed, his gaze still riveted on Beth.

Before she knew what he was about, he had captured her limp hand and brought it to his lips, pressing a kiss to her fingers, his eyes sparkling at her intimately.

"Well, Lady Elizabeth?" he asked, his breath warm on her hand. "Shall we dance?"

Coming July 2006

♥

A Bite to Remember

By Lynsay Sands

♥   ♥

When Vincent Argeneau's production of *Dracula: The Musical* closes, he suspects sabotage and calls in private detective Jackie Morissey. He quickly sees that she's more than just a tempting neck, but unfortunately, Jackie doesn't have a thing for vampires . . . that is, until she meets Vincent.

♥

Vincent Argeneau forced one eyelid upward and peered around the dark room where he slept. He saw his office, managing to make out the shape of his desk by the light coming from the hallway. Oh yes, he'd fallen asleep on the couch in his office waiting for Bastien to call him back.

"Vincent?"

"Yeah?" He sat up and glanced around for the owner of that voice, then realized it was coming through his answering machine on the desk. Giving his head a shake, he got to his feet and stumbled across the room, snatching up the cordless phone as he dropped into his desk chair. "Bastien?"

"Vincent? Sorry to wake you, cousin. I waited as late as I could before calling."

Vincent grunted and leaned back in the chair, running his free hand over his face. "What time is it?"

"Five p.m. here. I guess that makes it about two there," Bastien said apologetically.

Vincent scrubbed his hand over his face again, then reached out to turn on his desk lamp. Blinking in the increased light, he said, "I'm up. Were you able to get a hold of that private detective company you said was so good?"

"That's why I couldn't call any later than this. They're on their way. In fact, their plane was scheduled to land at LAX fifteen minutes ago."

"Jesus!" Vincent sat up abruptly in his seat. "That was fast."

"Jackie doesn't waste time. I explained the situation to her and she booked a flight right away. Fortunately for you, she'd just finished a big job for me and was able to put off and delegate whatever else she had on the roster."

"Wow," Vincent murmured, then frowned as he realized what Bastien had said. "She? The detective's a woman?"

"Yes, she is, and she's good. Really good. She'll track down your saboteur and have this whole thing cleaned up for you in no time."

"If you say so," Vincent said quietly. "Thanks, Bastien. I appreciate it."

"Okay, I guess I'll let you go wake yourself up before they arrive."

"Yeah, okay. Hey,—" Vincent paused and glanced

toward the curtained windows as a knock sounded at his front door. Frowning, he stood and headed out of the office, taking the cordless phone with him. "Hang on. There's someone at the door."

"Is it the blood delivery?" Bastien asked on the phone.

"Umm . . . no," Vincent said into the phone, but his mind was taken up with running over the duo before him. He'd never set his eyes on such an unlikely pair. The woman was blonde, the man a brunette. She was extremely short and curvy, he was a great behemoth of a man. She was dressed in a black business suit with a crisp white blouse under it, he wore casual cords and a sweater in pale cream. They were a study in contrasts.

"Vincent Argeneau?" the woman asked.

When he nodded, she stuck out her hand. "I'm Jackie Morissey and this is Tiny McGraw. I believe Bastien called you about us?"

Vincent stared at her hand, but rather than take it, he pushed the door closed and turned away as he lifted the phone back to his ear. "Bastien she's *mortal!*"

"Did you just slam the door in Jackie's face?" Bastien asked with amazement. "I heard the slam, Vincent. Jesus! Don't be so damned rude."

"Hello!" he said impatiently. "She's *mortal*, Bastien. Bad enough she's female, but I need someone who knows about our 'special situation' to deal with this problem. She—"

"Jackie *does* know," Bastien said dryly. "Did you think I'd send you an uninitiated mortal? Have a little faith." A sigh traveled down the phone line. "She has a bit of an attitude when it comes to our kind, but Jackie's the best in the business and she knows about us. Now open the goddamned door for the woman."

"But she's mortal and . . . a girl," Vincent pointed out, still not happy with the situation.

"I'm hanging up, Vincent." Bastien hung up.

Vincent scowled at the phone and almost dialed him back, but then thought better of it and moved back to the door. He needed help tracking down the saboteur out to ruin him. He'd give Ms. Morissey and her giant a chance. If they sorted out the mess for him, fine. If not, he could hold it over Bastien's head for centuries.

Grinning at the idea, Vincent reached for the doorknob.

Coming August 2006

♥

Never a Lady

By Jacquie D'Alessandro ♥

Colin Oliver, Viscount Sutton, is in need of a wife—a demure, proper English paragon to provide him with an heir . . . everything Alexandra Larchmont is not. She's brazen, a fortune-teller and former pickpocket. Clearly they're all wrong for each other . . . Aren't they?

♥

From *The London Times* Society page:

Lord and Lady Malloran's annual soiree promises to be more exciting this year than ever as the entertaining fortune-telling services of the mysterious, much-sought-after Madame Larchmont have been secured. As Madame's provocative predictions have an uncanny knack for accuracy, her presence at any party guarantees its success. Also attending will be the very eligible Viscount Sutton, who recently returned to London after an extended stay at his Cornwall estate and is rumored to be looking for a wife. Wouldn't it be delicious if Madame Larchmont told him whom it is in the cards for him to marry?

Alexandra Larchmont looked up from the tarot cards she'd just shuffled and was about to deal, intending to smile at Lady Malloran, the hostess for the evening's elegant soiree where Alex's fortune-telling services were in high demand. Just as Alex's lips curved upward, however, the crowd of milling party guests separated a bit and her attention was caught by the sight of a tall, dark-haired man. And the smile died on her lips.

Panic rippled along her nerve endings and her muscles tensed, for in spite of the fact that three years had passed since she'd last seen him, she recognized him instantly. Under the best of circumstances, he wouldn't be a man easily forgotten—and the circumstances of their last encounter could never be described as "best." While she didn't know his name, his image was permanently etched in her memory.

She dearly wished that's where he'd remained—not standing a mere dozen feet away. Dear God, if he recognized *her*, everything she'd worked so long and hard for would be destroyed. Did he normally move in these exalted circles? If so, more than her livelihood was at risk—her very existence was threatened.

Her every instinct screamed at her to flee, but she remained frozen in place, unable to look away from him. As if trapped in a horrible, slow-moving nightmare, her gaze wandered down his form. Impeccably dressed in formal black attire, his dark hair gleamed under the glow of the dozens of candles flickering in the overhead chandelier. He held a crystal champagne glass, and she involuntarily shivered, rubbing her damp palms over her upper arms, recalling in vivid detail the strength in those large hands as they'd gripped her, preventing her escape. Out of necessity, she'd learned at a young age how to master her fears, but this man had alarmed and unnerved her as no one else ever had, before or since their single encounter.

The tarot cards had repeatedly warned her about him—the dark-haired stranger with the vivid green eyes who would wreak havoc with her existence— years before she'd ever seen him that first time. The cards had also predicted she'd someday see him again. Unfortunately the cards hadn't prepared her for someday being *now*.

Looking up, she noted with a sickening sense of alarm that his gaze moved slowly over the crowd. In a matter of seconds that gaze would fall upon her.

WIN A BEAUTIFUL SET OF DIAMOND JEWELRY
COURTESY OF *Baby Doll Gems*
AND
AVON BOOKS

One lucky entrant will win her own
set of diamond jewelry from Baby Doll Gems...
As featured in

Christie RIDGWAY'S

THE
Care and Feeding
OF
UNMARRIED MEN

GO TO **WWW.AVONROMANCE.COM** FOR THE OFFICIAL RULES AND
ENTRY DETAILS
AND CHECK OUT BABY DOLL GEMS' WEBSITE AT
WWW.BABYDOLLGEMS.COM

Baby Doll Gems
FINE JEWELRY
WWW.BABYDOLLGEMS.COM

AVON BOOKS
Imprints of HarperCollins*Publishers*
WWW.HARPERCOLLINS.COM

BAD1 0506

Visit www.AuthorTracker.com for exclusive
information on your favorite HarperCollins authors.